Ralph Modder

The Red Cheong-sam
and Other
Old Tales of Malaya
and Singapore

Horizon Books

Singapore • Kuala Lumpur
www.horizonbooks.com.sg

First published in 2006
Reprinted in 2007

HORIZON BOOKS PTE LTD
Block 5 Ang Mo Kio Industrial Park 2A
#05-12 AMK Tech II
Singapore 567760
Email: horizon@horizonbooks.com.sg
Website: horizonbooks.com.sg

HORIZON BOOKS SDN BHD
Wisma Yeoh Tiong Tee
72C Jalan Sungai Besi
57100 Kuala Lumpur
Malaysia
Email: horizon@wismaytt.com

©2006 Ralph Modder

All rights reserved. No part of this book may be reproduced, stored in a retrieval system, or transmitted in any form or by any means, electronic, mechanical, photocopying, recording or otherwise, without prior written permission of the publishers

Cover design: Cheryl Marie Song

Model: Andrea Joy Dragon

Text layout: Clement Michael

ISBN 978-981-05-0390-1

Printed and bound in Malaysia by Vivar Printing

About the Author

Ralph Modder is a Singaporean writer and veteran journalist. He held senior positions with newspapers and magazines in Singapore, Malaysia and Hongkong. He was born in Chemor, in the state of Perak (British Malaya) in 1923. His family moved to Singapore in 1929 where he was educated. He was a Volunteer truck driver during the Japanese invasion of Singapore in 1942 and was in Singapore during the Japanese Occupation from 1942 – 45.

He wrote several stories and screenplays for Singapore film producers, including the Malay 'classic' *Sergeant Hassan* starring the legendary Tan Sri P. Ramlee. The story was about the heroic defence of the Royal Malay Regiment during the Japanese invasion of Malaya and Singapore in 1941– 42. The film had a royal charity premiere in Kuala Lumpur in aid of the families of members of the Regiment who were killed in action. The premiere was under the patronage of the king and queen of Malaysia.

Books written or edited by Ralph Modder and published by Horizon Books:

Souls The Gods Had Forsaken
Curse Of The Pontianak
The Singapore Chinese Massacre
The Boy Who Talks To Ghosts (editor)
Killer Vampires From Hell (editor)
Curse Of The Gamblers' Tree Demon (editor)
The Bomoh

Contents

Author's Note

'The English sent all their bores abroad and acquired
the Empire as a punishment.'
– From *Narrow Road To The Deep North* (Pt.2)
by Edward Bond.

This selection of thirty-one tales spans various periods of British colonial rule in Singapore and Malaya (now Malaysia) that lasted for 140 years following the founding of Singapore by Sir Thomas Stamford Raffles of the British East India Company in 1819.

An attempt was made to portray the seamy, steamy, humorous, sentimental and tragic sides of life at various levels of the segregated English and Asian communities in both territories during those times.

The lifestyle of the English 'upper class' *tuans* and *mems* (respectful Malay terms for English 'gentlemen' and 'ladies') was similar to that in other British colonies in the region: large bungalows in prime areas with retinues of servants and year-round programmes of entertaining. They got six months 'home leave' to England with their families once every three or five years (depending on the employer) and two weeks 'local leave' each year that was usually spent in the cooler climates of Malayan 'hill stations' such as Fraser's Hill and Cameron Highlands in the state of Pahang, Maxwell Hill in the state of Perak and Penang Hill on the resort island of Penang, where there were government-run 'rest houses', English-styled cottages and pubs that served English beer and food, libraries, golf, river fishing and jungle hikes. But, while *tuans* and *mems* in the towns enjoyed easy lives, there were others whose duties took them into the malaria-infested swamps and jungles where they slept under canvas and were isolated from civilisation for the most part of each year. They included those clearing jungle to plant rubber, tin miners, surveyors, forestry, police and medical officers who were stationed in some of the remotest areas that could only be reached by river and by hiking for days through dense jungle.

Many roads, bridges and other landmarks in Malaysia and Singapore to this day bear the names of British officials who had contributed largely towards the development and progress of both territories.

Behind the veil of 'upper class' pomp and snobbery was an ostracised English 'second class' made up of those in various non-executive positions in government, banks, trading companies and so on, who were in more direct contact with the 'locals' or 'Asiatics (as Asians were known, then) and who, because of this, became more unpopular than the aloof *tuans* and *mems*. But, it must also be said that there were those who were ostracised by the 'upper class' for marrying 'locals' and deprived of many benefits enjoyed by other expatriates. They raised families, regarded Singapore or Malaya their homes and became part of 'local' community life.

Under these two levels, was a third comprised of an illiterate *coolie* (labourer) class of mainly Chinese migrants and Tamils from south India. Above this level was a minority English-educated *kerani* (Malay term for 'clerk') class. In limbo were 'riff-raff' European drifters and adventurous women, many with criminal records in other British colonies in the Far East. Their presence did much to tarnish the image of the *tuans* and *mems* whose composure was somewhat restored by frequent deportations of these 'undesirables.'

There was also the 'soldier class' that comprised British military personnel. They were accommodated in cool, clean barracks or houses situated in self-contained 'villages' that had hospitals, bars and canteens, cinemas, stores and recreation facilities. They were seldom seen in the cities except during sports events in which they participated, weekly visits on pay-days to bars and 'cabarets' (dance halls) and when taking part in ceremonial parades.

They, like the others, lived in segregation.

Malays, Chinese, Indians and Eurasians formed separate community associations in Singapore and Malaya. Despite belonging to different religious faiths and cultural backgrounds, they existed in harmony sharing the same neighbourhoods, while their children attended the same schools.

After almost 130 years of British colonial rule, elections were introduced in Singapore in 1948 at a municipal level. Singapore was elevated from a Municipality to a City in 1951, a move that made way for a new City Council and for the creation of political parties.

It is hoped that the stories in this volume will create a picture of life as it was in colonial times in Singapore and Malaya. Aside from club life, occasional house parties and hunting trips with the same boring people, the 'upper class' English led rather restricted and secluded lives, confining their activities to within their own group. From time to time there were rumours of scandals and 'indiscretions' by *tuans* and *mems*, the most common being illicit love affairs that produced enthusiastic gossip, especially if these were outside their circle and involved 'local' women. Cases involving European homosexuals and prostitutes were rarely brought to court.

It had been the practice from the early 1900s that if a serious crime committed by a member of a prominent European demanded a court hearing, the trial was held *in camera* from which the public was barred. The brief newspaper reports while mentioning the nature of the offence, referred to the accused or defendant as 'Mr X' or 'Miss/Mrs X.' Names of witnesses were withheld. But, despite these precautionary measures there were 'leaks' that revealed names and other details that became topics with wide public appeal. Europeans sentenced to prison terms were segregated from 'local' convicts and spent only the first few months of their terms in Singapore and the remainder in prisons in Australia or Britain. Such 'preferential treatment' was not accorded the European 'second class' and to those below that level.

It was necessary to give fictitious names to the characters in most of the stories in this volume. The names of historical characters, places and dates are factual.

British rule was interrupted in Malaya from 1941 and in Singapore from 1942 up to 1945 because of the Japanese Occupation. It was resumed after the surrender of Japan and continued for some years following the end of World War II in 1945, when former colonies, protectorates and dependencies in the British Empire became independent. Singapore became part of Malaysia comprising Malaya, North Borneo (Sabah) and Sarawak. Singapore separated from Malaysia and became a republic in 1965. Later, Malaysia and Singapore became members of the British Commonwealth.

Ralph Modder
September 2006

The Red *Cheong-sam*

Irma Marshbanks looked at the seven dresses hanging in her wardrobe for the umpteenth time and sighed. She sat on the edge of her bed and a frown creased the forehead of her pretty, young face. 'It's no use,' she muttered.

The dresses that had been made for her while she was at school in England two years before still fitted her slim body perfectly but they were not the things fashion-conscious young women her age wore in 1929.

She had just turned eighteen.

Women were beginning to assert themselves and were being paid more attention. Women's suffrage had been approved of in Britain. George Bernard Shaw had published *An Intelligent Woman's Guide To Socialism And Capitalism* and Hollywood was producing 'talkies' with some of the world's most glamorous female stars – Greta Garbo, Clara Bow, Marlene Dietrich, Mary Pickford and the 'blonde bombshell' Jean Harlow, were revolutionising women's fashion.

Women were at last 'coming out of their shells' and Irma Marshbanks was most conscious of this fact. The cause of her unhappiness was because she had discovered she did not have a 'trendy' dress to wear to the Grand Fancy Dress Charity Ball to be held at Singapore's famous and ('Europeans only') Raffles Hotel, named after Sir Thomas Stamford Raffles of the British East India Company, who founded Singapore in 1819.

The lateness of her discovery came about when her father John Marshbanks, an assistant in a shipping company, arrived home to excitedly inform his wife and daughter that he had bought three tickets for the gala event that was only three days away.

'Imagine being in the company of the governor and his wife! It's the biggest social event of the year!' he exclaimed, hoping it would justify his extravagance for spending $15 (about two English pounds at that time) for the three tickets that would allow himself, his wife and daughter to experience the privilege of 'rubbing shoulders' with the elite of Singapore society.

From the look on his wife's face it was obvious she disapproved of his rashness. With the money he had squandered on the tickets she reckoned she could have fed her family and their Hokkien *amah* for three days – maybe four.

Because of their financial status, the Marshbanks were regarded as 'second class' Europeans. Their home was a rented 'shop-house' in Armenian Street at the foot of Fort Canning Hill where British army units were garrisoned. They had allowed themselves the luxury of a Chinese *amah* whose monthly salary was $5. They did little or no home entertaining and seldom went out, except for a walk in the evenings up the hill or, to see a silent film at the YMCA that was close to their home.

Life for them was dull and uneventful. Because of her husband's small salary Mrs Marshbanks gave piano lessons to help make ends meet. However, they had made further cuts in their expenditure in order to pay for their daughter's education at a girls' boarding school in Surrey for which they had incurred unforeseen debts and were now in the process of repaying.

Mr Marshbanks couldn't remember the last time he and his wife had attended a party or had a meal at a restaurant while Irma was away. Now that she had returned a grown-up and very pretty young lady, he thought the forthcoming fancy-dress ball would be a belated celebration for her success in her school examinations.

It was predicted in the social columns of the local newspapers that most of the ladies attending the event would seize the opportunity to display the latest fashions from London and Paris. Valuable prizes were being offered to the winners of the fancy-dress competition.

When Irma Marshbanks told her friends that she would be attending the event and when she was asked what 'fancy dress' she would be wearing she casually replied, 'Oh, something of my own creation, I suppose,' which of course, was a lie.

How could she have told them the truth?

The grand occasion was now only two days away and it gave her no time to create anything and even if she had, she knew she wouldn't be able find a tailor to perform a miracle at such short notice. Moreover, she knew her parents would not be able to afford the cost of a new dress.

Mrs Marshbanks, however, lost no time in selecting the clothes, shoes and accessories that she would be wearing.

'For heaven's sake remember to wear something sober and dignified! Remember the governor and his wife will be there – and the bishop and his wife, too!' said Mr Marshbanks, realising that his wife had a weakness for 'loud' colours.

Irma had only one presentable dress in pink organdie that she wore regularly to church on Sundays and also to birthday parties. When her mother suggested she could wear it to the fancy dress ball, she felt tears rushing to her eyes.

'I think you'll look charming in it, my dear,' said Mrs Marshbanks pleasantly, overlooking the fact that her daughter was a grown up young lady and no longer a child.

The thought of appearing before her friends in the same dress sent a cold shiver down Irma's spine especially since she had told them she would be wearing something of her 'own creation.' She felt the simple answer to the problem was not to attend the ball. She would give her parents the excuse that she had an upset stomach, or she could pretend to fall down the stairs and say she had sprained her ankle. Or she could . . .

But on second thought she abandoned the idea, realising her

parents would easily discover the real reason. Dejected, she felt there was no way out for her.

She was sitting in a chair in her bedroom and wishing the floor would suddenly open and swallow her when she heard a knock on the door. Opening it, she saw it was Ah Sum, the old *amah* with a tray on which was the afternoon tea.

Ah Sum had been in the family's employ since the time Irma was born and she loved Irma like her own daughter. At times when Mrs Marshbanks laughingly told her friends, 'Ah Sum is Irma's adopted Chinese mother,' she had meant it more seriously than must people may have thought.

Ah Sum put the tray down and looking at Irma, sensed at once that something was troubling her. She placed a hand on Irma's shoulder and said, 'Make sad face no good! Make happy face good!' After Irma had explained her problem to Ah Sum in 'broken' English and Hokkien, the old servant offered her a cup of tea and stroking the side of Irma's face, said, 'I know, I know. No sad face, okay?'

Irma tried to read to take her mind off her worries without success. It had started to rain heavily and as she went to close her bedroom windows she saw Ah Sum with an umbrella over her head hurrying down the road. Where could she be going in such terrible weather, she wondered.

The sun was setting when Ah Sum returned. With her was her eldest daughter, Ai Lin who was in her thirties. Together with her younger sister, Ai Lin had opened a small tailoring shop specialising in the latest Chinese fashions from Shanghai.

Mrs Marshbanks and Irma greeted Ai Lin warmly since it had been some time since they had seen her. They noticed she was carrying a brown paper shopping bag.

Ai Lin spoke English quite fluently. As they sat in the living room, Ah Sum told her daughter something in Hokkien and Ai Lin said to Irma and Mrs Marshbanks, 'As you know, my mother cannot speak English so well. So, I shall speak on her behalf. My mother wishes to give Miss Irma a humble gift to welcome her back home from England. My mother hopes Miss Irma will accept the gift, which I made myself.'

She paused to speak to her mother in low tones. She got to her feet and from the paper bag she had brought, held up a dazzling *cheong-sam* in flame-red silk.

Irma did not know what to say as tears rushed to her eyes. She ran up to Ah Sum and threw her arms around her, 'It's gorgeous! Oh, Ah Sum, thank you! Thank you!' she cried and looking at her mother said, 'I am going to wear it to the fancy-dress ball!'

Mrs Marshbanks clapped her hands and sat back in her chair, delighted. Ai Lin smiled broadly, happy that her craftsmanship had met with such enthusiastic appreciation while Ah Sum secretly congratulated herself for making such a wise decision.

Ah Sum spoke to her daughter again and Ai Lin said to Mrs Marshbanks: 'My mother says she is happy that you both like the *cheong-sam*. Such a fashion is now most popular in Shanghai and also in Hong Kong and is worn by many film stars and rich *tai-tai*. My mother is very happy that Miss Irma has decided to wear this dress to the ball. I shall be happy to make any alterations that may be necessary. My mother also wishes to say the colour of the *cheong-sam* is red, which we Chinese believe is a most lucky colour. My mother hopes it will bring Miss Irma much good fortune and future happiness. Thank you.'

Looking at Irma, Ai Lin said, 'Please, will you try on the dress?' and holding hands, the two delighted girls ran towards Irma's bedroom.

Mr Marshbanks returned home from work at that moment and before he could remove his hat, his wife excitedly told him about Irma's beautiful and unexpected gift that she would be wearing to the ball.

As she was speaking, Irma wearing her dazzling *cheong-sam* appeared and like a fashion model, twirled around in the centre of the living room.

'What a splendid creation!' exclaimed her father and then screwing up his nose to show his disapproval, remarked to his wife, 'But, don't you think bright red would be too glaring for such a dignified occasion? The governor, the bishop and their wives will be there, you know.'

He was quick to notice the reaction his remark had on Ah Sum after Ai Lin had interpreted it to her. The *amah* smiled without betraying what she was thinking but Mr Marshbanks knew from the look she gave him that she disagreed with what he had said about the colour of the dress being 'too glaring.'

'I don't think it is at all glaring,' said Mrs Marshbanks.

'I agree,' said Irma firmly.

Ai Lin smiled uncomfortably, realising that she had unwittingly scored a victory at Mr Marshbanks' expense and Ah Sum studied the clock on the wall, hiding her amusement.

If Mr Marshbanks could have read Ah Sum's thoughts he would have learned something quite startling because she was saying to herself: 'These *ang moh* think they know everything! Mr Marshbanks is a good man and a good father but why is he making such stupid remarks? He has lived in Singapore long enough to know that the colour red according to us Chinese is symbolic of good fortune and is the dominant colour at all important Chinese festivals and celebrations! Didn't he know that lucky *ang pow* money was always wrapped in *red* paper during the Lunar New Year Festival? Didn't he know that firecrackers for driving evil spirits away and to bring good luck were also wrapped in *red* paper? Didn't the fat, old *ang moh* named "Santa Claus" carry his presents in a *red* bag? And, didn't he wear a *red* suit and a *red* cap? He also had fat, *red* cheeks! Wasn't a popular Christmas decoration *red* holly? How could Mr Marshbanks have even the slightest objection to his daughter wearing a *red* dress!'

Realising that he had committed a *faux pax* by his remark about the colour of the *cheong-sam*, Mr Marshbanks made an attempt to 'save face' by remarking, 'Well, I suppose if some

Chinese ladies choose to wear western dress these days, why shouldn't English ladies wear Chinese dress? Furthermore, I feel Irma has every right to wear a *cheong-sam*, since she was born in Singapore!'

He was happy to note that what he had said was accepted with smiles from all concerned.

Mrs Marshbanks said happily, 'I feel quite certain Irma will be the only European girl at the ball wearing a *cheong-sam*. Valuable prizes are being offered to the winner of the fancy dress competition, you know. Wouldn't it be wonderful if Irma won?'

'Oh, indeed!' said Mr Marshbanks. 'Think of all the publicity in the newspapers! You're not sorry now that I bought those tickets, are you?' he said to his wife, who chose to ignore his remark.

As Mrs Marshbanks had rightly predicted, Irma was the only European lady at the ball who wore a *cheong-sam*. Admiring eyes followed her as she entered the Raffles Hotel ballroom with her parents who were delighted to overhear flattering remarks about their daughter. Across Irma's shoulder was a pink sash with 'Miss Singapore 1929' stencilled in red letters – her father's idea.

'Although there hasn't been a beauty contest to choose Miss Singapore, I think my daughter is pretty enough to claim the title!' he proudly told some of the guests.

A red rose nestled in Irma's long, wavy black hair. She looked stunningly beautiful. Young men from prominent families requested her to dance with them and she was the focus of attention each time she was escorted to the dance floor. It was a foregone conclusion as to who the winner of the fancy dress competition for ladies was and there was cheering and enthusiastic applause for the blushing Irma as she went up to receive her prizes.

In her speech before she called upon the governor's wife to present the awards, the bishop's wife, who was the head of a panel of judges for the fancy dress contest, congratulated Irma on her 'most original and beautiful choice of dress.'

Irma could only splutter her thanks, having won a beautiful diamond pendant, French perfume and a voucher for three made-to-order dresses of her choice at a leading French boutique.

Later, she was presented to the governor who said, 'You are indeed a charming and worthy winner, Miss Marshbanks!'

When Irma and her parents returned home it was after midnight. Ah Sum and Ai Lin were there to open the door for them.

'I won first prize for the best fancy dress!' cried an overjoyed Irma showing them her prizes, 'and I owe it all to you both, especially you, Ah Sum!'

Mr Marshbanks who could not contain his excitement, exclaimed, 'I still can't believe it! My daughter was the winner of the fancy dress contest and was presented to the governor! It was lucky that I bought those tickets!' hoping that he would at last be accorded some praise for making such a wise investment. But, his remark went unnoticed, again. He saw Ah Sum whispering to her daughter.

'Excuse me, sir,' said Ai Lin to Mr Marshbanks with a smile, 'my mother says that while your daughter is most charming and beautiful, her success in the competition was further assured because of the lucky red *cheong-sam* she wore.'

Mr Marshbanks paused for a moment and dismissed the comment with a laugh, 'I suppose the bright colour of her dress might have had something to do with it. It was very eye-catching.'

The old *amah* was sitting in a cosy chair in the living room. She was conscious of the discomfort her comment had caused Mr Marshbanks although it was not intended to cause him any embarrassment whatsoever.

'Poor man, he realises he would have "lost face" if he admitted that I was right about red being a lucky colour,' she told herself.

She turned her attention to the others who were chatting happily and grinned, revealing two gold teeth. But Mr Marshbanks knew she was watching him from the corner of her eye and that her grin was meant for him alone.

The Irrepressible Bah Chee

Bah Chee was a *peranakan* (Chinese domiciled in Singapore or Malaya) who was employed as a chief clerk by a British trading firm. He was one of the many colourful characters who patronised the hawker food stalls along the black, muddy banks of the Singapore River and at *Lau Pa Sat* ('old market' in Hokkien) in Teluk Ayer Street during the 1930s – where it stands to this day – and still a popular rendezvous for a variety of Asian cuisine.

Bah Chee had spent three years studying accountancy in London and seemed to have an inexhaustible supply of stories that he was able to blend with a unique sense of humour or a touch of sadness whenever required. He could imitate 'upper class' English, Cockney, 'local' as well as foreign accents almost perfectly.

At times there would be impromptu comic sketches by unknown 'artistes' highlighted by the hilarious mimicry of prominent English and 'local' personalities. These performances were also enjoyed by the 'second class' and 'riff-raff' Europeans who were present and who had as many 'axes to grind' as the 'locals' about the way they were being discriminated against. Such 'shows' helped to diffuse tensions and life became more tolerable as it jogged along.

Bah Chee had failed his accountancy exams in London. 'I spent too much time in pubs and at dog races and didn't study hard enough!' was his excuse when he returned to Singapore in 1931.

To those who thought he disliked the British, he would say: 'I have a lot of respect for them. It's only some of the policies of the colonial government that I, as well as a good many others strongly objected to. I think people should be treated fairly on their merits and without discrimination or prejudice because of the colour of their skins. You may be surprised to know that the English "working class" were discriminated against by the "upper class" snobs whom we know as *tuans* and *mems* in Singapore. We seem to judge all English people by the objectionable conduct of these people in their attempts to prove their superiority, not realising that by doing so, they were displaying their ignorance as well as their inferiority!'

He was an avid reader of newspapers and magazines published in London that were brought to Singapore by fast Pacific and Orient (P&O) mailboats. The knowledge Bah Chee obtained from these publications as well as from books on how the British built their empire gave him the advantage to speak with more authority on certain subjects than his audiences that comprised clerks and secretaries employed by trading firms, banks and government servants.

One day the conversation drifted to the subject of Chinese 'coolies.' Some of those present were of the opinion that *rickshaws* should be banned because this form of transport degraded the Chinese as a race (since all the *rickshaw* pullers were Chinese) and reduced them to the level of beasts of burden.

Bah Chee said: 'The Oxford dictionary described "coolie" as: "An unskilled native labourer in Eastern countries." I therefore expected the dictionary's definition of "labourer," which is the Western equivalent for "coolie," to be: "An unskilled native labourer in Western countries." Or, as I would interpret it: "A Western coolie." But, to my disappointment I found this description instead, that read: "One who labours; especially one employed to do unskilled manual work."

'The word "Western" had been omitted. Was it done to imply there are no "coolies" in the West?

'When I was in London many of my friends were from the "working class." I found them to be warm-hearted, nice people who didn't think there was anything strange about me because I came from the East and had a so-called "yellow skin" as some colour-blind Westerners had described Chinese skins.'

The status of Chinese in the eyes of Westerners was one of the subjects in which Bah Chee had 'specialised'. Reading from a typewritten speech, he said: 'Some races in Asia have been branded with insulting names by Westerners because of the colour of their skins, cultures, way of life or religious beliefs. I single out as an example, the treatment of the Chinese who are known as "Chinamen." There is nothing wrong about being called a "Chinaman." Natives of England are known as Englishmen, those of Holland are known as Dutchmen, the natives of France are Frenchmen, and so on. It was all right as long as there wasn't a racist slur attached. But, if you were a Chinaman, Westerners regarded you as something strange because you came from the "mysterious, mystical East" and therefore were inferior to Westerners. Didn't Chinese pull *rickshaws* and weren't Chinese "coolies" used as "beasts of burden" and pull carts? A Chinaman was considered a symbol of the backward, heathen Oriental who also spoke a strange-sounding language! Did Westerners expect Chinese to adopt English as their mother tongue?

'To Westerners, Orientals also had strange habits and cultures and worshipped strange gods and goddesses. These critics were ignorant of the fact that all the major civilisations and major religions, including Christianity, originated in the East – and not the West.

'However, Eastern races became the targets of ridicule, despite the great inventions and discoveries made by Egyptians, Arabs, Indians and Chinese in the fields of science, astronomy, agriculture, engineering, chemistry, medicine, navigation and mathematics and were in many instances, hundreds of years ahead of the West.

'As a Chinese, it makes me proud to know that before 2000 BC my ancestors in China were planting their crops according to calendars computed from the regular motions of the sun and moon. Two thousand years ago, Chinese mathematicians were using algebra to solve geometric problems and had invented the abacus that is still in use today - and a lot faster and more accurate than the hand-operated machines we have!

'Chinese astronomers in 240 BC were the first to record the passage of Halley's Comet that was only discovered by the English astronomer Edmund Halley, and named after him, in the late 17th century! The Chinese were using gunpowder in the 10th century in the manufacture of firecrackers and fireworks to celebrate festive events such as the Lunar New Year. But Western nations from the 13th century onwards started putting gunpowder into bullets and cannonballs that were used to great advantage by empire-builders against people armed with spears, bows and arrows.

'I was shocked to discover that some Europeans mixed gunpowder with their alcoholic drinks to give them an extra "kick"! Some sleazy bars in the British colony of Hong Kong were known to serve "gunpowder cocktails" that were popular among foreign sailors and Western "ladies of the night."

'The term "Chinaman" was in popular use along the Pacific coast of the United States in the early 1900s where Chinese migrants earned livelihoods as laundrymen or "coolies." They were also known as "chinks" because their eyes appeared to be narrower than those of Caucasians. The dictionary defined the word "chink" as: "a narrow opening; a slit; a peephole." And, so, Chinamen also became known as "slit-eyed chinks".

'Large groups of Chinese had migrated or stowed away to America in ships from Chinese ports and Hong Kong. They were the fortunate ones who had escaped the horrors and hardships that many millions of their countrymen continually suffered as a result of political or military turmoil, severe droughts, famines, epidemics or floods. Besides, in a densely populated and impoverished country with a huge population such as China, unemployment was a major problem. That was the reason why our forefathers came here to Singapore, Malaya, Java, Sumatra and Borneo and crossed oceans to strange Western countries. They did so with the knowledge that most of them would never again see the families they left behind.

'The Chinese who arrived in the United States were willing to do any kind of work for very low wages or for no wages at all, in exchange for shelter and food. Because of the illegal influx of Chinese, strict laws to limit their entry to the United States were necessary. Their frugal way of life and the fact that they did not understand the language of the country of their adoption (only a few could speak pidgin English) caused these Chinese immigrants to be segregated and ostracised, resulting in the formation of small, isolated Chinese communities. By hard work, enterprise and resourcefulness, bustling Chinatowns appeared in big American cities as well as those in Britain, Europe and wherever Chinese had decided to settle as had happened in Singapore and other countries in Southeast Asia.

'Chinamen had also become an object of much curiosity and ridicule. It was noticed, for example, that instead of a knife and fork, they ate their meals with the aid of two thin wooden sticks. Being practical-minded, most of the food in Chinese recipes is sliced into bite-size pieces before being cooked and since there were always many mouths to feed at a Chinese dining table, there were enough pieces to go around. Such oddities however practical only helped to cause more ridicule of the Chinaman. One researcher after visiting a Chinese "coolie" settlement in California, said: "Chinamen worshipped strange gods and named each month of the year after twelve different animals. They performed vigorous lion and dragon dances to the ear-splitting sounds of clashing cymbals, drums and gongs made worse by hundreds of exploding firecrackers! It is said

Chinamen invented gunpowder to create this dreadful noise!"

'This researcher also noted, and I quote: "Chinamen played a noisy and complicated gambling game called *mah-john* (he meant *mah-jong*) in which small bone cards or tiles the size of postage stamps are used, creating a maddening din when they were shuffled on top of a bare wooden table! While this was going on other Chinamen lay on divans smoking bamboo pipes filled with a black, foul-smelling substance known as opium to Westerners or *chandu* to Chinamen. It is a drug that is extracted from the poppy plant and widely used in China. Quite naturally, it was in great demand by Chinese immigrants in the US." End of quote.

'What these so-called researchers conveniently overlooked was the fact that millions of Chinese became addicted to opium because British and American traders had smuggled it into China after the Manchu emperor had banned the drug because he realised the evil effects it would have on the his people. The opium that the British smuggled into China was grown in Calcutta and Bengal by the British East India Company. The opium smuggled by the Americans was grown in Turkey and brought to China across the Pacific in fast 'clipper' sailing ships. It may be of interest to point out that the British East India Company was the same company that had employed Sir Thomas Stamford Raffles, who founded Singapore in 1819.

'The British were making enormous profits from opium smuggled into China. They even went to war with China twice to protect this illegal trade. These wars were known as The Opium Wars. One lasted from 1839 to 1842 and the other from 1856 to 1860, resulting in the downfall of the Manchu dynasty and the beginning of British rule over Hong Kong, its surrounding territory as well as forcing the Chinese to concede other unfair treaties.

'The British had also introduced the sale of opium to Chinese in Singapore and had an opium factory at *Bukit Chandu* or Opium Hill off Pasir Panjang Road on the west coast. (Note:

This hill is known today as Kent Ridge Park. – RM). The raw opium from Bengal was processed there and sold to registered addicts, the majority of whom were Chinese coolies or *rickshaw-*pullers. In those days, more than one-third of Singapore's annual revenue came from the sale of opium. The opium was also made available to addicts in Malacca and Penang and smuggled into Malaya, Borneo and Sarawak. When the manufacture and sale of opium was finally banned because of the thousands of addicts who were dying of tuberculosis and lung cancer, another serious problem was instantly created – the smuggling of the drug into these areas and widespread corruption involving senior civil service officers. Many of these men were never charged in court and were quietly "sent home" to England. This was done in an effort to maintain an "impeccable British image."

'Other curious people in the West unravelled "secrets" about the character of Chinamen whom they discovered were "conservative, sinister and inscrutable" while the food these "mysterious" people ate became the subject of close scrutiny and further ridicule.

'Hilaire Belloc, the French-born English poet apparently had had an unpleasant experience after eating a bowl of birds' nest soup. He was prompted to write some verse about it:

Birds in their little nests agree.
With Chinamen, but not with me!

'Obviously, the soup had upset Belloc's sensitive stomach. It is possible he might have composed those lines while sitting in a toilet!' said Bah Chee with a laugh.

Sadly, Bah Chee was one of the many thousands of Chinese who were massacred by the Japanese army after the British had surrendered Singapore in February 1942.

The Street Of Broken Hearts

'I don't think anything could hurt as much as a broken heart.' – 'Jenny' of Bugis Street.

When the American ship *President* arrived at the Tanjong Pagar wharves in Singapore in July 1950, among the large number of passengers was a small, middle-aged man. He might have easily been unnoticed if not for the pole he was carrying from which hung a square, white, cloth banner in a wooden frame. In the centre of it was the outline of a sheep embossed in black thread. In bold, red capital letters above it were the words: Church Of Lost Sheep.

Black had been chosen for the sheep's outline to emphasise a common belief that people became black because of their sins. Their skins magically turned white after they were forgiven for their misdeeds.

It was learnt that the designer of the sheep motif on the banner dedicated to the Church Of Lost Sheep had suggested it would have carried a stronger message if there had been an outline of a white sheep on a black background beside one of a black sheep on a white background with 'before' under the black sheep and 'after' under the white sheep. By doing so it would have clearly illustrated the transformation from evil to good. For some reason this advice was ignored.

The gentleman holding the banner was flamboyantly dressed in a shining, white 'sharkskin' suit, a white silk shirt, white satin clip-on bow and white suede 'cowboy' boots into which the ends of his trousers had been tucked. To complete his all-white ensemble, he wore a white cowboy hat over his shoulder-length silver hair. On his nose rested a pair of rimless spectacles that sparkled in the scorching mid-day sun. If not for the banner he carried, the Reverend Jefferson Pickford-Smith might have been mistaken for an entertainer, which indeed he was, in his own right.

He was what was known in the United States at the time as a 'hot gospeller' – a new breed of Christian preachers who combined high-spirited sermons with high-spirited singing by 'back up' choirs.

Some of these 'spiritual healers' as they called themselves, wore expensive robes emblazoned with gems and religious motifs as well as other symbols of their cults. Many claimed to have been 'sent from heaven to save the world and all its sinners.' However, unlike Jesus Christ, they were not too keen on the idea of being crucified on a cross to achieve this noble goal. Surrounded by young 'angels' in white gowns, large donations of money from sinners who wished to be saved rolled into the preachers' bank accounts amidst accusations of fraud and trickery.

One such person called himself 'Father Divine.' It was the stage name of George Baker, a Black American preacher and founder of the Peace Mission sect that was popular on the east coast of the United States. He demanded that his disciples worshipped him as 'God incarnate.'

The Rev. Pickford-Smith, who was fifty-two, had the qualities of becoming such a divine star. His wife was two years younger and a 'senior shepherd' of the church he had helped to found. They had been married fifteen years and had no children. She was at present attending to some unfinished church work in Manila and would be joining her husband shortly in Singapore.

At the dockside to welcome Rev. Pickford-Smith was a small, perspiring and excited group made up mostly of 'locals' and a few Europeans. They too, were dressed in white and waved a banner similar to the one held by the Rev. Pickford-Smith.

'There he is!' shouted one of the welcoming party excitedly as she saw the banner that was now being waved from side to side by the man in spotless white on the ship's deck. It prompted the spirited singing of *Onward Christian Soldiers* by the welcoming party.

One would have expected a person with the surname of Pickford-Smith to be English, since the English were rather fond of 'double-barrel' or hyphenated surnames. But, Rev. Pickford-Smith was a red-blooded American right down to his hand-made, buckskin boots.

He had spent the past seven months in the Philippines guiding 'lost sheep' back to the 'flock' and at the same time recruiting male and female 'shepherds' as helpers in his church were called, to assist in the task of shepherding the strays away from evil and sin. It was a formidable task since the presence of American servicemen in the Philippines had caused the mushrooming of bars, brothels and vice dens wherever there were military camps. It had been a one-sided battle in which the 'shepherds' were outnumbered not only by an ever-increasing flock of young, female 'black sheep' but also by pimps who had enticed them to these places of unrestricted sin.

Although the odds were stacked high against the 'shepherds' they had won over some 'black sheep' to their side, finding them domestic employment in homes or as office workers, salesgirls, nurses and welfare workers.

Most of the strays had come from broken homes or families in which there were too many hungry mouths to feed and too little money to buy food. They had been forced to work in bars and vice dens where they at least could depend on some income, the size of which was determined by their sex appeal and to what lengths they were prepared to go to please the men with the all-powerful Yankee dollar.

In the bars the girls sat on the laps of the GI-Joes, as

American soldiers were known, and sang a song made popular by the Andrews Sisters who appeared in several Hollywood musicals:

'Drinking rum and Coca-Cola
Both mother and daughter
Working for the Yankee dollar!'

In his report to his headquarters, Rev. Pickford-Smith wrote in red ink: 'We have set ourselves a formidable task. But, fortified by the blessing of our Lord Jesus Christ, we shall crush the obstacles in our path. Victory shall be ours! We shall proudly plant our flag in areas that were once in the evil clutches of Satan!'

He had been reluctant to leave his unfinished work in the Philippines but was persuaded by his superiors to go to Singapore that was being seriously threatened by the 'black scourge of sin.' He had been told, 'It is best that we try to arrest the spread of these devilish, soul-destroying maladies before they reached epidemic proportions, as has happened elsewhere.'

Since arriving in the Philippines two years before he had built up a reputation as being a fearless crusader and a 'holy terror.' He was known to enter some of the most disreputable vice dens alone and deliver fiery sermons after which he would read aloud from a notebook the names of well-known pimps, prostitutes, procurers, drug pushers and gang leaders and advise them to abandon their sinful ways or suffer the vengeance of the Almighty.

'Everybody deserved a second chance in life!' he would shout to his awestruck listeners. 'All you have to do is to ask our Lord Jesus to forgive you! It's as simple as that! And, you'll be saved – instantly! Believe me!' Then looking upwards and pointing, he would exclaim, 'Look! An angel from heaven is right here with us! Do you see it?' Everybody would 'cross' their chests and nervously look up to where he was pointing – expecting to see a heavenly vision.

Seizing the opportunity he would shout, 'The reason why you cannot see the angel of the Lord is because you have not been forgiven for your sins! In the name of our Lord Jesus Christ, I command you to get down on your knees and ask for His forgiveness and be saved! Everybody! Down on your knees! Right now!'

There wasn't a person who dared ignore his call. In this manner, he succeeded in changing the fleece of many sheep from 'black' to 'white.'

After his arrival in Singapore he went to work immediately at the church's headquarters that was in a house in Holland Road, a prime residential area. He had studied several reports by members of his church on Singapore's 'red light' areas that were marked with tiny, red paper flags on a map on a wall in his office. The reports were not encouraging. The people in these areas, the reports said, were followers of various religious beliefs and cults or were non-believers. Furthermore, the majority of prospective converts had only a limited knowledge of English, said the reports.

The Rev. Pickford-Smith had not encountered such problems in the Philippines. But, he was a man of steadfast determination and had his reputation to protect. He made up his mind that he would prove the reports wrong. 'There's no place on God's earth where God's work cannot be done!' he declared.

One morning he summoned his 'shepherds' to announce that he was going undercover in Bugis Street, one of the most notorious 'red light' areas, to see for himself how Satan went about his business.

The street had been named after early Bugis traders from the Celebes who brought their cargoes of spices, birds' nests and a variety of other products to Singapore in sailing boats. Bugis Street had since become a flourishing 'red light' district with a network of brothels, opium and gambling dens, attracting sailors from all over the world for more than a hundred years.

He had been warned against venturing into such an area alone and was advised not to make fiery sermons that he was noted for, until he had made a careful survey of prevailing conditions in the area. When he was told to take along a 'shepherd' as a bodyguard, he had laughed and said, 'I have the most powerful protector anyone could wish for – our Lord Jesus Christ!' and holding up a small prayer book, exclaimed, 'And, here is my trusty weapon!'

Shortly before midnight that night, he dressed like a tourist in slacks and a floral Hawaiian shirt and took a taxi to Bugis Street. As he was being taken there he remembered reading a report which said, 'Bugis Street catered to a variety of people with various vices and perversions. One had only to name what was desired and got it, for a price.'

Stepping from the taxi, the Rev. Pickford-Smith stood in the shadows at the entrance to the narrow street. The strong smell of Chinese cooking dominated by the pungent smell of fried garlic, hung in the air.

On one side of the street was a row of ancient two-storey, brick shop-houses (shops below, living quarters above) that accommodated Chinese liquor shops with small wooden tables and bamboo stools for customers. Outside on the narrow pavement were more tables resting on planks covering 'monsoon' drains and more tables on the street itself, leaving barely enough space for a car to pass.

The stench from the stagnant drains were to some extent lessened by cooking smells and the sickly odour of opium smoke from the nearby dens. Now and then, a gust of breeze momentarily cleared the air and permitted the strong, sensuous fragrance of frangipani and jasmine, both popular perfumes with the women prostitutes and their male rivals who came to Bugis Street each night to sell their bodies.

Rev. Pickford-Smith shut his eyes and said a silent prayer, 'O Lord, give me courage and make me victorious in my battle against Satan tonight!'

He walked between the tables at which sat men and women

of Asian races he had not seen before. Some drunken men were asleep with their heads resting on the tops of tables as their hopeful male or female escorts tried to revive them. He stood some distance away to observe the scene before him.

Sitting alone at a table was a tall, sinewy European who was dressed in a black T-shirt and black jeans tucked into his shiny, black riding boots. He had a shaved head, a drooping moustache and 'goatee' beard. A gold ring hung from the lobe of his left ear. Around his neck was a heavy gold chain and cross. On his table stood a bottle of Russian vodka and a packet of black Russian cigarettes. Seeing the cross the man was wearing, the Rev. Pickford-Smith was about to make his acquaintance when he saw a young woman with a bare mid-riff and the American flag tattooed above her navel go up to the man and say, 'What your name, handsome man?'

'Piss-off!' he replied.

The girl smiled and said, 'Oh, hullo, Piss-off! You buy for me drink? I give you good time!' She was about to take a seat beside him when a slim, young man with dyed ginger hair in a red T-shirt and white slacks, shoved her aside and embracing the man in black – and sat on his lap. The girl walked away muttering under her breath.

The Rev. Pickford-Smith saw effeminate young men and attractive transvestites in low-cut cocktail frocks and rubber padding in their 'bras' parading under the lights, their imitation jewellery sparkling. They might have got away with their impersonations had their masculine voices and traces of stubble on their chins not betrayed them.

In a corner of the street two of their 'tribe' were hissing, scratching and pulling at each other's hair. They fell over a table and rolled on the filthy street. A big, Black man wearing a yellow cowboy hat and boots and whose affections they were apparently fighting over, laughingly poured a bottle of Tiger beer over them. They stopped fighting, stood up and showered him with obscenities in English, Malay and Chinese. He laughed as he saw them walk away, dripping beer and embracing each other.

There were gaudily-dressed old whores, the wear-and-tear of the years of their demanding profession showing on their lined faces, despite the heavy make-up. These were 'the zombies of Bugis Street,' as someone had described them. Although they were willing to offer any form of sexual perversion for a fraction of what their young counterparts charged, they rarely found customers. They patiently stood away from the tables occupied by younger whores of both sexes and their clients, hoping for hand-outs to help buy a shot of cheap Chinese *shamshu*, a 'fix' of adulterated cocaine or a pipe of opium dregs to help chase away the demons that tormented them in their dreams.

Many people knew Bugis Street as 'The Street Of Broken Hearts' It was where passions could develop into wild infatuations that sometimes had tragic endings.

During his research on Bugis Street one of the Rev. Pickford-Smith's 'shepherds' had told him the story about a tragic love affair between Gracie, a Hokkien whore and Crazy Jack, a young English sailor that happened some years before.

Everybody in Bugis Street had thought Jack was crazy because he did crazy things when he was drunk, dressing like a transvestite and performing a striptease on top of a table. The *grand finale* of his act was to climb up a lamp-post and to sing *God Save The Queen*.

Standing on a table one night with Gracie in his arms, Crazy Jack announced to everyone that he was going to marry her and take her to England.

The wedding reception would be held in Bugis Street and everyone was invited. A cheer went up from the crowd at the tables and for two days a hat was passed around for donations to help pay for the cost of the wedding.

A few days before they were to be married by a Taoist priest, Gracie went out to do some shopping, leaving Crazy Jack asleep in the small apartment she shared with a young whore named

Fifi. Not to awaken Jack whom she thought could be still asleep, Gracie tip-toed to her bedroom on her return. She quietly opened the door and was horrified to see Jack and Fifi making love on her bed.

She went quickly to the kitchen, grabbed a long-bladed meat knife and burst into the bedroom. She pulled Jack off Fifi and stabbed her through the heart. She then pounced on Jack, cut off his penis and watched him bleed to death. She swallowed a bottle of sleeping pills and killed herself.

The Rev. Pickford-Smith was wondering how many others there were like Gracie and Crazy Jack in Bugis Street when he was approached by a dark, young woman wearing a transparent blouse of gold net over her black 'bra.' She was heavily made up and had a large red dot between her eyes. She flashed him a smile as she pointed to a vacant table beside a 'monsoon' drain.

As they sat at the table an old Chinese playing the *erhu* with a coloured lantern suspended from its neck began singing an operatic song very loudly through his nose. Those at the tables he stopped by and who were obviously irritated by the sound of his voice quickly gave him some money and he went away.

'The old chap practices a very subtle form of extortion by using his sharp, penetrating voice as an intimidating weapon!' remarked a professor from a university in England who was at a nearby table. He told the Rev. Pickford-Smith he had 'come to observe Bugis Street as part of a sociological survey' that he was conducting. A young man with long, wavy hair and mascara eyes snuggled close to the professor, holding his hand.

The girl with the Rev. Pickford-Smith told the *erhu*-player something in Chinese and he stopped singing. 'You pay him fifty cent, he go away,' she told the reverend. She spoke English with a Chinese accent, although she wasn't Chinese. He gave the man a dollar. He presented the reverend with a packet containing two salted Chinese plums and went to serenade the people at another table.

A Chinese in shorts, a T-shirt with 'Harvard University' printed on it and wearing wooden clogs, came up to the girl and the reverend. 'You want drink?' he asked.

'A small bottle of beer,' said Rev. Pickford-Smith as he brushed aside a few a 'blue-bottle' flies from the nearby drain. The girl grabbed his hand and squeezing it said, 'You can buy for me drink, okay?' He nodded his head. The girl said something to the man in Chinese. The man went away after making a note of her order in a small book. He would pay her a commission, later, which was the 'custom'.

The girl told the reverend her name was Varma and he lied to her that his name was Tim and that he worked on an American ship. The waiter brought a small bottle of Tiger beer for him and a large glass that contained Bulldog stout fortified with a double shot of Chinese *shamshu*, as she had instructed him. She quickly swallowed half the contents of the glass, lit a cigarette and squeezing his hand again, said, 'We go my room after you drink beer, okay? I give you good time. Short-time forty dollar. All night, sixty dollar. I clean girl. I go to clinic for check-up every week. I no tell lie.' From her coloured glass-beaded purse she produced a small blue card from a government VD clinic. It had her photo on it and had been stamped 'inspected' and a recent date. The Rev. Pickford-Smith glanced at the card and returned it to her.

She moved her stool closer to his and placing an arm on his shoulder tried to kiss him, but he moved his head away. She grinned and said, 'Hey, you no like girl, *ah*? Why you no tell me? It's okay. You want young man or girl-boy?'

The Rev. Pickford-Smith took a sip of his beer and a deep breath before he replied. 'No. I don't want anything, thank you. Could we just talk? I shall pay you for your time.'

She looked at him strangely. 'You only want only talk-talk?'

'Yes. Only talk-talk,' he said with a smile.

'Okay. One hour you must pay twenty dollar. Also, you must buy for me two more drink.'

He nodded his head, still smiling. He didn't mind the cost because he intended to ask her many questions.

'You pay money first, okay?' she said. He took two ten-dollar bills from his wallet and gave them to her. She stuck the money into her purse. As she sipped her second glass of supercharged stout she felt in a mood to answer his questions that were mainly about the girls who came each night to Bugis Street, their backgrounds, nationalities and religious beliefs.

When he had asked her, 'Have you heard of Jesus, the Son of God?' She nodded her head, 'crossed' her chest and laughed aloud, 'See? I know!'

'Would you like to know more about Jesus?' he asked. She grinned, wagging her head from side to side, declining the offer and said, 'If Jesus father is number one god who stay up there,' she pointed to the sky, 'Why he never save his son? *Hi-yah!* If people want to kill my son, I sure must try save him! Never mind I die!'

He looked at her steadily. He remembered what he had read in the reports about Bugis Street being a tough area. His eyes began to roam from table to table. The cosmopolitan crowd bothered him. What Varma had just told him also bothered him. Was everyone like her? He had planned on giving one of his 'surprise' sermons, like he had done with much success in Manila before coming to Singapore but changed his mind. He wasn't sure now of victory. In the Philippines he had dealt with people who were mainly Christians and who understood English. Bugis Street presented a different and complex problem.

When he asked Varma, 'Which god do you pray to?' she grinned and said, 'I pray so many god! I pray money god, good luck god, god for gamble!' She laughed aloud. 'But money god best! Because, if have money can have everything! If no have money, have nothing! Cannot eat! Cannot drunk! Cannot screw! Better die!'

He asked her if she had ever thought of marrying and settling down to a 'good life.'

She said, 'All girl like dream to marry good man, have baby and house. But, dream is all bullshit! Bugis Street girl only talk about how to happy, how to drunk, how to get money!' She laughed again.

The waiter came to inquire if more drinks were needed. 'No thanks,' said the reverend and looked at Varma's glass. It was empty. 'Have another drink?' he asked. Although he was getting nowhere with her he didn't wish to be left alone at the table. She told the waiter to bring her another glass of supercharged Bulldog stout.

He summed up the scene around him. 'A flock of lost sheep of various colours and tastes,' he thought, and sighed. He also noticed that the 'flock' had increased in size since his arrival an hour before.

He looked at his watch. It was almost 2 a.m. His visit had been unrewarding. He was about to leave Varma with her drink and take a taxi back home when looking towards the entrance to the street he saw something that captured his immediate attention.

A girl with a white skin and blonde, wavy hair had stepped out of a taxi. She wore a tight-fitting yellow satin *cheong-sam* that accentuated her shapely body. He noticed she was young, in her twenties perhaps. And, although he was some distance away, he saw she was beautiful. He was quick to notice, too, that around the high-neck collar of her *cheong-sam* hung a cross from a gold chain that nestled in her cleavage.

Varma said, 'Her name Jenny. Her father English soldier. Die already. Her mother Chinese. Also die already. Jenny speak English very good.'

He saw the men at the tables turning their heads as she passed by, some reaching out to touch her body. She pushed their hands away good-naturedly and went to a table occupied by a stocky Chinese with tattoos on his arms and sat in front of him. He said something to her and gave her a small paper packet. She opened her purse and handed him some money and he went away.

A huge Black man in a T-shirt, jeans and baseball cap came up and sat in front of her. A waiter placed two glasses and a bottle of Johnnie Walker whisky before them and a container with ice cubes. The man poured some whisky into the glasses, dropping in the ice. They began talking and laughing. The reverend was too far away to hear their conversation because of the noise coming from the 'flock of lost sheep' that surrounded him.

'Jenny have many boyfriend,' said Varma and sighed. 'She very beautiful. Every man want her.'

'I wish to meet her,' he said.

'When?' asked Varma.

'Tonight.'

She laughed. 'How can? She sure already book for all night.'

'How do you know?'

'Jenny never book for short-time. Only book for all night. Must pay one hundred, twenty dollar, you know?' she said.

'One hundred and twenty dollars?' said the reverend raising his eyebrows. 'She must be very rich.'

'I don't know. Maybe,' said Varma.

Jenny and the big Black man drank more whisky for half an hour and during all that time the reverend had kept his eyes fixed on her. Now and then the light from the naked electric bulbs at the food stalls reflected from the gold cross that hung around her neck, sending tiny flashes of light. Were they dots and dashes? wondered Rev. Pickford-Smith. Were they messages in heavenly Morse code? An SOS? Was the good Lord signalling to him that he must save her? He felt a shiver run down his back.

'Jesus is watching,' he told himself and looked upwards instinctively. He was somewhat annoyed that his view of the heavens was hampered by a low, stationary cloud of blue smoke caused by the cooking at the Chinese food stalls and from the smoke of a thousand cigarettes rising from the 'flock of lost sheep' at the tables.

When he looked towards Jenny's table again he saw her and her companion walking hand-in-hand towards a taxi. He stood up suddenly and said to Varma, 'Goodnight. I am going home' and walked away.

She wondered what had upset him. Obviously it had something to do with Jenny. Maybe he was annoyed because he couldn't book her.

Varma drank the balance of the concoction in her glass and wandered towards a table where a small crowd were playing dice. She thought she'd try her luck with the twenty dollars 'Tim' had given her for one hour of 'talk-talk.'

In the taxi on his way home, Rev. Pickford-Smith shut his eyes and tried to picture Bugis Street and some of the faces he had seen there. But he could only see one face – Jenny's. She seemed to be everywhere. He opened his eyes and looked out of the taxi's window and thought he saw her standing under each streetlight they passed by.

He slept restlessly and on awakening found himself thinking about her again. He stared at the ceiling above his bed for a long time. He tried to find the reason why he was thinking about her so much, but couldn't. He frowned as he thought of an old, wrinkled Jenny, like one of the 'zombie' ex-whores who hovered around the tables like vultures waiting to scoop up the left-over food before the waiters came to clean-up. Would she end up like one of them? Was she occupying so much of his thoughts because she was the only White girl in Bugis Street? He ignored what Varma had told him about Jenny's mother being Chinese.

As far as he was concerned, she was White and he had to save her!

What about the lost sheep? Didn't they need to be saved, too?

'They can wait!' he told himself.

He jumped out of bed.

He was guarded about what he told his fellow 'shepherds' about his trip to Bugis Street. He described it as 'most interesting' and said he would have to make a few more visits there before he could 'work out some strategies.'

There was a letter from his wife who said she hoped to leave Manila for Singapore in about a week's time. He placed the letter in a desk drawer and his thoughts returned to Jenny. He wondered if he should return to Bugis Street that night in the hope of meeting her, but decided against it. He went to the library and began reading a book.

Shortly before midnight the Rev. Pickford-Smith found himself in Bugis Street again and seated at a table close to the one he had occupied the previous night. He looked around for Varma and asked the waiter in the 'Harvard University' T-shirt where she was. He shrugged his shoulders and grinned, 'Maybe she go for short-time. You want Tiger beer?'

He nodded his head.

The crowd was increasing as it usually did around this time.

He sipped his beer and noticed the heavy shower of rain that afternoon had washed away the stagnant rubbish in the drain not far from where he sat, temporarily depriving the 'blue-bottle' flies and rats of a rendezvous. He looked at his watch. Almost an hour had passed and he was sipping his second small bottle of Tiger beer. He didn't like the idea of being alone. Supposing Jenny showed up. What would he do? Go up to her and invite her to his table? For some strange reason he knew he wouldn't have the courage to do so.

'Oh, where are you, Varma!' he said to himself, impatiently. He'd tell her to invite Jenny to his table. Yes, that's what he'd do – that's if Jenny wasn't already 'booked'.

Nearby, a group of young, drunken sailors were having fun with an old whore named Lucy.

Sailor: 'How many times have you had syphilis?'

Lucy: 'Same as your mother!'

Sailor: 'How many bastards have you given birth to?'

Lucy: 'Same as your mother!'

Sailor: 'You are a poxed-up old whore!'

Lucy: 'Same as your mother!'

The sailors roared with laughter.

Sailor: 'You're one crazy, old bitch!'

Lucy: 'Same as your mother!'

She had asked them for a hand-out but they demanded that she sang a song first.

One of her pencilled eyebrows had been rubbed away. The mascara around her eyes and her lipstick were a mess. 'No sing, no money!' said one of the sailors.

'Gimme two dollar! I sing!' she said. 'I'll give you fifty cents and a kick in the arse!' teased one of the group.

'You naughty boy!' she said and laughed. 'Gimme two dollar, I sing. Come on,' she said.

The young sailor relented. 'Okay. Here's two dollars. Now, sing *River Of No Return* and turning to his friends, said, 'I've heard her sing this before. You'll piss yourself laughing!'

Lucy cleared her throat and began to sing in her hoarse, tuneless voice:

'There ees a liver, a liver of no lee-tung
(There is a river, a river of no return)
'Sung-ti-eet pissful ang sung-ti-wai-an-flee'
(Sometimes it's peaceful and sometimes wild and free.)

The Rev. Pickford-Smith watched the young sailors holding their sides as they laughed and said to himself, 'May the good Lord have mercy on them!'

Another fifteen minutes passed. He heard a woman's voice behind him say, 'Hey, Tim!' He looked round quickly and was relieved to see Varma. He quickly offered her a stool beside him and asked, 'Where have you been?'

She smiled, not answering his question. 'How you feel tonight? You want only talk-talk again?' and laughed.

'Yes. Do you mind?'

'No. I no mind. You pay me twenty dollar for one hour and

buy for me two drink, same last night?'

'Sure,' he said. He signalled the waiter to bring drinks.

From the corner of his eye he saw Jenny leaving a taxi.

She was wearing a low-cut, scarlet cocktail frock with a short skirt that revealed her white, shapely thighs. There were some wolf-whistles and as usual the men at the tables pawed at her as she passed by.

'Ah! Her Majesty! The Queen of Bugis Street! Come sit on my lap, sweetheart!' said a man with a beard and an Australian accent.

She avoided his outstretched hand and went to an unoccupied table.

She had made it a point to accept invitations only from men who asked her to join them in a 'gentlemanly manner'. That was the reason why she was known as 'The Queen'. She was selective, demanded respect – and got it.

'Ask her to join my table,' the reverend told Varma.

'Sure? Jenny not same like me, talk-talk for twenty dollar one hour. Jenny only for all night. Must pay one hundred and twenty dollar. I tell you before.'

'Yes. I know. You've already told me! Don't worry about that. You go quickly and ask her to come here!' he said.

She stood up. 'Okay I go ask her.' She grinned at him and said over her shoulder as she walked away, 'Hey, Tim. I think you crazy son of bitch!'

He saw Varma whispering into Jenny's ear and point towards him. They spoke briefly. As Varma came towards him, he asked anxiously, 'What did she say?'

She smiled. 'Okay. She come.'

He took a sip from his glass of beer and waited impatiently.

He saw Jenny again talking to the stocky Chinese man with tattoos on his arms as she had done the previous night. She handed him something. Money, perhaps? He gave her a small packet. Drugs, perhaps? Whatever it was, she put it into her small purse.

She looked towards where the reverend was sitting and saw that he was watching her.

She began to walk leisurely towards his table conscious he was watching every movement of her body. She was used to being looked at in this manner. After all, a man had the right to inspect her. 'I am only for hire – not for sale! Nobody can own me!' she had told some of her clients.

She realised it would be a problem for her one day if men didn't hire her any more and she became like one of those old zombies who hung around the tables. But she had vowed she would never let such a thing happen to her. 'I'd swallow a bottle of sleeping pills and get it over with,' she had promised herself.

As she came closer to his table the reverend realised she was even more beautiful than he had first thought. In fact, she was the most beautiful creature he had ever seen.

He stood up with his hand outstretched and as he touched hers, he felt a sensation running through his body, like he had never felt before.

'Good evening, Jenny. I am Tim,' he said pleasantly.' Please sit down.' Her lips parted in a smile and he could see her teeth were white and even. 'Thank you for inviting me,' she said. She spoke with a trace of a London accent.

The 'Harvard University' waiter arrived. 'Would you care for a drink?' the reverend asked her. 'Yes, please. A double whisky on the rocks,' she said. He ordered another small Tiger beer for himself and supercharged Bulldog stout for Varma.

Jenny looked at him, still smiling. 'You are from a ship, Tim?'

'Yes,' he lied.

'American?'

'Yes.'

He couldn't help stealing glances at her well-formed breasts with the gold cross resting snugly between them. He felt the strange sensation return – the one he had felt little while ago when he shook her hand.

Their attention was temporarily attracted to a heated argument between a female whore and a young male with blonde hair, eye make-up and red painted lips. He wore a shiny black shirt, white slacks and white canvas shoes. Varma, who was listening to the argument with interest, giggled and told the reverend, 'Last night, she say he steal her boyfriend, so she very angry.'

The young man gave his female rival ten dollars. She grabbed the money and smiled, her anger instantly soothed. He had given her 'face.' They embraced. All was forgotten.

The waiter brought the drinks. The reverend raised his glass of beer and said, 'Here's to good luck and good health to all of us.' He felt his hand tremble slightly as he raised the glass.

Varma said she had to use the toilet. Jenny looked at him and smiled as soon as she left. 'Do you mind if I sat beside you?' she asked him.

'Please, do.' he said. As she did, her leg brushed against his and he got the smell of her perfume. It was delicate. French, perhaps. Unlike Varma's.

She took a sip from her glass and looked up at the sky.

He said, 'Do you think it'll rain?' making conversation.

'No. There are too many stars in the sky,' she said with a smile. 'No clouds – no rain. But, I wish it would rain. I love the rain. Do you know the song, *Singing In The Rain?* It's from the movie of the same name with Gene Kelly.'

He knew it, but pretended he didn't.

She began to sing softly:
I'm singing in the rain
Just singing in the rain
What a glorious feeling
I'm happy again
I'm laughing at clouds
So dark up above there's sun in my heart
And I'm ready for love

She stopped singing and said with a laugh, 'I used to play in the rain when I was a kid and looked forward to rainy days. Everything smelt and looked so fresh after the rain. And, it was cool and clean.' She paused to reflect for a moment before continuing, 'Did you play in the rain when you were a kid?'

He did not answer.

'You speak English very well,' he said 'Was it because of your English father – Varma told me.'

'Oh? What else did she tell you about me?' she asked, smiling.

'Also, that your mother was Chinese. I heard you lived in England for some time.'

She said, 'You are asking me to tell you my life story, aren't you? I must have told it at least a thousand times before to a thousand lovers!' She laughed. 'My father was in the British army here. He was not married to my Chinese mother. My father took me to England before the war. I was three years old. I attended school until I was about fourteen and began to hang around with bums. I was sixteen when I fell madly in love with a Greek guy who was much older than me. I ran away with him to a Greek island without telling my father. Six months later my lover dumped me. I returned home to find my father was seriously ill. He had quit his job and had spent all his savings searching for me. I guess he loved me very much. I had broken his heart by running away. I could understand how he felt, because my heart had been broken, too.'

She paused and looked away, her eyes suddenly sad. 'I don't think anything could hurt as much as a broken heart. When he died a few months later I came to Singapore and found my mother. We worked as waitresses in bars. An overdose of heroin killed her two years ago. That's it. Now, tell me your life story.'

He smiled.

He hadn't expected conversation like this in Bugis Street, not after what he'd heard at the tables for the past two nights.

The conversations had been vulgar and perverted. The young whores came straight to the point with their prospective clients. 'Short-time? All night? If you kinky, you pay more money! Okay?'

It had taken Varma less then five minutes after they'd first met to grab his hand and ask him if he wished to sleep with her and naming her charges.

But, Jenny was something entirely different; her appearance, the way she spoke and everything about her. She was so . . . intelligent, decent and White! She was someone whom you could take on your arm to a black-tie dinner or to the theatre and heads would turn as she walked by. People who came to Bugis Street didn't talk about pleasant childhood memories as she had and about the joy of playing in the rain! He wondered how any man could do anything obscene to one as lovely and decent - as her.

Why did she allow herself to be mauled and abused by the scum who came to Bugis Street each night? He gritted his teeth as he remembered what Varma had told him: 'Money is god . . if have money, can have everything. If no money, have nothing . . . die better!'

He took a deep breath. He was more determined than ever before that he must save Jenny, if it was the last thing he did.

After two frustrating days he had thought he had been defeated by Bugis Street and would have to surrender. But, now as he glanced at her he knew he was presented with a chance to 'save his face' by saving her. He couldn't bear to think of her surrounded by such evil for another day and ravaged by some perverted beast!'

There wasn't any time to be lost.

He had to save her tonight!

Varma returned to the table hugging a young European wearing dirty slacks and a T-shirt. He appeared to be either drugged or drunk. His eyelids were heavy and his long red hair was dishevelled. 'This my friend Hans. He German. He very drunk. I take him go my room. Goodnight.'

Before she turned to leave, she paused to stroke the side of Jenny's face affectionately and smiled strangely at the reverend.

As Varma left, Jenny looked at him and smiled.

He had expected her to say, 'Well, let's go to my place.'

He looked at his watch. It was almost 2.45 a.m.

'Would you like me to take your home?' he asked.

She smiled. 'Yes. It's getting quite late, isn't it.'

They got into a taxi. The driver drove quickly away without her having to tell him where to go. Like all the other cabbies in Bugis Street, he knew.

The taxi stopped outside a block of two-storey 'shop-houses' on Geylang Road.

'Three dollar, eighty cent' said the cabbie and the reverend gave him the money.

They got out from the taxi and walked across a narrow pavement. She slipped a key into the lock of the door and opened it. She entered the living room and switched on the light.

'Please come in,' she said.

A sleepy-eyed Chinese woman in a crumpled *samfu* and with dishevelled, greying hair appeared from inside the house and smiled at the reverend.

'This is my Auntie,' she said.

'Good evening,' he said.

The woman grinned, scratching her backside.

Jenny and the woman spoke briefly in Chinese. 'Follow me,' Jenny told the reverend but just as he was about to, the woman said to him, 'You pay money, first, okay? One hundred twenty dollar,' and stretched out a hand.

The reverend gave her the money from his wallet. He was smiling. What he was about to achieve was worth a great deal more to him, he told himself. 'I am going to guide a lost sheep back to Jesus!'

Jenny was halfway up the stairs. She pretended not to

have noticed the transaction between the reverend and her 'Auntie.'

She opened her bedroom door, switched on a dimmed light and parted the curtain for him to enter. But, before he did, the Rev. Pickford-Smith said a silent prayer: that he would be successful in his undertaking.

Jenny's room was small and cosy with pink and white furniture, pink curtains and a white double bed with a pink covering. In the centre of the room was a coffee-table with two pink and white easy chairs and a couch.

She smiled and indicated a chair to him.

'Would you care for a drink?' she asked, looking towards a 'dumb-waiter' on which were bottles of whisky, brandy, vodka and gin. 'There's beer in the fridge, too,' she said nodding in the direction of a small refrigerator near her bed.

'No. No thanks,' he said as he sat down.

She came up to him and stroked his face and went behind a screen. Moments later she appeared wearing a Japanese 'happy coat' that was loosely held together in front by a sash. She had combed her hair so that it fell over one side of her face, giving her a sultry, seductive look. As she walked slowly towards him her movements parted the front of her coat slightly and his eyes moved from her partly covered breasts and settled on her naked thighs.

He felt his heart pounding in his ears, faintly at first and becoming louder as she came nearer to him, her red lips slightly parted and her eyes soft. She stood before him, her white, perfumed body almost touching his face.

All notions of *decency* that he had conjured in his mind about her had suddenly vanished. His throat had become dry and it took all his willpower to dispel the thoughts that flashed through his mind as he looked at her. With some effort he reminded himself of the real purpose for his visit.

He sat back in his chair. Tiny beads of perspiration had formed on his forehead.

He took another deep breath and said, 'Please sit down. There's something important I have to say to you,' indicating the couch beside his chair.

She looked hard at him and smiled, knowing that whatever little resistance he could offer would only be brief. She had encountered such situations before. Some of her clients needed 'warming up' to put them in the mood for love. Some had special requests to make. She had always obliged if they paid her extra.

She stroked the side of his face again and lay down on the couch, her head resting on a cushion, her feet pointing towards him. She was still smiling at him with a triumphant look, like a cat would have given a cornered mouse.

He had not experienced a situation like this before with other 'lost sheep'. He had easily convinced them of his ability to 'wash away their sins.' Jenny, however, would require special attention because she was *intelligent*, forgetting that he had also thought she was *decent*.

He had told the 'shepherds' at the headquarters of the Church Of Lost Sheep that he would 'triumph with Jesus,' ignoring their warnings that he would find Bugis Street a 'tough nut to crack.' He had reassured them, 'Nothing is tough enough to stop me! Call me one-track minded, but I only think of victory – never defeat! Think positive! That is my success story!'

After his first visit to Bugis Street, he had reason to doubt the victory he had anticipated until Jenny appeared as though she had been specially sent to encourage him in his moments of despair. She had presented him with the opportunity to 'save his face' by saving her soul.

He was confident she would understand when he told her who he really was and the real reason why he had booked her for the night.

Supposing she wasn't interested in being saved and like Varma she also believed money was the 'god of everything'? What, then? He had no alternative plan to fall back on because until now, the possibility of failure had never bothered him.

These thoughts had flashed through his mind as he stared at the floor of her bedroom.

She waited to hear what he had to say.

He looked at her briefly, then lowered his eyes again and said, 'I am not the person I told you I am. I do not work on a ship. My name isn't Tim. I have not come here to . . . ' he paused.

'To sleep with me?' she said with a smile.

He nodded his head, his eyes still fixed on the floor, not knowing what her reaction would be. She got up from the couch and went to her bedroom door. She called out to the old woman downstairs and said something to her in Chinese. A few moments later the reverend heard footsteps coming up the stairs and there was a brief, whispered discussion between the two women.

Jenny came up to him. In her hand was the one hundred and twenty dollars he had given the woman earlier.

She held out the money to him.

'Please take this,' she said.

'No . . . no . . .' he began, pushing her hand gently away, feeling that if he had accepted the money he would not be paying for the time he wished to spend with her and that she would be freeing herself of any obligation to him.

She folded the money, stuck it into the top pocket of his shirt and stretched herself out on the couch again.

He looked at her with a slight frown.

'It's quite all right' she said pleasantly.

'Okay. If it's all right with you,' he said.

She laughed lightly. 'It would have been my fee if we were going to make love. I do not charge for the time I spend talking to people. That would be most unfair. Could I get you a drink?'

She got up and went towards the 'dumb waiter.'

'Could I have a glass of water, please?' he said.

'Only water? Sure?' she asked.

'Yes. Quite sure.'

She poured herself a double whisky on the rocks and a glass of water for him. She carried the bottle of whisky and her glass in one hand and the glass of water in the other. She handed him the water and placed the bottle of whisky on the table beside her.

He quickly swallowed some water and allowed himself a few moments to regain his composure.

Focusing his eyes on a vase of artificial orchids on the table before him and not daring to look at her, lest he became distracted. He took a deep breath and said:

'I have come here to ask you to take our Lord Jesus Christ into your heart and to ask him to forgive you for your sins – and be saved.'

He paused, waiting for her reaction.

She was silent for a few moments before she asked softly, 'You are going to save me?'

'Yes.'

She was silent again. From the corner of his eye he saw her drain her glass and pour more whisky into it from the bottle. She was watching him closely. He looked away from her.

During the next fifteen minutes he paced the carpeted floor as he gesticulated and explained in an incessant flow of words, instances of how other 'sheep' that had gone astray had been saved by him, abandoning their lives of sin. 'They were accepted into the flock of the Supreme Shepherd – the Lord Jesus Christ!' he said, raising his voice a little.

All the while he spoke she had sipped whisky.

He came to the end of the first part of his sermon with these rather startling words: 'An angel from heaven is here! I can feel its presence in this room! It has come to witness your rescue from sin! Prepare yourself for that glorious moment!'

He had now regained full confidence in himself. He was ready to begin the second and final part of his sermon. He took a sip of water from his glass and said, looking up at the bedroom ceiling and raising his arms slowly, 'I appeal to you . . . I beg of you! Please abandon your sinful life and be saved!' and quoting from The Book Of The Prophet Isaiah 40, 11, he said, 'He shall feed his flock like a shepherd: he shall gather the lambs with his arms and carry them in his bosom and shall gently lead those that are with young.'

He swung round to look at her and was surprised to see that she had fallen asleep with the empty glass in her hand. He also noticed the sash that held the front of her coat together had become undone. She was naked. He was in a situation he had not anticipated. He felt his heart racing again and the sound of his heartbeats were louder than before, like a drum being beaten rapidly in his ears. He removed the empty glass from her hand and placed it on top of the table beside her.

His eyes devoured every inch of her. He slowly bent his body over her and he touched her face with the tips of his fingers. It electrified him. He looked at her red lips that were slightly apart and only inches away from his own – and suddenly, his lips were pressing hard against hers as his hands feverishly found her breasts. The next moment, he was undressing himself with trembling, sweaty hands . . . and he was naked . . . and on top of her . . . and kissing her hungrily. He felt her arms around his shoulders and heard her whisper, 'Why did you take so long to come to me?' As he felt the heat of his passion, he told her how beautiful she was and how he had desired her from the moment he saw her.

Nothing else mattered to him now.

He lay next to her breathing heavily from his exertions, his face and body damp with perspiration.

The release of his passion had calmed him.

She was silent and motionless.

After a while he stood up and sipped some water from the glass on the table.

He saw she had fallen asleep.

He moved about the room noiselessly as he dressed, unaware that she was watching him. He stood before the mirror of her dresser and wiped his face with Kleenex and combed his hair. He sat on the chair beside the couch on which she lay and put on his shoes. He tip-toed towards the door.

As he reached it, he heard her call out, 'Hey! You haven't paid me!'

He stopped, realising the money was still in the top pocket of his shirt where she had put it. He should have given it to her because he had made love to her – and it was her fee. He removed the money from his pocket and offered it to her as she came up to him.

He could see she was angry.

'Forgive me,' he said. 'I forgot the money was still in my pocket.'

She snatched the money away from his hand and slapped him hard across the face, knocking his spectacles to the floor. 'Liar! I was watching you. You thought I was asleep. Why didn't you tell me you were leaving? I thought you were decent! I treated you like a gentleman and you tried to sneak away – like a thief! To think I had almost believed what you said about saving sinners!'

'Please! It isn't what you think!' he said.

'Why did you have to tell me all that bullshit? Why did you pretend to be a preacher? Shit! You're just another one of those kinky sons-of-a-bitches!'

'Oh, no! No! Please . . . please! Don't say such things! Let me explain!' he pleaded.

'You want me to hear more bullshit? Get out, you sick bastard!' she shouted.

The old woman hearing a commotion came into the room and Jenny quickly told her in Chinese what had happened. The woman screamed, 'You steal money! *Hi-yah!* You steal money! I call police catch you!'

The woman pushed him out of the bedroom. She followed him as he stumbled down the stairs in the semi-darkness. She opened the front door and he ran outside as he heard the woman shout, 'Son of bit-chee!'

She spat after him as he began to walk quickly away.

The first pink streaks of dawn were beginning to appear as he got into a Yellow Top taxi. He told the driver where to go and wound down the windows. He felt relaxed, although he could still feel the sting on the left side of his face where Jenny had slapped him.

He knew she would tell everybody at Bugis Street about what happened. He smiled and thought, 'Well, let her. I'll never go there again.'

He was glad he hadn't told her his name.

He felt she had deceived him by giving him the impression that she was decent. But, no decent person would have behaved the way she did . . . and the horrible things she had said to him! He had never been so humiliated in his life!

Satan had triumphed over him in a moment of weakness when he was unguarded and while he was about to save her soul. He would ask Lord Jesus for forgiveness.

He remembered what Varma had said about Bugis Street girls – that money was their god.

'Sinners! Let them all burn in hell! There were others who were more deserving of being saved!' he told himself.

He dismissed the incident from his mind and his thoughts went to his wife, who would be joining him within a few days. He would not tell her about Jenny, of course. It hadn't been his practice to inform her about certain other 'rescues.'

The breeze rushing in through the open windows of the taxi invigorated him. He sat back in his seat and remembered he was scheduled to speak at the Rehabilitation Home For Young Women the following day.

He smiled and began to hum softly to himself.

Snake Wine, Anyone?

It was June 1933 and Philpotts was about to attend his first cocktail party since arriving in Kuala Lumpur, the Federal capital of Malaya, a week before.

'I've heard Malayan cocktail parties were quite unlike those in England. They're supposed to have an air of the mystical Orient about them,' he said to Cutler with whom he shared an apartment.

'Indeed!' said Cutler who had been living in Kuala Lumpur for more than a two years. 'One must not forget the inscrutable cocktails prepared by inscrutable Chinese bartenders,' added Cutler dryly, stifling a yawn with the back of his hand.

Philpotts paused while tying a knot in his necktie to raise his eyebrows and ask, 'Inscrutable cocktails? Whatever do you mean by that?'

'I said "inscrutable," Cutler replied, 'because we don't really know what our Chinese bartenders put into the cocktails they prepared to give them such a distinctive flavour.'

'Oh? You also said, "inscrutable" Chinese bartenders. What makes them so?'

'Well, didn't you know that all Chinese were supposed to be inscrutable? Sinister? Mysterious? Haven't you read any books on the mystical East, old chap? Anyway, I think you should know that Chinese bartenders have long been suspected of secretly adding snake wine to their cocktail recipes'

'Snake wine? What the devil is that?'

'It's Chinese rice wine delicately flavoured by certain species of snake that were also chosen for their medicinal value,' said Cutler.

'You jest, surely!' said Philpotts grimacing.

'No, old chap, I jest not,' said Cutler. 'It is said that snake wine adds a certain distinctive zest to cocktails prepared by Chinese bartenders and not found in any European concoction. Personally, I find snake wine pleasantly invigorating. My favourite is Hainan cobra wine which has a far more aromatic "bouquet" and fuller "body" than Yunan puff-adder or Tsingtao green bamboo-viper wine. The last-mentioned is believed to be an aphrodisiac and therefore enjoys wide popularity. I'm also told that Foochow boa-constrictor wine packs the kick of a mule. It is supposed to relieve arthritic discomfort, besides rendering a person insensible in the process. There are a large variety of wines from China to choose from. I believe the snakes are drowned in tubs of rice wine. Special herbs are added to suit each individual species of reptile and human therapeutic requirements. Of course, the sacs containing the snakes' venom are never removed since, I am told, they added potency to the final product.'

Philpotts' face had taken on an unhealthy greyish-green hue and his jaw had sagged.

Cutler controlled a desire to burst out laughing and managed to continue, keeping a 'straight face.'

'Some wines are bottled with young snakes inside,' he went on. 'Besides being decorative they are quite crunchy and taste rather like pickled gherkins. I really must take you to a snake wine-tasting party. Unlike European wine tasting that is accompanied by disgusting gargling, mouth-rinsing and spitting, Chinese snake-wine tasters swallow every drop! A most practical and hygienic way of disposal, don't you think?'

Philpotts' face had now turned a sickly yellow. 'Good God!' he croaked.

They were both twenty-five and draughtsmen employed by a firm of structural engineers that was founded in 1911 by three very unpopular but very successful English gentlemen named Brooks, Baldwin and Beaumont (all deceased) who were despised for the unethical tactics they brazenly employed to secure lucrative contracts. They were known in certain circles as The Three B's.

Cutler had been with the firm for just over two years. They were going to attend a reception given by Mr Charles Porter-Smythe, the chairman of Messrs Brooks, Baldwin and Beaumont to celebrate the company's recent award of a contract from the Yat Fatt Prosperous Property Development and Investment Company to build Plum Blossom Mansion, a block of offices in the business district.

'I say, you must tell me a thing or two about what a newcomer like myself should expect at a function like the one we're attending this evening. I suppose there would be a fair number of Chinese among the guests? How does one go about communicating with them? Do they all speak English or does one have to resort to pidgin English, or sign language?' asked Philpotts, having recovered from the effects of Cutler's hair-raising revelations about Chinese bartenders and snake wine.

Cutler smiled. 'I shall advise you accordingly, later.'

With Cutler at the wheel of his battered MG sports car and Philpotts seated beside him, they roared towards the city. Philpotts seemed to be worried, frowning deeply.

'I say, we're not going to attend a bally funeral! Cheer up!' Cutler shouted above the roar of the car's engine.

'It's all right for you! You know what to do at these parties,' said Philpotts, sulking. To which Cutler replied, 'The only advice I could give you is not to get trapped in a conversation with a Chinese gentleman and find you have difficulty in understanding what he's saying because of his Chinese pronunciation of English words. In which case, don't keep saying to him, "Excuse me, but could you repeat what you just said?" This is where tolerance and good manners are called for because the gentleman could be one of the Chinese board members of our company. One is never quite sure whom one may meet at these parties. While some Chinese are only able to speak a smattering of English, or none at all, others have degrees from British universities and would be happy to spend a relaxing afternoon analysing the works of Chaucer, Lord Byron or Shakespeare! Your best bet would be to nod your head, smile pleasantly and cautiously adjust to the situations as they presented themselves. By doing so, I am confident you'll come through with flying colours.'

A shiver ran through Philpotts who nodded his head seriously although Cutler was enjoying every moment of the anxiety he was causing.

Philpotts had decided he would 'play it safe' and keep close to Cutler throughout the evening, not letting him out of his sight for a second.

A scale model of the four-storey Plum Blossom Mansion was displayed on a table at the entrance to the Town Hall's ballroom where the reception was being held. Beside it were bouquets of flowers in baskets tied with broad red and pink ribbons on which were written appropriate 'good luck' slogans in Chinese characters.

Some distance away was a long table behind which was a row of vacant chairs, soon to be occupied by board members of Messrs Brooks, Baldwin and Beaumont and the Yat Fatt (which means 'No.1 Luck') Prosperous Property Development and Investment Company who were supplying the money for the Plum Blossom project.

At the centre of the table was a microphone on a stand into which propitious speeches would be made before and at the conclusion of the official contract-signing ceremony, after which champagne would be served, toasts would be proposed and the guests set free to gorge themselves with a variety of food – and to get drunk.

Cutler and Philpotts stood close to the entrance, holding glasses of beer. They were watching Mr Porter-Smythe and his wife greeting a stream of guests.

Mrs Porter-Smythe a tall and bony woman was seen to sway slightly as she bared her long, tobacco-stained teeth in a perpetual grin and allowed her extended lace-gloved right hand to be shaken, gripped, pumped and squeezed. Her husband, a tubby, nervous man, greeted everyone as though they were long-lost friends. 'Wonderful to see you again! So nice of you to come!' he would say in his high-pitched voice.

Cutler remarked pleasantly to Philpotts, 'It is my considered opinion that Mrs Porter-Smythe is under the influence of alcohol and her performance this evening could create some concern.' Cutler saw the guests moving rather swiftly towards the buffet tables. 'Come on, let's get stuck into the food!' he said.

'What's the hurry?' asked Philpotts.

'It's time you learnt, dear boy, that eating is one of the two most popular activities of the people in this part of the world. So, if you don't wish to starve, follow me!' said Cutler.

'What's their other most popular activity?' asked Philpotts.

'A game called, Chasing The Dollar.'

A recording of a Strauss waltz coming from a loudspeaker attached to a pillar was halted abruptly. It was replaced by the sound of a small bell ringing, followed by the voice of Mr Porter-Smythe after the board members of both companies had taken their seats at the main table.

'Good evening ladies and gentlemen,' he said into the microphone over the sounds of slurping, sucking, swallowing and belching coming from the buffet tables. He paused, expecting the sounds of human feeding to cease, but they continued.

One of the European guests realising Mr Porter-Smythe's predicament, made a long and loud 'Shhhhhhh!' sound, like that of air escaping from a car tyre. The warning was transmitted by other guests, notably European, while directing freezing stares at the 'locals.'

Mr Porter-Smythe cleared his throat and began again, 'Good evening ladies and gentlemen,' he said, taking a deep breath as he began to read from a prepared speech he was holding.

'Welcome to this reception which is to witness the signing of the official contract between the firm of Messrs Brooks, Baldwin and Beaumont of which I am proud to be chairman and whose honourable board members are seen seated to my right and the honourable Yat Fatt Properous Development and Investment Company, whose honourable board members are seen seated to my left – and the reason why we are graciously assembled here this evening is to witness and to celebrate the signing of a contract awarded to Messrs Brooks, Baldwin and Beaumont for the construction of Plum Blossom Mansion, a building of modern offices and a model of which is prominently displayed in the centre of this hall and which no doubt has caught your attention because of its unique . . . . design . . . and . . . '

Mr Porter-Smythe stopped speaking suddenly and gasped. His face had turned a ghostly white since his asthmatic lungs had run out of air while attempting to read the long-winded opening paragraph.

He silently cursed Stevenson the assistant manager, who wrote the speech. 'Not a damn fullstop in it! Not a bloody semi-colon!' Nothing to give me the chance to pause and catch my breath! That swine Stevenson! I know he dislikes me as much as I dislike him! He is aware of the poor state of my lungs and did this on purpose to embarrass me, the fiend!'

Mr Porter-Smythe began to wheeze, cough and grind his dentures while he bowed and smiled apologetically for the sudden breakdown in communications.

During the brief hold-up, a distinguished-looking Chinese gentleman with a grey beard and wearing a long Mandarin gown who was seated in the centre of the Yat Fatt representatives began to applaud enthusiastically. He was obviously under the impression that Mr Porter-Smythe had come to the end of his speech because he had seen him bow. According to some practitioners of Chinese etiquette, a person only bowed at the beginning and end of a speech or a performance, a fact unknown to Mr Porter-Smythe.

Other Yat Fatt Company directors and Chinese guests began to applaud. The Europeans, not to be outdone responded with equal enthusiasm and soon the hall was echoing the sounds of an impromptu hand-clapping competition accompanied by shouts of 'Hear! Hear!' 'Bravo!' and 'Jolly fine speech!' from the European guests. This was met by the shouting of 'good luck' slogans in Chinese which went on for a few minutes before the contestants suddenly realised they were wasting valuable drinking and eating time and made a hasty return to the bar and food tables.

A dumbfounded Mr Porter-Smythe began to wave the two pages of his unread speech in the air. He saw to his horror that all the board members of the Yat Fatt Company had vacated their seats and were gathered in small clusters, chatting happily with other Chinese guests as they chewed on roasted spare ribs and swallowed brandy.

Mr Porter-Smythe suddenly spotted Stevenson. 'Ah! There you are! Don't just stand there gaping! Do something, dammit!' he panted.

Stevenson had courageously appeared from behind a pillar where he had hidden himself after Mr Porter-Smythe's brief and ill-fated opening delivery.

'Yes, sir!' said Stevenson without having a clue as to what he intended doing. He went quickly to the microphone and began to adjust its height, playing for time. He cleared his throat and opened his mouth twice but no words came from it.

He felt a sharp prod in his ribs and got a strong whiff of gin. Then he heard a woman's voice say into his left ear, 'Pish-off!'

Breathing the fumes of Old Colonial Gin into his face was Mrs Porter-Smythe who had shoved him aside with the point of her bony elbow. She stood before the microphone, swaying slightly. She quickly drained the glass of gin and tonic in her hand and taking a cake knife from the table began striking the side of her empty glass.

'This should be interesting' remarked Cutler to Philpotts who was standing beside him, 'the dear old thing is as drunk as a skunk!'

'Atten-shun please, everyone,' said Mrs Porter-Smythe, smiling pleasantly and winking a glazed eye at her husband who had begun to wheeze again. 'Pleash gather round to witnessh the contract-shining sherry-mony That's what we're here to witnessh anyway – and you gentlemen over there,' she said pointing a thin, shaky finger at a group of Yat Fatt Company board members, 'kindly return to your sheats.' She leaned towards her husband and whispered, 'I'd forget about making that shilly speech! Just get the bally contract shined!

She turned to address the puzzled Yat Fatt board members again, 'Come on, all you gentlemen . . . get back to your sheats!' baring her discoloured teeth as she waved them towards the main table.

'One never ceases to be puzzled by the strange conduct of these foreign barbarians,' a dignified-looking Yat Fatt board member was heard to mutter in Mandarin to another board member who was standing beside him.

The contract was quickly signed, hands were shaken and bows exchanged, camera flashbulbs and champagne corks popped and everybody quickly returned to the bar and food.

Philpotts, staggering slightly after several whiskies, accidentally bumped into a young Chinese with a pleasant face and well-greased hair that was parted in the middle.

'Oh, I'm dreadfully sorry!' said Philpotts.

The man replied casually with an Oxford accent, 'My fault, old bean. Had my eyes focused on a curvaceous female in a seductive *cheong-sam*. Were you on your way to visit the resident pharmacist?'

'The resident pharmacist?' echoed Philpotts, puzzled.

'Yes, that's what I call bartenders, old chap! Come along,'

he said cheerily as they went towards the bar.

Philpotts found it difficult to contain his joy at his sudden and unbelievable stroke of good fortune, because he had accidentally bumped into a species of human being that he had believed only existed in the minds of writers of fiction. Walking beside him was the perfect example of a WOG – a Westernised Oriental Gentleman! How wrong Kipling was when he wrote, 'Oh, East is East and West is West and never the twain shall meet,' thought Philpotts. The 'twain' had not only met, but had happily presented such a person in a navy-blue blazer with six gold buttons, white flannel 'Oxford bags', white buckskin shoes, red socks and a bright pink scarf tucked into the collar of a yellow silk shirt.

'Ah, how absolutely marvellous! A Bohemian WOG!' Philpotts almost shouted, feeling the urge to do a couple of cartwheels.

'I fancy a Black Velvet which is a combination of champagne and Irish stout,' said the WOG.

Philpotts controlled his feelings and chose to stick to whisky although he would have liked to have celebrated his anthropological 'discovery' with champagne.

'By the way, I'm Bertrand Chung. I also answer to the name of Bertie and if I had a tail, I'd wag it! Ha! Ha! Ha!' he said, offering his hand which Philpotts grabbed and squeezed as he happily announced, 'I'm Philip Philpotts! It's indeed a pleasure to meet you . . . a great pleasure!'

Philpotts couldn't wait a second longer to inform Cutler of his sensational discovery. He breathlessly said to Bertie Cheung, 'I've a friend and colleague whom you must meet! Shan't be a second!' as he ran up to Cutler. He paused briefly to catch his breath. 'I say, I've found him! I had never imagined one existed!'

'What the devil are you talking about?' asked Cutler.

'I've met an absolutely marvellous bloke! A thoroughbred Westernised Oriental Gentleman! A genuine WOG, old boy!

He's Chinese but English all the way down to his red socks and white buckskin shoes! You must meet him!' and grabbing Cutler by the arm led him quickly to where Bertie Cheung was standing and quietly sipping his drink.

'May I present Desmond Cutler…and this is Bertie Chung!' said Philpotts as he introduced the two men with a triumphant grin.

'Ah! A pleasure, old chap!' said Bertie.

'Ditto! Not a bad party. Enjoying yourself?' Cutler asked.

'Trying to, old boy,' said Bertie. 'This is my first cocktail party since my return from London a week ago! I've already started to miss the old village!'

'Were you there long?' asked Cutler.

'Six wonderful years! I managed to creep unnoticed into Oxford, bought myself a degree in economics and jumped on the first boat leaving for Malaya before they found out about me!' he said with a laugh.

'I say that was a bit of a cock-up just now,' said Philpotts casually. 'Some silly old ass in the Yat Fatt crowd evidently thought Porter-Smythe had ended his speech when he'd only just begun reading it!'

'Do you chaps happen to work for Brooks, Baldwin and Beaumont?' asked Bertie Chung.

'Unfortunately, yes,' said Cutler with a sigh, 'and what sort of work do you do?'

'Nothing at the moment,' replied Bertie. 'But, my father is very keen that I joined the group of companies he founded – the Yat Fatt Group,' he said, quickly adding, 'Ah, there he is, the one on the left in'the silk Mandarin gown and the long beard. The dear old soul doesn't speak a word of English – a Confucian scholar. I'm afraid he was the cause of that misunderstanding a while ago.'

Philpotts suddenly felt sick and wanted to make a dash for the toilet, realising he had called the man who had awarded the Plum Blossom building contract to Messrs Brooks, Baldwin and Beaumont, a 'silly old ass' – in front of his son!

Realising Philpotts had unwittingly committed a *faux pas*, Bertie Chung tried to put him at ease by quickly changing the subject. 'I say, I am giving a snake dinner party for some friends next week and I'd love you chaps to come. Loads of snake wine, too!' he said cheerfully, 'Eating snake, drinking snake wine and playing *mah jong* are among my die-hard Chinese habits, I'm afraid. Please say you'll come.'

Cutler said, 'Sounds wonderful!'

Philpotts looking pale and with a cold sweat forming round his collar, made some gurgling sounds.

Glancing at his watch, Bertie Chung said, 'Well, I must depart. I'll be in touch. Cheers!' as he went to join his father.

Philpotts was silent for most of the time on the way back home, making only grunting sounds in response to Cutler's efforts to engage in conversation. As far as he was concerned, the evening had been a total disaster. He was shattered and disillusioned.

Bertie Chung's craving for snake flesh and snake wine had demolished Philpotts' image of him as the 'perfect Westernised Oriental Gentleman'. The perfect WOG in Philpotts' estimation would not have a disgusting desire for 'heathen food' and would have indulged in a civilised steak and kidney pie, a pint of draught and a game of billiards or darts – not hideous *mah jong!*

'Had Bertie Chung other die-hard Chinese habits?' Philpotts asked himself. 'Perhaps Kipling was right after all! East is East and West is West and never the twain shall meet.'

He studied Cutler as he steered his MG through the traffic. He felt a growing pity for him. 'How sad! Another young English life destined for an Oriental gutter!' Philpotts thought as he remembered reading the stories of Maugham and Conrad and other tales about the Orient corrupting young, innocent Englishmen.

'Cutler enjoys eating snakes,' thought Philpotts to himself. He is a connoisseur of snake wine and probably enjoys the infernal din of Chinese opera, too!'

He grimaced.

The cool night air had helped to clear much of the alcoholic fog in Philpotts' brain and he recalled to mind a passage Kipling had penned in *Life's Handicap from The Man Who Was*, that said: 'The Russian is a delightful person till he tucks in his shirt. As an Oriental he is charming. It is only when he insists on being treated as the most easterly of western peoples instead of the most westerly of easterns that he becomes a racial anomaly and extremely difficult to handle.'

Philpotts wondered if these words in some way also described Bertie Chung.

He looked at Cutler who was humming a tune.

'Poor devil!' he thought, 'I suppose without realising it, he has become an Easternised Western Gentleman!'

The Man With An
Unforgettable Face

At the end of World War II in 1945, Cheng was one of many young men in Singapore who wished to become involved in the tourist business after having read articles in the newspapers describing the many lucrative possibilities it offered.

In the years immediately after the surrender of Germany and Japan, people were travelling to various destinations around the world by the planeload and shipload.

Seats on the few airlines that were operating at the time were heavily booked for months in advance. Few of the arrivals in Singapore were 'sight-seers.' They were all visiting places to re-establish contacts with relatives or friends from whom they had been separated because of the war or to pay their respects at the graves of loved ones who had died during the fighting in Malaya or Singapore. Others, too, wished to renew business contacts and to reopen offices for their companies that had been forced to shut down.

Cheng wished to become a tour guide although there weren't many scenic spots in Singapore in those early years after the Japanese Occupation with relics of the war still strewn about. There were only pre-war attractions; Malay *kampungs* (villages), old Chinese and Indian temples, mosques and churches, the Raffles Museum, named after Sir Thomas Stamford Raffles, the founder of Singapore (now the National Museum), the Botanic Gardens, Bugis Street with its varied, after-dark pleasures and overcrowded, shabby-looking Chinatown. There was nothing new to see.

He found a job as a trainee-guide with a small tourist agency whose owner was a pleasant old Englishman, a Mr Tea. He was interned at Changi Prison where the Japanese held British civilians after the fall of Singapore in February 1942.

Mr Tea had invested in an old British army Land-Rover, a veteran of the Burma campaign that he had bought from an army vehicles disposal dump and had it converted into a mini-bus with nine-seats: eight seats at the rear and one beside the driver.

Its camouflaged body was repainted an attractive metallic-blue. The engine had been thoroughly overhauled. The transformation was quite remarkable.

Cheng was proud to be the driver of this rejuvenated, old 'war-horse' and drove it with care as he explained the few sights of Singapore as best he could to his passengers, many of whom had been prisoners-of-war of the Japanese in other parts of South-east Asia and were visiting graves and the sites of former army POW camps. They all had bitter memories of the war.

Cheng's heart went out to these people although he did not show it. Like them, he too had painful memories – the pain tightly concealed within his heart. He had managed to control his feelings a long time ago. The years of a cruel Japanese Occupation had transformed his character to a certain extent as it had done to a great number of people.

During the Occupation a person became used to having his face slapped and his shins kicked by Japanese soldiers for the slightest reason or no reason at all. But worst of all was the fear of not knowing what was going to happen to you or to your family from day to day. People kept disappearing – taken from their homes or while walking in the streets by the *Kempeitai,* the dreaded military/secret police and not heard of or seen again. There was no way of finding out if they were alive or dead because people were too afraid to make inquiries for fear of being arrested.

The *Kempeitai* was the Japanese version of Hitler's *Gestapo*. They didn't need to have any evidence against a person. They simply accused him and gave him no chance whatsoever to prove his innocence. He wouldn't dare call any witnesses to help clear any suspicions against him for fear of them suffering the same fate as himself. A person eventually admitted his 'guilt' – that's if he survived the brutal torture.

One of the popular methods used by the *Kempeitai* to extract confessions was known as the 'water treatment.' The victim was made to lie flat on his back, his arms and legs secured by ropes. One end of a rubber hose was shoved down his throat and the other attached to a water tap. When the victim's stomach became bloated with water, his interrogators would take turns to jump on it. This process would be repeated several times, until the victim 'confessed'– if he was still alive.

There were many other ways for causing excruciating pain to extract confessions.

Death came as a welcome relief to the victims.

Under Japanese rule fear had become everybody's constant companion and Cheng grew up very frightened.

The nightmare had ended with the surrender of Japan in August 1945 after the atomic bombing of the Japanese cities of Hiroshima and Nagasaki by the Americans. But the effect the Japanese Occupation had on people still remained. However, Cheng felt that facing whatever challenges or hardships in a peaceful world was like living in paradise after what he had experienced under Japanese rule.

At times he envied the passengers in his van who had come to pray and to lay wreaths on the graves of their loved ones, either in Singapore or elsewhere, such as Kachanaburi in Thailand (formerly Siam) where many thousands of Allied prisoners-of-war had died of starvation, torture and disease. They had been used as slave labour by the Japanese to build the infamous Siam-Burma 'Death' Railway.

The reason for Cheng's envy was because he had no idea

what became of the bodies of his parents after they had been tortured to death by the *Kempeitai*. They were arrested on the day the Japanese had occupied Singapore in Feburary, 1942 and were among several thousand Chinese who were rounded up and executed in a massacre that lasted for more than a month. It is believed that some 50,000 were killed. The Japanese had admitted after the war to killing 5,000. Most of the executions took place at lonely beaches and the bodies disposed of in the sea. Nobody knows how many more were executed after the massacre because the campaign against the Chinese in Singapore and other territories occupied by the Japanese was an extension of the Sino-Japanese War that began in 1937 and in which atrocities by the Japanese army against Chinese civilians was commonplace. It was revealed at War Crimes Trials after the surrender of Japan that the massacre in Nanking in 1937 ('The Rape of Nanking') had alone claimed some 300,000 lives.

A total of 135 Japanese war criminals were hanged in Singapore after being convicted by a British War Crimes Court in 1947 for committing atrocities during the Occupation. Many were high-ranking officers whose troops under their command had taken part in the killings.

The day of Singapore's surrender to the Japanese (15 February 1942) was the most horrific day of Cheng's life because it was also the last time he saw his parents alive. His sister Lin drowned herself in the sea. She was raped by a *Kempeitai* officer and gave birth to his child, a son.

Lin had pinned a farewell note to Cheng's pillow while he was asleep on the day she killed herself. The note written in Chinese, said: 'I'm going to cast myself into the sea to end my shame and sorrow and be with our beloved parents. Please look after my child. Forgive me. I shall always love you. – Lin'

She was almost sixteen when she died; three years older than Cheng.

A tourist guide's job could be pleasant at times. It depended on who the tourists were. There was the time when Cheng was driving some tourists around in his mini-bus. One was German. He had been a prisoner in India for the duration of the war. The Shanghainese lady seated beside him was interned in Sumatra because her husband was Dutch. It was amusing to hear them converse in English; he in with a gruff German accent and she in her 'sing-song' Chinese-accented English. However, they managed to get along without too much difficulty.

The German was on his way to visit the graves of his English brother-in-law and sister, both killed in the fighting in Singapore while the Shanghainese lady was visiting the Bukit Brown cemetery to pray at the graveside of her father who died in an air raid. The cemetery was near the old Sime Road Civilian Internment Camp, where British civilians from Changi Prison were transferred in 1944 following a 'purge' at Changi Prison Internment Camp by the *Kempeitai* that resulted in several prisoners being tortured to death.

Cheng noticed that some of the British and Australian passengers were giving the German 'dirty' looks, muttering under their breaths. The German was the only former 'enemy' in the bus and Cheng wondered how the Australians, British and the Shanghainese lady would have reacted if there had been a Japanese passenger among them.

There hadn't been much affection between the Germans and the Japanese during the war although Germany, Italy and Japan were members of what was known as the 'Axis Powers' who had planned to rule the world together. There was no hope of such a thing happening according to the German passenger, who told the other passengers: 'Hitler despised the Japanese because they were not a white, Aryan race. He had thought the Italians were lazy, inferior people who were only good at preparing pasta!'

Perhaps, had there been a Japanese passenger he would have incurred the hostility of everybody, including the German – and Cheng, of course!

The hatred of the population of Singapore for the Japanese, especially among the Chinese was such that the British authorities had banned the entry of Japanese visitors. This was because their safety could not be guaranteed. Although the Chinese had been the most victimised by the Japanese, members of other communities had also suffered terribly.

The wounds the Japanese had caused to everyone in Singapore were still very fresh and very painful in their memories and Cheng had made up his mind that if he ever got his hands on a Japanese he would thrash him unmercifully – before killing him.

Lin's son, Kim, bore no resemblance to his sadistic, Japanese father. Thank God for that! Kim was slim and tall and not short and squat like his father. He also had his mother's finely-shaped mouth and nose – not his father's pig-like snout. Thank God for that, too!

Kim would never be told who his father was. Neither would he ever know that his beastly father had tortured his mother's parents to death.

The few people who did know the truth about Kim had either died or had moved to other areas in Singapore after the surrender of Japan They had their own bitter experiences of Japanese cruelty to haunt their memories.

Cheng never spoke about his family to Mr Tea, his boss, so there was no way of him knowing what bitter feelings were deep inside Cheng's heart. Cheng knew the day would come sooner or later when the British authorities would allow Japanese into Singapore and Mr Tea would expect him to take them around in his bus to visit the Japanese cemetery at Chuan Hoe Avenue off Yio Chu Kang Road where the ashes of thousands of Japanese soldiers who were killed in the fighting in Malaya and Singapore are buried as well as Japanese war criminals who had been hanged for their crimes. He would also have to take them to the old Ford Motor Factory on Upper Bukit Timah Road where General Percival surrendered Singapore to General Yamashita, commander of the victorious Japanese forces.

The YMCA building in Orchard Road was one of the many buildings used by the *Kempeitai*. Inside rows of cells had been constructed as well as torture chambers. An unknown number of people had died horrible deaths there.

It had crossed Cheng's mind that some of the Japanese tourists who would be arriving could be people who had lived in Syonan (which meant 'light of the south'). It was the name the Japanese gave Singapore. Or, perhaps they would be a different lot of people who had had nothing to do with the war. Even if this were so, it didn't alter the fact that they were *Japanese*. And, Cheng hated every Japanese with every drop of blood in his body!

What excuse could he give Mr Tea when the time came for him to show Japanese visitors around? Would he say he was ill? Supposing there were Japanese arriving every day? What would he do? Resign from his job and look for another? Doing what? He had no experience in any other kind of work. No matter which tourist agency he worked for he would be expected to show Japanese tourists around!

He always reminded himself about his responsibility to take care of Kim. Lin had asked him to do so in her suicide note. What would he do for income without a job?

There was no way out for him.

A couple of months later there was a report on the front page of the newspapers that the British authorities had lifted the ban on Japanese entering Singapore.

It made Cheng feel sick in the stomach. But, there it was in big bold type across the front page of *The Singapore Free Press:* Govt. Lifts Ban On Jap Visitors.

He flung the newspaper to the floor in disgust.

Mr Tea without knowing it made matters a lot worse for Cheng when he said, 'Ah! At last! The Japs are coming! I hate their bloody guts but if we didn't go after their business there are other tourist agencies that would! I think I'll have to get an additional tour bus in readiness!'

Cheng left the office early that day. He was disgusted with everything. He got on the Norton motor-cycle he had bought from a British army vehicles dump and took a slow ride home.

He and Kim had been living with his mother's youngest sister 'Fourth Auntie,' as they called her, and her two grown-up children for almost thirteen years – ever since Cheng's parents were arrested by the *Kempeitai*.

Kim, of course, had no memory of his mother. To him, Fourth Auntie was his 'adopted mother' and Cheng was his 'uncle.' He was told his parents had died in a Japanese air raid when he was a baby.

Cheng treasured a photo album with old family photographs. Many had been taken shortly before the Japanese Occupation. There were photos of his parents and of Lin and himself in their school uniforms. He shed tears whenever he looked at these photographs.

For many years, Cheng had tried to put the memory of that horrifying day in February 1942 when the *Kempeitai* came to his father's farm, out of his mind.

His family was a part of a small farming community in the district of Nee Soon. They were all quite poor and earned their livelihoods as vegetable, pig or poultry farmers. Cheng's father, Mr Wong, reared ducks.

As he sat in Fourth Auntie's garden under a *jambu batu* (guava) tree that evening after learning that the ban on Japanese visitors had been lifted, his mind wandered back to some of the carefree days he and Lin had spent with groups of children from the nearby farms; swimming in the duck ponds, diving amongst the huge lotus leaves and chasing ducks and geese about the place.

Then, everything changed abruptly because of the war and he suddenly felt his throat being gripped by cold, steel fingers as he thought about Lin, barely fifteen and pregnant with a half-Japanese child – and he going on twelve – both orphans! He saw Kim approaching him. He was returning from school and Cheng smiled. He was every bit a normal, healthy, Chinese boy.

Cheng got to his feet and embraced him as he ran up.

'You are back early, Uncle Cheng?' he said as Cheng reached into his pocket and withdrew a bar of chocolate. The boy grabbed it and said, 'Oh, thank you!' and ran towards the house where Fourth Auntie was waiting to give him his dinner.

Cheng had made it a practice to bring Kim chocolate or sweets each day when he returned home from work. On Sundays, if he had no work, he would take Kim on the back of his motorcycle to one of the beaches along the east coast for a swim.

From where he was, Cheng could see into the kitchen through an open window and smiled as he saw Fourth Auntie fussing over Kim who was seated at the round, wooden dining table.

Then suddenly Cheng got to his feet, not knowing why he had done so and walked down a little-used footpath overgrown with creepers and weeds. It led to his parents' unoccupied and dilapidated farmhouse that had been abandoned for more eight years.

He had never done such a thing before.

Cheng had come to hate the place because of what had happened there. But this evening he had felt drawn towards it by some mysterious force.

As he came closer to the farmhouse he could see only parts of the wooden fence that was covered with creepers. He had to pull away a mass of matted vines before he could see the rotting, low gate that fell to the ground at his touch.

Cautiously, he waded through the waist-high *lallang* grass that grew where there had once been a well-cared-for garden with roses and pomegranate trees – all planted by his parents.

A lump came to his throat and tears rushed to his eyes.

He stood there, weeping.

Some minutes later when he could see clearly again, he saw the door and windows of the wooden house were shut – just as he had left them. He gave the slim door a shove and it swung open.

By the glow of the setting sun he entered the semi-dark interior. He could make out the round wooden dining table in the centre of the room and six bamboo stools around it. Faded curtains drooped from loose wires over the doors to the two bedrooms; the one to the right being his parents' room and the other to the left, that he had shared with Lin.

His eyes fell upon the altar behind the dining table on which were the statues of Kwun Kong, the red-faced God of War and Protector and Kuan Yin, the Goddess of Mercy. In front of them, was a brass bowl filled with sand from which the purple stems of burnt joss sticks protruded and the melted wax of red candles on two white saucers. Beside them was the family photo album. He had left it there because he had thought it would invoke heavenly blessings upon the souls of those in the photographs.

He stood in the centre of the room for some time. He had the urge to run out of the place and never return to it. But, something held him back.

He shut his eyes and all that happened on that terrible February morning flashed before him. He gritted his teeth and clenched his fists and screamed at the top of his voice until the veins on his neck stood out like little pipes and there was no more breath in his lungs.

Late afternoon on 15 February 1942.

'Tell everybody that the British have surrendered! Japanese troops are occupying Singapore! Hide your daughters or they'll be raped! You know what happened in China! Be brave!' the headman of the village told a crowd of people at the market square.

Terrified, Cheng's mother and Lin hid themselves under the bed in his parents' bedroom. Cheng and his father sat at the dining table watching the front door in silence and for the inevitable to happen. It did, two hours later as night was falling.

There was loud banging on the front door and a voice calling out in the Teochew dialect, 'Open the door, Chinese pigs!'

'Be quiet!' Mr Wong whispered to Cheng who was crouching behind some bamboo stools beside the table.

Mr Wong, opened the front door and was confronted by a short, thick-set Japanese officer who had a pistol in his right hand. From his belt hung a sword in its scabbard. He wore rough, unpolished, brown riding boots. Standing beside him were three scruffy-looking soldiers with rifles and bayonets that they pointed at Mr Wong. They all wore white arm-bands with large red characters that meant *Kempeitai* that neither Cheng or his father knew the meaning of, then.

The officer scowled at Mr Wong, slapping him hard across the face, the force of the blow knocking him to the floor. Cheng cried out and rushed from his hiding place to his father's side. The officer kicked him in the stomach and he fell, screaming.

The officer stood over them, waving his pistol and shouted angrily, 'Stand up! Bow to me! I am a Japanese officer! Bow!'

Cheng and his father got to their feet with bowed heads.

The officer hit Mr Wong across the head with the barrel of his pistol and blood instantly covered his face, dripping on to his shirt.

'Bow!' the officer screamed. 'You do not know how to bow? I'll teach you! Like this!' He grabbed Mr Wong by his blood-soaked hair and forced him to bend his body right down from the waist, his head almost going between his legs. He did this many times. 'Now, do you know how to bow? Let me see! Bow!' he shouted.

Cheng and his father bowed low.

The officer shoved them aside and entered the house followed by the three soldiers. His eyes searched the walls. Then he took a slip of paper from his shirt pocket and consulted it briefly. Looking at Cheng's father he shouted, 'Your name is Wong? You are a branch committee member of the China Relief Fund? Isn't that so? You and your wife collected money to send to China to buy guns to fight the Japanese army? Isn't that so? Answer me!'

Mr Wong hung his head, wiping the blood from his eyes with his hand. He did not reply.

'Where is your wife!'

'She is dead' mumbled Mr Wong.

'How did she die!'

'She was killed in an air raid.'

'You lie!'

He punched Mr Wong in the face, knocking him backwards to the floor.

He entered the bedroom where Lin and her mother were hiding under the bed.

Moments later, Cheng heard them screaming.

The officer pulled aside the curtain across the bedroom door and roughly shoved Lin and her mother in front of him. They fell to the floor, terrified.

Seeing her husband covered in blood, Mrs Wong began to scream. Mr Wong said to the officer in the Teochew dialect, 'Please do not harm my wife and children. Kill me, Not them.'

This seemed to enrage the officer. He swung the barrel of his pistol across Mr Wong's face and more blood spurted. As he was falling to the ground, Cheng grabbed his father around the waist but let go as a soldier stabbed him in the thigh with his bayonet. He screamed, blood running down his leg.

Lin crawled up to her father and tried to embrace him. A soldier shoved her aside with his boot and began slapping her face. Mrs Wong screamed and lunged at the soldier. He stopped hitting Lin and kicked Mrs Wong in the stomach. She doubled up in pain momentarily and ran into the bedroom.

She reappeared moments later with her husband's .38 revolver in her hand. Pointing the gun at the officer's head she pulled the trigger. The bullet hit him in his left shoulder, knocking him slightly off balance but he steadied himself and kicked the revolver out of Mrs Wong's hand, punching her in the face. She collapsed beside her husband and lay still.

A patch of blood soon formed around the bullet hole in the officer's shirt. Blood dripped down his arm.

He barked an order to the soldiers and they dragged the limp bodies of Mr and Mrs Wong out into the garden and tied their hands behind their backs with wire.

The officer tore off a sleeve from his shirt and making a pad, placed it over the wound. He barked another order. One of the soldiers ran out of the house and down the lane. He returned a few minutes later driving a small van.

The soldiers dumped the limp bodies of Cheng's parents into the rear of the van and jumped in.

The officer looked at Lin and Cheng and shouted in Teochew, 'You stay here! I'm coming back! If you try to run away, I'll kill you!'

He sprang into the front seat of the van and it disappeared down the lane.

It was the last time Cheng and Lin saw their parents.

Lin and Cheng sat on the blood-spattered floor, too frightened to move and where they were still seated an hour later when the officer returned. He arrived riding a bicycle. As he entered the house they saw he was wearing a clean shirt and noticed a dressing over the wound on his shoulder.

He pulled Cheng up by the hair and taking him to the garden bound his hands and feet and gagged him with rag before tying him to a tree.

'Be quiet, or I'll shoot you!' he said, waving his pistol in front of Cheng's face.

He re-entered the house.

A few minutes later Cheng heard Lin screaming. Her cries were coming from his parents' bedroom. Tears streamed down his face and he shut his eyes tightly, biting into the cloth gag across his mouth.

A little while later the screaming stopped and he could hear Lin sobbing.

The officer appeared shortly afterwards, untied Cheng's hands and legs and removed the gag.

'Go and look after your sister!' he shouted, shoving Cheng into the house.

'I shall be gone for a little while! If you try to escape, I'll kill you both!' he said and jumping on his bicycle, rode off. He returned carrying a basket. In it were packets wrapped in newspaper that contained rice, gravy and pieces of roasted duck. He placed these on the dining table and sat down.

Not seeing Lin, he asked Cheng where she was.

Cheng told him she was in the bedroom and saying that, burst into tears because when he found her she was naked and curled up in a corner of the bedroom, terrified and sobbing. There was blood on her thighs. Her face was swollen and her lips broken and bleeding.

Cheng had lifted her up in his arms and laid her gently on the bed. He wiped the blood from her face and body with a wet towel. He poured some tea into a cup from the kettle his mother kept on a bedside table. She took a few painful sips. They did not speak.

'Come out!' the officer shouted to Lin as he tore open the paper packets containing the food he had brought. He immediately stuffed his mouth with it. He pushed some rice and roasted duck towards Cheng.

'Eat!' he said.

'Hey! You in the room! Come out! Do you want another beating?' he yelled.

Cheng saw the curtain over the bedroom door part slowly and Lin with a bath towel wrapped around her slim body stood looking at them, sobbing.

He glanced at her, his mouth full of food and said, 'Stop crying! Sit!' indicating a stool beside him.

When he saw Cheng wasn't eating he slapped him across the face and shouted, 'Eat! I told you to eat!' and going quickly up to Lin dragged her by the hair and deposited her on the stool beside him.

'You both eat or I shall beat you up!' he shouted.

Terrified, they both put some rice into their mouths.

After a while the officer said to Lin, 'Go! Take a bath!'

She left the table and went towards the outdoor bathroom at the rear of the house where her father had built a deeper well to replace the old one whose walls had collapsed.

Cheng sat at the table in silence, pretending to eat.

The officer seemed to be deep in thought as he stuffed his mouth with more food.

Lin appeared after her bath, her hair still damp. She was wearing a clean, yellow *samfu* that her mother had made for her only two weeks before.

'Sit!' said the officer, indicating the stool beside him with his chin. She sat beside him nervously.

He touched her chin with his forefinger and smiled into her face. She frowned, turning her face away. He grinned. 'You are very pretty!'

She glared at him.

'Oh! You are angry!' he said mockingly and began to caress her breasts.

She pushed his hands away angrily and tears filled her eyes.

'All right, I shall be good,' he said.

He got up from the table and stood by the door, deep in thought for some time. 'Your parents were so foolish!' he shouted. 'Your mother tried to kill me!' He glanced at his left shoulder. 'I should have shot your parents right there and then! They are misguided and stupid like Chinese everywhere who do not understand the honourable and sincere intentions of Japan!'

He lit a cigarette, inhaled deeply and said, 'I have forgiven them. The punishment for their crimes is death! However, I am appealing to my superior officer to spare their lives.'

Cheng got up from the table and taking care to bow very low, said, 'Sir, when can we see our parents?'

'That depends on how you both treated me and how much kindness and affection you show me.' He walked up to Lin and stroked her face.

'Think carefully about what I've said. I am going out for a while. Lock the door. Stay inside!'

In a moment he was gone.

Cheng and Lin were ravenously hungry and as soon as he left, they shared the remainder of the food. The fact that their parents were alive and there was a chance of seeing them was such wonderful news.

Lin made some tea and as they drank it Cheng said to her viciously, 'He's a beast!' She looked away as tears rushed to her eyes, her cracked, swollen lips trembling.

They did not speak for some time. She said softly, 'We have to obey him and do whatever he says, if we wish to save our parents' lives and ours. We have no choice.' They hugged each other tightly.

Later that day, 'Fourth Auntie, ' who lived with her two children on a farm not far away, stood at the gate calling out to her elder sister. Getting no response and seeing the windows and doors of the house were shut, she went away.

Cheng and Lin who had been peeping through a crack in a wooden wall saw her, but were too frightened to answer her calls in case the officer suddenly returned.

The officer was now sharing Mr and Mrs Wong's bedroom with Lin.

He brought food to them twice a day and they prepared tea or coffee for him.

He was drunk some nights and treated Lin roughly. Cheng would hear her cry out and after he fell asleep she would creep out of the room and come to his bed and they would hug each other and sob quietly.

A week passed and one day Cheng bowing deeply, asked the officer very politely, 'Pardon me, sir, but when could we visit our parents?'

He stared at Cheng and said, 'In a few days! Don't bother me!'

Cheng bowed low again and thanked him, his spirits soaring.

He couldn't wait to tell Lin the good news.

The following morning the officer awoke early, dressed and left without saying a word to them.

Two days passed. Cheng and Lin were without food and too frightened to leave the house. On the third day he said to Lin, 'I must look for some food for us! Supposing he doesn't return? We will starve to death! I am going to Fourth Auntie's house. You stay here. I shall not be long. If he returns and asks where I am tell him some of our ducks escaped from the pen and I went to the field to catch them.'

Cheng ran as fast as he could to his aunt's farm, arriving there breathless. He quickly told her everything that had happened.

Fourth Auntie wept and hugging Cheng said he and Lin must escape from the house and come to live with her. She would hide them.

That evening Cheng and Lin put some clothes into two paper bags and ran all the way to Fourth Auntie's house.

Fourth Auntie's husband was with the anti-Japanese guerrillas in the jungles of Malaya. But, she had told everyone he had been killed in an air raid. To add weight to her story that he was dead, she had pasted a cross of white paper over his photograph that she displayed on the altar at the front of her house. Her children and herself also wore little tabs of sackcloth pinned to the sleeves of their jackets to indicate they were in mourning.

Later, Fourth Auntie made inquiries among some trusted friends of the family and was told that the officer was a lieutenant in the *Kempeitai*, the secret police who had rounded up thousands of Chinese and executed them. He had set up an office at the village school that was now locked up. He had not been seen for some days. Nobody seemed to know where he had gone.

Although Lin and Cheng breathed sighs of relief at the news, they were also aware that without this officer's help their hopes of seeing their parents again would disappear. And, even if Cheng went in search of the officer, he didn't know his name – neither did Lin. They had been too afraid to ask.

There was nobody else they could turn to for help.

A few days later, Fourth Auntie was told in confidence by an old villager that Cheng's parents had been tortured to death by the officer. The old man did not know what had happened to their bodies.

'Fourth Auntie' had tried to conceal the terrible news from Cheng and Lin but she had burst into tears one day when Lin began to speak about her parents. As she wept Fourth Auntie told them the truth.

Fourth Auntie took very good care of Lin who was now three months pregnant. She did not allow Cheng and her out of the house since there were many *Kempeitai* informers about.

For most of the day she hid them at the bottom of a dried-up well that was covered by a mass of creepers. Access to the well was by a narrow, underground tunnel that had its entrance cleverly concealed amongst thick *lallang* growing beside a pigsty. Her husband built it before he left to join the guerrillas. He had meant it to be a place where his family could hide from marauding Japanese soldiers on killing and raping sprees.

It formed a perfect hideaway.

Fourth Auntie informed everybody that Cheng, Lin and their parents had gone to live with relatives in another part of Singapore.

When it was time for Lin's delivery, Fourth Auntie was the midwife and her eldest daughter Lian, who was a year older than Lin, was her assistant. Her son and Cheng busied themselves in the kitchen boiling water and tearing up old rags that they had been instructed to do.

Lin began to behave strangely after the birth of her son.

She refused to nurse him and avoided going near him. She would sulk and brood for hours and only nibble at her food, refusing to talk to anybody. As the weeks passed she grew thinner and began to have nightmares, waking up screaming.

Fourth Auntie and Cheng knew the cause of the trouble was the horrible memory of her rape by the officer and the fact that he had murdered their parents.

Now, she couldn't bear the sight of his son!

As the days passed Lin's health grew steadily worse. It was painful to see her wither away. Her bones stood out from under her pale skin. Her beautiful, young and radiant face had become haggard.

They knew she was going to die. She knew it, too. Perhaps, that's what she wanted to happen. One morning, Cheng found her farewell note pinned to his pillow.

After the ban on the entry of Japanese in to Singapore had been lifted the first group of tourists arrived in Singapore.

As Cheng drove the mini-bus to the Sunrise Hotel to pick up a group for a tour, a cold sweat came over him. He began to tremble slightly and felt sick and thought he was going to vomit. He prayed he would not allow his hatred for Japanese erupt into any violent behaviour.

He arrived at the hotel, parked his bus and was approached by a pleasant, young Japanese, followed by eight other young men and women.

They stood in line, bowed to him and said, 'Good morning'– in English! He couldn't believe what he saw and heard. Was he dreaming?

Here was a group of Japanese who were actually *bowing* – to him! And, greeting him in *English*, the language of one of their most-hated enemies! Unbelievable!

The young, smiling people looking at him were not in military uniform but in holiday clothes and carried cameras and not rifles with a fixed bayonets!

'Good morning,' he managed to mumble and took a deep breath to steady himself.

A young man who appeared to be the group's leader bowed again and taking a slip of paper from his shirt pocket cleared his throat and began to read from it in halting, heavily-accented English:

'Honour-able gree-tings-o to you, sir! We are all pri-mary school teacher from Hiroshima. We are most de-light-ful to arriving in Sing-a-pore for peace-ful visit! When it is the war-time, we are very young. So, we do not know about fighting! We are most de-light-ful to be your friend! Thank you! *Arigato gozaimasu!*'

He smiled and bowed again and the others did likewise!

Cheng quickly ushered them into the bus, remembering that these were some of the survivors of Hiroshima that was one of the two Japanese cities atom-bombed by the Americans in August 1945. The Americans had dropped another atomic bomb on Nagasaki a few days later killing an estimated 200,000 people! Thousands more were to die from radiation.

He glanced at the young faces of his passengers seated behind him and realised with sudden horror that every one of them could be a war orphan – like himself!

But, whatever feeling of sympathy he may have had for them vanished immediately when he thought, 'The atom-bombings of Hiroshima and Nagasaki were justified! It had forced Japan to surrender! Millions more lives would have been lost if the war had continued! I must not be soft-hearted! These young people from Hiroshima may have had no part in the war. But one of them could be related to the monster who killed my parents and raped my sister!'

The leader of the group sat beside Cheng.

As they drove along he said haltingly, 'My-name-is Oka-mo-to,' offering his hand.

Cheng thought: 'Oh, God! Spare me the agony of shaking his hand!' and looked away. He gritted his teeth.

'May-I-know-your-name?' asked the young man with a smile.

Looking away again, Cheng hesitated, then mumbled, 'My name is . . . er . . . Peter,' he lied and thought: 'Why should I tell this pig my name?'

'*Ah-so*. I am happy to know you, Mister Er Peter,' said the young man happily and turned round to inform the others in Japanese that the name of the driver of the bus was 'Er Peter-san.'

Cheng gritted his teeth and said, 'No! My name is not Er Peter! It is Peter – without the Er!'

The young man said, '*Ah-so*. So sorry for mistake,' and turning round again informed the others accordingly.

Consulting another slip of paper from his shirt pocket, he informed 'Mister Peter' that they would like to visit 'scenic-abode-of-native, garden-for-tropi-cal-fruit and frowers. Also, tree-for-making tyres for automobiles!'

Cheng drove like a speed demon to the Botanic Gardens to show them 'tropical fruits and (frowers) flowers' and then to a rubber plantation to show them the 'trees for making tyres for automobile.'

They were very excited to see all the tropical plants and blooms and were thrilled when they saw rubber trees and the white latex collected in cups that were attached to their trunks with wire. They took photographs of themselves embracing the trunks of the trees and others holding cups filled with latex! They also collected the brown seeds of the trees they found on the ground. A few of them attempted to crack open the shells between their teeth.

Cheng watched them with silent contempt. 'Monkeys!' he muttered to himself and spat.

He took them to a Malay fishing *kampung* on the west coast where a crowd of curious villagers came out to see the *monyet-Jepun* (Japanese monkeys) as the Malays had called the Japanese behind their backs during the occupation of Singapore. The crowd appeared to be hostile and he decided to make a hasty departure with his group. He took them to a Chinese and then to an Indian temple before returning to the hotel where they lined up in front of him and bowed, smiling broadly.

'Thank you Mister Peter. Japanese people say *arigato gozaimas*,' said Okamoto and handed Cheng an envelope. They all bowed again and said, 'Sayonara! Good-bye!' and turning on their heels, walked smartly away.

Later, when he opened the envelope, he found two, crisp $10 notes inside.

With each passing day more and more Japanese tourists arrived. Cheng did not seem to mind them at all and welcomed the 'tips' he received from them at the end of each tour. His passengers were mostly old men and women from farming districts and a mixture of fishermen, students, factory workers and clerks, shopkeepers and teachers.

He couldn't believe these people were of the same race as those who had tortured and beheaded, slapped and kicked people during those terrible years of the Japanese Occupation in Singapore. Where had all these pleasant and kind people been hiding during the war? Why hadn't they come to Singapore instead of those murderers in military uniform? If they had, his parents and Lin may still be alive – so would many thousands of other innocent people who died of starvation and torture!

Although a large number of Japanese were hanged at Changi Prison for atrocities committed during the Occupation of Singapore, Cheng believed that a large number of war criminals had escaped punishment – like that monster who had killed his parents and raped his sister!

However, as the months passed, Cheng looked forward to meeting Japanese tourists. They behaved like decent human beings and were polite. And, he was polite and helpful to them in return. He discovered his attitude towards Japanese had changed. He had even begun to learn to speak Japanese and could make himself understood with some difficulty. And, he had two Japanese pen-friends!

Life was being kind to Cheng in many strange ways – until that day in March.

He had gone to a hotel in Mr Tea's brand new mini-bus to pick up a group of visitors from Japan.

They were waiting for him, smiling and bowing as usual. They took their seats in the bus, the tour leader sitting beside him. He was a middle-aged man and pleasant.

He told Cheng his name was Kato-san. Cheng was still using 'Peter' as his *nom-de-plume*, a name he had come to like and that even Mr Tea had come to know him by.

But, he didn't approve of the way some Japanese pronounced it: 'Pee-tah!'

Kato-san, a schoolteacher, said. 'Please, we go first to Japanese cemetery. After, we go for sight-looking. Thank you! *Arigato gozaimas!*'

They were soon on their way to the Japanese cemetery. Cheng, looking in his rear mirror scanned the faces of his passengers as he always did but not for any particular reason.

It was only to familiarise himself with them.

There was one face which caused him to frown a little because he was sure he had seen it before, but he wasn't sure where. It was probably a tourist who had been in his bus on some previous occasion. But, that explanation didn't seem to satisfy him. He looked in the rear mirror again. The man had greying hair and was wearing sunglasses. Cheng could only get a look at his profile, since he was looking out of the window beside his seat.

There was no getting away from it, the man's face was most familiar. Cheng's curiosity increased as he kept one eye on the road and the other on the rear mirror, hoping the man would face the front – but he kept looking out of his window.

Cheng's impatience grew with each passing minute.

He hit upon an idea. He grabbed the inter-com microphone and said in halting Japanese, 'Attention please, ladies and gentlemen. If you wish to stop the bus to take photographs, please tell me. Thank you.' As he spoke, he kept looking in the rear mirror and then he saw the man turn his head and face the front.

Cheng's blood froze!

He had a striking resemblance to the *Kempeitai* officer who had come to his father's farmhouse and who . . .

A cold shiver ran down his back as those horrible memories flashed through his mind.

It was a face he could never forget.

Cheng's feelings must have been registered on his face because Kato-san, sitting beside him, was saying something but Cheng hadn't heard him.

The shock of suddenly seeing this man's face had been too much for him. He dared not look in the mirror again because if it was *him*, what was he going to do about it?

He felt as though a million tiny needles were pricking his skin.

He cursed under his breath. The timing of his discovery

had been so wrong! Had he seen this man on a street at night he would have taken him to a back alley and beaten him to death!

But, there was a lingering doubt in his mind. Was he absolutely certain this man was the *Kempeitai* officer? Japanese faces were so much alike. And, it had been thirteen years since he last saw his face – and he looked different then.

The tormenting uncertainty made him perspire.

He struggled to control himself and after a few minutes, looked in the rear mirror again.

The man was holding up a tourist map that hid his face!

He parked the bus near the entrance to the Japanese cemetery and waited for the passengers to get down.

While the group read inscriptions on the monuments and took photographs, Cheng stood beneath a large shade tree, his eyes focused on the man whom he tried to picture in Japanese army uniform strutting about his father's farmhouse in heavy riding boots. He had a shaved head then, and was much younger. The face of the man Cheng was looking at now had a few lines of age and he had a mop of long, greying hair.

'Those sunglasses! Why doesn't he take them off!' Cheng cursed under his breath.

He wandered slowly back to the bus and sat in the driver's seat. He rested his head on the steering wheel and shut his eyes trying again to match the man's face with the one he had seen every day for more than a month during those horrible days when the officer had stayed at the farmhouse and had made Lin his unwilling mistress. He didn't even know the officer's name. If he did, he could have checked the names of his passengers with the hotel's reception clerk.

He leaned out of the driver's window and spat. He felt like throwing up. He told himself again that he had to make absolutely sure about this man's identity.

If he was the same man he was going to kill him that night! They returned to the hotel just before lunch.

Cheng next saw him in a pair of white shorts and with a towel thrown over his shoulders – still wearing sunglasses! He was walking towards the hotel's swimming pool.

It suddenly occurred to Cheng there was a foolproof way of finding out if his suspicions were correct. There would be a scar on the man's left shoulder where the bullet fired by his mother with his father's revolver had torn off a piece of his flesh!

Cheng saw him remove the towel from his shoulders and spread it beside the pool. He took off his sunglasses and began to apply suntan lotion to his face and body from a bottle before lying facedown on the towel.

Cheng's heart was racing as he slowly made his way towards him and struggled to contain his excitement as he walked beside the pool. When he was a few feet away, his eyes fell on the man's left shoulder.

There was an almond-shaped scar just below his collarbone!

No mistake! It was him!

Cheng saw his face clearly for the first time and fought the maddening urge to crush his head with one of the heavy flowerpots beside the pool.

The man swam leisurely about the pool for a few minutes before he got out and after drying himself went towards the hotel's lobby.

Cheng went quickly ahead of him and was standing beside some potted palms when he saw him pause to admire two pretty girls as they passed.

Cheng said, 'You like pretty girls?'

He turned round quickly and seeing Cheng, said with a grin, 'Ah! You are bus driver, Peter-*san*! You have pretty girl for me?'

It was *his* voice! And, that leering grin that Cheng remembered so well!

Cheng said with a smile, 'You want young, beautiful girl?'

'You have?' he asked eagerly, coming towards Cheng.

'Yes. Beautiful Chinese schoolgirl.'

'How old?'

'Sixteen.'

'She is very beautiful? Sure? How much money?'

'Fifty dollars for a short-time.'

He looked hard at Cheng and Cheng was worried he would be recognised. But over the years, Cheng's features had changed. He was much taller and muscular, too. His hair was long and not short-cropped like it was, then. He wore spectacles and he had a rather deep voice.

'Okay. You bring girl to my room,' the man said.

'Not possible. You must go to the girl's house. If she comes here, hotel security will arrest you and the girl. Understand? She is a schoolgirl.'

He frowned and Cheng thought he was going to change his mind when he said, 'Business friend coming to see me tonight at eight o'clock.'

'That's all right,' said Cheng. 'Ask the reception clerk to tell your business friend that you went for a swim at the seaside and would be back shortly.'

He grinned. 'Good idea! Okay. I will tell clerk. What time we go to girl's house?'

'Six o'clock,' said Cheng with a smile. 'I'll pick you up in my bus. I don't want people to become suspicious, so wait for me in front of the Chinese coffee-shop that is about one hundred metres to the left side of the hotel's entrance. Don't be late. You must not tell anybody I am taking you to see a girl. This is a secret, understand?'

'Yes. Understand. Secret,' he said with a grin.

'See you at six o'clock, Remember. It's the Chinese coffee-shop one hundred metres to the left of the hotel's entrance. Is that okay?' said Cheng.

'Yes. Okay.'

Cheng returned to his office and lied to Mr Tea that his motorcycle had broken down and asked him if he could take the bus home that evening. Mr Tea agreed.

Cheng sat on a stone seat on the waterfront to plan the murder he was going to commit. To his surprise he discovered there was very little planning to be done. He had only to take good care nobody saw him picking the man up in front of the coffee-shop. The rest would be simple.

Cheng thought he might need a small flashlight and a box of matches later on and bought these from a shop. He had taken a heavy spanner from the toolbox in the bus and wrapped some cloth around its 'head.' He placed it under the driver's seat. He planned to hit the man over the head with it to stun him and finish him off later on.

Cheng parked his van in a side lane near the hotel and waited, listening to music from the radio. At fifteen minutes to six o'clock he drove his bus towards the appointed place, feeling very relaxed.

He arrived at the coffees-shop ten minutes later – and there he was, dressed in a floral, Hawaiian shirt, white slacks and shoes. He looked rather smart, Cheng thought. He grinned as he jumped into the front seat beside Cheng. The bus shot forward, quickly losing itself in the traffic. The strong, sweet perfume of his hair cream filled the bus.

'Girl is young, beautiful? Sure?' he asked Cheng eagerly after they had gone some way.

Cheng nodded his head and smiled.

The man folded his arms across his chest and began to whistle a Japanese tune through his teeth as he looked out of the window beside him.

Was he recognising familiar sights when Singapore was 'Syonan'? Cheng wondered.

As he drove along Cheng became aware that he was the master of this cat-and-mouse game and that very soon the cat was going to kill the mouse!

'You look handsome,' Cheng said easily.

'No handsome,' he said with a laugh.

'Is this your first visit to Singapore?'

He paused briefly before answering.

'Yes.'

'You like Singapore?'

'Yes. I like.'

'You've come to Singapore on business?'

'Yes. Textile business. Tonight I can be with girl only for short-time. Maybe, next time I come to Syonan . . . '

He stopped and quickly corrected himself. 'Next time I to come to Singapore, maybe I have more time. Can see many young girls!'

He laughed. Cheng laughed, too, pretending not to have noticed his mention of 'Syonan.'

Suddenly, Cheng had to fight a tremendous urge to shout: 'I know who you are! You are the *Kempeitai* officer who tortured my father and mother to death and raped my sister! You bastard!'

Cheng watched him from the corner of his eye as they left the city area. The sky was overcast with low rain clouds and soon it would be sunset.

'Girl house very far?' he asked.

'Five minutes more,' said Cheng.

Just before they reached Nee Soon village near where the old farms were, Cheng swung the bus into a red-earth side lane. He was taking a roundabout way to reach his family's farmhouse since he was making very sure nobody saw them. They passed by two abandoned farmhouses before he slowed down and switched off the headlights, keeping the sidelights on.

'Why you no use big light? Here is dark,' the man said.

'I do not want people to see us. Must be careful,' said Cheng.

'*Ah-so*,' he said, nodding his head approvingly.

Cheng turned the bus into an old cart track that led to the farmhouse.

He slowed it down almost to a crawl before coming to a halt outside the gate.

He turned off the engine.

It was quite dark and very quiet, except for the sounds of insects. He quickly reached for the heavy spanner under his seat and without a moment's hesitation hit the man on the side of the head with it. He slumped forward, his head coming to rest with a thud on the dashboard.

He dragged the man's limp body through the tall *lallang* and deposited it at the door of the house. Entering the house, he switched on the small flashlight he had brought, resting it on top of the altar table. The beam showed the statues of the Goddess of Mercy and Kwan Kung, the God of War. Beside the statues, he saw the family photo album. Everything was as he had left it on that day he had visited the house.

He switched off the flashlight and lit the stump of a red altar candle, using the box of matches he had also brought along. It produced an orange glow but it was sufficient for him to make out everything in the room: the dining table with six bamboo stools around it, the bedroom and window curtains and a peeling picture of the Kitchen God on the door that opened to the outdoor kitchen, storeroom and the two wells — the old, collapsed one and the new, deeper one which his father had built.

He quickly tore strips off a bedroom curtain and going outside tied the man's hands behind his back and made him sit up on the floor. He forced open his mouth and stuffed it with a strip of cloth and gagged him.

The man groaned. He went quickly to the rear of the house and returned with a pail of water from the new well, splashing it over the man's face and body. Cheng saw him open his eyes, look around and then up at Cheng who was standing over him.

He struggled briefly with his bonds.

Speaking to him in the Teochew dialect which Cheng remembered the man was familiar, he said softly, 'Don't you recognise this place? Don't you recognise me? I am the little boy who once lived here. You stayed here in that room over there with my sister for more than a month when you were a *Kempeitai* officer many years ago. Surely, you must remember?' He stared hard at Cheng.

'Maybe this would help you to remember!' said Cheng as he took a bamboo stool from under the dining table and swung it downwards on to the man's left shin – and then the right.

He shut his eyes tightly and let out a muffled groan, the veins on his forehead and neck sticking out like small pipes. Blood oozed from his broken shins and through his white cotton slacks.

'Now, do you remember this house?'

The man rolled over and groaned as tears ran down his face, red and bloated with pain.

Cheng went to his parents' bedroom door and pushed it open, drawing the curtain to one side. He lit two candles on a shelf, filling the bedroom with soft, orange light. 'Do you remember this bedroom?'

The man quickly turned his face away.

'You found my mother and sister hiding under this bed when you walked into this house on that morning in February 1942. Remember? Perhaps, if you went inside, your memory would be refreshed?'

Cheng crashed the stool on to the man's knees. He gave out a long, muffled howl of pain as he threw himself backwards, rolling from side to side on the floor, urinating as he did.

Cheng pulled him up by his hair into a kneeling position. He was groaning and shaking his head violently from side to side. He stopped momentarily to look at Cheng with pleading, bloodshot eyes.

Cheng dragged him by the hair into the bedroom and went to the altar outside where he had kept the family photo album. Holding a candle over a photograph of his mother and father, he said, 'Remember them, my mother and father? You killed them! Isn't that true?'

He stared at the photograph without replying.

'I want you to admit that you killed them!' said Cheng removing the gag from the man's mouth. 'Now! Tell me! Did you kill them?'

'Yes . . . yes! Forgive me!' he whined in the Teochew dialect. 'It was war-time . . . '

Cheng replaced the gag and pointed to a photo of Lin in her school uniform.

The man shut his eyes. His body trembled and he began to sob.

'Remember, her? She committed suicide! Do you know why? Because she was haunted by the terror of that day you raped her . . . right here! On this bed! You pig! And, the shame you left her to bear after she gave birth to your son!'

He tore away the left sleeve of the man's shirt revealing the scar of the old bullet wound on his shoulder.

'This scar was caused by the bullet my mother fired at you with my father's revolver! Isn't that so?'

He nodded his head slowly.

Cheng swung the stool into the man's face and he fell backwards, blood spurting onto his flowered shirt and pants. He dragged him out of the room and into the back yard. He began to struggle weakly.

Cheng lifted him up and placed his body half over the side of old well, with his head hanging down. He shone the flashlight down the narrow shaft, the beam reaching the almost dry bottom about ten metres below.

'See? That's where you're going to be buried and where nobody will ever find your rotten body!' he said softly and quickly tipped the man over the side.

There was a dull thud as his body hit the bottom. Cheng switched on the flashlight and saw the man's legs were curled backwards, his feet almost touching the back of his head.

Nearby was a pile of sand, bricks and stones. These were leftovers after the walls of the new well were built. Cheng went into the tool-shed, took a spade from it and began to transfer the sand and stones into the old well. He worked quickly in the darkness until the well was almost filled.

He was perspiring. He switched on the flashlight to examine his work and saw there was some blood on his white slacks. He ran to the bus collected a paper bag in which he had kept a change of clothes and hurried back to the well. He bathed and changed, placing his soiled clothes into the paper bag. He shone the flashlight about, making sure he had not left any clues and re-entered the house.

With the flame from the candle he set a bedroom curtain alight. He placed the bag with his soiled clothes on the dining table and with the family photo album under his arm, ran out of the house.

It was very dark outside. He drove the bus slowly and quietly away with the lights off. After he had gone some distance he glanced over his shoulder and saw flames shooting up from the *attap* rooof of the house.

When he returned home two hours later, Fourth Auntie said excitedly, 'Your father's house burned to the ground before the fire-fighters could arrive! It must have been the work of those young hooligans we see hanging around. They're always causing mischief!'

'There was nothing of value in the house and the wood was rotten,' said Cheng casually.

He realised he had committed murder. But hadn't the man whom he had killed tortured his parents to death and was also responsible for causing the death of Lin, whom he had raped?

He thought: 'If I had killed him and a hundred other Japs during the war, I would have been hailed as a hero! I would have been awarded a medal and made a big fuss of in the newspapers. But since we are not at war and if I confessed to the murder of this monster, I would have to stand trial and most probably be sent to prison for many years! Is this the way justice is done?

Did that bastard give my father and mother a fair trial? And, what about the rape of my sister?'

When the man hadn't returned to the hotel by the following morning the reception clerk informed the manager, who reported it to the police.

The clerk told detectives that the missing man had told him he was going to a beach for a swim and would return later. He said the man had not mentioned the name of the beach.

Police checked the popular swimming beaches and searched the sea for the missing man's body without success.

Nothing more was heard.

About a year later, a bulldozer cleared the burnt remains of the farmhouse. The whole area was levelled and lorry-loads of gravel were spread over the site. After a steamroller had done its work, the place looked like a car park. A signboard said a factory block would be constructed on the site.

Fourth Auntie's husband who was with the anti-Japanese guerrillas in the Malayan jungles was reunited with his family. She was paid compensation by a developer for her farm and moved into a new flat with her family, Cheng and Kim.

Cheng took over Mr Tea's travel agency when he retired a few years later.

Kim grew up to be a fine young man and became Cheng's manager.

Her Ladyship

There was an unmistakable stir among a small group of elderly people seated in the lobby of the Colonial Hotel in Kuala Lumpur. They comprised mostly 'non-executive' European government pensioners, some with wives, bachelors, widows and widowers as well as a few retired rubber planters and tin miners. They all rented rooms at the far end on the ground floor on a monthly basis and had their meals at the hotel, for which they were charged a special rate.

They had chosen to spend their remaining years in Malaya where they had lived and worked most of their lives and where they could still enjoy some privileges as *tuans* and *mems*. It was far better than what they could have expected 'back home' in Britain.

But, on that sunny July morning in 1933 they had spent less time over breakfast so they could hurry to the lobby to focus their attention on the hotel's main entrance. The reason was because they were informed by the manager of the hotel that a titled lady guest would be arriving by train from Penang Island, in the north.

Since there were only a few titled people in Selangor at that time; the British Adviser to the Sultan and the Chief Justice immediately coming to mind, the information the manager had imparted had generated excited discussion among the group – a welcome change in their otherwise uneventful daily lives.

'According to George Bernard Shaw titles distinguished the mediocre, embarrassed the superior and were disgraced by the inferior,' remarked a cynical old pensioner. 'Personally, I wouldn't expect too much and be disappointed. I once knew a certain lady who was the wife of an army surgeon who was knighted and a jolly decent chap he was, too! I wish I could say the same about his wife. Her title, like new wine, went straight to her head! The airs she put on! A pain in the posterior, she was!'

An hour later, the hotel's stately Rolls-Royce came to a halt at the entrance. The assistant manager quickly got out from his seat beside the chauffeur to open a rear door.

The French manager who had been anxiously waiting near the front steps behind a large pot of ferns, sprang forward like a panther in his newly-pressed black suit, his black, well-greased hair parted in the middle, his black eyes shining, eager to be of service. With a dignified bow he offered his hand to assist an immaculately attired and distinguished-looking lady from the vehicle and recited his well-rehearsed lines: 'Greetings, Your Ladyship,' he purred in his accented English. 'It is indeed an honour to have you as our guest. We hope you will enjoy your stay with us.'

A large Sikh doorman with a grey beard and wearing a blue and gold striped turban and a blue serge ceremonial uniform, displayed a row of military medals on his chest that were won in the 1914 – 1918 Great War. He had polished them specially for this occasion, He snapped to attention, and stuck out his jaw smartly as Her Ladyship entered the foyer.

She smiled pleasantly and paused to look at some paintings of Malayan wildlife on the wall. Pointing to one, she asked the manager in a cultured voice, 'Is that a Malayan tiger?' When she was told that it was, she raised an eyebrow delicately and said, 'Tigers are so handsome, aren't they?'

'Oh, indeed, Your Ladyship, indeed!' said the manager who gracefully waved her into the lobby. She smiled, aware that she was the centre of attention of a group of elderly people who were craning their necks towards her. Not far behind was a small caravan of her expensive suitcases.

The manager directed her towards the lift and in a few moments the vision of English aristocratic charm that had captivated the silent onlookers slowly ascended to the second floor where the VIP suite was located.

The young English assistant manager glad that the responsibility of attending the Very Important Person was no longer his, mopped his forehead with a handkerchief and proceeded to copy her particulars into the register from her British passport.

A male member of the lobby crowd rushed up to peer over the assistant manager's shoulder and whispered what was being entered into the register to a hawk-faced woman standing close behind him. 'Her name's Lady Beryl Carmichael,' said the man. She's English. Age: 42. Port of embarkation: Bombay,' and abruptly ended his commentary when the assistant manager quickly shut the register and gave him a cold stare.

This piece of information was quickly transmitted to the others in the lobby who seemed to share one common objective – to discover more details about her without any further delay.

The minutes ticked by as anxious glances were directed at the lift by which the manager would make his descent. 'There he is! I can tell by his rather short legs!' whispered a heavily made-up lady with silver hair, adjusting her spectacles, as the manager made his way down. As soon as he stepped out from the cage, he was quickly approached by the group and to their annoyance, he could only supply them with information they had already gathered.

They had hoped they would be given some general information about Her Ladyship, such as: Who was her husband? Why wasn't he accompanying her? Was she widowed or divorced? How did she acquire her obvious wealth? Why was she travelling alone? Why had she embarked at Bombay? Did she live permanently in India and if so, why and where? What was she doing in Kuala Lumpur? For how long would she be staying? Did she have relatives or friends in Kuala Lumpur? If so, who were they? Was she a friend of the Sultan, the British Adviser or the Chief Justice?

The manager had tactfully informed them he was in no position to provide them with the answers they sought since her personal background was no concern of his or anybody else's. He did reveal, however, that she had written to the hotel to reserve the most expensive suite some weeks before her departure from Bombay, travelling first-class on a luxury Lloyd-Triestino passenger liner to Penang from where she travelled first class on the express train to Kuala Lumpur.

The information-starved guests gathered in a corner of the lobby to draw their own conclusions about Her Ladyship and after ten minutes of pointless chatter quietly dispersed but obviously thrilled that they were living under the same roof of a titled lady.

A short while later, a tall and slim middle-aged man with close-cropped grey hair and moustache arrived by taxi with his luggage. According to his passport he was Major Dudley Chatsworth. Age: 45. He had arrived on the same ship as Her Ladyship. He was accommodated in a single bedroom at one end of the first floor.

The hotel guests did not see much of Lady Carmichael. Those who had a chance to exchange a few words with her said she was 'extremely charming and well-mannered.' She was also polite to the hotel staff, which, according to one of her admirers, easily distinguished her as a well-bred, upper-class English lady whose status had not 'gone to her head.' Another guest was heard to remark, 'One can always tell a person of good breeding, as in the case of Lady Carmichael. Well-bred people were pleasant and courteous to everyone, unlike second and third class English riff-raff who were rude and snobbish while pretending to be first-class. They gave the European community such a bad name!'

Lady Carmichael usually left the hotel by mid-morning in

one of the hotel's cars, returning late in the evening to retire to her suite where she ate her supper.

But, despite her busy schedule she had become a favourite with everybody in the short time since her arrival. One might even say that she had become a celebrity and had won the hearts of everyone at the hotel with her infectious charm. People seemed to go out of their way to bow, smile and greet her. Some would claim to have stopped and exchanged a few words with her, giving details of their conversations. These stories, whether they had been invented or not, had created a fair amount of jealousy among those who hadn't experienced such a privilege.

Nobody also saw much of Major Chatsworth.

The fact that Her Ladyship and the major occupied rooms on different floors did not prevent them from meeting each other that was done discretely and very late at night: the venue being Her Ladyship's bedroom where they would have supper together and drink French wine as they spoke in hushed tones before adjourning to her bed. The major took care to slip away quietly from her room before dawn.

Their purpose for meeting in secret every night was because the major and Her Ladyship wished to assess their 'takings' for the day, plan their next 'moves' and select their victims.

'Lady Carmichael' and 'Major Chatsworth' were accomplished frauds, pickpockets and jewel thieves. Their real names, according to Scotland Yard were Sybil Appleby and Henry King – pleasant-sounding names for two notorious criminals who had spent various periods of their lives in British prisons.

They had met by accident at a dinner party given by a London socialite that they had 'gate-crashed' some years before. They were unknown to each other at the time. Both had intentions of relieving some of the wealthy guests at the party of their valuables when they discovered to their embarrassment that they had unwittingly selected each other as prospective victims.

They saw the humour in their error of judgement and

immediately became friends, deciding to 'pool' their talents. Together, they embarked on a most successful and rewarding career in crime by using false names, clever disguises and an array of forged passports.

Her Ladyship had decided to describe herself as the widow of a millionaire-philanthropist who manufactured sun helmets in East Bengal and had received a knighthood for his charitable work. The major told everyone that he had spent some years 'jungle-bashing' with the Indian army in Burma and since retiring, had acquired 'substantial financial interests in Burmese teakwood.'

The major and Her Ladyship went about their 'research work' with professional efficiency; she making the necessary contacts and paving the way for the major to make a 'killing' among their unsuspecting victims.

She had memorised the names of well-known recreation clubs and hotels in the large Indian cities such as Bombay, New Delhi and Calcutta and popular 'hill stations.' She could 'name-drop' with effortless ease, rattling off the names of maharajahs and prominent people whom she claimed were among her circle of friends. She had also made it a point to remember important events on the social and sporting calendars, obtaining this information from Indian newspapers and magazines in London's public libraries.

With this background, Her Ladyship confidently entered the social arena with the major, making sure there would be no former residents of India or Burma among the guests at the events they attended and who might discover they were a pair of frauds.

Her Ladyship was always the 'receiver' at the scenes of their operations. She had a rather large and beautiful pearl-studded handbag which she said had been presented to her by the Maharajah of Jaipur for her welfare work in his state, into which she placed what jewellery she and the major had acquired, sneaking into bedrooms using 'master' keys and helping themselves to valuables while the guests were dancing and drinking.

As soon as they arrived (at different times) at a reception, it would be left to the major to select an inconspicuous pick-up point where he could discretely deposit his loot. He would make its location known to her later by secret signs. Their favourite places were popular racetracks. They would position themselves near the 'pay out' windows where big bets were made and winnings collected and relieve the lucky punters of their winning tickets or the cash they had won.

They felt they both needed a change of scenery and boarded a ship for Bombay, travelling first-class and making sure at the same time that the voyage was a most profitable one by relieving some of the wealthy passengers of their valuables and by cheating at card tables.

The major experienced a stroke of bad luck after two months of very successful operations in India when he became careless one day at the Bombay racetrack. He was about to pick the pocket of an English detective-inspector in civilian dress and might have been arrested on the spot had it not been for the timely arrival of Her Ladyship who, with her glib tongue, managed to 'smooth things over.'

It was after that incident that the major and Her Ladyship decided to take a holiday in Malaya, after being told exciting stories about its 'high society' and of vast sums of money gambled at the racetrack by Chinese millionaire tin miners and owners of rubber plantations.

After their arrival in Kuala Lumpur they began to carefully lay their plans. Soon, they were doing the 'social rounds,' meeting wealthy people and operating with much success while keeping a low profile at the hotel.

When some hotel guests had asked Her Ladyship why nobody saw much of her, she replied she was busy writing her memoirs. Meanwhile, the major had acquired a selected circle of friends who regarded him as 'a *pukka* English officer and gentleman and a polished poker player.'

But, an unkind twist of Fate was to abruptly end the criminal careers of Her Ladyship and the major in Kuala Lumpur.

It happened in the early hours of one morning when two thieves broke into Her Ladyship's bedroom and stole several items of expensive jewellery that the major and herself had recently 'acquired.' The culprits were caught by the hotel's security guards and handed over to the police.

Investigations revealed the items stolen by the thieves were among those that had recently been reported stolen from several wealthy Kuala Lumpur residents.

When police asked the two arrested men from where they had stolen the jewellery, they led detectives directly to Her Ladyship's bedroom where they found other items of stolen jewellery – and a red-faced Major Chatsworth in his pyjamas, hiding under Her Ladyship's bed!

Her Ladyship and the major appealed to the English investigating officer to be allowed to appear 'respectably dressed' and not to be handcuffed as they were escorted from the hotel, a 'face-saving' request that was granted.

As they passed the lobby on their way to a waiting police car, they were approached by some of their admirers who wished to know the reason for the presence of the police.

The quick-witted Lady Carmichael replied, 'Major Chatsworth and I have been the unfortunate victims of a robbery and we are assisting the police with their investigations.'

Pointing to the two handcuffed men, she said, 'Those are the miserable thieves!'

The newspapers, however, reported the shocking story of 'Lady Beryl Carmichael' and 'Major Dudley Chatsworth' on their front pages together with their photographs after they were charged in court on various counts of fraud and theft.

The small group at the hotel that had come to regard Lady Carmichael and the major with admiration and respect were shattered by the news. A ruffled old member of the group had angrily flung the morning newspaper aside and lost his appetite to eat his breakfast after reading that Lady Carmichael and Major Chatsworth had each been sentenced to two years' in jail. The man's wife wiped away her tears and was too upset to even sip her tea.

Like the others, they found the lights that had briefly illuminated their fading lives were suddenly extinguished.

The Cartwright Affair

Mariana Angelina de Carvalho was probably the most beautiful girl in Malacca and perhaps the whole of Malaya.

She had been a prime witness in a famous murder trial in Kuala Lumpur in 1931.

The deceased was a prominent English jeweller and diamond merchant named Herbert Gerald Cartwright who had a prestigious business in Kuala Lumpur. He was 51, married and the father of a son who was at Cambridge.

The prosecutor at the trial had said: 'Mr Cartwright had been a faithful and good husband to his wife for nineteen years, until the beautiful Miss de Carvalho who was in her twentieth year, appeared on the scene and stole his heart.'

As expected, Mrs Rosemary Cartwright was terribly shaken by this change of affection by her husband and as the prosecution at her trial attempted to prove, she had shot him with his own revolver. This was after she realised he was determined to divorce her and marry Miss de Carvalho whom he had already made the manager of his lucrative jewellery business and a substantial beneficiary in his will.

The newspapers had described the murder as a 'crime of passion.'

The prosecution had set itself the difficult task of proving that it was a case of premeditated murder and the charge was amended to one of manslaughter. Mrs Cartwright had maintained her innocence but was found guilty by a jury and sent to prison for four years.

She was released after serving just over two years of her sentence that was reduced because of her 'good conduct' while in prison.

She told reporters who were waiting for her at the prison gate, 'I shall search for my husband's killer or killers, no matter how much time or money it takes.' With her was her 23-year-old son, Richard, who had returned after graduating from Cambridge University.

Mrs Cartwright was short, on the plump side and had a flat, sallow face that called for her heavy dependency on cosmetics and when Mariana de Carvalho decided to capture the affections of Herbert Cartwright she did so knowing it would be quite easily achieved and there was nothing Rosemary Cartweight could have done about it.

Mr Cartwright knew nothing about Miss de Carvalho's background. She was young enough to be his daughter. But, 'love is the wisdom of fools and folly of the wise,' as they say.

Miss de Carvalho displayed her charms to an unfair advantage, using a devastating blend of innocence and sensuality for which her mentor, a Mr Horatio Wong, had to be given full credit.

She had made her entrance to Kuala Lumpur's social scene with the dramatic impact of a stage magician's beautiful assistant – materialising from out of nowhere – so to speak.

Nobody had heard of her or seen her until she walked into the elegant Queen Victoria Hotel one night on the arm of Mr Wong, a middle-aged racketeer, who was well-known for his liking for fast cars, fast women and fast money – not necessarily in that order.

As they were greeted by the manager of the hotel all eyes were focused on Miss de Carvalho whose stunning beauty created by a delicate mixture of Portuguese, Indian and Chinese blood, was accentuated by a daring, body-hugging gown of turquoise-blue silk.

Mr Wong and his curvaceous companion had arrived earlier

that day from Malacca and it was no coincidence that he had reserved a table close to the one occupied by Mr and Mrs Cartwright and their guests at the hotel's 'Royal Banquet Room' who were celebrating Mr Cartwright's fifty-first birthday.

Mr Wong's sole purpose of being there that night was to try and become better acquainted with Mr Cartwright, having met him only briefly some time ago.

He had planned to use Miss de Carvalho's eye-catching physical attributes to their fullest advantage in order to accomplish his mission.

As Mr Wong, with Miss de Carvalho on his arm, passed Mr Cartwright's table, he bowed respectfully. Mr Cartwright, having had knowledge of Mr Wong's shady reputation, would have ignored his greeting had Miss de Carvalho not looked at him with a shy smile.

As they sat at their table, it gave Mr Wong much pleasure to see that Mr Cartwright could not take his eyes away from Miss de Carvalho and wondered how long it would be before he made his 'move' – that came sooner than Mr Wong had expected.

Mr Wong and Miss de Carvalho were on the dance floor when Mr Cartwright, who was dancing with his wife, moved closer towards them.

They stopped dancing briefly and Mr Cartwright said, 'You must introduce us to your charming companion, Mr Wong.' After brief introductions, Mr Wong casually mentioned that Miss de Carvalho was 'the daughter of a good friend' and he was acting as her chaperon on her first visit to Kuala Lumpur.

Mr Cartwright was secretly delighted to hear she was unattached and impatiently waited for the music to end so that he could ask Miss de Carvalho for a dance.

Mr Wong chuckled to himself as he noted that Mr Cartwright spoke very little to Miss de Carvalho while they danced, choosing to focus his attention on what her low-cut gown revealed. She was aware of this and now and then looked up at him to smile shyly before lowering her soft, black eyes.

Mr Wong had good reason to feel satisfied from the way things were developing because he had personally coached Miss de Carvalho for the role she was now playing so well.

He had rescued her from a Malacca gambling den where she had worked as a hostess and whore six months before, shortly after her release from prison where she had served a sentence for theft.

He had installed her in a cheap hotel and lost no time to explain the ambitious plans he had for her.

'For the next three months I shall teach you how to behave like a respectable young lady! How to speak like a lady without using obscene words and expressions! I'll also teach you etiquette,' he said to her. 'I shall buy you expensive clothes and other things. I have big plans for you and we shall live in luxury. Just do as I say and don't double-cross me. If you do, you'll live to regret it!'

Miss de Carvalho had heard what happened to some people who had double-crossed Mr Wong; their bodies were found floating in Malacca harbour with their throats slit.

'He's not to be trusted! He is the kind of man who would happily sharpen a knife on his mother's tombstone to slit his father's throat!' she had been warned. But, life with Horatio Wong promised excitement and she was young, beautiful and adventurous. Who knew what the future held for her?

Her Chinese mother, a prostitute, had abandoned her on the front steps of a convent when she was a few days old. Bored with the strict discipline at the convent, she ran away when she was fifteen to become the concubine of an elderly opium smuggler who kicked her out after finding her in the arms of a younger man. She became the mistress of an English rubber planter for a while but left him for a more exciting job as a hostess.

She was spotted by one of Wong's bodyguards and as soon as Wong set eyes on her, he realised she was 'just the girl' he had been looking for to carry out some of his plans. 'With some grooming, she could be transformed into succulent bait to hook some big fish!' he had told himself, blackmail being one of his specialities.

Mr Cartwright's attraction to Miss de Carvalho was immediate and after he had danced with her he said to Mr Wong, 'Why don't you and Miss de Carvalho join my party? It's my birthday, you know.'

A delighted Mr Wong and Miss de Carvalho moved over to Mr Cartwright's table, Mr Wong making sure Miss de Carvalho sat beside Mr Cartwright while he seated himself some distance away from where he could watch how she performed.

Mr Cartwright had danced almost every dance with Miss de Carvalho to the silent delight of Mr Wong and to the obvious discomfort of Mrs Cartwright.

With that began a story of seduction, lies, blackmail and murder.

Mr Wong lay naked in bed beside Miss de Carvalho pleasantly recounting the events of the previous night when there was a knock on the door of his hotel room. He slipped on a dressing gown and opening the door saw a room attendant with a bouquet of red roses. The words on the attached card said, 'Mariana – Thank you for a wonderful evening! Could we meet tonight for dinner. Alone. With fond thoughts – Herbert.'

Mariana kissed and hugged Horatio Wong. 'Oh, Horatio! This is so wonderful! Nobody has ever presented me with flowers before!' she exclaimed. He laughed and said, 'You've seen nothing yet!'

The setting was a romantic one when Herbert Cartwright met Mariana de Carvalho for dinner at the Queen Victoria Hotel's French restaurant that night. He had earlier told the manager he wanted a secluded table, away from prying eyes, the best wine and a corsage of gardenias for his lady companion.

He sat impatiently at his table waiting for her to appear and when she did, his heart missed a beat. She was wearing a low-cut, white silk evening dress.

As she was being ushered to his table by the manager,

he rushed up to kiss her hand. 'You look so lovely!' he whispered.

As they sat at their candle-lit table, he handed her a small velvet-covered box. It contained a diamond mounted on a platinum ring. She was speechless for some time as she gazed at the glittering solitaire. She felt as though she was riding on a magic carpet among the clouds, like some princess in an Arabian Nights tale. When he slipped the ring on to her finger and kissed her hand, she realised she wasn't dreaming.

When she returned to her hotel, Horatio Wong was overjoyed by what she had to show him and to tell him. But, always cautious, he took the ring to a jeweller the following morning to have it valued. He was grinning on his return. The ring, he said, was worth about two thousand dollars, that in those days, was a small fortune.

As they drank whisky in their hotel bedroom, Wong said to Mariana, 'I can see he's very attracted to you. But, don't get carried away by his gifts. Rich men give young and beautiful women expensive gifts only to get what they wanted after which they kicked them out. Resist his advances. Play him along like a fish chasing after a tempting bait - and you are the bait! It's too early to surrender to his desires. He will have to part with a lot more expensive gifts and money before that happens. And, may I remind you, not to try any tricks behind my back. I'll be watching you closely.'

Mariana and Herbert Cartwright met for lunch the following day, spent the afternoon shopping and dined by candlelight again.

As they danced late into the night he said, 'As you know, I am very attracted to you. But I do not expect you to feel the same way about me because of my age and because I am married and have a son who is about your age. I do not expect anything in return from you and if you prefer for us to be friends and nothing more, it's all right. I shall do nothing to displease you.'

He paused and frowned slightly. 'This man Horatio Wong

who says he's your chaperon – he has a bad reputation. Be careful of him. I would not have invited him to my party the other night if it hadn't been for you. I wished to get to know you. I think a young and beautiful girl like you shouldn't mix with a character like him. I worry that you may find yourself in trouble because of him. I care about you. Please trust me.'

She was totally unprepared for what he had told her and was at a loss how to answer him. She smiled without replying and drew him closer to her as they danced.

Cartwright had not believed what Wong had said to him the other night – that she was 'the daughter of an old friend' and that he was her 'chaperon.' Men like him didn't have such honourable intentions towards beautiful, young women like Mariana de Carvalho.

When Cartwright had casually asked her about her family in Malacca she followed Wong's instructions and lied that she lived with an aunt who knew Wong. She got a job as a salesgirl in a textile store in which Wong had a share. Her holiday in Kuala Lumpur, she said, was a reward from Wong for 'exceeding her sales quota.'

Cartwright suspected she was indebted to Wong in some other way. It was his intention to lure her from him and away from possible trouble.

He had said to her, 'How would you like to work in my jewellery store at double what Wong is paying you? Plus commissions, of course. You could start work right away. What do you say?'

When she told Wong about this, he had said, 'I think you should take the job. It's too good to refuse and of course, it will open up many possibilities for me. You do understand that if you accepted his offer, you could also become his mistress?' She nodded her head slowly.

'My terms are eighty-twenty,' he told her.

'What do you mean by that?' she asked.

'That's the way we'll split everything you make – eighty

per cent for me and twenty for you. And, you will continue to do exactly as I say. I don't think you've had any reason to complain, so far? I've shown you how to hook a fat fish. For a start, tell him I am paying you five hundred dollars a month plus commissions – and let see if he would double that as he's promised you! If he does, then ask him for a thousand dollars in cash because you would like to leave some money with your sick, old aunt in Malacca before you moved to Kuala Lumpur. Do you see how one money-making idea leads to another?' He laughed and kissed her. 'You know, I had a feeling I was making a good investment in you!'

She was aware that she would soon become the mistress of two men and would play a major role in making Herbert Cartwright part with everything he possessed, never suspecting it would also include parting with his life.

Cartwright had acceded to her requests while realising that Wong was behind them. Even so, it was not a strong enough reason to extinguish his blazing desire for her.

When he had mentioned to his wife that he was employing Miss de Carvalho as a 'sales assistant,' she said with a strange smile, 'Well, I hope you won't be punished too severely for your folly.'

When he had asked her to explain what she had meant, she said, 'I am sure you'll find out for yourself in due course.'

'I hope you won't mind addressing me as Mr Cartwright in the store. It's for the benefit of the other staff and my wife who may pop in from time to time. And, I shall call you Miss de Carvalho – you know how people gossip,' said Cartwright to Mariana.

It amused her to know that she was already in a conspiracy with her employer. What other conspiracies were to come? She had another discussion with Horatio Wong before he returned to Malacca 'to attend to some important business.'

'Phone me every day. No tricks behind my back! I have spies everywhere!' he had warned her. 'I'd hate to make a mess of your beautiful face!'

She remembered hearing about a young prostitute in Malacca who had sulphuric acid thrown into her face for refusing to pay more for Wong's 'protection.'

Each day after work she waited in her hotel room for Cartwright's phone call. They would meet at a secret rendezvous for an hour or so before he returned home to have dinner with his wife. Later, he would stay awake, pretending to read. But his thoughts were with Mariana and wondering whether she was awake too – and thinking of him. Or, was she in the arms of Horatio Wong? His eyes narrowed and he felt the blood rush to his face at the thought.

Two weeks had passed and Herbert Cartwright could not bear the torment any longer. One evening while they were alone he said to her, 'Mariana, my dear, I find I cannot carry on with this farce. I want you so badly! It's driving me mad! I am going to move you to a house of your own.'

Embracing him, she said happily, 'Oh, that would be wonderful, Herbert! I can't wait!' knowing also that Horatio Wong would be overjoyed to hear of this new development when she phoned him later.

'Excellent!' he had said when she told him about it. 'But make sure about how much extra he's going to pay you for becoming his mistress. All mistresses are paid special fees.'

'How much should I ask for?'

'How desperate is he?'

'He can't keep his hands away from me!'

'Good! Tell him it will cost him two thousand dollars a month. That's beside what else you could get out of him in the way of gifts!'

'What? That's probably more money than the Chief Justice of Selangor earns a month!' she joked and they both laughed

'Try him and see! If he's so desperate to sleep with you, he'll pay anything! He's a multi-millionaire. To him, having to pay two thousand dollars a month would be like taking away two drops of water from the South China Sea! He owns a magnificent mansion in Bukit Damansara, a luxury yacht anchored at Port Dickson, holiday villas in Penang and Cameron Highlands, a chauffeur-driven Rolls-Royce and three bank accounts, one of which is in Switzerland. He also has shares in several big British companies – and that's before we start trying to figure out the value of all that high-class jewellery in his store!'

'You've been checking on him, I see,' she said.

'I don't fool around when I am trying to hook a diamond-studded whale, my dear!' said Wong with a laugh. 'This game is becoming more and more exciting! Don't do anything without informing me first!'

Cartwright had willingly agreed to Mariana's 'extra charge' and she moved to a secluded bungalow near Batu Caves. By doing so, he had found it increasingly difficult to tear himself away from her each evening and to go home to his wife.

He found he couldn't concentrate on his work, with her around him at the store. How he longed to be in her arms every moment of each day!

He had stopped going to the Selangor Club after work for drinks or to play bridge as he sometimes did. His wife's suspicions had already been aroused not only because he returned home late each night but also because when she had phoned the Club she was told he wasn't there. It did not require any stretch of her imagination to conclude where he might be spending his time.

After dinner one night while they were seated in the living room she calmly said to him, 'You're having an affair with that young Eurasian woman from Malacca, aren't you?'

He stared at her for some time before he slowly nodded his head.

'Is it just passion – or love?' she asked.

He did not reply and poured himself a drink at the bar.

'I had sensed this would happen from the night of your birthday party. I suppose you have installed her in a house? Are you planning to live with her?' she asked, her voice steady.

'The past weeks haven't been easy for me,' he said.

'Oh? Did she put up some resistance and tell you she was a virgin, when you tried to be intimate with her? I hope she didn't disappoint you.'

'I could do without your sarcasm,' he said.

She got to her feet and stood before him. 'It's best we come clean about this, Herbert. I refuse to be a part of any charade you may have in mind. Either you end this affair right away or I shall leave you. I am not going to put up with any lies. Besides, you don't expect this affair to be kept secret, do you?'

He swallowed some whisky from his glass and stared at the floor.

'I suppose you're worried about what your friends and business associates would say if you decided to live with her? Well, one cannot prevent tongues from wagging, could one?' she told him.

She began to climb the stairs that led to the bedrooms. 'I shall occupy the guest room tonight,' she told him.

'You needn't have to do that,' he said.

'Do you expect us to share the same bed with the scent of her perfume still on your body? For heaven's sake, be reasonable, Herbert. I am your wife, not some cheap whore.'

When he returned home that night, the *amah* informed him that his wife had packed some of her things and had left in a taxi, without saying where she was going.

He sat in the living room for some time deep in thought and steadily drinking whisky. He got into his car and went back to Mariana's house.

Three months passed.

Mrs Cartwright had been staying with friends for some time before moving into a rented apartment. She had returned to the house once, to pick up the remainder of her clothes.

Her husband, according to the *amah*, spent the nights away from home, returning early in the morning to bathe and change his clothes before he went to the office.

His wife had not tried to contact him. He didn't even know where she lived. Neither had he bothered to find out.

By now, it was common knowledge that Mariana de Carvalho was Hubert Cartwright's mistress.

He had received a cool reception from his friends when he visited the Selangor Club, because of his 'disgraceful affair with a half-caste woman.'

He decided to keep away from the place.

'You have him eating from the palm of your hand! Well done! It's time you moved ahead!' Horatio Wong told Mariana over the phone from Malacca. 'Make him sack his manager at the store.'

'What! Are you crazy? Mrs Lee has been in his employ for more than ten years and is a very competent person,' she said.

'So, what?' he replied. 'Find a reason to have an argument with her. Threaten to quit if she remained on the staff. I am quite sure he will give you her job. I was right about getting you extra money as his mistress, wasn't I? Just do as I say.'

He was right again.

Mrs Lee was dismissed and Mariana was appointed in her place.

At Wong's insistence, she made Cartwright give her $5,000 that she said was to pay for the funeral of her 'beloved aunt' who had looked after her from childhood and had died in Malacca, leaving many debts.

In fact, such a person only existed in the fertile imagination of Horatio Wong who needed the money to pay a debt he owed the boss of an illegal horse-racing betting syndicate who had threatened to kill him if he did not pay up.

According to their agreement, Wong should have given her twenty per cent of the $5,000 as her share, but he had conveniently forgotten to do so. When she had asked him about it, he told her he really owed that sum and would make it up to her later.

She knew he was lying.

It was to be the beginning of further demands of varying sums of money by Wong who was now 'living it up' at her expense.

'It's time we started making big money,' he told her. 'This would be done by the proven method of blackmail. I shall hide in the wardrobe in your bedroom and take photographs while the two of you are in bed making love. It's as simple as that!'

She knew what he was capable of doing to her if she had refused to carry out his plan.

When Cartwright received some intimate photographs of Mariana and himself by mail at his office, he immediately showed them to her. She pretended to be as shocked.

'It's the work of that swine Wong and no-one else!' he said angrily.

'But, how is that possible? He's in Malacca,' she said. 'It could be somebody else.'

The next day, he received an anonymous phone call demanding $50,000 for the negatives of the photographs, failing which prints would be circulated to his wife and his friends at the Selangor Club.

'How did the person who took these pictures get into our bedroom?' Cartwright asked Mariana who pretended to burst into tears.

'I'll tell you!' Cartwright went on, 'He let himself into your house with a duplicate key and hid himself in our bedroom, took the pictures and left after we had gone to sleep.' Then, grabbing her by the shoulders, he said, 'You had conspired with him to blackmail me!'

Mariana began to sob.

'Tell me! Did you have anything to do with this?' he demanded, raising his voice. 'I am not the fool you take me to be! I know you are still in contact with Wong! He has some hold on you and you will do anything he asks, like demanding money – the lies about your aunt's funeral, your move to get the manager's job in my store – and now, blackmail! Tell me the reason why you are afraid of him! I shall see he is put behind bars! To think I had instructed my lawyers to ask my wife for a divorce and to offer her a substantial settlement, because I had wished to make you my wife! I had also included you in my will so that you would receive half a million dollars in case I died before we were married! My intentions towards you have always been honourable, because I love you! And, now – this filth!'

She stared at him, speechless, then turned on her heel and ran out of the jewellery store, watched by the other members of the staff.

When he returned to her bungalow that night, she wasn't there. He waited for her until midnight and walked slowly along the deserted roads thinking about many things, until dawn.

During this time she had rented a room at a hotel from where she had phoned Wong in Malacca and told him what had happened.

He became excited when she told him that Cartwright had made her a beneficiary in his will for half a million dollars.

'Stand firm!' he told her. 'He may kick you out as his mistress and dismiss you as the manager of his store, but we must not give him the chance to cancel your name from his will! We stand to lose all that money! We shall have to move fast to make sure such a thing doesn't happen!'

'How are you going to do that?' she asked.

'I'll think of something. In the meantime, calm him down. Call me later,' he told her.

She went to a bar and drank until sunrise.

When she returned to her bungalow she was quite drunk and found Cartwright sitting in a chair in the living room, waiting for her.

He looked at her steadily, at her dishevelled hair and dress. Her lipstick and mascara were a mess. She stood before him with her hands on her hips and a cigarette hanging from her bottom lip. 'Hal-lo, dar-ling,' she said drunkenly with a smile.

She began to undress.

He suddenly realised he was seeing her for the first time as she really was, without the make-up and without the pretence. Was this the person he was thinking of making his wife?

She was naked.

She came towards him slowly, her arms outstretched.

'Come to me, dar-ling,' she lisped.

He got to his feet, roughly pushing her aside. She fell to the floor. He went to the door, opened it and went out, slamming it after him. She turned round as the door slammed shut and scowling, spat at it.

'You old bastard!' she screamed, furious that he had rejected her.

She grabbed the telephone and called Horatio Wong.

'Calm down. I'm leaving for Kuala Lumpur immediately. I'll contact you as soon as I arrive. Sober up!' he told her.

The first thing Herbert Cartwright did that morning was to call his lawyer from his home where he had gone after leaving Mariana. He instructed him to suspend divorce proceedings with his wife.

Next, he phoned his wife. 'I would like to meet you. It's urgent. Would you come home tonight for dinner? Please say, yes.'

'I'll be there,' she said. 'Don't send the car. I'll take a taxi. Are you all right? You sound terrible.'

'I'm all right. I'll see you around 7.30.'

When he met her later that night, he intended to ask her forgiveness; to tell her his affair with Mariana was over and if she would return to live with him.

When Mariana opened the door to let Horatio Wong into her bungalow that afternoon, she was still drunk.

'Well, how do you plan to solve the problem? And, what about my twenty per cent share of the $5,000 I gave you? You lied to me! I know, don't deny it!' she said angrily.

He slapped her hard across the face. She sank to her knees and began to sob. He hadn't struck her before. He stood over her, his eyes blazing. 'How dare you talk to me like that, you little bitch! Stand up!' he shouted pulling her up by her hair.

She tried to protect her face with her hands and arms as he continued to slap her.

'I am sorry! I am sorry! Please don't hit me!' she cried. She saw he had a revolver stuck in his belt.

'Sit down! I'm not going to shoot you – not yet! I still have use for you! Bitch!' he hissed. 'You had wanted to know how I was going to solve the problem. Well, here is the answer!' he said taking the gun from his belt and waving it in front of her face. It was a Smith & Wesson .38, similar to the one Herbert Cartwright carried in his briefcase, she remembered.

'Now listen,' he said. 'It's obvious he is not going to pay the blackmail money and that he's going to try and get back with his wife. He's also going to cancel you from his will, which means kissing half a million dollars goodbye! But, there's one way of making sure you'll still be paid that sum of money!'

'How?' she asked.

'By killing him before he removes your name from his will! It must be done without any delay!' he said quickly.

He saw her eyes widen.

'You are going to . . . kill him?' she whispered and a shiver ran down her back.

He smiled. 'We are going to kill him – the two of us! Remember, we're partners!'

She stared at the gun in his hand, suddenly feeling sick and weak.

'Smile! We're still going to be rich, after tonight!' he said.

'Tonight?' she asked nervously.

'Yes!' he replied with a grin. 'Now, have a bath and put some make-up on your face. You look terrible! We have things to do! First of all, we are going to keep a close watch on the movements of Mrs Cartwright!'

Wearing wigs and dark glasses they sat in a rented car and watched the entrance to the building in Ampang where Mrs Cartwright's apartment was located.

At about seven o'clock that evening they saw Mrs Cartwright get into a taxi.

They followed her at a safe distance.

'If my guess is correct, she's going to a reunion dinner with her husband,' he said casually and smiled when he saw Mariana who was sitting beside him, playing nervously with her fingers. 'Relax. The show is just about to begin,' he said.

After some time the taxi in which Mrs Cartwright was travelling was speeding towards Damansara and then entered a private road that led to her home. Wong parked his car some distance away from the entrance to the road. He got out with Mariana and they began to walk slowly in the shadows. The taxi that had carried Mrs Cartwright passed them on its way out. They moved among the trees and bushes in the garden and stopped close to the house.

Crouching behind a bush they saw Mrs Cartwright seated in a chair in the living room while her husband was at the bar preparing drinks. They saw him handing her a glass. He took a seat facing her.

Wong took the .38 from his belt and whispered to Mariana, 'One sound from you and I'll blow your head off!'

He disappeared in the shadows and seconds later she saw him crouching beside the French windows on the veranda. He picked up a pebble and threw it against the living room door and waited. He saw Cartwright stop talking after the stone had struck the door.

Cartwright got up and went to the door, looking out towards the garden before rejoining his wife. Wong waited a couple of minutes before he threw another pebble at the door. This time Cartwright came quickly to the door and said, 'Who's there!'

He presented an easy target. Wong was barely three yards away, hiding behind a large pot of ferns. He fired once, the bullet hitting Cartwright on the left side of his head. He fell, face down. At that moment he saw Mrs Cartwright remove a gun from Cartwright's briefcase and run to the door. Wong crouched as he ran in the shadows towards where Mariana was hiding. Mrs Cartwright saw a figure dashing through the bushes in the darkness and fired once at it, then dropped to her knees to attend to her husband.

Wong and Mariana ran towards the gate and heard Mrs Cartwright calling to the *amah*.

As they drove away in their car, Mariana asked Wong nervously, 'Is he . . . dead?'

'I hope so! I think I've just made you a rich little bitch!' he replied.

The *amah* said at the trial that she had heard two shots fired. This was in support of Mrs Cartwright's statement to the police that she was talking to her husband in the living room of their home on the night of the murder. He had told her he was going to end his affair with Mariana de Carvalho and asked her forgiveness. She had told him she was willing to return to him. As they were talking they heard a sound outside on the veranda and he had gone to investigate and had rejoined her after looking around. She thought an intruder was outside. There had been two recent armed robberies in the area.

They heard another sound coming from the veranda a few minutes later. Her husband went quickly to the veranda to investigate and as he stood at the doorway, she heard a shot fired and saw him fall face down. Convinced it was an intruder, she took her husband's .38 revolver from his briefcase. As she reached the veranda she saw a figure running among the bushes in the garden. It was very dark and she couldn't say whether it was a man or woman. She fired once at it.

She tried to offer aid to her husband and called out to the *amah* for help. Her husband was bleeding from a head wound.

He appeared to have stopped breathing. She tuned him over and placed her ear to his chest. There was no sound of a heartbeat. She immediately phoned the police.

The prosecution had said Mrs Cartwright's story was an invention; so was the *amah's* evidence that she had heard two shots fired – one by the killer followed by one by Mrs Cartwright. But, actually, only one shot had been fired. It was by Mrs Cartwright, using her husband's .38 Smith & Wesson revolver – and it was the shot that had killed him.

The prosecution also suggested there had been a heated argument between Mr and Mrs Cartwright over his affair with Miss de Carvalho before she had shot him.

Miss de Carvalho lied when she told the court that Cartwright had told her on the day before the murder that he was going to meet his wife the following night to try and make her agree to accepting terms for a divorce. 'He had warned me,' she said wiping away an imaginary tear, 'it wouldn't be easy. He said his wife wished to destroy him because he had left her. He had told her his wife would stop at nothing, that's why he had made her (Miss de Carvalho) a beneficiary in his will – just in case something happened to him.

When the prosecutor had asked her, 'And, what did you gather from that, Miss de Carvalho?' she had replied: 'He was afraid his wife might kill him,' she said.

Miss de Carvalho had denied suggestions by the defence counsel that Cartwright and herself were at a point of breaking up because he was being blackmailed by Horatio Wong and herself.

'I put it to you, Miss de Carvalho,' said the defence counsel, 'that you conspired with Horatio Wong to kill Herbert Cartwright because you both knew he would change his will in which he had made you a beneficiary for half a million dollars! You both decided to kill him before he could alter the will!'

'That's a lie! Herbert and I were in love!' she exclaimed, breaking into well-rehearsed sobs. 'I loved Herbert with all my heart – just as he had loved me!'

Horatio Wong told the court about the time when Miss de Carvalho met Cartwright at his birthday party. 'It was love at first sight,' he said with a shy smile. 'I treated Miss Carvalho as I would my own daughter. She told me she was going to work for Mr Cartwright. I later heard they were living together.'

Mariana de Carvalho, according to Cartwright's will was paid half a million dollars. She returned to live in Malacca and only gave Wong a couple of thousand dollars, investing the rest of the money in property and keeping a substantial amount in a fixed deposit in a bank. She also hired bodyguards to protect her since she feared Wong might kill her.

Mrs Cartwright believed that it was either Wong or Mariana de Carvalho who had fired the shot that killed her husband. Was it Wong she saw escaping in the darkness on the night of the murder?

A week after she was released from prison, Mrs Cartwright accompanied by her son, went to Malacca. She had heard Horatio Wong was in a hospital, dying of cancer.

Wong stared at her with sunken, glazed eyes for some time without speaking as she stood beside his bed. He kissed the rosary he wore around his neck and whispered haltingly, 'You have come to hear my confession . . . before I die, Mrs Cartwright?'

Tears rolled down his haggard face. 'May God have mercy on my soul! Forgive me! I killed your husband and Mariana saw me do it!'

Wong made a sworn statement to the Malacca police before he died a few days later.

At the re-trial, Mariana de Carvalho was charged with

conspiring to murder Herbert Cartwright. A jury found her guilty and she was sentenced to three years in prison. Upon her release she changed her name and returned to Malacca briefly to sell her possessions and was not seen again. It is believed she went to live in Portugal.

Mrs Cartwright wound up her husband's business, sold their property and returned to live in England with her son.

Ramona

The public performances by the band of one of the British garrison regiments stationed in Singapore before the Japanese invasion, was well received by audiences wherever it had performed – at parks, at the Victoria Memorial Hall, on the Padang and on ceremonial occasions such as the King's Birthday Parade and Empire Day.

Besides regimental marches it had shown its versatility and musicianship by including in its programmes popular and contemporary compositions and music specially arranged for ballroom dancing.

The band had accepted an invitation to perform at the 1938 Gala New Year Charity Ball at the Sea View Hotel in Tanjong Katong on the east coast of Singapore.

To the delight of those attending the programme selected by the band included the beautiful and somewhat melancholy song *Ramona* from the film of the same name. The arrangement for this popular melody featured a trumpet solo by Bandsman James Smith who although only eighteen, was regarded by his bandmaster as 'a most promising, young musician'. He had played the solo part in *Ramona* once before at a charity performance and had become, as one newspaper described, 'the band's star performer.'

The large crowd at the event included high government officials, members of the consular corps and prominent European and Chinese residents. Formalities over, the guests soon settled down to enjoy themselves. Now and then they turned their attention to Bandsman Smith whenever the trumpet was given prominence in the music being played. This was because the tones he effortlessly produced from his instrument were of a smoothness and clarity seldom heard. At times, there would be ripples of applause meant for him alone and his boyish face would redden as he cast an embarrassed look at the perspiring bandmaster who wondered why some of the audience's appreciation had not been directed to him.

During the first brief interval, the bandsmen gathered at a corner of the hall for some light refreshment and to hear the bandmaster's praise or criticism for the music they had been providing. But, he had no reason for complaint and looked rather pleased with life. When the others weren't looking he stood close to Bandsman Smith and said under his breath, 'Well done Smith, but take care not to lose your concentration,' to which Smith had stiffly replied, 'Yessir!'

The band was about to continue with their programme when Smith saw her.

She was wearing a bright pink *cheong-sam* and stood among a knot of people; her young, delicate Chinese face partially hidden by bunches of red and white roses that decorated the marble pillars of the ballroom.

She appeared to him as the most beautiful rose of all. He was mesmerised by her beauty. He felt his heart racing and a tingling sensation all over his body. He did not realise he was still standing while the other members of the band had resumed their seats – until he heard the bandmaster say, 'You all right, Smith?'

'Er, yessir!' said Smith and sat down, his heart pounding in his ears. The young man beside him who played 'second trumpet,' asked, 'You all right, chum?' Smith nodded his head as the band started to play, conscious that the bandmaster was watching him from the corner of his eye because he didn't want anything untoward to happen to his 'star.'

Smith stared at the music sheet before him as he played

with mechanical precision quite unlike his normal style, trying to keep his mind on the notes as the vision of her face kept flashing before him. He mopped his face with a handkerchief at the end of the piece and the bandmaster after bowing to the crowd, asked him again, 'Are you all right?' because next on the programme was *Ramona* – and Smith would play the solo part.

'Yessir,' he said taking a deep breath as he looked over the music before him that he didn't really have to do since he knew it so well. But, it was an excuse to avoid looking at the bandmaster and to overcome the gnawing temptation to steal a glance towards the pillar where he had seen her.

Leaning his body slightly to one side to avoid the bulk of the bandmaster, he plucked up courage and his eyes travelled slowly towards the pillar decked with roses. And, there she was! Her face was now in full view and she looked even lovelier because she was smiling and he could have sworn she was smiling at him! His heart leaped and he felt the blood rush to his face. Should he return the smile? But, was she smiling at him or at one of the other musicians? His heart sank and a frown creased his forehead, unaware that the bandmaster was watching him.

He recovered his composure when he heard the bandmaster say, 'Are you all right, Smith?'

'Yessir,' he said again.

He picked up his trumpet and moistened his lips in readiness as the bandmaster led his musicians into the introduction of *Ramona*.

Silence fell upon the crowd as Bandsman Smith stood up and closing his eyes, began to play as none had heard him play before that even caused a look of surprise from the bandmaster who wondered what could have suddenly possessed the young man.

He ended the solo by sustaining a high, lingering note, its beautiful sound filling the dance hall and floating out of the windows and to the sea and the islands beyond.

Bandsman Smith stood at attention, his heart still pounding as the General Officer Commanding British armed forces who was the guest of honour, led the applause that was punctuated with shouts of 'Bravo!' and 'Encore!'

The beaming bandmaster quickly invited Smith to stand beside him and they both bowed graciously.

The general's *aid-de-camp* approached the bandmaster and said something to him. With pride that swelled his broad chest, the bandmaster announced, 'We shall be honoured to play a special request by the General Officer Commanding. He has requested that Bandsman Smith play a solo of the ever popular *Danny Boy.*'

Bandsman Smith had made up his mind: He would smile at her even if she chose to snub him.

He slowly cast his eyes towards the pillar of roses again and suddenly felt his heart sink into his boots.

She was no longer there!

'Are we ready, Smith?' he heard the bandmaster say and he mumbled.

'Yessir,' his eyes anxiously searching the faces in the crowd.

The introduction was played and with a wave of his baton the bandmaster signalled Smith to commence his solo that was the last item on the programme.

Bandsman Smith brought his performance to an end with a flourish of unrehearsed high and low notes much to the surprise of the bandmaster and the crowd who responded with a standing ovation.

As he bowed in acknowledgement his eyes quickly searched the faces in the crowd again, but in vain.

'A very fine performance, Smith!' he heard the bandmaster say in a voice which seemed to come from very far away.

In the fleeting moments that he had seen her, Bandsman Smith had fallen deeply in love. He found himself in a most unenviable situation, not knowing whom to ask for information about her except to say that she was young, the most beautiful girl he had ever seen and that she was wearing a bright pink *cheong-sam*.

He told nobody the reason for his desire to be left alone at the regiment's barracks. He did not smile as easily as he did and seldom spoke to anyone that his rivals were quick to diagnose as 'the symptoms of a swollen head' because of his popularity.

Over the next few days when he was not rehearsing with the band and had a few hours to himself, he wandered in the crowded streets hoping she would suddenly appear from somewhere.

A shiver ran through him as he thought, 'Supposing she appeared in the company of a man who was her husband or lover?'

He felt like weeping at the thought of it.

His search for 'Ramona' as he had named her, took him to cafes and restaurants and among the crowds in Chinatown.

A month later, part of his regiment was on a troopship bound for England.

As he stood on deck watching the skyline of Singapore slowly sink behind the horizon, his sadness became unbearable.

He wept bitterly and felt like jumping overboard. What had prevented him was the hope that he would see her again.

Ten years passed.

It was 1948. World War II had ended three years before and the world was once more at peace.

The emptiness in James Smith's heart still remained. All through the war years he couldn't forget her. How he longed to see her, if only for another fleeting moment, to know she had survived the war!

There was an advertisement in the Singapore newspapers that a dance orchestra from London had been engaged to perform at the Sea View Hotel and the 'star' of the band was its leader, a trumpeter named James Smith, who was no stranger to Singapore.

The writer of an article in the *Tribune* happily recalled Smith's previous stay in Singapore when he was better known as 'Bandsman Smith, the man with the golden trumpet' and a member of a regimental band.

The writer recalled Smith's much-acclaimed performances, also mentioning that he was a bachelor and that he had chosen *Ramona* as the 'signature tune' of his orchestra 'for a very special reason that he had declined to reveal.'

The crowds flocked to the Sea View Hotel once more where Smith had won so many hearts but lost his own.

Patriotism And Prejudice

Elaborate preparations were completed well in advance of the date of arrival in Singapore of Sir Cecil Clementi, the new governor of the Straits Settlements that comprised Penang and Malacca (in peninsular Malaya) and Singapore.

Merchant houses, government offices, schools and *Johnston's Pier, where Sir Cecil would arrive by launch from the ship that had brought him to Singapore, were decorated with red, white and blue bunting, Union Jacks and gold-painted cut-outs of the British Crown.

The route by which Sir Cecil and his escort would take to the Padang (a large, green open space beside the waterfront) where he would inspect a ceremonial guard of honour would be flanked by hundreds of cheering, flag-waving schoolchildren and the 'local' population.

There would also be a gala banquet and ball at the Victoria Memorial Hall in Sir Cecil's honour as soon as he and his family had 'settled' themselves in Government House, his official residence.

The 5th of February 1930, the day of the new governor's arrival, was unusually hot despite the presence of the rain-bearing northeast monsoon during that time of the year.

It was declared a public holiday so as to give as many of Singapore's 'local' British subjects and the small English

---

*Johnston's Pier was built in 1855 and named after a Scottish trader named Alexander Lawrie Johnston who settled in Singapore in 1820. The pier was demolished in 1933 after Clifford Pier was built. It was named after Sir Hugh Clifford who was governor from 1927 to 1929.

community the chance to honour the representative of King George V.

Hundreds of people of various Asian races, representing the colony's population, had assembled at the waterfront from early on the morning of Sir Cecil's arrival.

Brindle and Muffin, two Englishmen who worked for a British bank in Singapore, were among the huge crowd.

Brindle, the older of the two, had been in Singapore for two years. He had brought along a fixed-focus 'box' camera while Muffin, who had recently arrived from England, was eager to 'shoot' the new governor with the latest Kodak 8mm cine-camera. The two men also wished to capture on film, some scenes of the military parade at the Padang.

Muffin had always felt a deep sense of pride after reading various accounts of exploits of the heros who had built and preserved the Empire. It had brought peace, justice and freedom to millions of people through what was known as *Pax Britannica* ('peace imposed by British rule.')

He had secretly wished he had been an officer serving under the legendary Sir Robert Clive of India or Sir Stamford Raffles of Singapore instead of being a 'pen-pusher' in a bank. He had often stood before a long mirror and imagined he was dressed in the resplendent uniform of an officer of the famed British East India Company.

'Ah! Only dreams!' he had said to himself.

Today, he would have the privilege to witness a rare display of British colonial pomp and pageantry and he found it difficult to contain his excitement as his heart swelled with pride and patriotism.

From the Padang, not far from where he stood a British army brass band was playing *Rule Brittania* and Muffin stuck out his chest and began to sing softly along with the spirited music. Suddenly he stopped singing – and a chill ran through his body at what he had seen.

A young English police inspector with a cane in his hand

was standing in the centre of the road and observing the crowd that was held back by rope barriers opposite the pier where Sir Cecil and his entourage would arrive.

A young Tamil in a white shirt and trousers and clutching a small British flag had ducked under the rope barrier and attempted to run across the road, apparently to a spot that would offer a better view of His Excellency.

'Get back, you black bastard!' yelled the inspector at the top of his voice, angrily brandishing his cane. The man tried to escape but stumbled and fell. The inspector began to thrash the man, ignoring his screams for mercy. The crowd watched in silence and horror. Unconscious and bleeding, the man was dragged away by two Sikh constables.

Muffin was speechless and nauseated and thought he was going to faint.

Brindle had seen what had happened but pretended to be interested in something else.

'You saw that . . . didn't you?' Muffin gasped. 'That poor man! It was ghastly!'

'My dear chap,' said Brindle soothingly, 'you'll have to train your eyes not to see such exhibitions of instant colonial justice. I have seen worse when I was in India. You would also have to remind yourself from time to time that you are in a British colony and not in England where a different brand of British justice is administered.'

'That poor man was brutally assaulted by an English police inspector! And, everybody just stood there and watched!' said Muffin, aghast.

'You didn't expect the crowd to riot, did you?' asked Brindle. 'It's the same kind of justice that is administered to the followers of Mr Gandhi in India, when unarmed men and women who offered no resistance whatsoever, were shot and killed or had their heads split open with rifle butts by British troops and police!'

'I feel so . . . ashamed!' said Muffin softly.

'I can quite understand your feelings,' said Brindle. '*Pax Britannica* my arse and to all the bullshit about justice and equality! You wouldn't have expected to have seen, not even in your wildest dreams, a similar performance by a constable who was controlling a crowd outside Buckingham Palace, would you?'

'Would you mind if I left?' he said to Brindle after a while. 'I feel I need a drink.'

'I could do with one, myself,' said Brindle. 'Mind if I came along?'

'No, not at all,' said Muffin.

The two men placed their cameras in a duffle bag they had brought and disappeared slowly into the milling crowd.

The 'special guests' had lined up inside the pier, awaiting the new governor's arrival.

On one side stood senior civil service officers in white helmets with shining brass chin-straps, starched white tunic jackets, shining brass buttons, medals on their chests and swords in scabbards hanging at their waists. Beside them were members of the legal service and the judiciary. Facing them were 'selected' *tuan besars* (the Malay equivalent for English VIPs) and their wives (the *mems*, short for *mem-sahibs*, as English 'ladies of leisure' were known in India) who had spent small fortunes on the ensembles that had been specially ordered from London or Paris for the occasion.

The *tuan besars* representing the Singapore British Chamber of Commerce and the Singapore British Bar Association were in tweed suits with waistcoats and wearing felt hats; their wives in satin and silk, organdy, voil and *crepe-de-chine*. Some held lace parasols over their hats from Paris that offered no protection from the towering heat that descended in invisible waves from the pier's roof of corrugated iron sheets and which, for some reason, was not insulated against the heat.

Widening rings of perspiration formed under the armpits of the ladies and around the brims of their felt or velvet hats;

some of which were decorated with clusters of celluloid fruit or flowers while others had feathers dyed in various hues that might have had their origins in French or English poultry farms.

The *tuan besars* cursed silently under their breaths as they mopped their red, dripping faces and waited for His Excellency to make his appearance. 'Apparently there's been an awful cock-up about the arrangements! The welcoming ceremony should have been over half an hour ago!' muttered a large, silver-haired *tuan besar*. 'Meanwhile, we're being roasted alive in this bloody oven!'

The welcoming party had already been waiting for more than an hour.

A 21-gun salute boomed from the direction of the Padang where *tuans* of less importance and their wives belonging to the 'riff-raff' society that included beachcombers and bums had gathered. The 'locals' were kept at a safe distance by rope barriers and burly Sikh constables with *khandar* sticks of black hardwood that had been imported from India where they were being used with much success in controlling demonstrators in Mr Gandhi's civil disobedience campaigns.

Favoured local residents were allotted seats in covered, wooden stands decorated with red, white and blue strips of cloth and small Union Jacks at one side of the spacious Padang where the military parade would be held. The front seats were reserved for those who had displayed their loyalty to the British Crown in more tangible forms than those who were seated in the rows behind. Many of those occupying front seats had been awarded the much-sought-after OBE (Order of the British Empire) in a very competitive game known among the English upper-class as 'Currying favour' and which the European 'riff-raff' and 'locals' called 'Bum-sucking' or 'Ball-carrying.'

Detachments of perspiring British troops and those from the Straits Settlements Volunteer Corps stood 'at ease' under the scorching sun. They had been rooted to the ground where they stood for almost two hours in silence. An English regimental brass band stood some distance away, soaked in perspiration, their brass instruments heated by a scorching sun, temporarily abandoned on the grass. An official understanding their plight and that there could be no music provided when Sir Cecil arrived, quickly ushered the bandsmen and their heated instruments under a canvas tent occupied by the Red Cross.

Meanwhile, at Johnston's Pier two single-engine seaplanes with open cockpits from the Royal Singapore Flying Club, raised more fears than cheers from the crowd when their floats narrowly missed removing two British flags fluttering from the masts of the *ss Mantua* that had brought the new governor and his family to Singapore, in what was intended to be (according to the official programme) an 'aerial salute.'

For the benefit of those who may have mistaken this hair-raising demonstration as a display of stunt-flying, the determined pilots made a second attempt. This time they roared over the governor's launch as it approached the pier, missing the pier's simmering zinc roof by inches. The planes' engines produced an ear-drum-shattering, rattling sound that reverberated through the pier's roof, considerably adding to the distress of the welcoming party below. Moments later, a sudden calm descended on the pier as word was quickly passed around, that Sir Cecil had (at last) arrived.

A tall, slim and distinguished-looking intellectual, Sir Cecil shook the hands of those who had waited for more than two hours in the maddening heat to experience such an honour, smiling into their haggard faces as he went down the lines.

He was not the sort of person to be shaken by the death-defying antics of pilots infused with wild patriotism. neither was he the sort of person to be overcome by the explosions of colour from sweaty, over-dressed English ladies and gentlemen who were there to welcome him.

He had been through all this before in Hong Kong where he was governor in 1925 and before that, when he had served there as a cadet in the Colonial Secretariat in 1899.

At ceremonial occasions at Government House during Hong Kong's sticky, humid 'summer' season, prominent Cantonese gentlemen appeared in frock coats, satin-lined tweed waistcoats, trousers, silk cravats, top hats, kid gloves and with spats on their patent-leather boots. Their wives (or favourite concubines) wore hats and dresses that were exact copies of those 'exclusively' worn by female members of the Royal Family as seen in photographs appearing in British high society magazines. It was an acknowledgement of the ingenuity of Hong Kong's Cantonese tailors and milliners.

Sir Cecil was one of the few colonial administrators to have distinguished himself as a Chinese scholar. Besides being able to speak Cantonese and Mandarin fluently, he composed Chinese poetry, wrote classical Chinese calligraphy and had published literary essays on the Chinese classics.

His knowledge of Chinese literature was held in high esteem and he was responsible for writing an illuminative introduction to a translation of *Cantonese Love Songs* (published by Claredon Press, London, in 1904), which also rather strangely dealt with the history of prostitution in China. It highlighted the romantic image of the Chinese courtesan in society and her contribution to China's economy. This was evidenced by a reference Sir Cecil had made to a thesis in the *Chronicle Of Sundry States* that was written in the 7th century BC. It was stated that a minister named Kwun Chung 'originated and put into operation the practice of prostitution as a masterpiece of political economy, making it a source of revenue to the country.'

Prostitution in Singapore, however, was not regarded as a boost to the colony's economic prosperity. It was prohibited by law but was also considered 'a necessary evil' in an effort to control the increase in cases of rape and molest.

'Conditions could have been a lot worse if not for our strict controls,' according to a statement issued to the press by a government official although the steady influx of prostitutes had reached the startling figure of 30,000 – or about ten per cent of Singapore's population. He said that efforts were being made to counter some 'unfair and uncomplimentary insinuations' in local newspapers that the efficient bunkering services provided to ships by the Singapore Harbour Board 'were not the only reasons why more ships and crews were being attracted to Singapore in view of the alarming increase in the number of brothels and cases of venereal disease in recent months.'

He gave the assurance that the government continued to regard prostitution as a social evil despite accusations to the contrary made by certain ill-informed people. These included the Anglican and Catholic bishops of Singapore who had long campaigned for stricter controls on those engaged in the world's oldest profession.

The sale and manufacture of raw opium imported from the vast poppy fields of Eastern Bengal, made up about 30 per cent of Singapore's annual revenue.

While opium addicts, mainly Chinese 'coolies,' were registered by the government and allowed to purchase the drug at government-run centres, no effort had been made to license 'ladies of the night.'

Singapore's development as an international port and business centre had made rapid progress after it came under British control in 1819. By the early 1920s a hundred years after it was founded by Raffles, the 'swampy, fishing village' as it was once known, was now a bustling trading port that was acclaimed as 'one of the most valuable assets in the British Empire.'

An increasing number of ships from all over the world bound for Western or Far Eastern ports called at Singapore for supplies and to load or unload a variety of cargo. These ships also brought with them large numbers of sailors with money to spend and who were in search of somewhere to spend it – preferably in bars or brothels for which other 'flesh ports' such as Shanghai, Hong Kong, Saigon (now Ho Chi Minh City) and Bangkok were already famous. To meet such a demand, vice dens mushroomed along Singapore's waterfront as well as in other districts within the city radius.

A sea captain commenting on the cluster of brothels near the Tanjong Pagar wharves remarked, 'These places are most conveniently situated. It's like rolling from the bunk in your cabin right into the arms of a whore in bed!'

The increase in the number of 'red light' districts that stretched from Tanjong Pagar to outlying districts also saw an alarming rise in cases of venereal disease that caused a serious problem since there were too few policemen (owing to the poor salaries offered) and too many prostitutes who had invaded Singapore.

One of the attractions in Singapore's booming vice trade in those days was The *Rickshaw* Parade in which 'ladies of the night' advertised their charms while being paraded in brightly-lit *rickshaws*. Two carbide lights on either side of the *rickshaw* seat provided the illumination for the heavily made-up 'queens,' since many of them wore tiaras of imitation jewellery. The more popular ladies had their own *rickshaws* decorated with peacock feathers, balloons, chrome-plated accessories and boasted velvet seat coverings embroidered in gold thread. Some *rickshaws* displayed small British, French, American, Dutch, Danish, Japanese and Chinese flags to indicate the international popularity that their lady passengers enjoyed.

There was keen competition among them and occasional territorial skirmishes broke out that also involved secret society gangsters to whom the ladies were obliged to pay protection money.

Popular routes for these nightly parades were along Stamford and Bras Basah Roads, Waterloo and Bencoolen Streets and Dhoby Ghaut. A customer would follow the lady of his choice in a separate *rickshaw* to one of the many brothels.

Business along the routes of the *Rickshaw* Parade was particularly brisk on Fridays when British soldiers stationed at Fort Canning and Tanglin barracks received their weekly pays.

Regular customers to brothels who may have found themselves short of cash were offered 'love now, pay later' credit with a small additional charge as 'interest.' Debtors who failed to pay their dues on the appointed dates were persuaded to do so by secret society gangsters.

Repeated public outcries by civic and church leaders stirred the government to finally crack down hard on vice and by doing so ended The *Richshaw* Parade, a colourful attraction of Singapore's nightlife.

The Unsung Hero

The last time Crosby and Captain Van Linden met was at the Long Bar at the Raffles Hotel some time before Singapore surrendered to the Japanese in February 1942.

The years of the Japanese Occupation saw Crosby in the jungles of Malaya as a guerrilla fighter while Van Linden was a prisoner in an internment camp near Palembang in Sumatra. He had been captured with some survivors after his ship carrying refugees from Singapore to Ceylon (Sri Lanka) was sunk in the Straits of Malacca by Japanese dive-bombers.

Crosby and Van Linden had known each other for some years before the war. Crosby was an accountant in Singapore in those days and they met at the Long Bar whenever Van Linden's ship was in port.

It was now 1947, two years after the surrender of Japan and Crosby and Van Linden had the opportunity to meet again.

'You know, I can still remember the last time they danced at the Raffles before the Japs entered the city,' said Van Linden to Crosby as he finished a glass of Bols at the Long Bar.

'It was on the 13th of February 1942, two days before Singapore surrendered. Of course, you were somewhere in the Malayan jungles at the time. Anyway, bombs and artillery shells were exploding all over the place. Fires were raging everywhere. We all realised there was no hope for Singapore, yet everyone believed something would happen to drive the Japs away. That feeling of optimism was quite evident at the Raffles. It had become a home for the homeless and a place where hundreds of wounded could get some medical attention.'

Van Linden paused to light a cheroot before he continued.

'The Raffles Hotel's orchestra turned up as usual and there was dancing at the Ballroom. Mostly everyone was in uniform instead of conventional dinner jackets and evening gowns. Amidst all this, sleep-starved surgeons and nurses were trying to save lives in makeshift operating rooms and attend to the wounded. At the same time, the number of those who had not survived steadily increased. It was a terrible scene for the graceful, old Raffles.

He paused to reflect momentarily and took a deep breath.

'It's quite astonishing how some people seem to be unaffected by adversity,' he went on. 'Although we were helplessly watching the last agonising days of Singapore, the hotel's waiters were dressed as usual in spotless, starched uniforms and making every effort to maintain their high standard of service although the Japanese were almost at their doorstep, so to speak.'

They were silent for a while then Crosby asked, 'Did you by any chance come across an American singer and dancer by the name of Laura? She was probably performing at the Raffles at that time.'

Van Linden stared at Crosby and it was some moments before he replied.

'You knew Laura?' he asked, his voice suddenly low.

'Well, sort of. I met her briefly when she performed at the E & O Hotel in Penang just before the Japs invaded Malaya in December 1941. I heard she moved to Kuala Lumpur to appear at the Selangor Club. When the Japs came further down the peninsula, she came to Singapore and began performing at the Raffles'.

Van Linden ordered another round of drinks and stared at the whirring ceiling fan above. The mention of her name had caused a sudden sadness to come over him. Without taking his eyes away from the fan, he said softly, 'Her voice was like soft moonlight . . . and when she danced, she became a moonbeam. She was the most beautiful creature I had ever seen'.

He looked at Crosby with a weak smile. 'Call me a romantic old fool who has had a little too much to drink. But when she made her entrance each night at the Raffles Ballroom the orchestra played her song *Laura* that she sang and then danced like a gorgeous butterfly trapped in the silver circle of a spotlight!'

He shut his eyes and began to softly hum the song, He stopped and ran his fingers slowly through his white hair and looked away.

'You seem to have fond memories of her,' said Crosby.

'Yes,' he replied and stared into his empty glass.

Crosby said, 'I believe she was half Cherokee Indian and half Italian. Everybody knew her as Laura. I remember the night I was at the E & O Hotel in Penang when she sang Cole Porter's famous ballad, *Night And Day*. The song haunted me on and off afterwards. In fact, when I was alone some nights in the jungle during the war I would shut my eyes and recall many things. At times I would see her so vividly in my mind. It's strange how one is able to bring back memories in such detail. Whatever became of her?'

Van Linden stubbed out his cheroot in an ashtray and began his story.

'I made a futile search to find Laura's grave after the war. She was buried on a hill behind a former women's internment camp that was some miles away from Palembang town. I was told her grave was not far from where the camp guards had buried her Japanese lover, an army officer. The Japanese guards had mutilated his corpse before throwing it into a hole'.

Crosby frowned. 'Her lover was a Japanese army officer?'

'Yes. I'll tell you about him later' said Van Linden, his face souring. 'But, first let me take you back to the 13th of February 1942. I had returned to my ship at about seven-thirty that night. The Tanjong Pagar docks and warehouses were ablaze, the flames lighting up the whole area for the benefit of the Japanese dive-bombers and fighter planes. I was supposed to sail for Colombo in Ceylon with evacuees. Three other cargo ships were lined up behind mine. Panic-stricken and hysterical people were fighting each other to get aboard the ships. Women with young children in their arms who had been pushed into the sea were screaming for help in the darkness. Heaven alone knows how many drowned. There were some terrible scenes and the Jap fighter planes would fly almost mast-high, machine-gunning and dropping incendiary bombs.

'My ship and the others were jammed with evacuees and although damaged, we managed to sneak out of the harbour and make for the Straits of Malacca. It must have been about three o'clock the following morning while we were somewhere off the coast of Sumatra when from out of nowhere Japanese planes dropped flares lighting up the whole area. Moments later, two dive-bombers roared over us. Flames shot high up as each bomb exploded. My ship, a rusty old tub, broke in two almost immediately and sank. I remember I was on the bridge with my chief officer at the time. As we were going down there was an explosion. When I came to, I found myself afloat on my back in oily, calm water. It was very dark. I could faintly hear voices calling out for help. Some were those of young children crying for their mothers. I tried to move but my right arm hurt a lot and I knew I had broken it. I was vomiting salt water and oil that I had swallowed. I must have lost consciousness again.

'When I awoke I found I had been deposited on a beach of a small island. The sun was scorching. Looking around I saw people scattered along the beach. Some were lying very still, the waves breaking over their bodies. Some had terrible injuries. I saw a woman staggering along the beach. Her clothes and face were black with oil. She fell. I ran up and knelt beside her and saw she had a gash across the side of her head that was still oozing blood. She was unconscious. I tore off the right sleeve of my shirt with my good left hand and began to wipe away the oil and blood from her face.

'I couldn't believe my eyes. She was Laura! I had no idea whether she had been aboard my ship or on one of the others that also sank. I had always wanted to be introduced to her when she was appearing at the Raffles. But, here she was, her head resting in my lap! I couldn't believe it!

'She was still unconscious some hours later when a native fishing boat appeared. On board were some Japanese with guns. Only survivors who were able to walk were taken aboard. Those who couldn't were left on the beach to die. But I managed to stagger on board, almost dragging Laura along with me.

'For a few days we slept in cattle sheds at a small river *kampung*, the women survivors separated from the men. I was able to find out that Laura was quite weak from the loss of blood. There was no medical aid available. I had no money with me, so I gave a villager my watch and told him to sell it and buy a bottle of antiseptic and deliver it to Laura after I had described her to him as best I could. I realised she wouldn't have known it came from me. Well, she wouldn't even have known who I was since she was unconscious for most of the time after I found her.

'My hope of making contact with Laura ended some days later when the male prisoners were moved some miles away to a logging camp in the jungle. However, we soon established what was known as a "bamboo telegraph" between the men's and women's camps and I managed to get some news about her. I learned that her health had improved. It had made me very happy.'

Van Linden took a sip from his glass.

'I was dying to see her again, only to tell her I was the person who had found her on that island. It was not because I was seeking her gratitude. I just felt she should know it was me, that's all. There were some of us who were thinking of escape, knowing we would be beheaded if we were caught. So what? We were doomed, anyway! The chances of us coming out of the jungle alive were nil. We would die of starvation, disease or a Japanese sword. When a person knows that such a fate awaits him, he is prepared to do desperate things. I had decided I would make a dash through the swamps and down the railway line to the women's camp that was seven miles away to see her, even if it was only for a few minutes and then I would kill myself before the Japs had the chance to torture me to death. I know it sounds insane when you come to think of it, but war makes everyone insane!'

Crosby lit his pipe and said with a half-smile, 'You had fallen in love with her, hadn't you?'

Van Linden looked away and paused before he faced Crosby again.

'I suppose I had, in a strange sort of way. I wouldn't have known for sure at the time. Like the other prisoners, I had nothing to live for. Without telling anyone, I planned my escape up to the last detail. However, something terrible happened that made me change my mind completely. An Indonesian who had been hauling logs in the area around the women's camp, told me a Japanese officer had taken an American woman as his mistress.

'My heart sank instantly because as far as I knew, Laura was the only American in the women's camp. I asked him if he was sure about this. He said he was and that the woman had moved into the officer's quarters. He had seen them together and he described her to me. There was no mistake. She was Laura. After I had recovered from the shock I discovered my feelings for her had turned to contempt and anger. How could she allow herself to be touched by a Jap! He must have forced her! Raped her! The bastard! But after I had cooled down a little I was told by my informant that this Japanese officer whose name was Oyama was a kind man who was trying to get more food rations and medicines not only for the women internees but for the men as well.

'I refused to believe any Japanese had kindness in his heart after I saw how they had ill-treated the wounded survivors from those refugee ships! They were brutal! I didn't wish to hear anything more about this shameful affair concerning Laura. But, as the weeks passed I found my interest in her was still very much alive and I began to make inquiries about her again from my Indonesian friend. He told me she and her lover were having problems. The Japanese army commander was furious about their relationship and ordered it to come to an end at once, which they were not prepared to do because they had fallen madly in love with each other.

'According to my informant, certain women at the camp were jealous of Laura because of the few luxuries her lover gave her. They made false reports against her to the *Kempeitai*, the Japanese secret police.

'They claimed she had a short-wave radio hidden in Oyama's quarters where she listened to war news from the Voice of America and the BBC in London. They also accused her of being connected to a spy ring based in Palembang that had contacts with American and British submarines that were operating against Japanese shipping.

'I now began to fear for Laura's life, having heard horrifying stories about the *Kempeitai's* torturing methods. I kept in close touch with my informant for further news.

'He told me later that Laura and Oyama had been arrested by the *Kempeitai* and were being held in two separate guardhouses at the women's camp. They were being tortured, he said, and their screams could be heard at all hours of the day and night.

'He said Oyama's quarters were searched because Laura's accusers claimed she had hidden a short-wave radio there. But, nothing was found. However, this did not put an end to the tortures.

Van Linden took a deep breath and lit another cheroot.

'Laura's screams stopped one day. A guard who was friendly towards Oyama told him she had died and was buried on a hill behind the camp. When another guard came to his cell with his food, Oyama knocked him unconscious, grabbed his pistol and escaped. He crept into the guardhouse where four *Kempeitai* officers and two guards were playing cards and drinking. He shot them dead. The other guards quickly surrounded him, but before they could arrest him, he shot himself.

'I was told the guards hung his body from a tree and used it for bayonet practice before throwing it into a hole on the same hill where Laura was buried.

'I searched in vain for Laura's grave on my release from the prison camp after the surrender of Japan. The whole area was thick with elephant grass and weeds.'

'When I visited the place a couple of months ago a construction company had levelled the whole area to build a low-cost housing estate.'

Van Linden sat back in his chair and fell silent.

Crosby said, 'A horrible end for both of them! But, Laura's death was avenged by her lover who died like a hero, didn't he?'

Van Linden sprang to his feet, suddenly angered. 'You called him a hero? Good God, sir!' he exclaimed fiercely.

He stomped out of the bar.

Crosby never saw him again.

A Matter Of Pride

Charles Forsythe had been advised as he made plans for his voyage from London to Singapore in 1934, that he should make an early reservation for accommodation at the prestigious Raffles Hotel in view of the heavy bookings throughout the year. But a series of farewell parties and his habit of putting things off until the very last moment caused this matter to be left unattended.

His uncle for whom he worked, had earlier written to some important business associates in Singapore informing them of his nephew's impending arrival and his intention to start a branch office there. He also thought it would add to his nephew's prestige to mention that he would be staying at the Raffles Hotel until other arrangements were made.

Arriving in Singapore, Charles Forsythe jumped into a taxi with his luggage. Twenty minutes later he was standing in front of the hotel's reception counter with his suitcases beside him and feeling his spirits quickly descending into his boots after being politely told by the manager that all accommodation was fully booked.

He felt quite foolish for not making a reservation before leaving England. Now, he was completely at a loss, not knowing what to do. The manager tried to be helpful by suggesting other hotels but Mr Forsythe was not paying much attention to what the man was saying. A feeling of deep despair had suddenly engulfed him, realising his situation was hopeless.

What did English gentlemen do in such situations?

'They blew their brains out!' he heard an imaginary voice whisper in his ear. 'Or, they changed their names and joined the French Foreign Legion, never to be heard of again!'

Then, an idea struck him: Surely the managers of famous hotels did special favours for special guests, as did the managers of popular restaurants – you know, when they suddenly 'remembered' an unoccupied table, or that there had been a last-minute cancellation when an important guest who hadn't made a reservation suddenly appeared?

Was it possible the manager of the Raffles Hotel had forgotten he had a vacant room that he had been reserving for some VIP in the event of such an emergency? Perhaps a subtle name-dropping exercise might help to achieve the desired result?

Forsythe drew the manager aside and said, 'You must have heard of my uncle Mr Andrew Douglas Forsythe, OBE, chairman of Forsythe & Forsythe the well-known and respected London trading house? Whenever he and my aunt visited Singapore they stayed here at the Raffles and nowhere else!'

The blank look on the manager's face indicated he hadn't heard of the young man's uncle or of Forsythe & Forsythe. But, Charles Forsythe was not one to accept defeat so easily. He quickly decided on three plans of action:

Plan A: He would try more name-dropping and combine it with mild intimidation.

Plan B: This would see a complete change in tactics. He would beg to be accommodated anywhere in the hotel, even in one of the storerooms.

Plan C: He would tell the manager that he had decided to end his life rather than stay in some disreputable hotel and destroy his family's good name. He would blow his brains out that very night. He would leave the usual 'suicide note' in which he would explain why he had decided to end his young and promising life, placing the blame squarely on the shoulders of the manager!

Forsythe became so carried away with Plan C that he could even imagine the headlines in the next morning's newspaper:

'Man Denied Room At Raffles Hotel Kills Himself'!'

'Excellent!' thought Forsythe.

He launched Plan A with quiet confidence and taking the manager aside again, said, 'It is imperative that I be given accommodation here without much further delay! I plan to entertain some very influential people this evening who are friends of my uncle, and the governor of Singapore, no less! Heaven alone knows what they'll do when they discover my predicament. I wouldn't like to be in your shoes!'

The manager sighed deeply and shook his head.

Noting this, Forsythe quickly launched Plan B. From the pompous young man he appeared to be a minute ago, Forsythe was now begging.

'But, you must help me,' he said in a pleading voice. 'Please! It's a matter of life and death that I stay at this hotel. I'm prepared to occupy one of your storerooms until a guestroom falls vacant. You cannot cold-bloodedly throw me on to the streets!'

The manager stared at the floor. He couldn't bear to see the anguish on the young man's face.

'I am very sorry, sir. How I wish I could help you. Please leave your name and contact address with the receptionist. I promise the first available room shall be yours.'

Saying that, the manager bowed sedately and quickly walked away not giving Forsythe the opportunity to launch Plan C which he had no intention of doing after realising how unconvincing it was and how foolish he'd look in front of the manager.

He was still standing beside his suitcases at the reception desk and feeling completely shattered when he saw from the corner of his eye a silver-haired lady sitting alone at a table in the tea-room nearby. She was looking towards him and smiling. Thinking she was smiling at someone else, he paid no attention. But, when he looked at her again she was still smiling – at him! There was no mistake.

He bowed cautiously in response not having the slightest idea who she was. Then he saw her pointing to the vacant chair beside her, inviting him to sit at her table.

Leaving his suitcases under the charge of the receptionist, he made his way towards her, not knowing what to expect. He noticed she was rather elderly, in her late fifties perhaps and that she was well attired.

Before he could introduce himself, she said pleasantly, 'Do sit down, young man. I couldn't help overhearing some of your conversation with the manager. Would you care for some tea?' Before he could answer she quickly poured him a cup from the pot on the table. She pushed the sugar bowl and the milk jug towards him.

'Go on, have a cup. It'll relax you,' she said with a warm smile.

He said, 'You are being most kind, madam.'

He introduced himself.

She tilted up her nose a little and proudly announced, 'I am Lady Beatrice Ascot-Holt of Burma. You must have heard of my late husband, Major-General Sir Aaron Ascot-Holt, MC, the hero of the Mandalay uprising and of his expeditions up the Chindwin River?'

He mumbled that it was his first trip to the East. She smiled and leaned her plump body towards him. 'I think I may be able to help you find a room here,' she said, her voice suddenly low.

He had his teacup raised to his lips and he quickly put it down on its saucer, his eyes widening. 'Oh, Your Ladyship! You think you could? I would be ever so grateful!'

She touched his hand lightly with her finger and said softly, 'Yes. I think it could be arranged, provided you agree to a few minor matters?'

'Oh, yes! Indeed! Whatever they may be!' he said excitedly.

'Hush!' she said softly, placing a forefinger to her lips. 'I'm afraid I must ask you to keep your voice down, Mr Forsythe.' She looked in the direction of the female receptionist. 'I fear that where we are at the moment is dangerously close to that eavesdropping tart at the reception desk. I suggest we repair to a place offering more privacy. Come along, Mr Forsythe,' she said and led the way out of the tea-room with her head held high.

They entered the Palm Court and she indicated a table and easy chairs under a bower of bougainvillea. As soon as they were seated she smiled pleasantly and said, 'Ah, this is much better, don't you think?'

Forsythe noticed she was wearing a necklace, ring and bracelet made from red stones of varying sizes that sparkled in the bright afternoon sun. Noticing his interest, Her Ladyship thought it was a proper time to tell the young man a few facts about herself.

'My late husband established the first British-owned ruby mines in Burma in 1851 in which my family has substantial interests, if I may add.'

She saw him admiring her jewellery again and went on. 'The stones I am wearing are from our personal collection of rare rubies.' She shyly avoided his gaze, changing the subject at the same time by saying, 'I hope you are not having the same irritating problems as I am with unnecessary delays in the transfer of funds?'

Forsythe thought for a while and said, 'No. None that I can think of, Your Ladyship.'

She smiled broadly. 'Ah, good! But I'm not as fortunate as you, Mr Forsythe. That's because I have to put up with stupid delays concerning the transfer of rather large sums of money from my bankers, the Bank of England, to my private account here. You see, funds have first to be transferred to London from the bank in Rangoon that seems to take ages. You have no idea how primitive banking conditions are in Burma, Mr Forsythe, when it should be such a simple procedure, really. Dear, oh dear!'

She sighed and continued, 'Well, I shouldn't be boring you with all this Mr Forsythe, if it wasn't for the fact that there has been another hideous delay that has put me in a rather uncomfortable situation. You see, I have kept a permanent room at this hotel for some years now and have been prompt in settling my bills. But there seems to be an unsettled account for a trivial sum, which the management appears not to be in the least concerned about but which I would like to settle without further delay. It's a matter concerning principle and keeping one's pride. You do understand what I am trying to say, don't you, Mr Forsythe?'

She looked at him, raising her eyebrows and he quickly said, 'Oh, indeed! I fear my reputation is being severely threatened with the prospect of living in some god-forsaken dump!'

She nodded her head sympathetically and said, 'I quite understand your distress, Mr Forsythe. However, I wouldn't have been at all concerned about this silly little hotel bill had it not been for the fact that I am supposed to leave for Kuala Lumpur tomorrow to join some old family friends and I would like to settle this outstanding account before I left.'

She sighed, looking at him from the corner of her eye and at the same time unnecessarily adjusting her necklace whose brilliance caught Mr Forsythe's attention again.

'It grieves me to see you so upset, Your Ladyship,' he said. 'If I could be of any assistance at all please don't hesitate to tell me!'

She looked at him, her eyes suddenly soft. 'Oh, I thank you for your kind concern but I should hate for you to do me a favour without being able to do one in return . . . one that perhaps could solve both our little problems?' She looked away.

'Oh, please do tell me what you have in mind, Your Ladyship,' he said eagerly.

She looked at him steadily and said, 'Would you care to take over my room for two weeks while I am away on holiday, Mr Forsythe?'

He was speechless for a few seconds before he excitedly replied, 'Yes, of course, Your Ladyship! Please tell me how this could be arranged. I shall be most happy to pay whatever the sum involved!'

She extracted a crumpled statement of accounts from her handbag and handed it to him. There were a lot of entries on it that he didn't care to inspect and quickly handed it back to her.

'Just tell me the amount, Your Ladyship,' he said.

She returned the document to her handbag and smiled. 'Well, I owe the hotel the sum of three hundred and twelve dollars,' she said. 'But there is another small matter. I seem to be short of cash. Do you think you could lend me a hundred dollars, in addition to settling the hotel bill? Of course, I shall repay the loan in full as soon as funds from my bankers in London arrive. As for the three hundred and twelve dollars, that would go to pay for the rent of my room for two weeks. Is that all right with you, Mr Forsythe?'

'It would be a pleasure, Your Ladyship!' he exclaimed. 'In fact, I think it would be most unfair if I did not compensate you in some way for your kindness that has saved me from some awful embarrassment. Please accept the hundred dollars as a small token of my gratitude, paltry as it would seem to a lady of your financial standing.'

'If you insist, Mr Forsythe,' she said. 'You would have to give me four hundred and twelve dollars in cash, if you please, since I would like to settle the bill personally and make the necessary arrangements with the manager for you to occupy my room.'

'Oh, of course, Your Ladyship!' he said.

She glanced at her gold wristwatch and said, 'If you hurry to the cashier you could make the necessary arrangements for the amount you have to pay me,' she said, smiling sweetly.

He rushed off and returned a short while later with the money in an envelope and handed it to her. She counted it and put it into her handbag.

'Well, Mr Forsythe, we seem to have been of mutual assistance, haven't we?' she said happily.

'I have to thank my lucky stars that I met you, Your Ladyship!' he said as she stood up. They shook hands.

'Very well, I shall make the necessary arrangements and vacate my room within the hour,' she said with a smile. She got to her feet and was about to walk away when she said, 'Of course, you would have vacated my room by the time I returned in two weeks?'

'Oh indeed, Your Ladyship,' he said.

'Excellent!' she said. 'And, one more thing, I trust you will keep our little transaction to yourself.'

'Oh, most definitely, Your Ladyship!'

True to her word, she vacated the room within the hour. Breathing a long sigh of relief, Forsythe took over the room and congratulated himself on his stroke of good fortune although the sum of money involved was not as 'trivial' as Her Ladyship had described it, considering the rent of her tiny room at the rear of the hotel was only one hundred dollars a month – a special rate.

The manager came into the room to inquire if there was anything Forsythe required. 'I trust everything is to your satisfaction, sir?' he said.

'Oh, yes, indeed! Couldn't be better, thank you!'

He smiled at Forsythe as he left the room.

Later, while Forsythe was dining at the restaurant the manager came up to him and said, 'I am delighted things turned out well for you, sir.'

Mr Forsythe grinned. 'Yes. It was most fortunate that I met Lady Ascot-Holt. It happened quite by accident, you know!' The manager attempted to hide a smile.

'Ah, yes. She describes herself to some people as Lady Ascot-Holt, the wealthy widow of a fictitious owner of some non-existent gem mines in Burma,' he said. 'But, I suppose, there's no harm in that, is there?'

Forsythe's expression quickly changed to one of concern. 'And just what do you mean by that?' he asked, slightly annoyed.

Coming nearer to Forsythe and lowering his voice the manager said, 'Well, sir, Miss Bertha Jones, the name she used when she was a stage actress and which, by the way, is her real name, has been residing at this hotel for the past three years. As far as I know, she arrived in Singapore as a member of a small Shakespearean theatre company that ran into financial difficulties. Having some savings of her own she came to stay here, paying her rent a month in advance as she has done ever since. With the increase in the number of short-term guests and tourists she appears to be making a fairly decent living by subletting her room at a good profit to persons such as yourself, sir, who arrive without having made prior reservations.

'The people concerned are in the habit of keeping their transactions with Miss Jones strictly private and are in fact rather grateful to her for her assistance. We understand that after sub-letting her room she moves into cheaper lodgings. But, that again is no concern of ours since she always settles her bills on time. Personally, I find Miss Jones a most pleasant and cultured person. I dare say she must have been quite a talented actress in her day. I might add, sir, she wears what is known as costume jewellery that is quite worthless.'

Forsythe didn't know what to say, remembering the promise he had made to 'Her Ladyship' that he would not discuss their transaction with anyone. And, Forsythe was a man of his word.

The manager was about to walk away when he said, 'Of course, sir, I trust what I've told you will be kept strictly between ourselves. After all, Miss Jones is a respected guest of this hotel like everyone else.'

'Yes . . . yes, of course,' said Forsythe absently, a deep frown creasing his forehead.

He pushed aside a bowl of oxtail soup that a waiter had placed before him.

He had suddenly lost his appetite.

He got up from the table and began to walk in the direction of the cocktail bar.

He decided a stiff glass of whisky was what he needed to revive his spirits and not a bowl of soup.

The Masquerade

The year was 1918. The Great War had ended. The world was at peace again and Mrs Henrietta Fairmount breathed a sigh of relief to know that young Christian Fellows whom she had high hopes of having as a son-in-law, would soon be returning to Penang from the war.

His marriage to her daughter, Isobel, would be a most timely event, from a financial point of view, since the young man came from a wealthy family.

Mrs Fairmount had been a widow for the past nine years and the money she earned as a teacher hardly made ends meet. Her late husband had left her with a mortgaged house and two young daughters. The modest amount of money from his life insurance policy was almost exhausted.

Isobel was 21 and her sister, Frances, a year younger. Both were pretty and rather charming. Mrs Fairmount thought that if she indulged in some diligent social manoeuvring, she would be able to find suitable sons-in-law with healthy financial backgrounds. She was a woman who loved putting words into the mouths of other people and if given half a chance would use her persuasive skills to get her own way whenever she could.

This didn't do much to improve her popularity.

Being the type of woman she was she failed to see that young men kept their distance from her daughters because of her overbearing and patronising attitude.

Isobel considered herself to be prettier than her sister Frances, an opinion shared by her mother, who seemed ever willing to sing her elder daughter's praises.

Frances on the other hand was mild-mannered and soft-spoken. She minded her own business and stayed out of family arguments. According to Mrs Fairmount's own assessment, Frances didn't have Isobel's 'magnetic charm' and thought her chances of securing a husband were rather poor.

Isobel was Mrs Fairmount's 'best bet.'

The favouritism Mrs Fairmount showed towards Isobel was the subject of discussion by some of her friends who wondered why this was so. The reason that they would never learn about was because of Mrs Fairmount's guilty conscience over what had happened between Isobel and a dashing, young army lieutenant by the name of Edward Fulton-Bowen whose family belonged to the English aristocracy.

This happened while Christian Fellows was away in France fighting the war.

It had occurred to Mrs Fairmount that her hopes of having Christian Fellows as a son-in-law could suddenly end if he were killed. Being a cautious and resourceful person, she thought it would be wise if she made some 'contingency' plans.

'It would have to be a first-come-first-served policy as far as Isobel is concerned from now on,' she said to herself.

Isobel had met Lt. Fulton-Bowen at a party. Perhaps it was the young man's smart uniform and his swashbuckling manner that had attracted her. It could have been her flaming red hair, alabaster skin and green eyes that proved irresistible to him. Whatever the reasons, it was soon obvious they had fallen head over heels in love.

Mrs Fairmount, optimistic that the whirlwind romance would lead to an early announcement of their engagement, allowed the young couple to spend much time together without the presence of herself or a chaperone that well-brought-up young sweethearts were obliged to tolerate. Having an older woman present to see that the affections displayed by courting couples did not go 'out of bounds' was an unpopular practice and such people became to be known among frustrated young lovers as 'old chastity belts.'

Lt. Fulton-Bowen and Isobel had no reason whatsoever to regard Mrs Fairmount as a hindrance to their frequent outbursts of passion because Mrs Fairmount made sure she was somewhere else on such occasions.

The thought of Isobel becoming pregnant did cross Mrs Fairmount's mind. And, should this happen, she would make very sure Lt. Fulton-Bowen married Isobel without any delay. In fact, that was what Mrs Fairmount secretly wished for since her inquiries about the young officer revealed he was the heir to a fortune.

Then, quite suddenly, he disappeared.

Mrs Fairmount was aghast to discover the young officer and his regiment had been secretly shipped out of Penang to help quell a rebellion in Burma.

Lt Fulton-Bowen wrote a long letter to Isobel from Rangoon in which he described his sadness at being parted from 'the only girl I shall ever love.' His regiment was on its way back to England and he would inform his parents of his love for her and seek their blessings for their marriage.

'It may be some time before I see you again since my regiment will soon be sent to the war. But I shall return to Penang to make you mine. Please wait for me,' he wrote.

He had also written to Mrs Fairmount about the matter. However, as far as Ms Fairmount was concerned, 'the canary had escaped from the cage and there was no hope of it returning'

Mrs Fairmount's doubts about Lt. Fulton-Bowen keeping his promise were more than confirmed when Isobel told her mother that she was no longer chaste.

Mrs Fairmount whose nerves were in tatters over the loss of a wealthy and prospective son-in-law fainted as she heard her daughter's confession. When she recovered, she said angrily,

'Since he's succeeded in getting what he set out to get with your wholehearted encouragement, you'll never see him again! All men were the same!' She sighed as she was reminded of her own experiences.

'Don't put the blame entirely on me for what happened! You must share the responsibility!' said Isobel hotly.

'How dare you accuse me! I didn't ask you to surrender yourself to him!' cried Mrs Fairmount. 'Oh, the unbearable shame I shall have to suffer if anyone found out! I can well hear the whispers and giggles. No decent man would have anything to do with . . . to put it crudely . . . a broken pot! That's what you are! A broken pot!' Mrs Fairmount quickly prostrated herself on a couch and announced to her daughter that she was going to faint.

To which Isobel said, 'Faint, if you wish, mother! But its not going to stop me from what I am about to say! You knew that Edward and I were passionately in love and yet you allowed us to spend long hours alone, putting temptation in our way! But you didn't seem to care, did you? You were hoping I would become pregnant so Edward would be forced to marry me! I was the bait in your scheme to catch a rich son-in-law, like you had plans for Christian Fellows! Don't deny it, mother! But, I want you to know that I love Edward and he loves me!'

Mrs Fairmount apparently decided to postpone her 'fainting spell' because she suddenly sat up and hanging her head said in a tearful voice, 'Well, it's no use crying over spilled milk, I suppose,' said Mrs Fairmount. 'I think I should be glad that you are not carrying that scoundrel's child!' She pretended to wipe a tear from the corner of her eye. 'Of course, as your mother, I shall make every effort to see you are respectably married as soon as possible and saved from disgrace!' she said.

Without informing Isobel, Mrs Fairmount wrote a nasty letter to Lt. Fulton-Bowen in which she called him a 'blackguard and scoundrel who should be publicly horsewhipped' for what he had done and for having caused humiliation to her daughter and herself. She made it clear that Isobel wished to have nothing more to do with him.

Mrs Fairmount quickly changed her tactics in the days that followed. Before tongues began to wag, she informed everybody that Lt. Fulton-Bowen and Isobel were 'only friends and nothing more', adding with a broad smile, 'Of course, it's no secret I suppose that my daughter has been patiently awaiting the homecoming of Christian Fellows who had stolen her heart. They have been sweethearts since childhood, you know.'

She was determined not to fail in her efforts to see that Christian Fellows and Isobel became engaged even if it meant resorting to gentle blackmail in order to remove the skeleton that Isobel had installed in the family cupboard.

There was nothing to support Mrs Fairmount's belief that Christian Fellows had any desire to make Isobel his wife since he hadn't even sent her a postcard in the three years he had been away. But that didn't seem to deter Mrs Fairmount. She somehow believed that the more people were told of her daughter's impending engagement to him the better were the chances of it happening.

She had also considered the possibility of Christian Fellows not wanting to marry Isobel. But, think of his embarrassment when he tried to explain to everybody why he had suddenly abandoned his 'childhood sweetheart' who had remained loyal to him all these years. If Christian Fellows persisted in being stubborn Mrs Fairmount was prepared to play her 'trump card', which would be to spread the rumour that Isobel had confessed to her that he had deprived her of her innocence before he left to fight the war. And she would go as far as to offer medical evidence to prove it! How could Christian Fellows deny such an accusation – if Isobel said it were true?

'I'll have Christian Fellows crawling on his hands and knees!' Mrs Fairmount told herself. 'But I must first be absolutely sure of Isobel's support in whatever I do!'

The two families had known each other for several years and

the children almost grew up together. Christian Fellows being about the same age as Isobel had found himself in her company more often than her sister's. They went horseback riding together and attended the same parties and dances.

Isobel's sister Frances had deliberately avoided Christian at parties, talking to the girls and dancing with other young men. The times when he asked her to dance she had made polite excuses. But, when she found herself forced to, she put on a serious face and moved mechanically to the music for the benefit of her mother whom she knew would be watching her like a hawk. She didn't wish to give her mother any reason to accuse her of trying to seduce Christian Fellows as she once did after a Christmas ball – and all Frances had done was allow him to kiss her under the mistletoe.

As far as Mrs Fairmount was concerned she had earmarked Christian Fellows to be Isobel's husband – and that was that.

Mrs Fairmount's anxiety to have Isobel married as soon as possible may have been caused by the fact that she herself had been 'left on the shelf' until she was twenty-five after having had a few illicit love affairs. She was having fears of spending the rest of her life a spinster in London when she met a young accountant named Cedric Fairmount whose parents were missionaries. He was on his way to Penang to take up a government appointment when she succeeded in seducing him. When she informed him that he had made her pregnant, he had no choice but to marry her.

Then, Isobel was born.

After Isobel's 'humiliating disaster' with Lt. Fulton-Bowen, as Mrs Fairmount wished to call it, she expected her daughter's full support for the success of her plan.

'You are going to do exactly as I tell you or I'll see to it that your life is going to be a very miserable one, young lady! Do you understand?' Mrs Fairmount told Isobel who was tormented by her mother's constant nagging. She would have agreed to anything her mother wished, if she could only be left in peace.

To add to Isobel's distress, the absence of any letters from Lt. Fulton-Bowen had caused her to doubt his promise that he would return to marry her. She was beginning to believe her mother could be right about him after all.

'The fact that he hasn't bothered to write can mean only one thing, that he has forgotten about you, as I had correctly predicted!' said Mrs Fairmount.

What Isobel didn't know was that her mother had intercepted and destroyed the many letters Lt. Fulton-Bowen had written.

It had become obvious to Christian's parents, Dr and Mrs Montague Fellows, what was in the mind of Mrs Fairmount as far as Isobel and their son were concerned.

Dr and Mrs Fellows decided they would leave their son's choice of a bride entirely to him and if it happened to be Isobel, well and good. So long as they loved each other, what could anyone say?

What nobody had any reason to suspect, however, was that Christian Fellows and Frances Fairmount were secretly in love and had taken great care to hide it.

They had decided to be married after Christian came home from the war.

In the meantime Frances had no wish to arouse her mother's vicious temper by upsetting the plans she had so carefully laid for Christian and Isobel.

Matters would be sorted out later, Frances decided, after Christian returned. Now that he was returning, she secretly shed tears of joy. However, the thought of their love for each other being discovered by her mother threw her into despair. She could well imagine what her mother's reaction would be when she found out.

At times Frances would hear her mother talking in undertones to Isobel and mentioning Christian's name. On one occasion she heard her mother say, 'You leave Christian to me! You just do as you're told and there'll be no trouble!'

Christian Fellows returned home shortly before Easter and

at a secret meeting with Frances, he told her he would inform her mother and his parents of their love for each other and their intention of becoming engaged. He had been promised a responsible job with a leading bank in Penang and he intended to marry Frances as soon as possible.

When Frances expressed fear that her mother was up to some mischief, he said, 'I am quite prepared to face anybody and any obstacles if you are by my side!'

Meanwhile, Mrs Fairmount was busy spreading the rumour that there would be an announcement of the engagement between Christian Fellows and Isobel.

Hearing this Frances and Christian decided to make a surprise announcement of their engagement at the Grand Easter Masquerade Ball to be held at the Oriental Hotel in a week. It was a gala annual event that would be attended by the elite of Penang society.

A few days before the ball, a letter arrived for Isobel. As usual, Mrs Fairmount took delivery of it from the postman. It was yet another letter from Lt. Edward Fulton-Bowen and had been posted in Bombay. She opened it and read it.

'I still love you Isobel. I am on my way to Penang to marry you,' he wrote. He also wanted to know why she had not replied to his many letters. Mrs Fairmount destroyed the letter as she had done with the others.

It was a night of Victorian charm and elegance at the stately Oriental Hotel's ballroom: the ladies in pompadours and lace; the gentlemen in wigs, tights and black leather pumps, all displaying various colourful masks.

During an interlude Christian Fellows seized his chance. He dashed across the floor and taking Frances by the hand ran with her to the orchestra stage from where he proudly announced their engagement.

It was greeted by applause and good wishes.

The announcement came as a pleasant surprise to all, including Christian's parents.

A dumbfounded Mrs Fairmount collapsed to the floor in a cold sweat.

As Isobel watched her mother's reaction she suddenly had the wonderful feeling of being free from her domination and wondered what future plans her mother had for her.

Isobel was walking towards Frances and Christian to offer her congratulations when she was swept into the arms of a masked gentleman.

'Don't you think we should announce our engagement too, my sweet Isobel?' said Edward Fulton-Bowen as he removed his mask and kissed her.

Tears of joy rolled down Isobel's cheeks.

'As I told you in the many letters I wrote, I would return to marry you!' he said.

Looking towards her mother who had been revived and was being assisted to her feet, Isobel knew at once that it was she and nobody else who had reason to intercept Edward's letters.

Mrs Fairmount's eyes almost popped out of her head at seeing Isobel in the arms of Edward Fulton-Bowen.

To everybody's surprise, Mrs Fairmount fainted again.

The Amazing Professor Brown

There was an air of excitement at a table in a corner of the Royal Tea Room in Kuala Lumpur on that afternoon in June 1935. Four ladies, two English and two Chinese were seated at a table and one of the English ladies was reading a letter in a hushed, excited voice. From the manner in which she and the others reacted it was easy to tell that the letter contained news of much importance to them.

After she had finished reading the letter she returned it to its envelope. She placed it in her handbag and said to her companions excitedly, 'Well, I think we should reserve suitable accommodation for the professor without further delay!' The other ladies nodded their heads in agreement and smiled.

Three of the ladies were the wives of wealthy gentlemen in the community. The other, the recipient of the letter, was a recent arrival in Kuala Lumpur. She was a gem-dealer by the name of Fiona Daffodil.

After leaving the Tea Room, they crossed the street to the Grand Hotel where Fiona Daffodil booked a suite in the name of 'Professor Thomas Brown.'

The letter that the four ladies had become so excited about was posted in Calcutta where he was lecturing. He said he would be arriving in Kuala Lumpur 'within a week.'

Professor Brown was a spiritualist.
Spiritualism was sweeping the United States, Britain and

Europe at the time and those with Professor Brown's 'special powers' were eagerly sought after. It was said that he could communicate with spirits of the dead while in a trance. By staring into a person's eyes he could also tell the person's past and predict his future – for a fee, of course.

Professor Brown's expenses at the Grand Hotel would be borne by a small and dedicated body of wealthy men and women who had formed the Spiritualists Society of Malaya of which Mrs Daffodil was chairwoman. She was also in charge of the society's Donations Box. The money that was collected would go towards funding the World Society of Spiritualists that Prof. Brown had founded.

Mrs Daffodil was the first contributor to 'The Box' with a donation of $500 that was quite a sizeable sum in those days. But she chose to describe it as 'a modest token of my admiration for Professor Brown and his magnificent contribution towards the progress and better understanding of spiritualism, the science of the future.'

She revealed that she had written to Prof. Brown and persuaded him to agree to conduct séances for members of the Spiritualists Society of Malaya.

'Professor Brown is doing us a special favour by agreeing to come here since we are a very small organisation,' said Mrs Daffodil. 'Five hundred dollars is perhaps too little considering the fact that he is an internationally famous spiritualist. Members could donate whatever sums of money they wished. All donations would be kept strictly confidential.' Using her charm and persuasive powers she saw to it that each member's donation equalled her own or bettered it.

Within a few days, money from donations had reached more than ten thousand dollars, a small fortune in the 1930s.

Mrs Daffodil, who was a newcomer to Kuala Lumpur, had described herself as a gem dealer and a representative of some leading gem merchants in Antwerp, London, New York and Cape Town. The genial Mrs Daffodil was an attractive blonde of forty-one. She said she was a widow.

While in the process of selling diamonds and other gems she had managed to get her clients interested in spiritualism in a casual manner, never failing to amuse them with her story about her attempts to communicate with her deceased husband that had so far ended in failure. 'I'm such an amateur, really! But, I am sure with Professor Brown's help, I'll succeed!' she said.

Having aroused her clients' interest in the gems she had for sale, her next step was to make them members of the exclusive Spiritualists Society of Malaya and supply them with the latest publicity about Prof. Brown whom she said she hadn't yet had the pleasure of meeting.

Mrs Daffodil made sure she also collected valuable information about prospective members of the Society that they were required to provide in their application forms. Mrs Daffodil filed such data in alphabetical order and kept it in her room in a locked cabinet. It would be passed on to Prof. Brown when he arrived in Kuala Lumpur.

The reason for her doing so was because Mrs Fiona Daffodil and Professor Thomas Brown were in fact husband and wife and had been working as a very successful team for a number of years, fleecing large sums of money from their gullible victims through fraud and blackmail. They each were fluent in some European languages and had several passports made out in different names. He was also known as the Reverend Edgar Peachtree, Baron Siegfried von Hindenburg, Dr Andre de Lavant and Senor Theodorico Santa. Some of Mrs Daffodil's bogus names were Mrs Otto Heinrich, Sister Mary Magdalene, Senorita Carmelita Estella and Lady Florence Windsor.

On her arrival in Kuala Lumpur she had rented a house in a prime residential area from where she conducted her business in gems, getting to know some influential people including wealthy Ipoh tin-miners and racehorse owners as well as the wives of some of Kuala Lumpur's many Chinese millionaire-bankers.

She saw to it that for the protection and security of its members, the Society met in secret since she felt that their activities were better 'kept in the dark' – not because there was anything illegal about holding séances, she explained, but simply as a precaution because some people who were ignorant of what spiritualism was all about and could easily arrive at the wrong conclusions.

The members, of course, welcomed this as a wise move by Mrs Daffodil in whom they had placed implicit trust.

'Imagine being able to communicate with my beloved in one of Professor Brown's séances! How absolutely thrilling!' said one of the members who had just presented a cheque for $1,000 to the Society's 'Donations Box.'

None of the forty-six members of the Society had yet experienced the pleasure of meeting Prof. Brown and had only seen some photographs of him through the courtesy of Mrs Daffodil.

'I am told that he is a tall, gaunt man with deep-set, penetrating eyes. He wears a trimmed beard and has a low, booming voice,' said a report published in a London magazine called *Wonderful*, copies of which were distributed by Mrs Daffodil to Society members. He was forty-five and a bachelor, added the report.

Of course, there was no such magazine by that name. The copies Mrs Daffodil distributed had been specially printed and were part of Prof. Brown's publicity campaign that included several other articles about his amazing powers – all written by himself.

People who practised spiritualism were believed to be worshippers of the devil or involved in witchcraft besides being charlatans and cheats. While it was true that some 'spiritualists' had been exposed as fakes and had been imprisoned for a variety of offences nothing of a criminal nature had been proved against Prof. Brown. While wires, special sound-producing gadgets and lighting effects had been uncovered by investigators during raids on séances held by these charlatans, no such 'props' had been found at the meetings conducted by Prof. Brown. The absence of such evidence only reinforced the claims by his supporters that he was 'a man with genuine supernatural powers.'

Prof. Brown's real name was James Chestnut. He was born in the slums of London and put into an orphanage at the age of ten from where he escaped and began a life of crime. Chestnut was impressed by the impersonations performed by actors on the vaudeville stage and soon developed similar talents that he later used with much success as a confidence trickster.

Fiona Daffodil's real name was Valerie Wheat, the product of a girls' reformatory in London. She had become a member of a travelling circus, married an Italian acrobat and learnt to speak Italian, German and French from some of the performers. She later deserted her husband in favour of a more exciting and rewarding life as a pickpocket.

James Chestnut met her under strange circumstances. While travelling on a train in London one day she tried to pick his pocket. Caught in the act, she went on her knees and begged his mercy saying she was starving and homeless. She so impressed the other passengers and Chestnut that they contributed some money for her and sent her on her way.

They were to meet again soon when he saw her putting on the same act after attempting to pick somebody's pocket at a railway station. He went to her rescue and saved her from arrest, since he was in search of a talented female assistant to broaden the scope of his own act.

They became a successful partnership and were married a year later.

So as not to arouse any undue attention, Mrs Daffodil decided she would be the only representative of the Spiritualists Society to greet Prof. Brown when his ship arrived at Penang.

Members saw this 'precautionary measure' as yet another example of Mrs Daffodil's concern for their welfare and were most grateful for her wise counselling.

This move by Mrs Daffodil allowed her the opportunity to meet her husband and to give him a full account of what she had accomplished in the two months she had been in Kuala Lumpur. She would also explain the programme she had drawn up for him.

Mrs Daffodil had advised members of the Society that in order to prevent any unwelcome publicity about Prof. Brown's visit, his presence in Kuala Lumpur would be treated as inconspicuously as possible. This was seen as a further manifestation of her genuine concern for the Society's members.

A private tea party to welcome Prof. Brown was held at the Royal Hotel and attended by all the Society's members who were each provided with a numbered card by Mrs Daffodil that also bore her signature. This was done, she explained, to prevent any 'gate-crashers'. She pinned these cards onto the lapels of the jackets of male members and onto the blouses of women members. The numbers on each card corresponded with those in a file containing private information about each member that Mrs Daffodil had compiled earlier in readiness for her husband's arrival. She had selected the names of three members from the file who would unknowingly assist in exhibiting Prof. Brown's 'remarkable talents.' It was a simple matter for the professor to memorise the three names, numbers and information regarding the members that Mrs Daffodil had pre-selected.

His dark, mascara-lined eyes scanned the anxious, excited faces of those seated before him and came to rest on his first victim, the wife of a prominent architect, who was informed two days previously by her doctor that she was pregnant with her first child.

'Begging your pardon, madam,' said Prof. Brown as he smiled at the lady, 'but may I be permitted to offer you my congratulations on the forthcoming happy event?'

The lady could only gape in wonder because she had only told a few close friends about her pregnancy and was unaware that her husband had casually mentioned this fact to Mrs Daffodil.

'Amazing!' said the dumbfounded lady.

To a gentleman who had lost his mother a few months previously, Prof. Brown said, gripping his hand, 'I shall be in communication with your beloved mother in just a moment, sir.' He shut his eyes and frowned in serious concentration for a few seconds. Opening his eyes he said, 'She is very happy where she is and sends her love to you and Violet. May I know, sir, who is this lady named Violet?'

Violet was the name of the man's wife who was seated beside him. The man rose to his feet and exclaimed, 'This is truly incredible! How did you know of my recent bereavement and my wife's name?'

The professor smiled kindly at the couple without replying while Mrs Daffodil joined in the appreciative applause and shouts of 'Bravo! Bravo!'

His next victim was a well-dressed Chinese gentleman to whom he said, 'Your good fortune at the racetrack will continue, sir! And, do I hear wedding bells?'

The man was a prominent member of the Selangor Turf Club and had been having many successes with the horses he owned. He had recently announced his engagement to the daughter of a wealthy Perak tin-miner.

The members of the Society were ecstatic. They had never seen anything so astounding before.

Soon news got around about his incredible powers. People who were non-members of the Society consulted him about important business and personal matters and paid handsomely for his advice.

Working closely with his wife who had 'volunteered' to be his secretary, substantial sums of money were added by members to the amount of money already donated to the Society's 'Donations Box.'

Curious about reports he had heard about the professor's great powers, an English detective superintendent of police in Kuala Lumpur contacted Mrs Daffodil and said he wished to meet the professor.

She pretended to be delighted by the detective's interest and made an appointment for a meeting the following week.

Always careful to keep as far as possible from the police wherever they went, Mrs Daffodil and the professor were convinced the detective superintendent was investigating them.

They decided it was time they departed from Kuala Lumpur, having collected more than $40,000 in cash, a very substantial sum at the time.

Without a word to anyone they took a train to Singapore from where they boarded a ship bound for Australia, using bogus passports.

Nothing criminal had been discovered by the Kuala Lumpur police about Mrs Daffodil and the 'professor,' who might have confidently extended their stay without fear of running into any trouble with the law.

In fact, all those who had come into contact with the pair of confidence-tricksters were sorry to learn of their sudden departure and seemed puzzled as to what had caused it.

It was later learned that the English detective superintendent was most anxious for Prof. Brown to communicate with the spirit of his late father – and for no other reason.

The Evil Island

There are many islands situated off Singapore. Most are beautiful and green with white, palm-fringed beaches. Gorgeous coloured fish inhabit the coral reefs. One of the islands was smaller than the others and barren with greyish-black granite in some places. Its hard, yellow soil only permitted coarse scrub to grow.

Evil spirits of the earth, wind and sea were believed to have made their home there. They stuck out their long, green, phosphorescent tongues from behind the sharp rocks on stormy nights waiting to devour those who ventured too close. Who, if not these demons caused shipwrecks and loss of life each year during the howling storms brought by the northeast monsoon? And, who if not these demons made those terrifying howls?

The island was Pulau Hantu Hitam. In Malay it meant 'island of black ghosts'.

Carrington and Freeman were bachelors. They had worked as government clerks for more than twenty-five years, joining the service at almost the same time. The year was now 1936 and time for retirement and a chance to enjoy their pensions. Both men had quite substantial personal savings despite their low wages. Both were in their sixties and had decided they were too old for marriage.

They got on extremely well together and were dedicated amateur fishermen. They knew quite a lot about the seasons for certain fish, where they could be found and everything else fishermen needed to know about fishing in the waters off Singapore. One of their favourite fishing spots was around the

Riau Islands that were an hour's journey by motor launch from Singapore.

Since retiring both men were at a loss as to how they would spend their remaining years.

Months went by and they hadn't yet made up their minds.

One afternoon as they were walking by a fashion shop they were attracted by a display of ladies' shoes, handbags and men's belts made from python and crocodile skins.

Carrington, who had always wanted to own a crocodile-skin belt, walked into the shop. But after being told the price, decided not to buy it. The prices of other items made from python and crocodile skin were also far too expensive. The Chinese manager of the shop informed Carrington that he paid 'top prices' for reptile skins that he also supplied to fashion stores in Paris and London.

The two retirees were on a weekend fishing trip to the Riau islands when the question of what they were going to do with the rest of their lives popped up again and Carrington said to Freeman, 'I tell you what, how about us breeding pythons for their skins?'

Freeman laughed aloud. 'Stop joking!' he said.

Carrington said, 'There's a lot of money to be made from dealing in reptile skins. Didn't you hear the manager of that reptile skin store say there was a big demand for python skins?'

'Forget it. We don't know the first thing about pythons except that Chinese restaurants make soup with their meat,' said Freeman.

They did not discuss the matter further.

But some days later Carrington returned to the small apartment they shared and deposited three books on top of the dining table.

'These books contain everything one could probably wish to know about pythons – their food, habitat, breeding habits, everything. I borrowed them from the library,' he said with a grin.

They were fascinated by what they read, especially about giant reticulated pythons that grew to lengths of seven to nine metres and weighed as much as two hundred kilograms. They were commonly found in the jungles of Malaya, Siam (Thailand) and Sumatra and were capable of swallowing prey as large as wild boar and even humans!

'Can you imagine how many pairs of ladies' shoes and handbags could be made from a couple of skins?' asked Carrington. 'Just suppose we started a farm to breed these creatures. After we'd taken their skins, think of the amount of fresh python meat we could supply the restaurants in Chinatown! We'd be millionaires in a couple of years! Just think about it, my friend!'

All the years they had known each other, the thought of becoming wealthy had never crossed their minds. But now, the idea of becoming the 'Snake Skin Kings Of Singapore' was tremendously appealing, The famous Aw brothers – Boon Haw and Boon Par were the manufacturers of various Chinese medicines for common ailments, of which the most popular was 'Tiger Balm' that was for soothing sprains, tired muscles – even toothache.

Carrington said, 'The Aw brothers built the splendid Haw Par Villa on the west coast of Singapore and Aw Boon Haw, the elder of the two, had a luxury car specially made for him in England. I remember seeing it once. He had it painted with gold-and-black stripes, like a tiger's skin. The front of the car was fashioned like a tiger's head. It attracted everybody's attention.'

Freeman looked at Carrington with a grin and said, 'Sounds wonderful!'

For the next couple of days Freeman did a lot of serious thinking and said to Carrington, 'I agree there could be a lot of money to be made by breeding pythons for their skins But, where are we going to locate such a breeding spot? You know how people feared and hated snakes!'

It was the season for sea bass again.

One weekend they hired a motor launch and went fishing around Singapore's southern islands.

While passing Pulau Hantu Hitam, Carrington focussed his binoculars on its grey-black rocks.

'That island is bald, black and ugly,' he said to Freeman.

'Nothing grows on it except coarse grass. It might be an ideal place for breeding pythons.'

'Why do you say that?' asked Freeman.

'Because the island is uninhabited and there'll be nobody to raise any objections,' said Carrington.

The Chinese launch-driver overheard their conversation and said, 'Be careful! Evil spirits live on that island!'

Carrington went to see a lawyer and asked him to find out if the island could be leased. He was informed later that there would be no problems.

The two men decided to explore the island one Sunday morning.

'I wonder why it is so ugly when all he other islands near it are so beautiful,' said Freeman as they came closer to it.

'You didn't expect a place that's supposed to be the home of various demons to look like some island paradise, do you?' said Carrington and they both laughed.

They anchored close to a small rocky beach of grey sand and rowed ashore in a dinghy. They climbed the side of a cliff without difficulty and reaching the top saw it was covered with thorny bushes. The island was almost flat except for a formation of rocks rising from its centre. On closer inspection they found several large holes among the rocks that pleased Carrington who said, 'We could erect an enclosure here for the snakes and a shallow pool of water for them to lie in. We could plant a couple of shade trees over the enclosure. Pythons are quite remarkable creatures and can go without food for a few months by living on water!'

As they viewed the island Freeman said, 'This rather barren scene will look much brighter after we erected a small bungalow and planted a few trees and some flowering shrubs.'

The enthusiasm for their unusual business venture increased.

'What are we going to do about the supply of water?' asked Freeman.

'We will have a large open-top tank to store rainwater collected off the roof of the bungalow,' replied Carrington. 'For a start we'll obtain water from one of the neighbouring islands and have oil lamps and kerosene stoves to provide heat for the incubators for the pythons' eggs.'

Freeman smiled. 'I see you have been doing your homework and digested those books you borrowed from the library.'

On their return to Singapore they registered a company. In the meantime they set about designing a bungalow for themselves and the layout of the enclosure for the snakes, the shallow pool, the water tank and a hatchery. The bungalow would be built of wood with corrugated iron sheets for the roof, asbestos ceilings to minimise the heat from the sun and glass-panelled windows.

They were granted a renewable two-year lease on the island and work on their project started within a couple of weeks.

The two men were seated under beach umbrellas watching workmen go about their jobs when Freeman said, 'I forgot to tell you. I met an old Chinese shopkeeper from one of the nearby islands the other day and I happened to tell him about our project. He said he knew about it. He didn't appear to share my enthusiasm about our future plans. He suggested that we get someone to exorcise the evil spirits on the island. He said the island was the scene of some horrible murders in the days when piracy was rife in these parts. The tormented spirits of those who were killed would take their revenge on any intruders, he warned me.'

Carrington shrugged his shoulders. 'Superstitious nonsense!' he said.

They didn't discuss the matter again.

Construction work on the bungalow, water storage tank,

snake enclosure and hatchery was completed in six weeks. A wooden jetty was also built at the small beach where a second-hand, motorised Chinese junk they bought would be moored.

After moving into their new home they took turns preparing simple meals and shared the housework. Fresh food supplies were easily obtained from the nearby islands and stored in their kerosene-powered refrigerator. Life for them was pleasant and free of fuss and bother. They had erected a high aerial for their battery radio and were thrilled to listen to broadcasts from as far as London and San Francisco.

There was much excitement when two half-grown male reticulated pythons and four young females arrived by ship in Singapore from Bangkok.

Newspaper reporters and cameramen were invited to the island. The two men were interviewed and spoke about their future plans as suppliers of python skins.

The pythons settled down quickly in the enclosure, exploring the holes and crevices in the rocks and resting in the shallow pool under a canvas awning to provide shade from the scorching sun.

The two men had started to rear poultry to feed the snakes and themselves and had made an effort to grow some vegetables in the hard soil with the aid of manure. They seldom left their home and when food and other supplies were needed one of them would go in their junk to a neighbouring island to do the shopping.

They had grown beards and their hair had reached their shoulders. There were patches of dirt on their sun-bronzed bodies and they went about barefoot and bare-bodied in filthy khaki shorts.

As the weeks passed there was a change in their behaviour towards each other. They seemed to have less to talk about and at times allowed a day or two to pass without exchanging a word, even at meal times. They were beginning to dislike each other's company and there were arguments over trivial matters.

They went for walks alone and would sit at different points of the island to watch the waves crashing on the black, jagged rocks below, returning to the bungalow at sunset to eat their dinners in silence before retiring to their bedrooms.

Some nights the two men would have terrifying dreams of being tormented by devilish creatures emerging from the floors in their bedrooms. The creatures Freeman saw had Carrington's face and those Carrington saw had Freeman's face.

They mentioned nothing to each other about their dreams.

In the weeks that followed the two men noticed that the female pythons were nesting. Later, when the eggs were hatched, twenty-three baby pythons were placed in boxes filled with dry weeds in the nursery that was located at one end of the hatchery.

The two men went about their work in silence, avoiding each other and even had their meals in their bedrooms. They rarely listened to their radio. They had ceased to care what went on beyond the shores of their island.

To keep visitors away they had put up a notice at the jetty that said: Strictly No Admittance Without Written Permission.

A villager from one of the neighbouring islands who caught a glimpse of them told the other islanders, 'They are possessed by the devils that live on the island! There is something evil about them!'

The northeast monsoon in November brought heavy rains, vicious winds and huge waves.

There was a storm one night and when the two men awoke the following morning, it was still raining and blowing heavily.

Carrington put on a raincoat and stood on the veranda of the bungalow looking out to sea where a huge mass of low, black clouds had gathered. He wandered down to the beach to inspect the wooden jetty where their junk was moored. By the time he returned, the sky was a mass of black, boiling clouds. Flashes of lightning appeared every few seconds, followed by frightening explosions of thunder.

It was quite dark, almost like twilight, although it was eight-thirty in the morning. The two men went about securing the doors and windows of the bungalow and inspected the snake enclosure and nursery where the young snakes were kept.

Carrington lit the kerosene lamp that hung from the ceiling of the living room as the howling winds increased their strength.

Freeman looked up at the ceiling and said, 'Hear those sounds?' He grinned, baring his yellow teeth. Carrington nodded his head. 'Those are the corrugated iron sheets on the roof rattling!' he said. 'They'll be flying away soon!' he added with a laugh.

It was the first time the two men had spoken to each other in four months.

Carrington got up from his chair and peering through a glass window saw swirling clouds low over the sea and close to the island. He tried to catch a glimpse of the snake enclosure but his view was obscured by billowing sand whipped up by the ferocious winds.

The asbestos ceiling above them began to tremble and water dripped through the loose zinc sheets on the roof. They flapped rapidly against each other, producing sounds like machine-gun fire.

Similar sounds were coming from the direction of the kitchen. They went to the rear in time to see the asbestos ceiling cave in and crash to the floor. Some of the sheets on the roof had been torn off, leaving gaping holes that allowed the wind and rain to rush into the kitchen, sweeping pots and pans off their hooks on the wall and overturning a wooden cupboard.

Streaks of blue-white lightning ran through the house, leaving an acrid stench before disappearing in the haze of flying sand, splintered wood and glass.

As the two men fought against being swept away by the terrifying winds, they wound their arms and legs round two wooden pillars near the kitchen.

It had become very dark and in the flashes of lightning their faces looked blue and grotesque. The sitting-room ceiling crumbled to the floor and the few remaining loose sheets on the roof were torn off like pages from a book.

The howling wind rushed in, ripping apart everything it touched.

The wooden kitchen wall collapsed and was carried into the garden by a blast of wind. Broken glass from the kitchen windows were swept towards the two men who had shut their eyes tightly against the flying debris.

When Freeman opened his eyes a fraction he saw Carrington's face was covered in blood from a wound on his forehead.

They locked their legs and arms more tightly round the pillars. The next instant, a violent gust carried Carrington upwards as though he was a paper kite. His body became lodged in the rafters above Freeman's head. His eyes seemed to glow like red-hot coals. Another violent gust swept him away and Freeman heard his fading screams as he disappeared in the darkness.

The next instant a steel plate from the kitchen stove crashed into Freeman's chest. He screamed in pain and released his grip on the pillar. A pair of gigantic, hairy hands reached down from the rafters and hurled him along the corridor like a child's doll, his body smashing against a low, brick wall at the front of the bungalow.

The storm raged for two days and nights.

A police launch with a sergeant and three policemen arrived at the island the day after the storm ended. They found part of the junk belonging to the two men deposited on some high rocks. The jetty where it had been moored was no longer there.

Below the pillars of the bungalow was a thick carpet of

splintered wood, broken asbestos and glass smeared with yellow mud and sand.

From beneath a pile of debris, a human hand protruded. When they dug Freeman's body out his mouth was open and filled with sand. His eyes were missing.

The water tank lay on its side and the wire fencing around the snake enclosure was a twisted mess. The shed that had housed the hatchery and nursery had been blown away.

Reports in the next day's newspapers said Freeman had died in the storm and a search was being made for Carrington. His body was never found.

The Meteorological Department described the storm as 'one of the most violent on record.'

Some years later the British army in Singapore constructed a stone jetty and 'secret' underground chambers on the island for the storage of high explosives.

Japanese espionage agents got to know about this rather loosely kept 'secret' and the island was blasted to rubble by Japanese bombers during the invasion of Singapore in 1941–1942.

All that remained of it were some small black rocks that protruded above the surface of the sea. These were removed after the surrender of Japan in 1945 in order to make the approaches to Singapore harbour safe for shipping.

Wrong Conclusions

Respectable European young ladies, like their Asian counterparts, rarely went about unescorted in Singapore and Malaya in the 1920s when others their age in Europe and America, were guilty of unladylike or 'tarty' behaviour; such as wearing heavy make-up, above-the-knee skirts and strapless 'tops' in bars and at private parties . . . performing the outrageous 'Charleston' or the Spanish tango during which a female's modesty was continually at risk of being outraged . . . or, sipping cocktails and exchanging 'smutty' stories with their male 'escorts.'

Many of these enterprising young ladies acquired 'celebrity status' by having their photos on the front pages of newspapers after being named in illicit *affaires d'amour* with well-known gentlemen. It was no surprise that one 'society' magazine chose to publish a rhyme that summed up the London 'scene' at that time : *

When Lady Jane became a tart
It almost broke her father's heart
But blood is blood and race is race
And so, to mitigate disgrace
He bought her a most expensive 'beat'
From Asprey's up to Oxford Street.

However, there were other mature and adventurous English ladies took life more seriously.

They belonged to what was known as 'The Fishing Fleet,' a derogatory term for ladies who had not succeeded in their search for husbands. They were known to embark on 'fishing' trips in the hope of 'hooking' lonely English bachelors in trading posts, tea and rubber plantations and military camps in the far-flung British Empire.

When South Africa and India became threatened by 'over-fishing,' these ladies sought new 'fishing grounds' in places such as Burma, Malaya, Borneo, Sarawak, Hong Kong and Singapore.

The unescorted Mademoiselle Marie Petain caused a fair amount of concern at the Raffles Hotel in Singapore in June 1921, where she was a guest. There were whispers accompanied by corner-of-the-eye glances directed at her by the other guests while she sat alone at a table having her meals.

She spoke to no one. As soon as she had finished, she returned to her room that was a few doors away from the one occupied by the Reverend and Mrs James Shepherd.

Mademoiselle Petain was tall, slender, pleasant-looking and in her early twenties. Her long, golden hair was plaited and neatly coiled in rings at the back of her head. There wasn't even the slightest hint of rouge or powder on her clear face.

Her dresses had high necklines and long sleeves that buttoned at the wrists. Around her neck was a gold chain from which hung a cross of gold.

Mrs Beatrice Shepherd, wife of the Reverend Shepherd, had reason to pay more attention to the rather reserved and lonesome Mademoiselle Petain than the other guests because of some unpleasant experiences she had had with certain ladies of 'questionable character.'

'I fear she could be one of those dreadful creatures from the Fishing Fleet who was trying to create a false impression,' she said to her husband who was seated next to her having tea while she kept her eyes fixed on the young lady. Then turning to Mrs Partridge, an acquaintance sitting beside her, she said with a snort, 'One can never be too sure about young women these days. As I've always said, one cannot judge a book by its cover. We came across many strange females during the course of our work in Madras, didn't we James?' she said glancing at her husband. 'Some very innocent-looking types turned out to be common . . .'

Mrs Shepherd paused and leaning towards Mrs Partridge whispered, 'They turned out to be common whores!'

She went on, 'Of course, there were also those who were easily identified. They were brazen, vulgar ones who had nothing to hide and no dignity to lose! It's appalling to think to what levels English society has sunk.'

Mrs Partridge nodded her head gravely and sipped her tea. Reverend Shepherd would like to have said to his wife, 'The women you speak of belong to the world's oldest profession and seem quite happy with their choice.' But as usual, he chose to keep his views to himself, especially when his wife was expounding her own.

Mrs Shepherd's face darkened for a moment as she remembered the embarrassment she had suffered during an encounter with a drunken member of the 'Fishing Fleet' at a charity ball in Madras. The woman had called her 'a narrow-minded and interfering old bitch'. This happened after Mrs Shepherd had broadly hinted that 'certain women of questionable virtue and character were invading respectable society' which, no doubt, was meant for the woman in question.

Rev. Shepherd and his wife were on their way to Sarawak where he would become the principal of a missionary school. They had decided to have a short holiday in Singapore before catching the next boat to Kuching in Sarawak.

They had met Mrs Partridge, a widow, who was on the same ship that Mrs Shepherd and her husband had taken from Calcutta. She had travelled from London to Singapore to attend the wedding of her only son, a rubber planter in Malaya. He had fallen passionately in love with 'a simple and absolutely marvellous English girl,' as he described her in his letters to his mother. He had met her at a party in Kuala Lumpur.

Mrs Partridge would like to have offered Mrs Shepherd her own opinion about young women of 'questionable character and virtue' with her future daughter-in-law in mind but chose to dismiss the thought with a deep sigh instead. There was nothing to be gained by crying over spilled milk, she decided, since she was also to become a grandmother that, according to the maternity hospital doctors, would be about a week after the date of her son's wedding.

'A fine place to be spending her honeymoon – in a maternity hospital!' thought Mrs Partridge and sighed again.

Mrs Shepherd put on her 'distance spectacles' and focused her eyes more comfortably on Marie Petain who had finished her tea and was reading a letter that Mrs Shepherd had seen doing several times previously.

'It is her third day at this hotel,' said Mrs Shepherd to her husband. 'She's been reading the same letter over and over again and from what I am able to observe, she is clearly distressed by its contents. I wonder who she is and who the writer of the letter could be – a lover, perhaps? And, have you noticed, she always seems to have her eyes fixed on the hotel's entrance, as though she's expecting someone special to walk in at any moment. One cannot help but notice her expression of anxiety. Very odd behaviour indeed, don't you think, James?'

Reverend Shepherd pretended to be occupied with a crossword puzzle in the newspaper resting on his lap and did not reply while his wife resumed her observation of the young lady.

Mrs Partridge sighed deeply again as she thought about her impending 'grand-motherhood'.

Mrs Shepherd felt she had been put on earth for the sole purpose of saving wayward female souls and regarded her marriage to 'a man of the church' as proof of the saying that 'marriages were made in heaven'. Furthermore, she felt it was her 'Christian duty' to expose women of loose morals.

'They must be made to suffer shame and repent,' she had often said. 'There's no other way.'

She was grateful in her prayers for having been blessed with keen powers of observation and intuition to assist her in her mission in life and Reverend Shepherd had been unpleasantly reminded all too often of the sharpness of his wife's tongue during the twenty-seven years they had been married. He had often been tempted to tell her what S. J. Perleman the American writer, had once told a certain lady: 'You've a sharp tongue in your head, madam! Look out it doesn't cut your throat!'

But Rev. Shepherd had learnt from past experiences that there was much to be gained by remaining silent in the presence of his wife. He looked up from his newspaper and after glancing at Mademoiselle Petain, said cautiously, 'She appears to be a rather reserved and decent young lady. She doesn't wear cosmetics, like some . . .'

He didn't get a chance to complete what he wished to say because his wife interrupted him. She gave him a freezing stare and hissed, 'You were about to say that only women of loose morals used cosmetics? How dare you even think of such a thing! If you cared to notice, I only apply the minimum amount of lavender-scented powder to my face and use the palest of red lipsticks, only because my lips are so tender and get chapped rather easily in this tropical weather.'

He ignored what she had said and returned to his crossword puzzle, which annoyed her. She cleared her throat noisily to attract his attention and said, 'I feel I have to warn you to be extremely careful about the rash remarks you make. You could find yourself in some very hot water!'

He thought to himself that she should practice what she preached but smiled at her instead. She got up from the table and sauntered into the Palm Court where a group of Indian snake charmers were entertaining some children and hotel guests. Unable to bear her curiosity any longer, Mrs Shepherd decided to find out more about Marie Petain.

The following morning when the hotel receptionist was busy elsewhere, she peered into the register and discovered some facts about the young lady. She had a French passport. She was twenty-two and had embarked on her voyage to Singapore from Marseilles. There was no mention of her occupation.

Mrs Shepherd took her husband behind a pillar and excitedly whispered to him about what she had discovered. He couldn't understand her concern about some very ordinary information.

'What's so unusual about a French woman having a French passport?' he asked her. 'Don't British women have British passports?'

Disappointed that her husband had shown no interest whatsoever in her skills as an investigator, she left him and made her way towards Mrs Partridge who was just about to enter the hotel's Antiques Room.

'Dear me! She's French, you say?' said Mrs Partridge after hearing what Mrs Shepherd had discovered. 'Then there has to be a man involved in whatever she's up to! You know what these French tarts are like!'

Mrs Partridge was known to partake in nips of whisky 'for therapeutic reasons' as she had said, and found the dimly-lit Antiques Room a convenient place to self-administer such relief, required more frequently now as the date of her son's wedding drew nearer.

The information Mrs Shepherd just made known about Mademoiselle Petain had provided Mrs Partridge with the excuse for an intake of whisky. She quickly dug her hand into her satchel where a flask of Johnnie Walker whisky reposed.

'You must excuse me. I have to steady my nerves,' she said as she unscrewed the cap on the flask and took two quick swigs. Wiping her mouth with the back of her hand and dropping her voice Mrs Partridge remarked, 'Have you noticed a foreign-looking man with a moustache watching her while she is in the restaurant or strolling in the garden? He keeps an eye on her from a distance. Most sinister!'

As she was about to return the flask to her satchel, she gripped Mrs Shepherd's arm and whispered, 'There he is! Behind that palm tree!'

Mrs Shepherd felt her hands suddenly turn to ice as she saw a stocky man with a 'handle-bar' moustache. There was no doubt he was watching Mademoiselle Petain who had just appeared in the Orchid Garden. She was looking sad as she took a seat on a garden bench.

Mrs Shepherd thought quickly, 'What if the man with the moustache, who could be her jealous lover or husband, pulled out a gun and shot her dead? The French were famous for their so-called crimes of passion. I'd be an eyewitness to a murder and would be called upon to give evidence at the trial! It would have been all right had the victim been someone of importance and not a French whore! Oh, dear! What would people say!'

She shut her eyes momentarily and shuddered at the thought. When she opened them she saw Mrs Partridge holding the flask of whisky to her mouth again. Then, looking at Mrs Shepherd, Mrs Partridge offered her the flask, saying, 'Here, have some of this. You look as though you've just seen a ghost!'

Mrs Shepherd grabbed the flask and took a few quick sips from it as she crouched behind a hibiscus bush.

Noticing this, Mrs Partridge said to herself, 'I see the Reverend's wife and I have much more in common than I had thought.'

'There's something very strange going on,' said Mrs Shepherd to her husband later that day and informed him what Mrs Partridge and herself had witnessed in the garden. Then she said with finality, 'That foreign-looking man must be her lover! All French women have lovers!'

He pondered over what his wife had said and replied, 'Well, if this chap has been watching her like a hawk, as you say, and no harm has come to her after four days, there seems to be no cause for alarm. However, if you wished to know the reason why he is following her about the place, I suggest that you asked him yourself.'

The drama of the mysterious young lady was about to enter its fifth nerve-racking day, as far as Mrs Shepherd and Mrs Partridge were concerned.

The two women met whenever they could in the Antiques Room, behind two life-size wooden carvings of Balinese dancers. It was an ideal spot for an exchange of information and welcome swigs from Mrs Partridge's flask.

Reverend Shepherd's obvious disinterest in his wife's speculation about Mademoiselle Petain prompted her to say to him with some bitterness, 'You never seem to see things the way I see them!'

'Thank God for that!' thought Rev. Shepherd to himself.

It was a humid night and Reverend Shepherd began to perspire in bed despite the ceiling fan. He thought he got the faint smell of whisky in the room – or was it the new mouthwash his wife was using? He noted with satisfaction that his wife had dropped off to sleep. He placed his hands behind his balding head and in the semi-darkness stared at the slowly rotating fan.

The humidity in the room had increased. He got up from bed and poured himself a glass of water from the decanter on the bedside table. He looked at the alarm clock on the dresser. It was almost midnight. He gently opened the bedroom door and went out onto the veranda overlooking the Palm Court that was bathed in bright moonlight. He remembered similar scenes during the years he and his wife had spent in Madras. He had always thought the beauty of a tropical scene by moonlight was beyond compare.

Reverend Shepherd was about to re-enter his bedroom when he saw a figure of a woman appear in the Orchid Garden. She took a seat on a bench. After a few moments he realised she was none other than the young lady who had been the subject of his wife's concern over the past few days.

'Whatever is she doing by herself at this late hour in the garden?' he wondered. His thoughts were interrupted when he saw a movement in the shadows near some palm trees. He became tense as he saw a man hiding behind a tree, not far from the woman. Realising she could be in some danger, Reverend Shepherd silently re-entered his bedroom, put on his bathrobe and slippers and as quickly and silently as possible made his way along the veranda, down the wooden stairs and into the shadows of the garden. From where he was he could clearly see the young woman but had lost sight of the man lurking in the shadows. His heart beat faster as he moved to where he had last seen the man. He concealed himself behind the trunk of a Traveller's Palm and waited. There was another movement in the bushes and he came face to face with the man for a second before he disappeared into the shadows again. The man had a moustache and Reverend Shepherd was sure he was the same man he had seen watching the young lady while she was having her meals at the restaurant.

Then he heard quiet sobbing and saw the young lady wiping her eyes with a handkerchief. She stood up and took a couple of steps, when she fell. Reverend Shepherd dashed out from his hiding place and in a couple of quick strides was kneeling beside her.

At that moment he heard a rustling sound in the bushes and the man he had seen earlier rushed up and spoke briefly to the young woman in what sounded like Russian. She said something in reply and he went away.

Reverend Shepherd helped the young lady to her feet. 'Are you all right, madam?' he asked.

She buried her face in her hands and said softly, 'Yes, thank you. I felt a little giddy.'

He offered her his arm and as they were walking slowly away

he heard a woman's voice cry out, 'Caught you red-handed, James Shepherd!'

A moment later, Mrs Shepherd appeared from the shadows.

'This young lady is ill and needs help,' said Reverend Shepherd.

'Liar! Oh, I cannot believe my eyes!' sobbed Mrs Shepherd.

Ignoring his wife, Reverend Shepherd led the young lady into the hotel building. He made her sit on a settee in the lobby and said to the night clerk, 'Is there a doctor available? This young lady appears to be ill!'

The clerk ran his finger down the names in the register and replied, 'Dr Thompson is in Room 42. I'll get him, sir!' and disappeared down the corridor.

He returned after a few minutes with a middle-aged man in a dressing gown. After Reverend Shepherd had described to him what had happened, he briefly examined the young lady who appeared to have fully recovered. She took a few sips from the glass of water the clerk had brought.

Mrs Shepherd stood some distance away. Her tears had suddenly vanished.

'Allow us to help you back to your room, madam,' said the doctor who had been joined by his wife. As she was being helped along, the young lady thanked Reverend Shepherd for his help.

'You realise the scandal that you have caused by having a midnight meeting with that French tart? Oh, the disgrace! Everybody in this hotel will be talking about it!' said Mrs Shepherd tearfully to her husband as soon as they returned to their bedroom.

He explained how he had come to meet the young lady in the garden but Mrs Shepherd refused to believe him, saying that he was having 'a sordid affair with a common whore'. She spent a sleepless night and wished she had Mrs Partridge's flask of whisky with her. She was still awake at dawn.

'You have as usual jumped to the wrong conclusions. I have told you the truth which you have refused to believe,' Reverend Shepherd told his wife. 'There is nothing more I wish to say to you.'

He got dressed and went downstairs to the restaurant where he joined Dr Thompson and his wife for breakfast.

'The young lady appears to be rather worried about some personal matter and told me she hadn't been getting much sleep during the past few days. I gave her a sedative last night and when I visited her this morning she seemed to have recovered rather well. I invited her to join us for breakfast,' and looking towards the corridor, he said, 'Ah! Here she is now!'

The young lady was looking very much better as she sat down at the table and thanked Reverend Shepherd and Dr Thompson again for their assistance.

Their attention was suddenly directed to the hotel's entrance. A gleaming, black Rolls-Royce had pulled up. Behind it was another car with some foreign-looking men in smart, colourful uniforms with medals, sashes and gold braids. A British army officer saluted as the rear door of the Rolls-Royce was opened. Out of the car stepped a beautiful woman elegantly attired in a dress of silver and gold. Accompanying her was a tall, handsome man with greying hair, elegant in a dark blue suit and wearing a bowler hat.

Everybody in the hotel was taken by surprise and wondered who these important visitors could be as an excited hotel manager hopped about in attendance.

The young lady suddenly sprang to her feet as she saw the distinguished-looking couple being ushered into the hotel. Tears welled in her large, brown eyes.

'Father! Mother!' she cried happily as she ran up to them, throwing herself into their arms.

Dr Thompson and Reverend Shepherd exchanged puzzled looks, as did the others in the restaurant and the hotel staff as Prince Boris and his wife Princess Tanya were escorted to the Royal Suite.

After a short while the happy and tearful young lady who had been known as 'Mademoiselle Marie Petain,' reappeared in the company of the hotel manager and a stocky man – with a moustache – who was now in military uniform. She stood beside the table where a rather confused Dr Thompson, his wife and Reverend Shepherd were seated.

Bowing sedately, the manager said, 'May I have your attention please, ladies and gentlemen. Her Imperial Highness, Princess Tamara, daughter of their Imperial Highnesses, Prince Boris and Princess Tanya of the House of Tsar Nicholas the Second of Russia, wishes to make an announcement.'

A crowd that had quickly gathered, began to applaud and the young lady said, 'I think I owe some of you an explanation. My parents and I escaped from Russia under assumed names and forged travel documents, since there were people who wished to harm us for being members of the Imperial family. Using the name of Marie Petain and a French passport, I made my escape from St Petersburg to the south of France where I was smuggled aboard a British ship bound for Singapore by friends loyal to my grandfather, the Tsar. I had no idea whether my parents were dead or alive neither did they know what fate had befallen me. They escaped from Moscow and across Siberia to Vladivostok. They arrived in Singapore this morning and only then did they know I was alive. Our movements had to be kept secret until now. I thank God we are safe! My parents and I shall be leaving for Australia today. From there we shall go to the United States of America where we shall live in exile.'

She paused to wipe her tears and said with a smile, 'And now, I would like to invite you all to join my parents and myself in a small celebration. I am most grateful to Dr Thompson, his wife and to Reverend Shepherd for their help when I briefly took ill last night.'

Her speech was greeted with more applause.

The stocky man with a moustache who was standing some distance away from the princess was the same man Reverend

Shepherd saw in the garden the previous night and who had been keeping a watchful eye on the princess. He looked different now in the ceremonial uniform of a Russian army colonel. Going up to Reverend Shepherd he clicked his heels and bowed stiffly. 'I am Colonel Yuri Ivanovich, Princess Tamara's personal bodyguard,' he said. 'I wish to thank you for your assistance last night, sir. I knew Her Highness was in safe hands when you offered your help, because I was at a loss, not knowing what to do to assist her.'

'Well, well! What do you think of that!' said Dr Thompson to Reverend Shepherd.

As he was making his way to the Royal Suite to attend the celebration, Reverend Shepherd saw his wife and Mrs Partridge peering from behind a pillar. They had watched the arrival of the royal couple, listened to the speech by the princess and were feeling rather foolish.

He went up to them and said with a smile, 'Aren't you joining in the celebration?'

Mrs Shepherd and Mrs Partridge exchanged embarrassed glances and Mrs Partridge said uncomfortably, 'The princess certainly took us all by surprise!'

'Yes, she certainly did, didn't she!' said Reverend Shepherd glancing at his wife whose face had turned a bright red.

'Come along, ladies. It isn't every day that one gets a chance to meet royalty, you know,' he said as he waved the two women on, trying hard to keep a straight face.

As Mrs Shepherd walked past her husband, he burst out laughing. She knew the reason why he had done so, but decided to ignore him.

As far as she was concerned, she would soon be in the presence of royalty for the first time in her life. The thought thrilled her beyond words and she didn't wish anything to spoil the occasion.

A Conqueror's Choice

'I was eight, going on nine in 1934,' said William Foo. 'That was eight years before the Japanese invaded Singapore, but I have to take you back to those days because of the rather strange story I am about to tell also because it concerned a man whose name will always be remembered in Singapore history books.'

William Foo was among a small group of friends who had survived the Japanese Occupation of Singapore and were recalling their experiences under Japanese rule from 1942 up to 1945, when Japan surrendered.

'One of the joys of my parents, my sister and myself was watching the spectacular sunsets at Pasir Panjang on the west coast,' William continued. 'It was something quite unforgettable. Although many years have passed, I have only to shut my eyes and those glorious scenes will magically reappear.

'We would leave our house in Sembawang in the north and travel to Sunset Beach to watch the sun's awesome displays. I had remembered my father, a keen amateur photographer, saying to his friends: "Sunset Beach is the place for spectacular views and photographs. The coastline with coconut palms stretching out to sea presented breathtaking silhouettes against a backdrop of a setting sun." '

'I'd jump into the back seat of our car, followed by my sister Pansy who was two years older than me. With Jalil our Malay chauffeur at the wheel we would all set off for Sunset Beach.

'Our car was a huge, grand-looking chrome and beige creation. It had eight cylinders and as many lights at the front, in addition to a chromed spotlight with adjustable height mounted on the footboard beside the driver's seat. My father told me it was to be used only in case of 'emergencies', whatever that meant. I persuaded my father to switch it on one night and I stared in wonder as its broad, silver-white beam instantly transformed darkness into bright moonlight. Two gold-plated claxon horns shaped like trumpets terrified all those who heard them sound warnings of our approach.

'Our car could seat ten passengers if required, although it was designed to carry seven hefty adults. The rear seat, that to me seemed as large as the settee in the living room of our house, could easily accommodate three large persons. In front of it were two folding seats. Embedded in the backs of the front seats was a cocktail cabinet with the necessary liquors in bottles, a silver shaker, four stemmed glasses, paper serviettes and a small Thermos for ice cubes. Beside it was a battery-operated cigar-cutter-and-lighter and below it a small compartment with a humidor containing a supply of my father's favourite cigarettes, black Balkan Sobranie (Russian blend) with gold tips. Chrome-plated ashtrays affixed to the doors were within easy reach.

'There was ample room for two adults beside Jalil who sat before a spectacular array of mysterious meters, coloured lights and switches artistically arranged on a walnut dashboard.

At the rear of the car was a massive trunk (or boot) in which the whole family could have hidden themselves. Clamped to it were two spare tyres in chrome casings.

' "But why only two spare tyres and not four, when our car has four wheels? Supposing all four tyres suffered punctures? What would we do?" ' I asked my father as we were about to set off for Sunset Beach one day.

'My mother happened to be standing beside him at the time. She gave me a freezing stare.

'My father chose not to answer me. I could tell what they were thinking: Didn't I know talking about punctures and other common mishaps before setting off on a journey was strictly taboo? Didn't I realise there were evil spirits who would be in hiding along the way, waiting to cause (among a hundred-and-one other things) flat tyres, brake failures and overheated engines? Didn't I know that some spirits could suck every drop of petrol out of a tank? Didn't I know that . . .

'No, I didn't know! Because I was eight years old and couldn't be expected to know all the superstitions and taboos my parents and other adults believed in.

'Our car was an immaculate American aristocrat. It glided silently on white-wall Goodyear tyres that encircled dazzling, chrome-plated disc wheels.

'It showed its contempt for everything on the road including some 'bluebloods' like the Lagonda and Daimler but demonstrated its respect for age and elegance by always giving the right of way to a Rolls-Royce.

'This impertinent upstart whom we all loved dearly bore the name of 'Packard' – that was among my father's inheritances from his late father, a prosperous spice merchant.

We simply relished the luxury it offered and we were thrilled each time people on the road stopped to turn their heads to gaze as we passed by like a gentle breeze. The bolder ones would wave to us and children would cheer as though we were royalty. We would wave in return and smile.

'Jalil, the show-off, would slow down whenever we came to a *kampung* so that the villagers could feast their eyes on this magnificent vehicle – and its occupants. I was to learn later on that the Packard was one of the favourite luxury automobiles of American "royalty" that was made up of movie "kings" and "queens" of Hollywood, playboy "princes" and "princesses" who were heirs to vast fortunes; oil "barons," "moguls," and "tsars."

'It was difficult to believe that a Chinese family such as mine on an almost unknown island called Singapore was able to enjoy some of the luxury that had been created exclusively for the rich and famous of the world.

'You don't see grand old cars like the Packard anymore these days unless they're displayed at a vintage show or appeared in movies with "oldie" stories. They don't make cars like that any more! What a pity!

'Our Packard was a 'tourer' model and it gave its passengers an all-round, unobstructed view that sedans or limousines couldn't offer.

'It had a white canvas hood that at the touch of a button came to life with a gentle whirring sound, unfolded itself from behind the rear seats where it rested, stretched full-length and descended gracefully to latch on to two small hooks on top of the windscreen, And, *voila!* The magic was done in a matter of seconds!

'Our journeys aboard this "magnificent beast" (as my father called it with affection) became thrilling adventures. My sister and I would secretly pray for rain, so that we could watch the hood perform its spellbinding magic. I think you would have been surprised, had you been around then, at the large number of people of all ages who came by car or by some other means of transport to view the spectacular sunsets at Sunset Beach. Not surprisingly, the crowds attracted an army of vendors selling all kinds of delicious food and drinks.

'There were no other cars at the beach that could have matched the beauty of our Packard and Jalil always parked it some distance away from the others so that it could be admired more effectively. He was envied by all the other car owners and chauffeurs and would every now and then go up to wipe away an imaginary speck of dust with a yellow polishing cloth. This was his way of making it known to all concerned that he was this American beauty queen's chief bodyguard.

'But, one day when we were at the beach the unchallenged supremacy of our Packard was severely threatened. It came from another American aristocrat, a new Buick in two tones of blue. It had gleaming chrome fittings and white-wall tyres and a long, mysterious, chrome-plated rod attached to the side of the windscreen that reached way above the roof. I was to discover later that it was a radio aerial – and, in a car of all places! Why a radio, when Singapore didn't have a radio station?

'Glass direction indicators shaped like arrows and illuminated by encased red bulbs shot out from the sides of this amazing car when the driver wished to make a turn. Three red lights at the rear appeared at the touch of the brake pedal.

'When my father saw this exquisite car, he immediately went along to view it with the rest of the family. He started chatting with its owner, a pleasant man by the name of Mr Song, who was about his age.

'Mr Song admired our car, too. Whether he did so out of politeness, I wouldn't know.

'Mrs Song and my mother started chatting and my sister Pansy and Mr Song's beautiful daughter Jennifer who was about my age, exchanged smiles. I found myself talking to her brother David, who was two years older than me.

'My father invited the Song family to join us for dinner on the beach and in no time we were all eating and talking happily as though we'd been friends for years. As I looked at the lovely face of Jennifer Song I knew I loved her with all the love in my eight-year-old heart.

'We were a happy group, the Song family and ourselves. Mr Song and my father, being the eldest sons in their respective families had inherited their wealth. Mr Song owned three pawnshops and a lot of property.

'My father had inherited the large house in Sembawang where we lived and another in Victoria Street. He had also inherited a grocery store that supplied hotels with all their needs. The Raffles Hotel was his store's most distinguished client since it was the largest and the most famous hotel in Singapore, if not the whole region.

'While Mr Song may have been wealthier than my father, our Packard was bigger than his Buick! I had made this heart-warming discovery after I had measured both cars with my school ruler one day at the beach when nobody was looking. Our car was a good nine inches longer – thanks to the two spare tyres sticking out at the rear. Also, our car had eight lights at the front and Mr Song's had only six. I did not tell anyone about my discovery, as I didn't wish Jennifer to think I had gone out of my way to make her father's car look inferior to ours. It might have hurt her feelings for which I would never have forgiven myself!

'My family liked Mrs Song, or "Auntie" Song. She was such a happy-go-lucky person and would giggle for the slightest reason. She was warm-hearted and was never heard to say an unkind word about anybody. I suppose that is why my mother liked her so much.

'Uncle' Song was also kind-hearted and although he was wealthy, he was most unassuming. My father and 'Uncle' Song got on well, as did Pansy and David, while I had secretly surrendered my heart to Jennifer without her knowing, of course. I thought she loved me too, from the way she looked at me. Or, was I mistaken? Could she have been thinking how ugly I was? To allay my fears, I asked my sister Pansy whether she thought I was good-looking and she replied in the affirmative and began to giggle. It only made me have more serious doubts about my looks.

'The years passed quickly. I was thirteen and so was Jennifer – and she was more beautiful than ever. There was nothing my parents would have done without informing the Songs and vice-versa, and we became like one happy, closely-knit family.

'By now it had become quite clear to all about how Jennifer and I felt about each other. The symptoms we showed were clearly related to a common 'disease' that affected adolescents. It was known as 'puppy love'. That's what they all thought. Well, Jennifer and I decided we would let them stew in their ignorance!

'Jennifer and I would meet at some secluded place at her home or mine, just for a minute or so to exchange secret letters we had written to each other. We would kiss hurriedly and make that moment last until our next secret meeting.

'At the same time there was something going on under our very noses and to which we seemed quite oblivious; it was the affection Pansy and David were showing for each other. They were both fifteen, he a few months older. Their "budding romance" was casually discussed by Auntie Song and my mother that caused a few giggles and when they informed their respective husbands about it the two men seemed amused, offering no comments. I seemed to think they were quite delighted but didn't wish to take the matter too seriously.

'It had suddenly occurred to me that if I married Jennifer and Pansy married David we would also become brothers and sisters in law! What a strange and wonderful way things seemed to be working out for our two families. Not only were we great friends, we would also be related by law.

'Quite suddenly, Jennifer and I were sixteen. David and Pansy had become engaged. David was studying accountancy. Pansy was already working as clerk-typist in my father's office.

'When war came to Malaya and Singapore in December 1941 the British army took over the Song mansion near Bukit Timah Hill and our house in Sembawang since we were told that they were located in 'strategic military areas.'

'My father insisted the Songs moved into our house in Victoria Street. It was old, but it had six bedrooms and two garages, one of which housed our Packard.

'We only occupy three bedrooms and you could park your Buick in the other garage. So, you see, there is accommodation for all!" ' said my father happily. ' "Besides, now that there is a war on, it is important that we should stay close," ' he said.

'The Songs moved in with us, to everybody's delight.

'When the Japanese increased their bombing and shelling of Singapore early in February 1942, our house was hit and badly damaged. So we locked up the place and the garages containing the Buick and Packard and moved into temporary accommodation that my father had arranged for us at the Raffles Hotel's staff quarters that were at the rear of the main building. Many of these double-bedroom units had fallen vacant. The occupants had returned to be with their families now that a Japanese invasion of Singapore was imminent.

'After the surrender of Singapore in February 1942 we were told that there had been widespread looting of homes and shops and we were anxious to know whether our house and the two cars had escaped the attention of the looters.

'One morning my father and Uncle Song decided to find out. From the looks on their faces when they returned we could tell the worst had happened.

' "Everything of value is gone! The two cars, too!" ' my father said. My mother and Auntie Song burst into tears so did Pansy and Jennifer. I cried, too.

'A month went by and we all found ourselves on the staff of the hotel that now accommodated senior Japanese army officers. We were glad to be doing any sort of work in exchange for a roof over our heads and some food. Pansy, Jennifer, David and I joined the cleaning staff. Auntie Song and my mother became kitchen helpers to three Japanese cooks while Uncle Song and my father had the task of searching for fresh food each day. They set out before sunrise in a small van in the company of a young Japanese army corporal named Tanaka, not daring to return empty-handed and face the wrath of a grumpy old sergeant named Hashimoto who was in charge of the hotel and who gave daily instructions to the local staff in Japanese – that none of us understood.

'Uncle Song discovered to his surprise and to our great relief that corporal Tanaka spoke a smattering of English and was able to interpret the sergeant's daily instructions. In exchange for this service, he wanted Uncle Song to give him English lessons – without the sergeant's knowledge. He explained that

English was the language of the British and American enemies of Japan and its use was strictly forbidden. It was obvious the corporal did not subscribe to such sentiment and told Uncle Song in confidence that he was attending high school in Osaka at the outbreak of war. He wished to continue his English studies – in secret.

'The first thing the Japanese did when they took over the hotel was to remove the portraits of British royalty, former colonial governors of Singapore and other well-known British personalities that had occupied prominent positions on the walls of the banquet rooms where Japanese bamboo screens, low dining tables of Japanese pinewood and large cushions on matted floors replaced antique teak dining tables and chairs while large stocks of Japanese beer and *sake*, Japanese rice wine, were stacked in the cellars.

'One morning there was sudden excitement. Sergeant Hashimoto barked orders to Corporal Tanaka who quickly mobilised the 'local' staff. Arming us with brooms, mops, buckets of water and polishing cloths, he set us to work. 'Must quickly make very clean, everywhere!' he whispered into Uncle Song's ear. Some Japanese officers arrived in a car and immediately carried out inspections of the hotel. The Japanese chefs were handed a menu and they set to work preparing delicacies for lunch. Quite obviously a VIP was expected.

'Our cleaning jobs done to Corporal Tanaka's satisfaction, Sergeant Hashimoto assembled the local staff, barked something at us in Japanese and went away.

'Corporal Tanaka explained to Uncle Song that the hotel would be visited later that day by the general who had conquered Malaya and Singapore. His name was Lieutenant-General Tomoyuki Yamashita who was known as "The Tiger of Malaya."

'Sergeant Hashimoto reappeared later, He checked and rechecked the names of all the staff and we were counted and recounted before being locked in a large empty room at the rear of the hotel. As soon as the sergeant left, Corporal Tanaka appeared and told Uncle Song that everybody in the room had to stay silent.

'About two hours later, we heard the sound of cars and motorcycles, followed by sharp commands in Japanese coming from the hotel's entrance. Obviously, the "Tiger of Malaya" had arrived and I wondered what he looked like. I had only seen an unclear photograph in a newspaper of General Yamashita with the defeated British commander General Percival after the surrender of Singapore. They were both seated at a table at the Ford Motor Factory at Bukit Timah where the surrender took place. Some said that the "Tiger" was short and had a big belly. Others said he was stocky and had a red, ferocious face, like a tiger's.

'The wooden windows of the room in which we were, were also locked. As my eyes wandered around, I noticed a ventilation slat was missing from one of the windows. I wondered what view of the outside it offered. I edged myself towards the window. The others were dozing in the stifling heat or talking in whispers.

'I could hear shouts of *Banzai*!

'I gradually bent my knees to bring my eyes level with the opening in the window. I was presented with an almost unobstructed view of the hotel's entrance. Come to think of it now, if I had a rifle at the time I could have probably shot General Yamashita dead as he entered or left the hotel.

'I felt myself tingling with excitement and I didn't really care whether the others in the room saw what I was doing.

'There were more shouts of *Banzai*!

'Another hour passed. Then I saw him. He was walking slowly up to the entrance from the Banquet Room flanked by two officers in uniform. They all had rows of coloured ribbons on their chests and carried *samurai* swords in scabbards that hung from their waists. They stopped to exchange stiff bows and smart salutes with some other men in uniform.

'General Yamashita was a short man with a big belly. He had a red, chubby face and a toothbrush moustache. He didn't look anything like a ferocious tiger to me. I thought he looked more like a well-fed pig.

'What I saw next caused me to hold my breath and my eyes to almost pop out of my head as I gaped at the car that had stopped at the entrance to pick him up. It was our Packard!

'I was at the point of shouting out my discovery to my father who was only a few yards away but remembering the harsh penalty such rashness would bring not only to myself but to the others in the room for breaking the silence imposed on us, I held my breath and bit into my bottom lip as I watched in agony.

'Our Packard looked more dazzling than it ever did before, I thought. No wonder General Yamashita had chosen it for his personal use from among the thousands of cars captured after the fall of Singapore. Tears blurred my view. I wiped my eyes with the backs of my hands as I fought the maddening urge to cry out, 'Yamashita, you thief! You stole our car!'

'Wild, angry thoughts flashed through my mind. I thought if I had a hand grenade, I would force open the window and make a dash for the entrance and blow our Packard and this pot-bellied robber to smithereens!

'I saw him climb into our car and sit on the rear seat where my parents used to sit with Pansy and me! His aide-de-camp sat in front next to a grim-faced Japanese chauffeur; not kindly old Jalil, who to our deep sorrow had died in an air raid.

'Four motorcycle outriders led the way out – and "The Tiger Of Malaya" was gone!

'It was the last time I saw our Packard.

'There were tears in my father's eyes when I later described what I had seen. My mother and Pansy wept so did Auntie Song and Jennifer while Uncle Song stared sadly at the floor, remembering there had been no news about his Buick. It was like a funeral gathering.

'When some other members of the staff wanted to know the

cause of our sadness, my father said we had just come to know of the death of a much-loved member of the family – which was the truth!

'Uncle Song and my father made unsuccessful inquiries about their cars following the surrender of Japan in 1945.

'David and Pansy were married a year later. Jennifer and I were married the following year. The Songs and our family moved into a block of apartments on the west coast, near to where Sunset Beach used to be. Coconut trees along that stretch of beach had been felled and concrete machinegun turrets were built by the British in readiness for a Japanese invasion from the sea – that never took place!

'On the wall of our new apartment was a large photograph in a polished teakwood frame taken a long time ago in front of our house in Sembawang. It showed my father at the wheel of our Packard, my mother seated beside him with Pansy and myself standing on the rear seat.

'Although some years had passed since the war ended we still had faint hopes that our Packard and Uncle Song's Buick had somehow survived, despite the fact that the Japanese army had shipped to Japan thousands of vehicles captured after the surrender of Singapore to be melted down and turned into weapons of war.

'My father feared this fate could have befallen our beautiful Packard. But, would General Yamashita have condemned it to such a ghastly end? My father recalled reading a newspaper article after the Japanese occupation of Singapore in February 1942. It said General Yamashita wrote poetry about the beauty of nature when he wasn't fighting wars and that he was "a man of honour and culture." '

Note: Following the surrender of Japan in 1945, General Yamashita was convicted by a US military court in Manila for committing war crimes in the Philippines, including the massacre of many thousands of Filipinos while he was commander of Japanese forces. He was hanged at Los Banos, Philippines, on 23 February 1946.

Murder: With Love And Kisses

The attention of the silent, sombre crowd staring at the coffin resting on wooden supports above a grave at the Christian cemetery in Kuala Lumpur was suddenly interrupted by a frail woman in black who was making determined efforts to get closer to the grave. She had now begun to scream in a shrill voice, 'Wait for me, Pop! Don't leave me!' as she tried to free her wrists from the grips of two tough-looking policewomen on either side of her.

She was Gina Honey, the widow of Pop Honey whose remains reposed in the coffin.

The chances of Mrs Honey succeeding in joining her husband in his neatly-excavated resting place were very much against her for two reasons:

First, the two hefty policewomen gripping her wrists were determined no such thing was going to happen. This was because Mrs Honey was being held on suspicion of murdering her husband by drilling a neat hole in his skull with a bullet from a 9mm pistol.

Second, the practice of people burying themselves alive with their deceased loved ones was forbidden by law; the reason for this wise piece of legislation being that the burial or cremation of those who had passed on was a procedure strictly reserved for them alone and not the living.

Apparently, the grief-stricken Mrs Honey was unaware that this well-meaning law had been designed specially to keep people like herself alive. Otherwise, she would not have been directing dirty looks at the two policewomen restraining her.

One of the policewomen threw a huge arm round Mrs Honey's waist anchoring her firmly to the spot on which she was standing. Mrs Honey thereupon decided to use her shrill voice to its best advantage. Filling her small lungs with all the air they could hold, she yelled, 'I'm coming, Pop!'

People were known to react differently at funerals of loved ones. Some cried more loudly than others. There were those who didn't cry or showed any remorse, having their own private reasons. Yet, there were some who felt secretly happy that the deceased had been permanently removed from Planet Earth.

Mrs Honey, however, decided to become suicidal although the possibility of ending her life by throwing herself on top of her husband's coffin was rather doubtful. This was because Mr Honey's coffin being a *de luxe* model and almost one metre in height would have reduced Mrs Honey's fall into the grave to less than five feet. There was little hope of a person dying by falling from a height as low as that, no matter how optimistic he or she might have been about the outcome. At best Mrs Honey would have only succeeded in causing minor bruises to her flat chest or bony back, depending on which way she proposed to fall.

Mrs Honey suddenly fell limp over the long arm of one of the policewomen. This coincided with the sound of a dull thud indicating that the coffin containing her husband's remains had hit the bottom of the grave. It was caused when the funeral parlour attendants who were lowering it with ropes, decided to speed things up since it had started to drizzle quite heavily. More sounds of dull thuds followed as two men began to shovel earth on top of Mr Honey's expensive coffin in an impressive burst of speed.

Mrs Honey's only brother was 'Hands' Wang, so nicknamed because of gesticulations he made with his hands when he spoke. He was about to rush to his sister's aid when he saw the policewomen carrying her to a big, black car that looked like a hearse. They got in and drove off.

Hands Wang was watching his sister's dramatic departure from the cemetery when Joe Smith a 'small time' lawyer, joined him. Smith was Mrs Honey's legal adviser and an old friend.

Hands scowled as he looked at the small group of mourners watching the diggers pat the wet, red earth down into a neat mound with the backs of their shovels and arrange the wreaths on top of Pop Honey's grave.

'Look at those hypocrites!' he said to Smith indicating the graveside crowd with his chin. 'They all hated Pop Honey's fat guts. But there they are! All dressed in black and wearing black, "funeral glasses" to hide their "crocodile" tears! To make matters worse one of them had the nerve to deliver the eulogy that described Pop as a fine guy and devoted husband although everyone present knew it was a lot of crap! But they all joined in the farce!'

'Is that why you are here? As part of the farce?' asked Smith. 'You hated Pop Honey's fat guts too, didn't you?'

Hands pretended to be shocked. 'Are you accusing me of being a hypocrite? I'm shattered and flattered!' he replied. 'Yes, of course! I'm putting on an act like the rest of them. It takes talent to be a hypocrite and a lot of dedication to reach Pop Honey's high standard. He was a superstar when it came to conning people and hypocrisy!'

He paused, then said, 'Let's leave this depressing place and have a drink. May I suggest the Coliseum Bar?'

'In celebration?' asked Smith with a chuckle. Hands grinned.

As they walked towards the road where their cars were parked, Hands said, 'There should be a law against it!'

'Against hypocrisy?' asked Smith.

'Oh, for heaven's sake, no! What would become of our illustrious society without hypocrites, liars, frauds, conmen and politicians? They're so colourful. What I meant was, there should be a law against burying pigs like Pop Honey in cemeteries! Pigs aren't buried. They are slaughtered, cooked and eaten, by some people!'

They sat at a corner table of the bar drinking whisky. Hands said, 'I remember what Pop said to me one day and I quote, "The secret of success is effective public relations. Nobody can do without it. As a communications consultant I specialised in image repair, image maintenance, image building, image creation and also when necessary, image destruction. My job is somewhat similar to that of a plastic surgeon except it's a lot more intricate because I am not concerned with reshaping faces. My job is reshaping people as a whole and to make them look presentable in the eyes of the public. In other words, to give bums, liars and hypocrites some respectability for a fee, of course!"

Hands paused and said reflectively, 'He was a pig! The way he dominated my poor sister with shameless impunity. He got her to do anything he wanted and to believe anything he said.'

Gina loved Pop Honey with all her heart. (He had Anglicised his name from Paw Hon Yee to 'Pop Honey'). She was thirty-six years old with a very slim hope of finding a husband when he showed up like a knight in a suit of shiny Italian silk and driving a borrowed Mercedes. In no time he had carried her off to dreamland.

From the way Pop behaved nobody would have suspected he was flat broke. Neither did they suspect the same of Gina who always pretended to be financially sound although she had mortgaged the old family house she inherited. Her boutique was in the red. What she needed desperately was some cash, lots of it, to get her out of the financial mess she was in. When Pop Honey came into her life she began to think the chances of that happening were very much brighter, as we shall see.

Hands tried to warn his sister that she was going to be 'taken for a ride by a wolf who was masquerading as a pig'. To which she dreamily said, 'But he's such an adorable pig! I love him!'

Well, when you come to think of it, no other man had given Gina a second look. And, here was Pop, a man-about-town, who was crazy about her.

What did he see in her?
What did she see in him?

He was shapeless, had a fat, oily face, thick lips and a bullet-shaped head. He was never out of debt and he was unfaithful to Gina and dishonest to others at the slightest chance. But, despite all this, Gina adored him.

Smith ordered another round of whisky.

'What's going to happen to Gina?' Hands asked seriously.

'Oh, I suppose the police will try to dig up some quick evidence to prove she shot him while trying to make it appear someone else committed the murder so she could collect the half a million US dollars he was insured for,' said Smith. 'I'll watch things closely'.

'Did you know she was almost broke?' asked Hands. 'Whatever little money Pop had, he spent on gambling, booze and women! He never gave my sister a cent. But she wasn't one to complain. She's a saint, I tell you!'

'Well, if she was broke, it would have given her more reason to kill her husband for his insurance money,' said Smith calmly.

'I suppose you are aware that my sister was also insured for the same amount of money?' asked Hands.

Smith nodded his head. 'Yes, as her legal adviser, I knew about that.'

'You don't believe she killed him, do you?' asked Hands.

Smith shrugged his shoulders. He looked hard at Hands and asked, 'Did you kill him?'

Hands laughed. 'Have you suddenly gone crazy? You don't waste a good bullet to kill a pig. Pigs have their throats slit! But seriously, I don't think the police will be able to prove she murdered him. She loved him too much to do a thing like that, although he treated her so badly. They even stayed in separate bedrooms on different sides of the house because he made her believe he had important clients visiting or phoning him up at all hours of the night and hadn't the heart to disturb her sleep! Can you beat that? The things he made her believe! Poor Gina!'

Smith was silent for some lime. Then he said, 'Do you know if your sister had a secret lover?'

Hands laughed. 'Are you drunk? As far as she was concerned, there was no other man alive on this planet except her darling Pop!'

The police had interviewed the gardener who said that on the day of the murder Gina had returned home as usual around six in the evening and her husband about an hour later. They went to their separate sides of the house. The maid who had a room downstairs next to the kitchen said she seldom prepared dinner for them since they always brought back food.

Just before midnight the gardener said he saw a car pull up in front of the house. A woman got out and let herself in with a key. He didn't pay much attention to her since Pop often had women visitors at all hours of the night. The woman came out from the house about fifteen minutes later and drove off. The gardener was uncertain of the make or colour of the car since it was quite dark. He did not hear a shot fired, neither did the maid.

The identity of the woman who had visited Pop on the night he was killed was a mystery.

The gardener and the maid told detectives that an elderly woman visited Gina about twice a week, usually after six in the evening. She left after about two hours, but at times would stay the night and leave very early the following morning by taxi. From their descriptions the woman was of medium build, she wore spectacles and tied her hair in a bun at the back of her head. The maid said the old woman was Gina's aunt. That's all she knew about her. They had never met this woman face-to-face. She always arrived by taxi and Gina was waiting at the front door to meet her. They would go upstairs to Gina's side of the house. This woman had not visited Gina for some lime. Police ruled out the woman as a suspect.

It was the maid who found Pop's body slumped in a chair behind a desk in his study early in the morning. He had a neat hole in his forehead where the bullet had entered. There was only a trickle of blood. On the desk was an answering machine and when the police played the tape there was a recording of a woman's voice. It said, 'Just to remind you, sweet lips, I'll be around at about midnight. See you.'

There were earlier messages but this one, the last on the tape, was the most important because it tallied with the gardener's story about the mystery woman he had seen entering and leaving the house around midnight. Investigators carefully studied all aspects of the scanty clues and came up with this theory:

1 The woman who had made the mysterious phone call and the woman who had visited Pop Honey on the night he was killed, were the same person.
2 If they found this woman, they would also have found the killer.
3 They hadn't the slightest idea who she was.

After considering the gardener's story about the mystery woman who had visited Pop Honey around midnight, there was no way the police were going to detain Gina as their prime suspect.

The morning after Pop's funeral Smith received a phone call from the Homicide Department saying they were letting Gina go.

The weeks went by without the police making any progress in discovering who had murdered Pop Honey. The coroner's inquiry ended with the usual 'open verdict': Murder committed by a person or persons unknown.

Gina seemed to be in no hurry to claim the insurance on Pop's life and had to be reminded twice by the insurance company to collect the cheque. It only went to show all concerned that she wasn't impatiently waiting to become a 'rich widow.'

Each month on the anniversary of her husband's death a tearful Gina would place a bouquet of red roses on Pop's grave. But as the months passed she relieved herself of this heart-breaking duty, passing it on to a florist who did it for a small fee, minus the tears.

Gina had changed her entire wardrobe to black after Pop's death and some of the gossips referred to her as 'The Black Widow' insinuating that she, like the deadly spider by that name had killed her mate. Eight months passed.

Then, quite suddenly, Gina ended her prolonged spell of mourning. She gave a cocktail party at the exclusive Coral Lagoon Nightclub to announce her forthcoming marriage to none other than her lawyer, Joe Smith! She proudly told the two hundred guests, 'Joe is not only my legal adviser but also my dearest friend. He stood by me during those very sad days after my dear husband's tragic death.'

Gina paused to dab her eyes with a lace handkerchief, taking good care not to make a mess of her eye make-up.

Everyone present including her overjoyed brother Hands saw a new and rejuvenated Gina who appeared in a rather daring, low-cut cocktail frock that showed most of her small breasts. Her hair was exquisitely styled, her face made up with a careful choice of colour tones while she displayed the beneficial results of her training at a well-known modelling school.

Her transformation was stunning and a bashful Joe Smith was heard to remark, 'I must have loved her even before she transformed herself from a grieving widow to what she is now!'

She had sold her house after collecting Pop's insurance money, paid her creditors and bought a new apartment where she and her husband would live after they were married.

Smith seemed delighted with the new arrangements. Gina with her many new connections introduced a few clients with impressive bank accounts to him and they were both climbing up the social ladder quite steadily. They were married in a simple ceremony three months later.

There were a few people who had known Pop Honey and Gina in the old days and who wondered how it was possible for Gina to have transformed herself from a faded wallflower into a lively, social butterfly and to have fallen so deeply in love with Smith.

Hadn't she threatened to kill herself over the loss of her 'darling Pop'? And how could anyone forget in a hurry the sorrow and anguish she had displayed at his graveside?

They couldn't believe she was the same woman, looking at her now. They reckoned no wife would have put up with the treatment she had received from Pop Honey, allowing him at the same time to carry on a separate life while living under the same roof. If she had loved him as much as she made people believe she did, she would have reacted differently to his shameful behaviour with other women and displayed fits of jealousy or kicked him out of her house.

What nobody knew was that Gina was playing the role of a 'very-much-in-love and obedient wife' until she decided it was time she put an end to her 'darling' Pop's life that would make her a rich lady.

Unknown to Gina, Pop had a similar plan for her. In fact he was just about to take her on a scuba-diving vacation from which she wouldn't return when someone put a bullet in his head.

Had Gina found out about his plan to kill her and killed him first? Maybe she had. Maybe Pop had become careless, believing his wife was dim-witted and left a few clues about the place.

It was she who had suggested as soon as they were married that they insured themselves.

At times when they met in his study in the evenings and he held her in his arms, she knew he was only pretending that he loved her. But, when she snuggled up to him, it had never crossed his mind that she was also 'putting on an act.'

Of course, they had planned to murder each other from the time they met.

This may be a good time to reveal the identity of the 'old aunt' who visited Gina at her house each week and sometimes stayed overnight. She was none other than Joe Smith in disguise. They had been secret lovers long before Pop appeared on the scene.

This is what happened on the night of the murder :

At about ten o'clock Gina telephoned Pop from her side of the house and made him believe she was about to give him the money he needed to pay off a gambling debt. She put on a pair of silk gloves, stuck a loaded nine-millimetre pistol with a silencer under her Japanese 'happy coat' and went to his study.

He was sitting behind his desk. He grinned as he saw her and called out, 'Darling!'

She smiled and said, 'Darling,' locking the door.

She stood before him still smiling. Suddenly she whipped out the gun and shot him once in the forehead. It was all over in a few seconds, just like she had seen it done in the movies. The sound that her pistol made with a silencer attached was like someone coughing lightly into a handkerchief.

She switched on the answering machine on his desk and returned to her side of the house. She had a luxurious bath, put on a cocktail frock and a wig of short, brown hair. She sipped a vodka-lime and watched TV. It was almost eleven o'clock.

The phone rang three times and stopped. It was a signal from Joe Smith that he was waiting in his car at a pre-arranged spot up the road near her house.

She quietly let herself out of the house, keeping to the shadows and met him. She gave him the gun and took the car, driving back to the house. (Gina was the 'mystery woman' the gardener saw driving up in a car, entering the house and leaving after fifteen minutes.)

Meanwhile, Smith had walked a little way up the road to use a public phone and called Pop's number. Disguising his voice to sound like a woman's, he left a message on the answering machine. (The voice of the 'mystery caller' that police had later discovered.)

216

After killing Pop, Gina returned the car to Smith and walked back to the house a little after midnight. The servants were fast asleep. She changed into a nightgown and after watching a tape of *Love Story* for a while, went to bed.

Smith later buried the gun.

No matter what unkind things people might have said about Pop, to Gina he was worth a lot of money – dead! Not many dead bums were worth half a million US bucks and two years – being the time they had been married – wasn't all that long to wait to collect that kind of money.

They never did find out who killed Pop Honey and except for the police, nobody seemed to care.

Three years passed.

Gina was often reminded that Joe Smith was the only person who knew her secret: that she had killed Pop Honey. She hadn't paid much attention to this fact but now the thought began to trouble her. She remembered what Benjamin Franklin once said: 'Three may keep a secret, if two of them are dead.'

Joe was younger than her by a couple of years and was quite a charmer. She was aware that a few young women were attracted to him. She suspected he was being unfaithful to her but couldn't prove it.

She thought: 'Supposing Joe found another woman and wanted to get rid of me?'

She weighed the possibilities in her mind. He could threaten to tell the police all he knew about how Pop Honey met with his 'mysterious' death if she didn't give him all she owned as well as a divorce!

Gina and Joe had each insured themselves for a million US dollars and there was another two million dollars tied up in property that could be inherited by the one who survived the other. If he wished to claim her life insurance money and the property, he wouldn't have to kill her – not if she was sentenced to death by a court for Pop's murder! Joe would get a couple of years in prison for conspiracy in the crime, but she'd be hanged or would spend the rest of her life in prison and would be as good as dead! He remembered also that Joe had told her that he had buried the gun that killed Pop. Did he really get rid of it? Or, did he still have the gun hidden somewhere and which he would produce at the right time?

Joe would be a very rich man when he came out of prison with enough money to start life anew. She wondered if Joe was capable of doing such a thing to her, like having her convicted of murder – and killed by a hangman.

Well, Pop was planning to kill her for the same reason when she became wise to what he was up to and messed up his brains with a 9mm bullet! What was she going to do about Joe?

They were sitting opposite each other at the breakfast table at home reading the newspapers when suddenly, for some unexplained reason, a cold shiver ran down her spine as she realised just how vulnerable she was. Her eyes became momentarily blurred with the horrifying thought and when she looked up from the newspaper she was trying to read she saw Joe staring at her – and he was smiling.

What was he thinking? Had he been reading her thoughts?

Although she blew him a kiss, she had at that moment decided she could no longer trust him. 'Some adjustments had to be made in life,' she thought.

A few days later as she stood looking at a wedding photograph of Joe and herself hanging on a wall, she sighed and whispered, 'Dear Joe, I'm afraid the time has come for us to part.'

She suggested they went to Kathmandu, rented a car and drove around the foothills of the Himalayas to celebrate their coming wedding anniversary.

'What a splendid idea!' Joe had said.

'Think of the wonderful photographs you could take with your new camera, darling! You could probably hold an exhibition later on,' she said.

Joe was killed in a car accident while they were on holiday. He was driving down a mountain road in Kathmandu to a scenic spot not far from their hotel where he had intended to take some photographs when his rented car plunged more than a thousand feet down a rocky ravine.

Police could only presume the car had skidded off the narrow, wet, mountain road. Search teams found the charred wreck of the car a week later and put Joe's remains into a plastic bag.

Gina was to have accompanied him on the day he met his death, but she had a sudden migraine and decided to rest in their hotel bedroom.

Earlier that afternoon, Gina had put two sleeping pills into Joe's cup of tea. While he was asleep she sneaked into the garage and let out almost all the hydraulic fluid from the brakes of their rented car, rendering them useless. She had watched how this was done by mechanics at a service station in Kuala Lumpur. She had secretly tested her skill in this operation on the brakes of her own car, twice, before leaving on their holiday and was quite pleased with her performance.

Of course, she pretended to be devastated by Joe's tragic death, just as she had been when Pop had met his 'mysterious' end.

After selling their apartment and her boutique and collecting the money on Joe's life insurance, she suddenly disappeared from Kuala Lumpur without saying a word to anyone.

It was rumoured she had married a French millionaire. There was also talk that she was living in New York . . . or was it Rome?

Agreeable Arrangements

Edward Traff tossed the stump of his Havana cigar into the large onyx ashtray on his Chinese blackwood desk and deposited his bulk into a leather chair. It caused a loud hissing sound as his ample buttocks forced pockets of trapped air out of the upholstery.

It was a little past eleven o'clock in the morning according to the gold calendar-clock on his desk, which also informed him it was 16 March 1937.

He had just arrived at his office that was located in Raffles Place in the heart of Singapore's business district. He had then begun a morning 'ritual' in which he allowed his eyes to feast upon some of his art acquisitions in a leisurely manner. On the rosewood-panelled wall facing him was the most recent one, a Picasso.

'I was lured into paying a hideous price for a monstrosity showing a bald female with one huge eye, one square breast and a plant growing out of her right ear!' he had remarked to some friends later. 'But such is the genius of Picasso. Either you understood his work, pretended to, or hadn't a clue what it was all about!'

Edward Traff hadn't a clue what Picasso's abstract art was all about but he was a good actor.

To celebrate his latest acquisition, he gave a cocktail party at his palatial home and told his guests, 'I could have added an English thoroughbred racehorse to my stable for the sum I paid for the Picasso. But then, one cannot place a horse in a picture frame and hang it up on a wall! Could one? It is widely believed a person's position in society was greatly enhanced by owning expensive status symbols. I must admit that I may have unwittingly contributed towards this trend that the more one paid for a symbol the better one's status became. But, from my personal observations over the years, wealth and status were meaningless without power. Power was the essential ingredient that made the world go round!

'Some people used their own money or someone else's to buy themselves powerful positions and in the process of climbing the ladder to fame and fortune eliminated their opponents, some of whom were disposed of in a rather callous and cold-blooded manner. But, that was the way in which the Power Game is played. Each contestant made his own set of rules by which he played, lived or died! If he survived he made his own laws – not rules – that everyone was expected to obey without question. Those who didn't were regarded as subversive elements. They were swiftly reduced to nothingness because society had to be protected from such dangerous people.'

A woman who wrote a weekly social column for a popular newspaper had jokingly asked, 'But surely that isn't a democratic way of doing things?'

Traff replied, 'There are several shades of democracy, my dear. Which one are you referring to?'

It drew chuckles and titters from those who had gathered around.

'Did you become rich and famous by playing the Power Game?' asked the woman with a disarming smile.

The onlookers fell silent, expecting a sharp retort from him. But, he laughed and said, 'I'm too much of a coward to play such a dangerous game.'

A week later the woman columnist was sacked from her job. 'Staff restructuring' was given as the reason. She had no reason to suspect that Edward Traff had anything to do with her dismissal because shortly after she left the newspaper, he invited her to lunch and promised to let her know if he heard of any suitable position for her, a promise he had no intention of keeping.

Looking at the collection of artefacts in his palatial home he thought that there was something lacking in his 'personal set up.' He felt his wealth didn't seem to boost his image.

He found himself unconsciously staring at his reflection in an ornamental Ching period mirror. He imagined he saw his reflection speak to him and it said, 'Ah, my dear Edward, I think what you need most of all is some proper form of recognition. What about an OBE . . . or a knighthood? Yes, a knighthood! Why not!'

He snapped his fingers and exclaimed happily, 'Why hadn't I thought of it before! Let's start doing what has to be done to get me a knighthood! Sir Edward Traff! It sounds marvellous!'

Not long afterwards he married Louise Squires in what he believed was a very important step towards the realisation of such an achievement.

That morning as he sat in his luxurious private office in the chambers of Edward Traff & Company, Advocates, Solicitors and Notaries, his eyes settled on the Maruyama Okyo painting on a paper screen near the entrance. On a wall were two portraits of Japanese *kabuki* theatre performers by Sharaku Toshusai, the famous 18th century Japanese colour-print artist and *noh* dancer.

On a mahogany table with dragon and lotus motifs inlaid in gold leaf was a fountain. In the centre of a bowl of green jade, a white jade dragon stood on its tail, a fine jet of water coming from its open mouth. It fell in a small, sparkling arc, creating the gentle sound of tiny bells chiming.

He closed his eyes. The soothing sound caused him to doze off. He could easily have fallen asleep. But he was not going to allow such a thing to happen. Not today of all days.

He yawned loudly and looked through the one-way glass screen in front of him and saw his Asian staff hard at work in an open office. He didn't really need to watch them. He paid them well according to 'local' standards and the work they produced was satisfactory.

Behind them, closeted in small, wood-panelled offices that he called 'The Stables,' were four English 'thoroughbreds': two barristers and two solicitors whom he had recruited in London some years before. From the 'in-out' signs on their doors and by consulting a diary on his desk, he could tell exactly where they were and more or less what they were doing. He paid them well according to English standards with extra fringe benefits and they produced satisfactory work.

He had read the morning newspapers over breakfast at home and pushed aside the copies on his desk. There was nothing in the news that interested him. His shares were looking healthy on the stock market and that, as far as he was concerned, was what mattered most.

He absent-mindedly rubbed the soles of his black patent-leather shoes on the Persian carpet under his desk and belched loudly, causing his double chin to quiver slightly. 'Must cut down on onions and garlic,' he told himself.

He swivelled his chair round and looked out of the large, tinted glass window behind his desk and broke wind loudly. He studied the small coastal ships in the harbour for some time with a pair of binoculars and looked further beyond at the islands of the Riau Archipelago.

He was killing time. He yawned again. He extracted a gold monogrammed Piaget watch from the pocket of his waistcoat. It was one minute past noon. He pressed a button on the intercom on his desk and told Mrs Gilbert, his English secretary, to have the chauffeur of his Rolls-Royce pick him up from the entrance of the office building in exactly fifteen minutes. He got up from his chair and stood before a long Cheval mirror and studied his huge, balding head and stuck out his tongue. He withdrew it quickly and grimaced. 'Damn garlic!' he muttered, forgetting the amount of brandy he had consumed the night before at a cocktail party.

He was about to proceed to the Raffles Hotel where he was to be the guest of honour at a luncheon to celebrate his recent knighthood.

When the anticipated announcement was made in the King's Birthday Honours List, Sir Edward had said to himself with tears in his eyes, 'Well, I jolly well deserved it, after all I've been through!'

Sir Edward had been in Singapore for just over twenty-five years, arriving as a young solicitor from England. He started a small firm. By a fair amount of hard work and the cultivation of some influential people he became a prosperous and respected member of European 'upper class' society.

He was now fifty-one. He had recently been married and divorced within the short space of eighteen months and swore 'by all the stars in the heavens' it would not happen again.

'I never dreamed for a moment that an innocent-looking document such as a marriage certificate could be used as an instrument for committing deceit, treachery and blackmail. Since it is nearly always the husband who finds himself at the losing end of this devilish, one-sided partnership called marriage, I would strongly advise any sane male contemplating such an important step to do so with the utmost caution and only after considering the legal aspects that may arise later. It's quite surprising, really, how most people seemed to believe a marriage certificate guarantees a life of everlasting bliss with a storybook ending, never thinking that those passion-filled honeymoon days would ever come to an end. But quite suddenly, the participants are rudely made aware that all marriages are not made in heaven, as some people stupidly believe. Then a bitter and ferocious battle is waged between husband and wife with one intention: to cause the maximum amount of pain and humiliation to one another!'

At times he could be heard saying, 'I lead a simple life, really. I only drop in at my chambers each morning as an excuse to break journey from my home in Mount Pleasant to the Raffles Hotel, where I go to experience that wonderful old colonial atmosphere; to sit in the library and have the pleasure of reading Maugham, Conrad and Kipling all over again; to play snooker and perhaps some bridge; to sit down to a civilised lunch prepared by excellent chefs and to be served by well-trained servants. And, finally, adjourn to the Long Bar for a drink and a chat. That about describes how I spend each day. I allow my legal assistants to get on with their tedious work and only advise them now and then. Things seem to have worked out rather well for all concerned, after some adjustments . . . and some agreeable arrangements were concluded.'

He would reserve such remarks when he was in the company of those who could not possibly enjoy such privileges. He would derive much pleasure watching his listeners nod their heads in agreement with what he said and would say to himself, 'Look at them! Nodding away like a lot of bally ducks! As though they understood what I was saying!' He would smile into their uncertain faces, his blue eyes twinkling with hidden scorn and walk away.

Sir Edward owned an old Moorish-style mansion on a hill near a large forest reserve beside a reservoir. It had six bedrooms, a banquet room, a ballroom, an antiques room, a study, and a billiards and cards room. The first owner was a wealthy Arab merchant. Sir Edward had bought it from its second owner, a Chinese rubber dealer who became bankrupt during the great slump of 1929.

Sir Edward had named the splendid white building 'The Manor'. He would tell his friends with a degree of modesty, 'I have three acres of landscaped gardens and a magnificent view of the undulating jungle-land. There are my prize-winning orchids and my collection of antiques and the joys of being pampered by a devoted and most efficient Chinese house staff. I think Chinese servants are the best, no matter what may be said of the Japanese and Filipinos.'

Sir Edward or 'Tiny Ted' as he was popularly known from the Governor down, had been the Bar Association's president for a number of years. He resigned 'in order to give some aspiring chap the chance to bask in the spotlight, which I have become rather tired of doing,' he had said.

Sir Edward was generally well liked. He selected his European and Asian friends with care. He was known at times to make indiscreet remarks about the influence he had on people in high places. He was genial and polite to all.

'You can always tell a genuine, upper-class Englishman by his polite and impeccable manners,' he had told his friends one day. 'It's the second and third-class trash who gave the British community a bad name by pretending they came from well-bred families. They resorted to rudeness and snobbishness in an attempt to establish their so-called superiority.'

He could be charmingly vicious when the occasion arose. There was that unforgettable example of the sharpness of his tongue when he reduced the wife of a well-known *tuan besar* to tears at the Governor's New Year Ball. It happened when she had asked him the reason why he was still a bachelor, since there were several eligible English ladies in Singapore.

'I shall endeavour to explain, dear lady,' he had said with his characteristic charm. 'I think it was Noel Coward who was heard to remark at a reception in his honour in Singapore that after meeting English ladies belonging to our so-called upper-class, he could well understand why there was such an acute shortage of charwomen in England. Besides, dear lady, why must one be burdened with maintaining a cow when milk is cheap and so readily available?'

He was called by his critics (behind his back), 'a pompous and insufferable braggart . . . a perpetual pain in the arse . . . a snob who believes sarcasm is the highest form of wit . . . and very dangerous at all times with the venom of a king cobra. His surname spelt backwards and with one 't' instead of two, would describe him admirably.'

Edward Traff had remained a bachelor up to the age of forty-nine. To everybody's surprise, he announced he was going to marry Louise Squires the widow of the late Henderson Squires, the financier, who was killed in an air crash in Argentina, He had left her with very substantial means. There were no children.

Edward met her for the first time when she made a brief visit to Singapore in connection with some of her late husband's business affairs. She had appointed him her legal adviser. A whirlwind romance followed and she accepted him when he proposed. It was the 'Wedding of the Year.' More than five hundred guests, including the Governor and his wife, *tuan besars* and their formidable *mems* and members of the diplomatic corps attended the reception at the Victoria Memorial Hall. This happened a year before he was knighted.

Mrs Squires was thin and tall, had a bony face and straight, close-cropped hair. She was never known to use make-up. She wore skirts below her knees and long-sleeved shirts buttoned at the wrists – and used spectacles with thick frames. She was altogether a rather unattractive lady.

Her large number of friends knew her as a warm-hearted, sincere and helpful person. She was a staunch Anglican and a prominent charity worker. She was the founder of an organisation in Britain that rendered financial aid counselling to unwed mothers and was decorated with the Order of the British Empire (OBE) in honour of her services.

'A typical missionary type, I would say,' said someone. 'What could have attracted that old buzzard Traff to her? Certainly it wasn't her money. He has loads of it. I cannot imagine him being faithful to any woman when he has a string of attractive ladies around him. Neither can I ever believe he is in love with Mrs Squires because Edward Traff has never loved anyone except himself! I suspect he has an ulterior motive for marrying Louise Squires which we shall learn about in good time.'

He had had affairs with various married and unmarried women whom he 'paid off' before they became 'difficult'. He had called it 'cheque-book diplomacy' and went on to explain, 'Independence and freedom are noble ideals that people sacrificed their lives for in revolutions and wars. Do you think I am prepared to surrender my precious liberty by becoming permanently manacled to some woman who would immediately take away my independence? Good, Lord! I shall never allow that to happen! By using "cheque-book diplomacy," all traces of unpleasantness between the two parties concerned are seen to vanish, wounds of the heart are miraculously healed and everyone begins to smile again and all because an offering of magic dollars had been happily accepted! That is how agreeable arrangements are concluded, my friends! All this was made possible by using the universal language of money that adventurous women seem to understand best.'

His well-known affair with Carmen Chang that happened several years before was different from his many other illicit relationships. There was talk at the lime that the elusive Edward Traff, twenly-five years younger, was finally 'caught.' There were a few bets laid making Carmen Chang the favourite to become the 'first official Mrs Traff,' an honour that had eluded some hot favourites in the past. His foes and friends would not have minded in the least if Carmen Chang became his wife despite the fact that she was Chinese. 'A most charming, intelligent and beautiful girl, who is far too good for a damn reprobate like him!' an envious bachelor had remarked.

Their much-anticipated wedding never took place.

Edward Traff had made no mention to Louise Squires about Carmen Chang and their son Rupert, who was twenty-three and a law student at Cambridge. He had given the matter considerable thought. He felt Louise Squires had some rather old-fashioned and narrow-minded ideas about such matters and that it would be 'highly dangerous to predict how she would have reacted in such a situation.'

She came to learn about Carmen Chang shortly after her marriage and in most embarrassing circumstances. She was among a small group of *mem besars* at a cocktail party when one of them, who had had an affair with Edward some years before, said sweetly, 'Tell me, Mrs Traff, do you see much of Carmen Chang? I suppose you have met her? How is she? It's been ages since anyone has heard anything about her. I suppose Edward still supports her and their son?' Having injected her venom, the woman withdrew her fangs and departed.

Louise Traff froze. It took some moments before she was able to absorb the sudden shock. She called after the woman in a shaky voice, 'Wait! How dare you say such . . . ' but stopped, words suddenly trapped in her throat.

The other *mems* exchanged glances and drifted away, leaving Louise alone and devastated. She felt weak and helpless and wanted to burst into tears.

'How could there be any truth in what that woman said?' she asked herself. 'Edward would have told me about this Chinese woman and the son he had by her. That woman wanted to humiliate me, for some reason!' She thought again. 'But, that woman would not have fearlessly said such vicious things if there wasn't some truth in what she said!'

Louise Traff kept her composure and behaved as normally as she could for the remainder of the evening.

On the way home in their car, he had noticed she was rather quiet and when he asked her about it, she said she had a headache.

Later, when they were in their bedroom, she calmly questioned him about what the woman had said. She saw him frown for a moment. Then, putting an arm about her bony shoulders, said, 'Oh, that? It happened a very long time ago. It was one of those silly affairs that should not concern you at all, my dear. You must have heard the old familiar story about young, lonely Europeans and native girls?'

He kissed her lightly on the cheek. 'Cheer up, my dear! You are my wife!' He tried to kiss her again but she pushed him away and backing up against the wardrobe, she gave him a strange look.

'Did you expect me to dismiss from my mind the fact that you have a mistress and a grown-up son by her?' she asked.

He was about to say something but she held up a hand and continued, 'Didn't you think it was proper for you to have told me about it before we were married?'

He began to approach her with both arms extended. She moved out of his reach. He stopped and smiled at her. 'Please, try to understand. The woman concerned ceased to be my mistress many years ago!' He came towards her slowly, smiling. He tried to hold her arm.

'Don't touch me!' she snapped, her face now flushed and angry.

Why all this unnecessary hostility? I realise it has come as a bit of a shock to you, but would it make you feel any better if I told you that I have had nothing to do with Carmen Chang for almost twenty-five years? We haven't even spoken to each other. She gets a monthly allowance. She's well provided for. I bought her a flat after we parted. Her son is in his final year as a law student at Cambridge.'

He paused and said to her with a smile, 'Carmen and I came to an agreeable arrangement.'

She glared at him and said, 'You refer to this young man as being "her son." He's your son, too! He bears your name!'

He laughed lightly.

'Bears my name? Oh, good heavens, no! Whatever made you think so? He was registered in his mother's name which is the usual sort of thing that happens in the Far East in such circumstances when a local woman has an illegitimate child by her European lover.'

Louise's eyes hardened. She was quite familiar in dealing with such circumstances because of the work carried out by the organisation she founded in London, offering aid to a large number of unwed mothers and their children.

'So, you have a son and you're quite content to know he will be illegitimate for the rest of his life! Why didn't you register him in your name? Was it because he has Chinese blood?'

He lowered his eyes and did not reply.

She stood before him, her eyes blazing. 'You are a respected member of this community and you are almost sure to receive a knighthood this year. However, your behaviour in this matter has been devious, selfish and loathsome!'

He held up a hand. 'But Louise, my dear, I was only . . . '

She interrupted him. 'Listen to what I have to say! It is hard to believe a man of your position would stoop to such low and contemptuous behaviour! You disgust me!'

She brushed past him, went to a cupboard and removed some clothes from it.

'Please, Louise! You are over-reacting. Let me explain,' he pleaded.

'I do not wish to discuss this sordid affair any further! I have never been so humiliated in my life! I want you to understand that from this moment I do not wish to live with you as your wife. You have deceived me! My opinion of you has changed completely. You are a man of low morals and a disgrace as a Christian, that's if you still have the courage to call yourself one! I wish to be left alone by you and your horrible friends. I hope I have made myself clear!'

She went to the bedroom door and opened it.

'Louise, please, you're being very childish about this. If you would only try to understand I am sure you would be able to adjust to the situation,' he said and began to move towards her.

She went out, slamming the door in his face.

She slept in one of the spare bedrooms that night. He came twice to her door, pleading with her to open it. Getting no response, he went downstairs to his study where he drank some brandy and spent an uncomfortable night on a couch.

Louise awoke late the following morning. From her bedroom window she saw him leave in his car. After removing all her clothes from their bedroom she went downstairs and sat on a settee on the veranda facing the beautiful Japanese garden. She was deep in thought.

'Good morning. Madam want eat blek-fuss?'she heard a voice say behind her. It was Ah Ling, the head *amah* who was in her sixties and had been in Edward Traff's employ since he bought The Manor.

'No thank you, Ah Ling. Perhaps a little later,' Louise said, forcing a smile. The woman went away.

Louise felt herself trembling slightly and decided to walk in the garden in the bright morning sunlight. Olive-green *mata-putih* darted in and out of the Indian rose and jasmine bushes, their long black beaks searching for nectar. She watched them for a while then sat on a marble seat in the summer-house that was surrounded by tree ferns and yellow, purple and white orchids hanging in wooden boxes from the eaves. She turned to look at the huge, old mansion that became her home two months ago: white and gleaming in the sun. It was beautiful.

Louise thought how happy Carmen Chang must have been when she was mistress of the mansion and how sad she must have been when she had to leave it.

She shut her eyes and pictured Carmen as a beautiful, young girl running through the garden, collecting flowers . . . as a charming hostess dancing in the ballroom . . . and Ah Ling serving her breakfast in bed.

Bed?

The word hammered in her head and she opened her eyes and felt her blood run cold for a moment. Could it be the same bed she had been sharing with Edward for the past two months?

She began to tremble again. She caught a glimpse of Ah Ling as she swept the entrance of the mansion and wondered what the old *amah* thought of her. Was she resentful that a White woman had become the mistress of the mansion instead of Carmen Chang?

232

Tears rolled down Louise's face. As she walked slowly in the garden she thought of Carmen Chang again. What had gone wrong between her and Edward? Why hadn't he married her? Why did she leave? Was she told to go when he discovered she was pregnant?

Louise realised her relationship with Edward, like Carmen's, had come to an end. Her marriage to Edward had been a bad mistake.

She felt she had to meet Carmen Chang and to tell her she was leaving Edward and returning to England. She decided to take Ah Ling into her confidence and to ask her to arrange a meeting with Carmen as soon as possible.

Edward Traff did not go to his office that day. Instead, he went straight from his home to the golf club. He felt he needed to think things over alone, without interruption. He realised Louise felt she had been severely humiliated and deceived by him. But what worried him most was her decision not to live with him as his wife from now on. She was being childish and pig-headed. She would have found out about his affair with Carmen and about their son in due course, he reckoned. So what? Damn it! Couldn't she appreciate his position? He felt he had to do something to repair the damage before things became worse. Supposing his efforts to patch things up failed and she decided to leave him? A scandal . . . divorce? Heavens, no! Not at a time when he was almost certain of receiving a knighthood!

It was something he valued more than anything else in the world and for which he would be prepared to pay no matter what it cost. A divorce would ruin everything and drag out old skeletons in his cupboard for a most untimely and unpleasant airing.

'Such a thing must never be allowed to happen!' Edward told himself as he sipped a whisky.

Why didn't he come to an agreement with Louise as he had done with other women in somewhat similar situations in the past? No dirty linen would be washed in public and no reputations destroyed. Everyone concerned would be satisfied and happy! Yes. That's what he would do. He would offer Louise a very substantial cash settlement – the old 'cheque book diplomacy.' Money had always proved an irresistible 'carrot' to dangle before anybody's eyes, even if they were well off as in the case of Louise. People always wanted to add more to their bank balances. And, all they had to do was to keep their mouths shut – or to open them, when told to do so! If an offer of cash failed, he would offer Louise a 'silent' partnership in his company or anything to make her agree to remain married to him for the next twelve months until he received his knighthood!

He sat back in his chair and smiled. 'After I became Sir Edward, she could do any damn thing she liked!' he muttered under his breath.

He was reminded what Cummings, an old resident, had told him when he first arrived in Singapore. Cummings had said, 'Have all the fun you can my boy, but for Christ's sake, don't marry a local woman. When you get tired of her, pay her off! If you wish to marry, choose a White woman. They are always a safe investment, although when it comes to the bedroom, I'd choose a little local lass any time! Many of our chaps have a White woman as a Number One wife and a local mistress or two if they can afford it. But, should you have trouble with a local woman, make what is known as an "agreeable arrangement" and offer her money. Local women appreciate that sort of thing. It gives them "face." A White man's dirty linen should never be washed in public. Remember that always!'

But Cummings had not explained how an 'agreeable arrangement' could be concluded with a prim-and-proper White woman of substantial means who had suffered public humiliation caused by her husband's lies and misconduct with another woman who was his former mistress.

When Edward Traff left the golf club he had decided on a plan of action. He would appeal to Louise's sense of reason and compassion and beg her to react in a manner expected of a decent, well-bred, English lady. This was one case Edward Traff knew he had to win, out of court.

He would speak to her that night.

As Louise re-entered the mansion from the garden, she saw Ah Ling dusting and cleaning. The other servants were busy elsewhere. Louise approached her uneasily.

'Ah Ling I wish to speak to you, please,' she said. Ah Ling noticed Louise's eyes were red from crying. She sat on a settee and made room beside her for the *amah*. 'Please sit down.'

Ah Ling remained standing, looking at Louise with a slight frown. 'What I have to say is very important. Please sit down,' said Louise again. There were tears in her eyes.

Ah Ling sat down cautiously, on the edge of the settee. She had never seen a 'foreign devil' woman cry before. She had heard stories from some of her friends who also worked for European households, that these strange *ang moh* seldom displayed their emotions, rarely shed tears at funerals and didn't even care to hire professional criers and mourners to perform that duty as was done at Chinese funerals.

Why didn't this *ang moh* woman mind losing so much 'face' in front of a Chinese servant? Ah Ling wondered.

Louise stared briefly into the old woman's eyes and looked away.

'Oh, Ah Ling! I am so miserable! I am sure you know the reason why, don't you? I spent last night in a spare bedroom.'

The *amah* knew about it but chose to stare at the floor without replying.

'I have only just found out about Carmen Chang, you see, Mr Traff never told me about her and their son before we were married.' She took a deep breath and her face suddenly hardened. 'He has deceived me! He hid the truth from me! And I heard about it from some woman at a party last night. It was terrible!'

Tears rolled down her bony face again. 'Oh, Ah Ling, please try to understand how I feel!' she said gripping the *amah's* hand, then quickly releasing it.

Ah Ling continued to stare at the floor.

'Please say something, ' Louise cried.

The *amah* looked at her and to Louise's surprise, saw her grin, displaying four gold teeth.

'No cry! Why you cry? You Number One wife! You must happy!'. Ah Ling's grin widened.

Louise sprang to her feet, fresh tears brimming in her eyes.

'You must never say things like that to me again, Ah Ling!' said Louise, raising her voice a little. 'It may be all right for some Chinese men to have a Number One wife and a Number Two wife and a string of concubines, but I am English and a Christian and so is Mr Traff! Christians are not allowed more than one wife!'

She paused to catch her breath. 'I don't suppose you understand a word I am saying, do you?' Then, realising she may have hurt Ah Ling's feeling by what she had said, she quickly resumed her seat. 'I am sorry if I have offended you. Please forgive me. I am so confused and miserable,' she said softly.

The *amah* continued to stare at her.

Louise took a deep breath. 'Ah Ling, I have to ask you to do me a big favour. I wish to meet Carmen Chang. I'll be most grateful if you could arrange it.'

The woman stared at Louise for some time. 'Why you want see Carmen?'

Louise took another deep breath before answering. 'I wish to tell her I shall be leaving this house and returning to England as soon as possible!'

The *amah* frowned and nodded her head slowly. 'How soon could you arrange a meeting with Carmen?'

'Tomollow, okay?'

'Oh, yes! Tomorrow would be fine!' said Louise.

Ah Ling stood up and took a few steps. She stopped and

turning round, said, 'You no tell Mr Traff I take you go see Carmen tomollow, okay?'

'No. I won't say anything to him! I promise!'

When Edward Traff returned home that evening he found Louise in the study, reading a book.

'Ah, so this is where you are!' he said, quickly stooping to kiss her on the forehead before she had time to avoid it. He put his briefcase on a table and said, 'I thought you'd be in the garden enjoying the sunset.'

She took no notice of him and continued reading.

Edward sat on the arm of a chair in front of her, gently twirling some brandy in a glass. He looked at her steadily. Small talk was not going to get him anywhere with her, he decided. He would come straight to the point. He got to his feet and taking a sip from his glass, stood before her, his short legs apart, a favourite courtroom stance when arguing a case.

'Louise, my dear,' he began, 'I wish you to do me a great favour, for which I shall forever be grateful.'

He was watching her closely, but she pretended he wasn't there. 'I am asking you . . . begging you to forgive me. If that's not possible, then I am prepared to do everything I can to compensate you most handsomely!'

He paused to take another sip from his glass. 'But I beg of you, don't leave me!' he pleaded in a low, wavering voice and shut his eyes as though he was fighting back tears. When he opened them, he fully expected to see her in a more responsive mood. But instead he saw her staring at him in a most hostile manner.

Snapping her book shut, Louise stood up and faced him. 'You are afraid that if I left you and started divorce proceedings your chances of receiving a knighthood would be adversely affected. Isn't that so? If you think I was fooled by your emotion-filled voice just now, you are mistaken. What a very devious man you are! You expect me to continue with this charade for which I shall receive payment? Like some street woman who is prepared to be paid for her favours? Is that what you want me to do?' she said, her face flushed with anger.

He lowered his eyes.

'There is no hope of a compromise?' he asked softly.

'No!'

'Are you thinking of leaving me?'

'Yes!'

'When?'

'As soon as possible!'

He felt his blood freeze. He sat down heavily in a deep leather chair and placed his head between his hands, his elbows resting on his knees. He shut his eyes and sighed deeply.

'Can't you please wait until the end of the year? I beg you,' he pleaded. 'Have you no feelings at all for me?'

She glared at him. 'Whatever feelings I had have been destroyed by you! I can see your scheme so clearly now! What a fool I've been! But how was I, a stranger to Singapore, to have known? I never suspected for a moment the reason why you wanted me to be your wife. It was simply because I didn't have any idea about your past. You lost no time in proposing marriage. I fitted the part so well, didn't I? I am a respectable woman of some standing and substantial means and of course by marrying me you would have been able to hide all the skeletons in your cupboard and cleared the way for your knighthood! But your plan has exploded in your face, Edward Traff!'

There was a knock on the door. It was Ah Ling who had come to say that dinner was served.

Louise went directly upstairs to her room and locked the door.

Edward sat at the dining table alone. He took his time eating and enjoyed his food, as he always did. He returned to the study after dinner to drink some more brandy and to think of a way in which he could change Louise's attitude towards him but nothing came to mind.

The visions he had of himself at the investiture ceremony at Buckingham Palace to receive his knighthood began to fade rapidly and he spent another restless night on a couch in his study.

Louise came down from her room the next morning and went to the far end of the garden to enjoy the bright morning sun. She had expected to see Edward at the breakfast table but an hour passed and there was no sign of him. When she went into the house, Ah Ling said, 'Mr Traff go out. No eat blek-fuss.'

Louise sat at the table. Ah Ling poured her a cup of tea and said, 'Last night you no eat dinner. You must very hungly.' Louise looked at the clock on the sideboard. It was nine o'clock.

'Ten o'clock, taxi come. We go see Carmen, ' Ah Ling said.

Louise nodded. 'Did Carmen ask why I wished to see her?'

'She no ask.'

'I think I'll take her some flowers,' said Louise.

'I or-leady buy present for you to give Carmen.'

'Oh? What present did you get for her?'

'I buy the Chinese sweet cake. Very good for good luck! For much money! For much happy!' Ah Ling laughed.

Ah Ling sat beside the Chinese taxi driver as they whizzed down Mount Pleasant Road. Twenty minutes later they were in River Valley Road. She said something to the driver in Chinese and the taxi began to slow down. It halted in front of an ancient row of shop-houses, the mouldy-pink limewash hanging in greyish-green strips.

The *amah* paid the driver and said to Louise, 'Carmen stay here.' She got out quickly, opening the rear door for Louise. She pointed to a flight of wooden steps between two ground-floor apartments. 'Carmen stay upstair.'

The staircase was dark and the wooden steps creaked under

their weight. They reached the top of the stairs and stood before a wooden door that had once been varnished. Ah Ling pressed the doorbell. A young Chinese girl in a *samfu* opened the door. Seeing Ah Ling, she bowed and greeted her.

'Go inside,' said Ah Ling gently pushing Louise through the open door.

They entered a small sitting-room furnished with some old cane chairs, a settee and a low table. On a shelf below the table were newspapers and magazines. Dusty pink and blue cloth flowers drooped from small vases on the walls. From the ceiling hung a long black-and-red electric wire with a bulb attached that was covered by a paper lampshade.

Ah Ling pointed to a chair and said, 'Please sit,' as the young girl ran inside.

Louise sat on the edge of the chair, her eyes still roaming the room.

'Soon, Carmen come,' said Ah Ling who watched Louise nervously clasp and unclasp her hands.

There were sounds coming from the corridor that led to the rear. Louise gripped the arms of her chair and momentarily held her breath. Approaching her in a wheelchair that was being pushed by the girl was a grey-haired Chinese woman in a black silk *samfu*.

She smiled at Louise as she drew nearer. 'Mrs Traff, how good of you to come!' she called out cheerily.

'I am Carmen Chang,' she said offering her hand to Louise.

Louise got up and shook her hand, muttering, 'How do you do,' as though she was coming out of a daze. Then she heard Carmen say, 'Please be seated.'

It was a while before Louise recovered from the shock of discovering that Carmen Chang was a cripple. Carmen wore neither jewellery nor make-up but she had a beautiful face and clear, black eyes that sparkled. There were faint lines at the corners of her eyes. Her mouth was well-formed and her skin was creamy-white.

A feeling of pity and shame gripped Louise and she felt like crying. Why hadn't Ah Ling informed her that Carmen was a cripple? Did she keep it away from her on purpose to embarrass her even further?

Ah Ling spoke to Carmen briefly in Chinese and gave her the box containing the 'good luck' cake and went to the rear of the flat.

'How nice of you to have brought me a present. Thank you. Sweet things are supposed to bring good fortune to the giver as well as the receiver, according to the Chinese,' she said with a light laugh.

Louise heard herself mumbling, 'Oh, it was Ah Ling's choice, really.'

'However, it was very nice of you to come. I don't get many visitors, you know,' she said. 'I suppose it's because I'm such a terrible bore. Now, don't say you haven't been warned!'

Her cheerfulness only added more confusion to Louise's mind and she was totally at a loss as to how she should deal with this unexpected and embarrassing situation.

What was she to say to this woman who seemed quite unaffected by the fact that she was meeting, for the first time the wife of her former lover with whom she had a child? She seemed so irritatingly relaxed, so devastatingly composed, so fluent and articulate . . . and she was beautiful! She must have looked like a Chinese goddess twenty-five years ago, Louise thought. Why hadn't Edward married her?

The young girl appeared with a tray of tea that she placed on the table in front of them and filled two cups from a Chinese teapot.

'I'm afraid it's Chinese tea without milk or sugar. Or, would you prefer a soft drink instead, Mrs Traff?' asked Carmen.

This was the second time Carmen had addressed her as 'Mrs Traff' and her casualness was discomforting.

'Chinese tea is fine, thank you,' said Louise, adding quickly, 'Will you please call me Louise?

Carmen looked into her eyes and smiled. 'Then you must call me Carmen.'

Louise sipped her tea thoughtfully, her eyes on the wall vases with those pathetic, faded cloth flowers. Then looking at Carmen, she said, 'I realise you have tried to put me at ease. I am much obliged. It was something that I had least expected in the circumstances.'

Carmen smiled. 'Circumstances are conditions of life like different sets of rules by which one has to live and which affect us in different ways. It is how we adapt that's important, don't you think?'

'Yes, I suppose so,' said Louise uncertainly, 'but at times there are circumstances that could be rather exceptional.'

'Is that the reason why you have come to see me? To discuss exceptional circumstances?'

Louise did not reply. Without realising it, she found herself staring at Carmen's legs.

'How did it happen?' she asked softly.

'Oh, shortly before Rupert, my son, was born, I had a bad fall. There were complications later. There was nothing the doctors could have done. My spine was damaged.'

She quickly changed the subject. 'My son Rupert is twenty-three and in his final year reading law at Cambridge. I have a photograph of him. Not a recent one, though.' She reached for a photo album from under the table before them and removing a large, loose photograph from it, handed it to Louise. She sat back in her wheelchair, watching Louise's face.

It was a photograph of a bespectacled young man. His face could have been Chinese if not for his Caucasian nose. He had a plain, honest face, Louise thought. She returned the photograph and said, 'He looks like a fine young man. You must be very proud of him.'

'Oh, yes, indeed,' said Carmen with pride, admiring the photograph briefly before returning it to the album.

They were silent for some moments. Then Louise,

looking away said, 'I have come here to tell you I am leaving Edward.'

'Why? Is it because you've only just found out about me?' asked Carmen smiling.

So, Ah Ling had told her everything! 'That's one reason. There are others. Did Edward tell you he was marrying me?'

Carmen raised her eyebrows. 'No. Why should he have done so? There hasn't been any communication between us since the time I left The Manor twenty-five years ago. I only knew about your marriage to him when I saw your wedding photograph in the newspapers.'

Louise's face reddened suddenly. 'He never told me about you and your son,' she said, her eyes wide. 'It was only two days ago that I learned about it at a party, from one of those awful women and in a most humiliating manner!'

She paused to control her anger that had suddenly returned when she heard Carmen say, 'But that shouldn't upset you. After all, you're his legal wife.'

Louise felt her face had become suddenly hot and raising her voice a little, said, 'It all seems so wrong! So very wrong! The way I was manipulated by him! I've been made to look such a fool! But how was I to even suspect . . . '

She bit her bottom lip and shook her head from side to side.

'Manipulated by him?' asked Carmen.

'Yes, manipulated!' said Louise hotly. 'It's only now that I realise he married me because I knew nothing about his past because he's expecting a knighthood at the end of the year and he didn't want anything to spoil his chances of getting it!'

She looked at Carmen, her eyes red with anger and continued, 'He is begging me not to leave him and is willing to pay me handsomely to keep up the farce of being his wife until he is knighted!'

She paused to control herself and said after a few moments asked, 'Why didn't he marry you?'

Carmen looked at Louise's unhappy face and wondered if she should tell her how it all happened, but changed her mind. She said, 'I suppose it was a case of exceptional circumstances, to use your expression. And, a person placed in such circumstances cannot expect too much. I am Chinese, you have to understand.'

'What has being Chinese got to do with it? Many Europeans are married to Chinese. Wasn't there some love between you two?'

'I am not quite sure now whether it was infatuation or just youthful, passionate giddiness. I was only nineteen at the time. I got a job as a typist in his office and certain things happened. I gave up my job and went to live at The Manor as his mistress for two years. I became pregnant and I came to live here.'

Louise stared at her for some moments. 'You mean it ended just like that? Didn't he ask you to marry him?'

'No,' replied Carmen with a smile. 'As soon as he knew I was carrying his child he moved me out of The Manor and into this flat that he had bought for me. I realised marriage was out of the question. He promised to provide for me. I accepted the situation. It was an agreeable arrangement.'

'An agreeable arrangement on his terms, you mean! But couldn't a beautiful, intelligent woman like yourself have married someone else, instead of being an abandoned mistress and condemned to spend the rest of her life in a wheelchair?' Louise asked, tears in her eyes.

'I am sorry I have upset you so much,' said Carmen noticing the tears rolling down Louise's face. 'But, you see, there are some things that may be difficult for a European to understand. No Chinese would ever take me as his wife. As his mistress, perhaps, but not as his wife, not after I had been the mistress of a European. And, to make matters even worse, I had a child by him. One becomes ostracised, you know. The only hope for a woman in similar circumstances is for her to marry a European. They are rather broad-minded when it comes to such matters.'

Louise was aghast. 'How horrible!' she cried. 'You have far better manners and character than some of the dreadful European women I've had the displeasure of meeting in the short time I've been in Singapore. And you've shown such admirable courage.'

She wiped the tears from her face with a handkerchief and shut her eyes. Her depressed mood left her suddenly. She jumped up smiling, as though she had just remembered something very pleasant and exciting.

As Carmen looked at her in surprise, Louise took her handbag from the settee and said, 'Excuse me, but I think I have to be going. Would you please call out for Ah Ling?'

They shook hands.

'Thank you. I am so glad we met. May I visit you again?' Louise asked.

'Yes, of course,' said Carmen. 'Drop by any time.'

When Louise returned to The Manor she went directly to her room, had a bath and changed. She came downstairs and sat on a settee on the veranda. She called out to Ah Ling to make her some tea and when she brought it to her, Louise said, 'Thank you again for taking me to meet Carmen.'

The *amah* nodded her head and said with a smile, 'Carmen, very good! You, very good! I very happy!'

She poured a cup of tea for Louise and left.

Louise thought about Carmen. 'I am going to try and put things right for Carmen if that's the last thing I do on this earth!' she said to herself.

She poured herself another cup and began to hum a tune.

The phone rang.

She answered it. It was Edward and her mood instantly soured. She fought a tremendous urge to slam the phone down.

'Oh, hello, my dear,' he said smoothly. 'I called earlier but was told you were out with Ah Ling.'

She did not reply.

'Well, I hope you had a pleasant time wherever you went,' he said. 'I have to attend a business dinner and shan't be back until about ten o'clock. I wish to speak to you when I get back. It's important.'

She put the phone down. The sound of his voice nauseated her.

Louise was reading a book in the study when Edward joined her. He handed her an envelope.

'Please read what's inside,' he said pleasantly, lighting a cigar. He took a seat opposite her, his eyes fixed on her face.

It was a draft agreement couched in legal phraseology stating that he was willing to give her ten per cent of his total assets on condition she remained his wife for a period 'not less than twelve months from the date the agreement became legal,' etc.

She replaced the document in the envelope without reading it completely and their eyes met. He smiled uncomfortably and went to the bar to pour a brandy. He stood before her waiting for her to say something.

She was still staring at him.

'I am sorry it had to be worded in such a manner, my dear. But circumstances being such as they are, there was no other way.' He paused to sip his brandy as she continued to stare at him.

'It's only a draft agreement and you are quite free to suggest any amendments subject to my approval.'

She stood up slowly not taking her eyes off him and said icily, 'Another one of your agreeable arrangements?' as she went towards the door.

'When could I expect a reply?' he called after her.

'Tomorrow!'

She went out, slamming the door after her.

It was nine o'clock when Louise awoke the following morning.

She felt fresh and rested, something she had not experienced for some days. She had read the draft agreement Edward had given her several times before she fell into a deep, peaceful sleep. Now, awake, she felt so happy she wanted to sing at the top of her voice.

While she was at Carmen Chang's flat, a thought had suddenly crossed her mind. How wonderful it would be if she could find a way for Carmen to be compensated for her suffering all these years? Now she had found a way to make that possible. Ironically, the answer had been provided in the draft agreement written by Edward Traff himself!

She took her time in the shower and dressed unhurriedly, spending a little more time in front of a mirror. She enjoyed her breakfast, much to Ah Ling's satisfaction.

The *amah* had sensed something was going on in Louise's mind, but didn't ask what it was, although she knew it had to do with Carmen.

Louise went to the telephone table and picked up a book with some private telephone numbers. She thumbed through the pages and came to the name she was looking for. It was that of James Orr, a solicitor whom she had met at a church fair. He had a Chinese wife and two young children. He would be just the right person to draw up an agreement on her terms that she would present to Edward Traff!

They met for lunch. She showed Orr the draft agreement Edward had given her. He read it without comment. She told him about her meeting with Carmen.

'Oh, how is she?' he asked smiling. 'My wife and I visit her when we have the time and she spends the weekend with us sometimes. Her son Rupert will be returning to Singapore soon as a lawyer. She saved every cent she could from the allowance Edward gave her for Rupert's studies in England. Carmen is quite a remarkable lady!'

'Oh? She didn't say a word about this to me. From what Edward told me, I was under the impression that he had paid for everything. Dear, oh dear! What that poor woman has been through!'

'What do you want me to do with this?' he asked, holding up Edward's draft agreement.

Her face brightened.

'Well, my late husband left me with very substantial means, Mr Orr. I don't want a cent of Edward's money. He is offering me ten per cent of all his assets so long as I remain his wife for twelve months, until he received his knighthood. Well, I would like you to make an agreement stating I am quite prepared to do so but only on condition that he agrees to pay Carmen Chang twenty-five per cent of his total assets; that I shall live apart from him and that I shall be free to divorce him after a period of twelve months.'

James Orr seemed to be taken aback momentarily. Then he burst out laughing.

'What's so amusing?' asked Louise.

'The thought of the look on Edward's face when he reads your terms!' he said.

'Could you please have a draft agreement ready by this afternoon?' she asked happily. 'I wish to show Mr Edward Traff that he is not the only one who can make agreeable arrangements!'

'Oh, of course!' he replied happily.

'And do you think you could have the same agreement stamped and ready for his signature and mine tomorrow morning at your office?'

'You seem rather certain he will agree to sign it?'

'Oh, he will! You'll see!'

'It gives me great pleasure to do this,' said Orr as they shook hands. 'You are a very remarkable woman.'

'Doing this has given me such a wonderful feeling of joy! It's quite hard to describe, really!' she said.

When Edward Traff read the draft of his wife's terms that James Orr had prepared, he looked up at her from his chair in his study. His eyes were blazing. He flung the document on the floor, springing to his feet.

'This is outrageous! It's damn blackmail!' he shouted. 'That swine, Orr! He hates my guts! He set you up to this filthy conspiracy with Carmen because he and his wife are friends of hers! You'll never get away with this! Never! Do you hear? I'll use all my influence! I'll expose this devilish plot!'

Louise sat in a chair in front of him, smiling.

'Hush!' she said. 'You don't seem to be your usual calm and resourceful self. But let me tell you, James Orr and Carmen had nothing to do with this. It was my own little idea. Try to be fair for once in your life.'

She picked up the document from the floor and threw it onto his lap.

'Agreeable arrangements cannot be one-sided. Of course, you wouldn't agree with that, would you?' she said with a smile.

Edward stared at the floor for some time and when he looked up she saw his bottom lip was trembling. His face was red and there were tears in his eyes.

She was on her way to the door when she stopped and said over her shoulder, 'Oh, by the way, Mr Orr will be expecting us at his office at ten o'clock tomorrow morning for our signatures. I'm sure you will do your best to attend, won't you?'

He left his chair and came towards her.

'Don't do this to me!' he said, tears rolling down his fat cheeks.

She stood in the doorway looking at him with a smile. He reminded her of a very large, pathetic pig. She closed the door behind her.

Carmen Cheng was surprised to receive a phone call from Louise about noon the following day.

'Of course, you can come right away,' said Carmen. 'You sound so happy!'

'You'll know why later, my dear. I'm leaving for London tonight!' said Louise.

It was a brief but warm meeting. They exchanged addresses and Carmen gave her Rupert's address in London.

'But you haven't told me the reason why you are leaving so suddenly,' said Carmen.

'You'll know the reason after you've read this!' she said, handing her an envelope containing a copy of the agreement Edward and she had signed before James Orr earlier that morning.

She kissed Carmen quickly on both cheeks. 'I'm in an awful rush. I'll be in touch,' she said cheerily.

'But, please tell me what this is,' said Carmen holding up the envelope.

'It contains the terms of a most agreeable arrangement!' said Louise with a grin.

She quickly opened the door and with a wave of her hand, went out.

Esprit de Corps

'That typically English characteristic for which there is no English name – *esprit de corps*.'– Sir Frank Adcock

'A great pity about Carruthers', said Edwards as he sipped a beer at the Malacca Rest House.

'Yes' said Loveridge thoughtfully. 'He was fine officer and a *pukka* gentleman!'

The two men had served under Police Superintendent Carruthers for almost ten years in Kuala Lumpur during the 1960s and had now retired. Carruthers had been asked to stay on in an advisory capacity because of his vast experience with secret societies.

'I'd give it a year or so more and then retire, too' he had told them. Edwards and his wife had gone to live with their married son in England while Loveridge had become a partner in a private investigation agency in Kuala Lumpur.

Edwards was visiting old friends in Malacca and was staying at the Rest House. He had informed Loveridge of his impending arrival and Loveridge had made a special trip to Malacca to meet him. Both men and Carruthers had joined the British colonial police force together, some forty years before.

'The London newspapers only had a couple of paragraphs about Carruthers' death,' said Edwards. 'What a terrible accident.'

Loveridge said: 'The local papers had splashed the whole

251

thing across their front pages since Carruthers was so well known, together with his photograph and service record,' said Loveridge. 'A revolver was found near his body. The newspapers said the police didn't suspect foul play. The coroner's inquest was short and sweet. The ballistics report said the bullet had been fired from the same .38 found beside him. There was a wound on the right side of his head and evidence to show the gun could have been fired accidentally. The coroner's verdict was "death by misadventure", which was expected and it pleased all concerned, especially Blake, the Chief of Investigations. He had personally taken charge of the case.'

He paused to take a sip from his glass of whisky before he continued. 'I'm glad the whole affair ended the way it did. Carruthers was too fine an officer to have finished a distinguished career with a black mark in his record book.'

'What do you mean by that?' asked Edwards.

'Well, the truth is, just between ourselves, Carruthers had committed suicide,' said Loveridge.

'Suicide?' repeated Edwards, raising his eyebrows. 'But he seemed such a happy sort of chap with a nice family and was fairly well off. His daughter had married well and I remember him telling me he was thinking of buying a house in Kuala Lumpur which had made his wife, Tammy, very happy.'

Loveridge nodded his head and lit his pipe.

'I don't think you knew that Carruthers and his wife had separated?' asked Loveridge, noting Edwards' increased surprise.

Loveridge went on, 'Well, it happened a year after he took his new job as consultant with Investigations at Kuala Lumpur. Carruthers took me into his confidence one night after a few drinks and made me promise what he told me would not be repeated to anyone. 'He said his wife had found out he was having an affair with a Vietnamese woman by the name of Michelle. She, incidentally, had escaped from Saigon before the North Vietnamese took over and managed to arrive in Kuala Lumpur on a forged passport.

'Well, she soon became the mistress of a wealthy Chinese businessman who died shortly afterwards under rather mysterious circumstances. But nothing was proven. She had quite a bit of cash from the old fellow with which she opened a Vietnamese restaurant in Kuala Lumpur where Carruthers first met her. Although she was in her early forties and had suffered the ravages of war in Vietnam since she was a young girl, she managed to retain her good looks and I must say, she was still a very attractive and desirable woman. She spoke fairly good English and excellent French, of course. I also found her to be a most charming and intelligent person on the few occasions I met her when Carruthers took me to lunch at her restaurant.

'At the beginning, his relationship with her was platonic. But, as you can well understand, such relationships have a way of turning into serious affairs, especially when there's an attractive woman involved. I remember someone saying it was impossible for a man and a woman to be good friends without sex eventually playing a major part in their relationship. Well, that's exactly what happened.

'Anyone could easily see he had become very attracted to her and it was around this time that boatloads of Vietnamese refugees began to arrive along the east coast of Malaya. The authorities were thrown into a flat spin. They had to arrange accommodation and food, medical facilities and so on for these poor, half-starved people. Whole families arrived in open boats. I'm sure you must have read about this in the newspapers?'

'Oh, indeed,' said Edwards.

Loveridge continued, 'With the arrival of more refugees Investigations was faced with a security problem since nobody knew how many undesirable people were among them. This meant having to screen each refugee thoroughly and at the same time having to keep the secret societies and gangsters from getting at them, since most of them carried gold and jewellery. This was when Carruthers was called in to help. He was asked by Investigations to head a special unit that would interrogate the refugees that was a most difficult and painstaking job and he was told to set up his unit as soon as possible.

'He was in urgent need of a Vietnamese interpreter and without any hesitation asked Michelle to fill the position. She joined Carruthers' team and was well paid for her services, I might add. They saw a lot of each other. They worked late into the night and he began to spend days away from home with her, of course.

'His wife, Tammy was understanding to a point, until she discovered he had rented a flat that he had conveniently forgotten to tell her about since it had become his secret love nest.

'His wife had found it difficult to contact her husband by phone at his office and one day decided to pay him a visit at his flat. She must have obtained his address from someone and when she got there, he was at work. But the *amah* had let her in after she told her who she was. Tammy was horrified to find the only bedroom occupied had a wardrobe full of women's clothes as well as those belonging to her husband.

'Tammy went to his office and took him to a restaurant where she, in her usual calm manner, asked him about what she had discovered. He didn't try to deny he was having an affair. Tammy, quite surprisingly accepted the situation although it was the first time in the twenty-two years they had been married that anything like this had happened to either of them.

'Tammy had asked him to give up his job and to end the affair. All would be forgiven and forgotten. They would buy a bungalow and settle down to a quiet, happy life, that I thought was most generous of her. But he seemed to be confused and not at all keen to discuss any plans with his wife. Before their meeting ended she informed him she was going to live with her mother in Australia that would give him time to sort things out.

'By now his affair with Michelle was well known. But what could anyone have done about it?

'On the day I met him, he told me his wife had written several letters so had his married daughter in Canada, pleading with him to end his affair. He did not reply to these letters.

'Some time later he received a deed of separation from his wife's lawyers in Sydney for his signature, which he signed.

'By now, he had fallen hopelessly in love with Michelle who was taking full advantage of her relationship with him by assuming she was in full charge of interrogating refugees; which he had foolishly allowed her to do. He told me that Michelle had become overbearing and bossy. At the same time her affection for him was declining rather rapidly.

'He said she was treating him like a dog. He tried reasoning with her but to spite him she began spending nights away from home. He had good reason to suspect she was seeing other men since she loved gambling, drinking and dancing.

'There had been some terrible fights. Carruthers wanted to leave her but hadn't the courage to do so. He even thought of contacting his wife to patch things up but was afraid she would reject him since it had been more than a year since they had separated.

'He told me his mind was "in one awful turmoil", to use his own words. I couldn't help but feel sorry for him despite the stupid thing he had done and the mess he had got himself into. The only advice I could have given him was to leave this woman and to seek his wife's forgiveness. But I didn't offer this advice to him because he had made it rather clear to me he was still very much in love with Michelle.

'I didn't meet Carruthers for some time after that meeting but one morning while I was at my office, I was surprised to get a phone call from him. He sounded very distraught and asked me if I would meet him at a restaurant. I agreed.

'I was shocked to see the state he was in. His hair was uncut, his face looked haggard and unshaven. His clothes hung on him. Could you ever imagine the smart, spit-and-polish Superintendent Carruthers appearing like that? But, there he was! A mess!

'He grabbed my hand, led me to a corner table and sat down. His eyes were bloodshot. There was an unfinished glass of whisky on the table.

' "I'm so glad to see you!"' he said. ' "I'm in one bloody awful mess. You're not going to believe what I tell you, but every word is true!" '

'He ran his fingers slowly through his hair and he clenched his fists. Then he said, "Do you know Michelle's been robbing the refugees of their gold and jewellery? It's been going on for some months now and right under my nose! I didn't have the slightest idea such a thing was happening until a couple of days ago when one of my detectives told me what she was up to! He hadn't told me earlier because he knew she was my mistress and didn't wish to interfere.

'He told me he had made the detective promise not to tell anyone else what he knew, but at the same time realised the detective wasn't the only person who knew what Michelle was doing.

'Carruthers gripped my arm tightly and said, "The detective told me something that made my blood freeze. Michelle had told the refugees the gold and jewellery she was taking away from them was for me! And if they didn't hand over their valuables, I would send them back to Vietnam!" '

'Carruthers was on the verge of tears, not because of self-pity, but because of the humiliation and disgrace he had brought upon himself and the whole police force.

'I was too shaken by what he had told me and the pathetic state he was in, to offer any advice except that he should tell Blake, the Chief of Investigations the whole sordid story.

'He replied, "But what good would that do? Michelle is quite capable of getting some others who were in this racket with her to say the whole thing was my idea, like she had told the refugees. The chief will throw the book at me! You know what he's like! Do you expect him to believe I didn't know this was going on all these months? Why had I allowed her to assume such high-handed authority? Could I tell him it was because I loved her? Good lord! My brother officers would spit in my face! I'll be charged in court and sent to prison – which I deserve! But think of the shame I've brought to everybody – to my wife and daughter!" '

'He stood up suddenly and without saying another word ran out of the restaurant. I went after him but he was nowhere to be seen. He blew his brains out that night.'

Loveridge paused to finish the whisky in his glass and said, 'I was told he had written a long letter to the chief before he killed himself. As a result of what he had revealed in it, investigations were able to crack down on the whole filthy business Michelle and her accomplices were involved in. Heavy prison sentences were imposed. Of course, Carruthers' name was kept out of all the proceedings – the chief saw to that!'

'What became of this woman, Michelle?' asked Edwards.

'The bitch was deported to Vietnam. She had pleaded guilty, fully expecting the judge to send her to prison in Kuala Lumpur. But he told her she was going to be deported back to Vietnam. Hearing this, she became violent, accusing the chief of tricking her into admitting her guilt. She said the chief had promised her that she would be imprisoned in Kuala Lumpur.

'She went on her knees to the judge, pleading with him not to send her back to Vietnam because she said the North Vietnamese would kill her. She had been a spy for the South Vietnamese during the war, so she claimed. However, she was packed off without much delay. The chief personally put her on a North Vietnamese freighter bound for Haiphong. The North Vietnamese authorities probably shot her. If they did, she bloody well deserved it after what she had done to Carruthers! He had become a lump of clay in her hands!'

'But why did she accuse the chief of being a liar in front of the judge? Did she have any reason to?' asked Edwards.

Loveridge paused for a moment and said, 'Strictly between ourselves, old chap, Chief of Investigations Blake had told

Michelle after her arrest that if she pleaded guilty to the charges and kept Carruthers' name out of the case, he would see to it that she received a light sentence and sent to Pudu Prison in Kuala Lumpur. Blake had realised she was determined to blame Carruthers for everything. She said what she had done was with his approval!'

Loveridge looked at Edwards steadily.

'Did Carruthers have a finger in the pie? Did he know what she was up to and kept quiet about it because of his love for her?' asked Edwards.

Loveridge shrugged his shoulders and grinned. 'Rather late in the day to try and find that out! But, Blake knew the truth, you could bet your last dollar on that! Anyway, he was not going to allow a Vietnamese whore to disgrace an officer of the colonial police force and tarnish our good image – even if she had been telling the truth! It stands to reason, doesn't it, old fellow. I'd have done the same for you and you for me. *Esprit de corps* and all that, old chap!"

Edwards said seriously, 'Full marks to Blake! It was damn fortunate that he took charge of the case from the start and saw that matters were properly handled. You know how court cases sometimes throw up such unnecessary filth about innocent people?'

'Quite,' said Loveridge.

'And what became of the gold and jewellery this woman stole from the refugees?' asked Edwards.

Loveridge replied, 'She kept about a million dollars worth of valuables in Carruthers' private cabinet at his office. Carruthers told Blake in his letter where the loot could be found. The refugees were asked to submit claims and descriptions of the articles taken away from them. It took a bit of time but I think everything was returned to their rightful owners.'

Loveridge told the waiter to refill their glasses.

'Carruthers was buried with full honours, you know,' said Loveridge with a satisfied smile. 'Blake delivered the eulogy.'

'Jolly good show! It makes me so happy to hear that!' said Edwards.

'Did Mrs Carruthers have any reason to suspect her husband had committed suicide?'

Loveridge grinned. 'Good Lord, no! Blake saw to that, too!'

'To the chief!' said Edwards raising his glass.

'To the chief!' said Loveridge, raising his.

Potpourri

'There Are No Chinamen In Singapore!'

Various uncomplimentary terms were used by Asians to describe their British colonial masters. In Singapore and Malaya they were known in the Hokkien (Chinese) dialect as *ang moh kwai* ('red-faced devils.') In Hong Kong the Cantonese called them *gwei-lo* ('red devils'). They were also known by unprintable names by people in other British territories in Southeast Asia.

The resentment against racial discrimination and being economically exploited were rarely expressed, or not at all. The 'immoral, uncultured and ignorant White barbarians' were tolerated and held in silent contempt – which didn't seem to bother them in the least.

The following story may help to illustrate the White man's 'ignorance' as seen through Chinese eyes :

A young Englishman arrived in Singapore in 1929 from England to join a well-known British merchant firm. Getting off the ship at the Tanjong Pagar wharves. He looked curiously at the Chinese clerk from his new company who was sent to meet him and asked, 'You are a Chinaman aren't you, my good man?'

The clerk replied with a smile, 'There are no Chinamen in Singapore, sir! Only Chinese.'

'Oh? And, what's the difference between Chinamen and Chinese?' asked the surprised newcomer.

The clerk who was a Chinese *peranakan* (see Note on next

260

page) pointed to his hair and said with a smile, 'Singapore Chinese have short hair like mine. Chinamen from China have plaited long hair known in Chinese as *tow-chang*.'

'You mean pig-tails?' asked the Englishman.

The clerk thought to himself, 'This *ang moh kwai* is so stupid! How is it possible to grow the tails of a pigs on one's head?' But, remembering an old Chinese saying that "one must be patient with those who are ignorant," he smiled again and said, 'Pig-tails are for making soup, sir. *Tow-chang* are used for chasing away flies.'

Obviously the clerk had not heard of the term 'pig-tails', thought the young Englishman who said with a laugh, 'Yes, of course! Only Chinamen from China have long hair. How silly of me not to have remembered!'

The clerk frowned as he thought, 'This *ang moh kwai* admits he is foolish and laughs about it! He is prepared to "lose face" to me, a humble clerk! It will take much effort on my part to respect a fool!'

On returning to his office, the confused Chinese clerk explained what had happened between him and the new arrival to the elderly Chinese chief clerk who smiled and said, 'In order to survive in this harsh and unpredictable world, one must be prepared to adopt many attitudes but without losing one's identity or dignity. One of them is to become a good actor by not displaying your true feelings about controversial issues and the ignorance of others, no matter how tempted you are to do so. Restraint and tolerance exemplify wisdom, self-discipline and good manners. Sadly, these virtues are unrecognised by Europeans who call us "inscrutable Chinamen." '

Note: Straits-born Chinese were those who were domiciled in the Straits Settlements under British colonial rule. The settlements comprised Penang, Malacca and Singapore and were under a governor. The majority of Chinese had arrived from China to work as 'coolies.' Having lost all physical and cultural contacts with China over the years, they considered themselves distinct from immigrants from China, marrying Malay and Javanese women. Later when their population grew, they married their own kind. They were known as *baba* or *peranakan*, the Malay terms for 'local born' Chinese. Through hard work and enterprise many were able to amass large fortunes in the tin, rubber and spice trades and became wealthy property owners. They were educated in English and spoke Malay at home. Their women dressed in the Malay *sarong* and *kebaya*.

The *babas* were also known as the 'King's Chinese.' They formed the Straits Chinese British Association in Singapore and Malacca in 1900, pledging their loyalty to the British Crown. Many chose to dress like English gentlemen and were quite willing to suffer the tropical heat in tweed suits, with waistcoats, 'sporty' white flannel trousers and striped 'blazers.'

They wore starched shirts with stiff collars and ties, bowler or straw hats and carried walking sticks and rolled-up umbrellas. They also played cricket, soccer, rugby, billiards and lawn bowls to keep apace with their English counterparts. Many had sent their children to be educated at schools, colleges and universities in Britain. So deep was their loyalty to Britain that they wanted to send a contingent of Straits Chinese to assist British troops to fight the Chinese 'boxers' (a martial arts organisation supported by the Dowager Empress Tz'u Hzi during the 'Boxer Uprising'in China in 1900.) The 'boxers' were against growing British, French, Russian and American influence and commercial exploitation of China. The European powers sent troops to protect their nationals in China, resulting in hostilities.

The Straits Chinese had formed a Chinese infantry company of volunteers that performed guard duties in Singapore during World War I (1914–1918) and the Straits Chinese British Association made generous donations to the British war effort that they repeated in World War II (1939–1945). Chinese volunteers went into action against the Japanese when they invaded Singapore in February1942.

Except for those who had been converted to other religions, *peranakan* Chinese to this day observe Chinese customs such as ancestor worship, marriage and funeral ceremonies.

The 'Chinaman' Stigma

Min-Ch'ien T.Z. Tyau, the author of the book, *London Through Chinese Eyes*, wrote a letter to the *Manchester Guardian*, the newspaper, while he was a student in London in 1912 in which he said that the term 'Chinaman' was used to describe Chinese laundrymen and coolies on the Pacific coast of the United States. Thereafter, the term became commonly used to describe Chinese irrespective of their professions or social status. He said the term 'Chinaman' apart from being used in a degrading and prejudicial manner by Westerners was also ungrammatical. He pointed out that the term should rightly be 'Chineseman' or if the noun were dropped, it should be 'Chinese.'

Tyau said that efforts were made by Chinese students in London, many of whom came from Malaya, Singapore and Hong Kong, to change the term 'Chinaman' to 'Chinese' and appealed to the government minister in charge of Chinese Affairs to have this done. They also presented a stage play to support their campaign. But, all to no avail.

Tyau had remarked: 'It seemed the forces of tradition and convention were impregnable and we failed signally.'

Divide And Rule

After he signed a treaty with the Johore sultanate in 1819 that placed Singapore under British control, Thomas Stamford Raffles, an officer of the British East India Company who was later knighted, decided that the island's population that consisted mainly of Chinese, some Malays, Javanese, a few Arabs, Indians and Europeans should settle in different areas of the island.

The Chinese were moved to the south, west of the Singapore River; the Malays, Indians and others to the east and the Europeans to the hilly north, well away from the 'native dwellings' and the Singapore River's unpleasant odour.

A policy of 'divide and rule' was born and that was to last for more than a century.

The governors of the island who were the king's or queen's representatives, ruled with supreme authority. (There were no political parties or trade unions until after the end of World War II in 1945.)

Under colonial rule the population was allowed to practice their respective religions and cultures, build churches, temples and mosques so long as they did not interfere with government policies and the peculiar and secluded lifestyles of the European *tuans* and *mems*.

Government and mission schools employed English teachers and attracted European as well as 'local' students. Although there was a prevailing 'colour bar,' schoolchildren were not segregated in government and mission schools. There were also schools run by the various communities where students were taught in their respective mother-tongues such as Chinese, Malay and Tamil.

There were no official 'Whites Only' areas in Malaya and Singapore although such restrictions were in force at certain 'exclusive' clubs and hotels. There was no necessity to put up notices to this effect. The 'locals' knew, without having to be told that they should avoid such 'White reservations.' There were many prominent 'locals' who had rejected this display of colour prejudice. However, their resentment was placated somewhat when a prominent Chinese doctor pointed out, 'I cannot see the reason why we "locals' are so resentful about not being permitted into "Europeans only" clubs and hotels. We should in fact be grateful that such rules existed because they quarantined us from being contaminated by some disgusting Western habits! I think I'd spare myself the embarrassment by not explaining what these are!'

The various communities had their own recreation and community associations that were funded by themselves. There was keen rivalry on the paying field between 'local' and European teams, some made up by members of the British army. However, Malayan states and Singapore included Europeans in their representative teams.

According to a Colonial Office report, 'feelings between the British and "local" communities were cordial but aloof.'

This was in sharp contrast to the sentiment between the British and Chinese communities in the British Concession in Shanghai's International Settlement and in Hong Kong where a 'Whites Only' restriction was imposed by law, much to the humiliation and anger of Chinese in these places.

After the outbreak of the Sino-Japanese war in 1937 an International Settlement was created in Shanghai separating areas occupied by the Japanese from those by Westerners. At the entrance to the Public Gardens (now known as Huangpu Park) that was modelled on the lines of a typical English garden and which was looked after with meticulous care, was a notice board with regulations that park users had to observe. One such regulation prohibited the entry of 'dogs and Chinese.' In Hong Kong a 'Whites Only' residential area was established on Victoria Peak (also known as 'The Peak.')

In government and private offices in Singapore and Malaya, European staff had keys that admitted them to 'European wash rooms.' Local staff were prohibited from smoking while working at their office desks and obliged to do so in toilets. Smoking in front of Europeans was 'not done' and considered 'disrespectful' except at some places of entertainment such as cinemas where the 'locals' usually occupied the cheap seats which were nearest to the screen and at a 'safe' distance from the *tuans* and *mems*.

The 'first class' was reserved for Europeans on trains operated by the FMSR (Federated Malay States Railway) with connections to the various states in Malaya and Singapore and on passenger ships owned by the Straits Steamship Company that ran services from Singapore to Penang, Sarawak and British North Borneo.

At the Singapore General Hospital, there was a 'European Ward' staffed by European doctors and nurses. Blood transfusions were made with blood only from European donors.

When Singapore's defence forces were mobilised to resist the Japanese invasion in 1941, a 'local' private in the Singapore Volunteer Corps (SVC) was paid 50 cents per day while a European conscript private was paid $1.06 cents per day.

Spotted Dogs

Although this incident took place in Kuala Lumpur it has a Singapore 'connection', since it concerns a well-known Singapore Chinese *towkay* ('wealthy Chinese businessman') and his first visit to Kuala Lumpur in 1929 that he would have good reason not to forget in a hurry.

While in Kuala Lumpur, Towkay Tan, as he shall be known, was staying with his brother-in-law who, like himself, was the owner of several Dalmatians, a breed of large, white, dark-spotted dog.

The day after his arrival in Kuala Lumpur, Towkay Tan decided to do some sight-seeing by himself and took along two of his brother-in-law's Dalmatians for company in a car driven by his nephew. While passing by the Padang and the well-kept grounds of the 'Europeans only' Selangor Club, he was informed by his newpew that the Club was also known as 'The Spotted Dog.'

'You mean spotted dog, like Dalmatian, *ah*?' asked Towkay Tan.

'I suppose so, ' replied his nephew who was at a loss to explain a strange 'British tradition' to name pubs and clubs after animals, remembering there was a British-owned pub in Kuala Lumpur that was called, The Fox And Hare.

'*Wah!* They got special club for Dalmatian in Kuala Lumpur!' exclaimed Towkay Tan and asked his nephew to take him to the club.

Towkay Tan walked happily into the building and was met by a short-tempered, old Scotsman who was the club's secretary. Since, the only non-Europeans permitted in the club's premises were Chinese waiters, office staff and gardeners, the secretary was curious to know the reason why a Chinaman had so brazenly entered 'forbidden territory.'

The following conversation took place between Towkay Tan (TT) and the Club Secretary (CS) :

TT: Good morning, sir! Excuse me. Are you club owner?

CS: No! Get out!

TT: I understand this club name is Spotted Dog?

CS: What if it is?

TT: It is so good!

CS: Why?

TT: Because you have club for spotted dog! You see, I have many spotted dog in my house in Singapore. Maybe you are knowing my brother-in-law Mr T.T. Foo? He is board member of Yat Fatt Prosperous Property and Investment Company in Kuala Lumpur. He also have many spotted dog! In my car outside have two spotted dog who belong my brother-in-law. Very beautiful! You want to see?

CS: No, I don't want to see your bloody dogs! Get out!

TT: Sir, I want to also starting club for spotted dog in Singapore. Maybe you can advising me?

CS: No! And, this is not a club for dogs, you idiot!

TT: Oh? Then why your club is call 'spotted dog'? I cannot understand.

The Club Secretary's face turned purple with rage and he yelled for the *jaga*, or watchman.

CS: Havildar Singh! Where the hell are you! Having a second breakfast of *chappatis*, are you?

A burly Sikh in khaki uniform hurriedly appeared, wiping his curry-stained fingers on the seat of his trousers.

CS: Get this man out of here! Now!

The CS disappeared into his office, slamming the door behind him.

The watchman escorted TT to his car.

TT said to the watchman as he departed: '*Hi-yah!* English most crazy people!'

The watchman stared after the car and muttered, 'You're not the only one who thinks so!'

The Privileged Class

There was a wide disparity in the treatment of 'Asiatics', as Asians were known in British colonial days. European civil servants and those employed by commercial firms enjoyed such privileges as six months' full-pay leave after every five years of service, plus two weeks' 'local leave' each year, free first-class passages by ship for themselves and their families to and from England, subsidised accommodation and children's school fees, free family medical treatment, servants' allowances, etc., etc

A European who had taken a 'local' wife and his family were barred from 'Europeans only' accommodation and subsidised school fees for their Eurasian children. While he was allowed first-class passages to and from England, his Asiatic wife and children, however, had to pay for their fares and were confined to the ship's 'second-class' areas.

Although there were many Asiatics who were graduates of British universities, they were barred from reaching positions of importance they were qualified to occupy. Top jobs had been 'traditionally' reserved for British expatriates, many of whom were less qualified than the 'locals' who were their subordinates.

'These White barbarians have strange, unpredictable ways,' said an old Chinese with a long, grey beard to a group of Chinese youths who were about to seek their fortunes in colonial Singapore. 'They imagine they are superior human beings and behaved intolerably because they think they are entitled to do so. They didn't realise that such behaviour only revealed their ignorance and inferiority!' said the old man.

If a class existed below the 'upper class,' it would not have been worth knowing about because everyone who belonged to it would have been thrown together with the low-paid, 'working class' Europeans. Attempts were made to 'separate the wheat from the chaff' since those arriving in Singapore from other British possessions such as India, Ceylon (Sri Lanka), Hong Kong and Burma (Myanmar) may have suffered 'a lick of the tar brush.' It was another way of saying that there was suspicion of a person having Asiatic blood.

At 'Europeans only' clubs members were not asked to pay in

cash for services rendered which included food and liquor. They signed their names on the bills. This privilege was introduced in almost every bar, hotel and restaurant patronised by Europeans and became known as 'chit-signing.' At clubs, the 'chits' were submitted to members for payment at the end of each month. Defaulters were penalised by having their names displayed on notice boards.

At local bars and restaurants, however, this embarrassing practice was not followed. European patrons were usually allowed to repay sums of money they owed by instalments. If the amounts were large, they were obliged to transfer the registration of their cars to the names of their creditors as 'security' until full settlement of their debts was made.

It was not uncommon, therefore, to find that owners of local pubs or restaurants had many cars belonging to financially embarrassed *tuans* and *mems* registered in their names. Debtors could also he asked to surrender their passports as a precautionary measure, since there were many cases of debtors 'doing the bunk' as it was known, or, absconding.

Some European ladies discovered that there was a simple and rather unique way of repaying their debts. This was by offering certain 'favours' instead of cash. The practice became so popular that the local owners of pubs, restaurants and stores selling ladies' merchandise discovered they could restrict the number of permitted debtors to attractive ladies only and who were agreeable to exchanging sex for service.

A *mem* who had not been offered such facilities because of her obvious lack of sex appeal, snorted angrily at one of the favoured ladies, 'You and your kind are nothing but whores!'

To which the favoured lady replied: 'Don't you wish that you were one, too?'

The 'Offensive' *Durian*

During the *durian* season in Malaya and Singapore stalls selling the fruit spring up in almost every street in the suburbs to meet the tremendous 'local' demand. Such a practice goes on to this day.

In British colonial times, the stalls were kept well away from the 'European areas' because of the fruit's rather pungent smell which irritated sensitive European noses and was known to cause nausea and vomiting.

For weeks the air was heavy with the peculiar smell which some Europeans preferred to call 'stench' and held handkerchiefs liberally sprinkled with lavender water or *eau de colonge* to their noses. The 'locals' however, found the odour only increased their appetites to take part in *durian* feasts!

An official from the Colonial Office in London who had arrived during the *durian* season in 1924 was badly shaken by the 'pong' in the air and was said to have added to his official report, this interesting information :

'It was my misfortune to arrive in Singapore while on my way to Kuala Lumpur, when this most offensive fruit was in season. I found the *durian*, as it is known, to be Mother Nature's version of a cannonball with sharp thorns and an unbearable stench! In my opinion the fruit is totally unfit for human consumption. Within its thick, thorny, muddy-green shell are large seeds covered with yellow, putrid flesh. I dare say that had Sir Stamford Raffles arrived in Singapore during the *durian* season in 1819, he would not have been so anxious to sign a treaty with the Johore sultanate, placing the island under British control. He probably would have fled the island in a hurry!

'The *durian's* taste could be compared to that of crushed garlic mixed with a particularly strong-smelling cheese that is consumed in close proximity to a horse breaking wind!'

When asked to comment on these remarks, an indignant 'local' resident and a *durian* 'addict' (who wished to be unnamed) had this to say: 'While eating a mixture of crushed garlic and high-smelling cheese may be part of the rather strange English diet, consuming it in the presence of a horse that is breaking wind would have been considered disgusting by even local "coolies."

'The gentleman making these remarks was ignorant of the fact that the *durian* is the undisputed "king of fruits" in this part of the world. Long may it reign! Its unchallenged popularity is further enhanced since it is also regarded as an aphrodisiac.

'I wish to point out that the gentleman was also wrong in assuming that Sir Stamford Raffles, the founder of Singapore, would have been so abhorred by the smell of the fruit that he might have beaten a hasty retreat from the island without signing a treaty with the Johore sultanate to place it under British control. On the contrary, I have heard from good authority that Raffles enjoyed eating *durian* at his residence with his many Malay, Chinese and Indian friends and had described its taste as *banyak bagus!* which in Malay means "very good!" Perhaps he may have also (secretly) had the same comment for the *durian's* legendary power as an aphrodisiac?'

'Local' Festivals

A *tuan besar* of a trading company was overheard briefing a new staff member from England about some of the 'local' festivals in Singapore and Malaya (Note: The correct spellings of the following festivals are in italics with their correct phonetic pronunciations).

He was overheard saying:

'There is Harry Rayer (*Hari Raya*, pronounced: ha-ri-rai-ya) that is celebrated annually at the end of the Muslim fasting month of Ramadan; Deeper Valley (*Deepavali*, pronounced: dee-par-var-li) which is the Hindu Festival of Lights) and Tie

Possum (*Thaipusam*, pronounced: thai-poo-sum) when Hindus pierced their bodies with skewers and hooks and walked barefoot on red-hot coals as penance for their sins and for the fulfilment of vows. And, of course, there is the rather unique Chinese Lunar New Year Festival that is named after a different animal each year. It is a time when every Chinaman seems to come under the moon's giddy influence.'

The *tuan besar* continued: 'During this festival, millions of firecrackers are set alight, their explosions causing an incessant din from dusk to dawn. The streets are covered with thick carpets of red cracker wrappings and to add insult to injury is the sound of loud drumming and clanging of cymbals as groups perform lion dances to chase away evil spirits as well as the European residents who fled from the awful noise and clouds of smoke with the acrid stench of gunpowder caused by the exploding firecrackers!

'Chinese household servants went on holiday for a week to celebrate the New Year each year. Offices were closed and everything else came to a halt, except for the essential services. It was a time when the Singapore Fire Brigade had plenty to do, putting out fires caused by exploding firecrackers.

'It was also a time when most Europeans and their families found sanctuary at Fraser's Hill or Cameron Highlands in Malaya where life was peaceful and with an almost English spring climate prevailing that invited the cultivation of English flowers and vegetables. There was golf, croquet and darts in English-style pubs with typical English names such as the Pig And Whistle and the Fox And Hare that served good English beer, steak and kidney pies, fish and chips and sausages and mash. There were quaint English-style stone cottages with fireplaces and staffed by English-speaking Chinese servants who were trained to cook delicious, civilised English meals; a dairy farm with Jersey cows that produced fresh, creamy English milk and a poultry farm that produced fresh eggs that were laid by English hens!

'Everything is so marvellously English, old chap! You'd wish you could spend the rest of your days there!'

'Boys' With Grey Hair

It was 1950. A young Englishman who had only recently arrived in Penang was at the Cricket Club in the company of two old *tuans*, when one of the *tuans* snapped his fingers and shouted to a grey-headed Chinese waiter, 'Boy! Three whisky *setengahs*!' (*Setengah* means 'half' in Malay. To a bartender it means 'half a peg of whisky or brandy.')

When the drinks were placed before them the younger man asked the waiter his name. 'Lim,' replied the waiter somewhat surprised. He had never been asked his name and was called 'boy' since he began working at the Club there forty-two years ago.

'Thank you, Lim' said the young man politely.

The two old *tuans* raised their eyebrows and exchanged critical glances since they thought the 'young squirt' had behaved rather stupidly by asking the 'boy' for his name and thanking him for bringing the drinks.

The young man noticing he had caused the old *tuans* some discomfort, said to them: 'There are two questions I would like to ask. Firstly, could you tell me the reason why Chinese servants are called "boys" by Europeans? We seem to have "boys" for everything. There are bar "boys", bedroom "boys" – without anything lewd intended – office "boys," ball "boys" at tennis courts, "boys" who are waiters – even grey-headed "boys" like the one who is serving this table and who is probably a grandfather. Frankly, I find the term "boy" not only absurd but also very rude! Negroes in some states in America are also called "boys" in a derogatory sense by Whites. There's no reason why racial prejudice must continue to be practiced in British colonies.

I think it's something we should be ashamed of! Secondly, why is it necessary to snap one's fingers to attract the attention of a "boy"? I've seen it done scores of times, especially in bars and restaurants – only by rude Europeans.'

One of the old *tuans* explained, 'To answer your first question: It goes back a very long time, when English army officers as well as those in the civil service had "boys" as their personal servants, such as valets. I had a "boy" myself when I first came to Singapore thirty-three years ago. Most of these "boys" were in their teens and because of their youth and for the want of a better name I suppose, were called "boys" as they have been called ever since – even when they became old and grey. To answer your second question: We usually snap or fingers to attract the attention, or to awaken "boys" in bars since they were particularly fond of dozing off in some secluded corner and neglecting their duties.'

The young man said, 'I think your explanations are bigoted and childish. However, I see no reason why we shouldn't address these people by their names. As far as I know, a person snaps his fingers when he wishes to attract the attention of a dog and not a human being! Would you like someone to snap his fingers to attract your attention? Apparently this rude behaviour was reserved for local people only! It's not surprising, therefore, why the locals disliked Europeans so much!'

The young man drained his glass, got up from the table and walked away.

Said one old *tuan* to the other, 'Well! What do you make of that?'

The other replied: 'Oh, he's just a silly young fart! There are quite a few like him around these days! They belonged to what is known as "the new breed of liberal English!" A frightening thought, isn't it? God save the Queen and God save England!'

'Sorry To Disappoint You, Sir!'

An English civil servant who was keen to learn the Malay language was in a *perahu* that was being rowed by a Malay along the Kelang River in the state of Selangor one day in 1916. Every now and then he asked the oarsman the Malay names for the many things of interest he saw and the oarsman readily obliged. The Englishman recorded this information in a notebook.

As they moved through a stretch of water with a patch of strong current, the oarsmen was seen to strain his muscles to maintain progress. The exertion caused him to break wind. The Englishman promptly asked the oarsman what the Malay term was for 'breaking wind.' The oarsmen said it was *'kentut'* which the Englishman didn't quite hear.

'Lagi sekali.' ('once again.') he told the oarsman and waited for him to repeat the word in Malay.

The oarsman stopped rowing and the Englishman noticed that he was grimacing and straining rather hard. He was about to ask the oarsman what the matter was, when the man said with an apologetic smile, *'Maaf, tuan. Ta-boleh kentut lagi sekali.'* ('Sorry, sir. I am unable to break wind again.')

An Imperial 'Slap In The Face'

The 'Imperial Edicts' of Chinese emperor Ch'ien Lung (AD 1736 -1795) that restricted English merchants and others from trading in China did not make him a popular figure with Westerners eager to exploit China's vast, untapped resources.

When he banned British merchants from importing opium to China that could have turned it into a country of drug addicts, he won more disfavour including the British government's.

Undeterred, the British persevered in their diplomatic approaches to try and make the emperor change his mind. But, the 'Son of Heaven' was not to be moved. To him, the 'foreign devils' were the 'descendants of dogs' and should be treated as such.

One of his most stinging 'slaps in the face' was delivered to Lord Macartney, envoy of His Most Gracious Majesty, King George III of England in 1793.

Long after the overthrow of the Manchu empire in 1912 in which Britain played a major role, the emperor's disrespect for the British monarch was still being spoken about with contemptuous snorts by *pukka sahibs* in India, *taipans* in Hong Kong and *tuan besars* in Singapore and Malaya.

It was said that when Macartney appeared before the emperor in Peking to present his credentials and also to convey King George's greetings on the occasion of the emperor's birthday, Macartney had failed to perform the customary *kow-tow* demanded by imperial protocol, by prostrating himself before the emperor and touching the floor three times with his forehead. He was reported to have refused to do so and instead had gone down on one knee, as he would have done before his own monarch.

The emperor was infuriated but since he was celebrating his birthday he was prepared to be generous and ignore Macartney's 'uncivilised, barbaric and insulting' behaviour that only supplied further proof to the emperor of the White man's inferior culture.

The emperor instructed his Minister of Protocol to read the Imperial Edict he had prepared in response to a request by King George for the British to be allowed to open diplomatic relations with China and also trading posts in Chinese ports.

The Imperial Edict (in part) to King George read as follows:

'It is noted that your country lies across the oceans but that you humbly wish to acquaint yourself with civilisation and that your envoy has journeyed to this Court to *kow-tow* to the Celestial Emperor and to congratulate him on his birthday.

Such humility and respectful obedience meets with our approval
... In reply to your request, your envoy will convey to you our
desire that your country over the seas must further demonstrate
its loyalty to the Celestial Empire by swearing perpetual
obedience to the Celestial Emperor before such requests could
be granted.'

This followed, among other things, two armed conflicts: the
Opium Wars between Anglo-French and Chinese forces; the
overthrow of the Manchu empire, the opening up of China to
European traders, the possession of Hong Kong by the British
and the large-scale smuggling of opium into China by British
merchants under the protection of Royal Navy gunboats based
in Hong Kong.

'Eating' Some Fresh Air

A popular Malay expression is: *Mari, kita pergi makan angin.*
Or, 'Come, let's take some (fresh) air' that was usually done by
taking a trip to the beach or to a park to enjoy the cool breeze.

(*Note:* The word *makan* in Malay means 'to eat' or 'to consume.'
Makan angin would literally mean, 'to eat or to consume the
air.' Also, the Malay word for air is *angin* and the word for dog
is *anjing* that some foreigners had difficulty in pronouncing
correctly.)

The year was 1925 and Brown had arrived in Ipoh, the capital
of the state of Perak, to become a police inspector. With him
was his wife. She did the best she could to cope with the many
hazards that confronted newly-arrived European wives in the
East, such as: the unbearable humidity; the horrible mosquitoes
(which, it was rumoured, had been trained by anti-British
elements to bite only English residents) and the inscrutable

Chinese servants who didn't understand English (the 'red-faced devil's' language') or pretended not to.

However, Mrs Brown was encouraged by other *mems* to cultivate a 'stiff upper lip'and determined to adapt herself to the 'primitive conditions.' She was even making an attempt to learn Malay.

Since they had no children her only companion, while her husband was busily arresting criminals, was her Scottish terrier pup that she had appropriately named 'Scottie.'

Like other adventurous English ladies who had decided to make their homes in far-flung colonial outposts of the Empire, she had read a few books about the strange customs of the inhabitants of the region. One of the things she vividly remembered was that the Chinese diet included snakes, octopus, birds' nests, sharks' fins, bears' paws – and dogs!

This explained why Scottie never left her side, more especially since she had employed a Chinese cook-boy and his wife as an *amah*. She even fed Scottie in her bedroom where he also slept each night. She was always on the lookout for the slightest cause to set off alarm bells in her pretty blonde head, when it came to protecting Scottie.

One night as her husband and herself lay in bed with Scottie at their feet, she said to him nervously, 'I thought I saw Ah Seng, the cook, looking at Scottie in a strange way this morning. You know what they say about the Chinese – do you think he maybe thinking of eating Scottie? The little thing has become rather plump and could be just right in Ah Seng's opinion for the cooking pot! Oh, dear! Imagine! Instead of sweet-sour pork – there could be sweet-sour Scottie!'

She began to cry.

Although her husband tried to tell her that her fears were totally unfounded, she kept a close watch on the attention Ah Seng and his wife paid to Scottie.

One Sunday, during the Festival of the Hungry Ghosts, while Mrs Brown and her husband were gardening, they saw Ah Seng and his wife all dressed up and on their way somewhere. They also noticed that Ah Seng was carrying a package wrapped in paper under his arm. Mrs Brown thought she saw four legs of an animal protruding from it. Furthermore, the legs appeared to have been roasted! Instinctively, she quickly looked around for Scottie, who was nowhere to be seen! Instantly, the cold fingers of panic gripped her throat. Her worst suspicions about Scottie's fate were confirmed when she heard her husband call out to Ah Seng in Malay: *Mana pergi*, Ah Seng? (Where are you going, Ah Seng?) and Ah Seng answer: *Saya pergi sembahyang, habis itu, saya pergi jalan-jalan makan angin.* (I'm going to pray and then I am going for a stroll to 'eat' some fresh air.)

Mrs Brown hissed in her husband's ear: 'Monster! Stop him! He had the nerve to tell you with a big grin that he's going to *makan anjing* – to eat dog! And, the dog in question is poor Scottie whose roasted remains are in that package under his arm! You're a police officer! Arrest the brute!'

While Brown did his best to calm his tearful wife, Ah Seng and his wife had walked on towards the main road on their way to the nearby Taoist temple where he would offer the roasted suckling pig he carried under his arm to the ravenous ghosts of his deceased relatives who were paying their annual visit to Earth from Hell.

Jumping on his motorcycle with his wife clinging on behind, Brown set off to investigate, determined that justice would be done.

As they approached the main road Mrs Brown heard her husband say, 'Look! Ahead!'

Peering from behind her husband's back she let out a huge sigh of relief as she saw Scottie romping about with some other dogs and Ah Seng trying to grab him by his leash. Scottie had obviously broken loose and run away from home to have some fun.

A sheepish Mrs Brown told her husband later, 'I definitely heard Ah Seng tell you he was going to *makan anjing* – and not *makan angin*'.

Her husband, however, didn't seem to be impressed by her explanation for her rather silly behaviour.

'Anyway,' thought Mrs Brown, 'it would be a nice story to tell the other *mems* at the club!'

The Dishonourable Cocktail

The following is part of a letter written by a Chinese student to his parents in Singapore, shortly after his arrival in London in 1920.

'London is a very a big and strange city. Shortly after my arrival Uncle Tong took me to a corner of the city where there are Chinese restaurants. The food wasn't too bad, but very expensive.

'I was surprised to learn that none of my English colleagues at my school had heard of Singapore. And, when I told them I came from there, one of them said, "It's some place in India, isn't it?"

'I quickly said Singapore wasn't anywhere near India. But, another student said there was an easy way of finding out because all British possessions were coloured red on maps. We consulted an atlas. He ran a finger along the map from India to Burma and down the Malay peninsula, to Singapore.

"See? Those places are all in red because they are a part of the Indian sub-continent or British India!" he said and giving me a strange look asked, "What race are you?"

When I told him I was Chinese he said, "Don't be silly! If you came from this place called Singapore you must be Indian, because Singapore is part of British India – didn't I just prove it to you?"

'As he walked away with the others, I heard him remark, "Poor chap, he doesn't know what race he is!" and they all laughed.

'I made a most surprising discovery the other day. It concerned the preparation of an alcoholic beverage known as The Cocktail that is widely enjoyed by Western people including the King and Queen of England, members of European royalty and other distinguished people such as the President of the United States!

'I imagined The Cocktail which I believe was invented by the Americans, must contain rare, health-giving herbal ingredients for it to enjoy such high esteem and popularity. However, I was to receive a great shock.

'An English fellow-student named Charles who is also called "Char-li" by his friends. (Isn't it strange that he has a Chinese-sounding name?) He told me that The Cocktail was made from the feathers that grow from the backsides of common farmyard cockerels and from which it derives its name! According to Char-li the feathers were placed in a specially designed steel container called a Cocktail Shaker together with certain potent brews, then capped and vigorously shaken. He explained there was a special art employed in the shaking process that is required so as to completely dissolve the cockerel feathers. After this was accomplished, the concoction was poured into specially invented drinking receptacles known as Cocktail Glasses and graciously sipped at special events known as Cocktail Parties at which ladies wore Cocktail Dresses and indulged in conversation known as Cocktail Gossip while devouring Cocktail Sausages pierced with coloured Cocktail Toothpicks made from a special, edible wood which, I was told, was chewed and swallowed together with the sausages!

I am puzzled as to why there is such elaborate preparation and ceremony for what appears to be a dishonourable and most unhygienic concoction with cockerel feathers as the main ingredient!

'I was also informed by another English student named "Hen-ri" (who also has a Chinese-sounding name!) that Char-li was a well-known 'prankster' (one who plays jokes on people) and apparently had "pulled my leg" when he told me about The Cocktail being produced from the rear feathers of cockerels.

"Pulled my leg?" what a peculiar thing to say! I assured Hen-ri that Char-li had not committed such a discourteous act nor had he interfered with any part of my body!

'Hen-ri's reaction to my embarrassment was to laugh heartily and walk away shaking his head.

What had he found so amusing, I wonder? I think it will be some time before I begin to understand English humour that is as strange as their way of life.

'None of my English friends at school seemed interested when I attempted to tell them that we Chinese considered the feathers growing on the backsides of cockerels only fit for being used as feather-dusters for the purpose of house cleaning!'

THE END